Praise for *The Better Liar*

"[Tanen] Jones's writing is strong and offers a gripping, suspenseful plot that keeps readers engaged and wanting more. The characters are deep, complex and unpredictable—exactly the kind of characters a thriller should deliver. . . . The story makes a bold and thought-provoking statement on women, sisterhood and motherhood."

—Associated Press

"Jones's sensational debut has the bones of a thriller but reads like literary fiction: lean, shrewd, and gratifyingly real."

—*Entertainment Weekly*

"Who'll love it? Those who enjoyed the literary style of *Gone Girl*. This thriller is smarter . . . than others in the genre."

—*Cosmopolitan*

"Jones's debut novel is clever, absorbing, and full of red herrings. No one is trustworthy—Leslie is hiding her reasons for needing the money; Mary has ulterior motives and rarely tells the truth. A stunning twist ending will leave readers waiting to see what Jones will give them next."

—*Booklist*, starred review

"Jones debuts with a taut, twisty thriller. . . . [She] sneakily builds suspense via a trio of narrators—Leslie, Mary, and Robin—none of them reliable. . . . Jones arrives with an undeniable splash."

—*Publishers Weekly*

"A darkly complex relationship between two sisters lies at the heart of Jones's debut psychological thriller. . . . A blistering debut from a promising new talent."

—*Kirkus Reviews*

"A twisty, fast-paced read with a sly sense of humor and an engine that won't quit, *The Better Liar* is emotionally surprising and deeply moving, making it a perfect book-club choice. Smart, sinister, and utterly engrossing—this debut delivers."

—JOSHILYN JACKSON, *New York Times* bestselling author of *Never Have I Ever*

"A tale of two dangerous women in a toxic embrace that winds relentlessly tighter, *The Better Liar* is a brilliantly claustrophobic thriller with a gasp-inducing sting in the tail—tense, controlled, and masterly."

—CHRISTOBEL KENT, author of *What We Did*

"With a gritty, suspenseful story unspooling in gorgeous prose, Jones expertly ramps up the tension and then delivers twists and turns at breakneck speed. This is an impressive debut, with an ending you won't see coming."

—ELIZABETH KLEHFOTH, author of *All These Beautiful Strangers*

"Jones's sharp debut is an expertly plotted, gritty thriller rooted in the sun-bleached landscapes of New Mexico. This dangerous story of sisterhood and inheritance will make you question how well you really know those closest to you."

—MADELINE STEVENS, author of *Devotion*

"*The Better Liar* is a dazzling debut that weaves a haunting past into a dangerous plan. Tanen Jones shifts effortlessly between narrators and storylines, and delivers one hell of a twist. I couldn't wait to finish but did not want it to end. This is the best kind of thriller!"

—WENDY WALKER, internationally bestselling author of *The Night Before*

The
Better
Liar

The Better Liar

A Novel

TANEN JONES

BALLANTINE BOOKS
NEW YORK

2021 Ballantine Books Trade Paperback Edition

Published in the United States by Ballantine Books,
an imprint of Random House,
a division of Penguin Random House LLC, New York.

BALLANTINE and the HOUSE colophon are registered trademarks of
Penguin Random House LLC.

Originally published in hardcover in the United States by Ballantine Books, an imprint of
Random House, a division of Penguin Random House LLC, in 2020.

Grateful acknowledgment is made to Farrar, Straus & Giroux for permission to reprint
an excerpt from "Averno" from *Poems 1962–2012* by Louise Glück, copyright © 2012 by
Louise Glück. Reprinted by permission of Farrar, Straus and Giroux.

Library of Congress Cataloging-in-Publication Data

Names: Jones, Tanen, author.
Title: The better liar: a novel / Tanen Jones.
Description: New York: Ballantine Books, [2020]
Identifiers: LCCN 2019034777 (print) | LCCN 2019034778 (ebook) |
ISBN 9781984821232 (acid-free paper) | ISBN 9781984821249 (ebook)
Subjects: GSAFD: Suspense fiction.
Classification: LCC PS3610.O6299 B48 2020 (print) | LCC PS3610.O6299 (ebook) |
DDC 813/.6—dc23
LC record available at lccn.loc.gov/2019034777
LC ebook record available at lccn.loc.gov/2019034778

Printed in the United States of America on acid-free paper

randomhousebooks.com

123456789

Book design by Diane Hobbing

To Jean and Janet
for teaching me
the world is wide.

Nothing is safe.

You get on a train, you disappear.
You write your name on the window, you disappear.

There are places like this everywhere,
places you enter as a young girl,
from which you never return.

Like the field, the one that burned.
Afterward, the girl was gone.
Maybe she didn't exist,
we have no proof either way.

All we know is:
the field burned.

—LOUISE GLÜCK, "AVERNO"

The
Better
Liar

Robin

Like most of the dead, I want to be remembered.

The lucky dead leave ghosts of themselves everywhere: an impression on a mattress, a name in the mouth. My name has almost disappeared now.

Robin Voigt—my old boss said it this year, going through the tax folder for the fiscal year 2011–2012, preparing to throw it out. It was one in a list: Krista Ungert, Maria Villanueva, Robin Voigt. My face rose up briefly before him, half-remembered; I had reminded him of his daughter.

Robin Voigt, written in eight-point font underneath my name in the yearbook. Kevin Borrego's youngest daughter smeared her finger over my face. *Who's that?* she asked. *She's pretty.* Kevin said, *Oh, Robin. She was a couple years below me. I think she moved away.*

Robin, in script high on my ex-boyfriend's inner arm, so that I pressed into the ripe furry creases of his armpit, pocked with eczemic scars.

Flimsy, shitty ghosts. I'm fading.

The only people who can keep you alive are the ones who loved you. Not the ones who panted after you, bought you flowers, kissed your palms. I mean the ones who saw your disgusting insides and loved you anyway. The people who really knew you.

I only had one person like that. Leslie, my sister.

My ghost wakes up with her in the morning, chews on her hair like I used to when we were children. It holds her hand at night. I'll never leave her. No one loved me more than Leslie. She loved me so much she sat my ghost up and breathed into it, made it walk around our home again, the way the living do. She bound herself to me a long time ago, but she won't say my name aloud anymore.

If I tell you how it happened, maybe you'll remember me as well.

Maybe you'll say my name to each other, a little chant, like a dirge.

1

Leslie

By the time I found her she was dead.

I groped for somewhere to sit down. The only place other than the bed, where the body lay, was a wooden dining-room chair half-buried under a pile of wrinkled clothes. It had a cushion hanging off the seat, patterned with cartoon bees, and as I moved to straighten it a cockroach, startled by the movement, hurried up the chair leg. I jerked my hand back and closed my eyes. Then I opened them again—helplessly.

I didn't want to look at the body. The body—Robin—Rachel. I'd never seen her as an adult, but as a teenager she'd been round-faced, milk-fed. Now she was so thin as to be impossible to look at. My vision unfocused itself when it encountered her ribs, visible through both the fabric of her RUNNIN' REBELS T-shirt and the sheet in which most of her body below the shoulders was tangled. Her hipbones, too, projected, cradling the vacant, starved abdomen.

A little vomit had dried in the corner of her mouth and on her tongue, the color of burned things. She had been unconscious when she'd choked on it.

Iker was panicking. "Should I call the police?" he said, directing his gaze at the close yellow walls, the popcorn ceiling. "I'm really sorry about this, I'm so sorry. I'll call the police. I'll call." He wore a white polo with the logo of the housing company on it. Crescent-shaped sweat stains gathered underneath his sagging pectoral muscles, like a pair of closed eyes. They twitched as he began digging in the pockets of his khaki pants for his cellphone.

"No," I said, trying to think fast. "No, I'll call. You go outside. I just want—" I swallowed. "I just want to be with her for a minute."

"Yeah," Iker said, wiping his upper lip. "Okay. Okay. I'll wait. Outside. I'll be . . ." He pointed. "I'll be right down there if you need me."

He went down the stairs into the living room below, taking his proprietor's key but leaving the door ajar. After a minute I could hear him shuffling on the front porch, audible through the mosquito screen on the open window.

She was still on the bed. The fact of her was as sweltering as the room.

In my imagination I reached for my phone. In another version, I didn't. I lived these two visions simultaneously for several long minutes, my hand twitching in the air above my purse, unable to choose between them.

If I called the police, then Robin would be dead—absolutely dead. Legally, governmentally dead. I would have to identify her, and arrange somehow to take her body back to Albuquerque to be buried, and have a funeral, and then everyone would know she was dead and it would be over.

I could contest, maybe—but contesting could take a year or more. I couldn't wait a year. If I didn't call the police, then she would still be dead, but—

I took her wallet off the dresser and looked at her ID. "Rachel Vreeland" stared out at me from the hypersaturated photograph. She'd been pretty as an adult, the pale skin I remembered from childhood turned slightly orange by the sun or the DMV's printer. *5'-09"*, the text next to her face said. *Eyes: BRO.*

Her real name wasn't anywhere in the wallet, or anywhere in the rest of the room. She had a lot of stuff, but most of it was clothes, strewn across the floor and piled in the closet. I picked through the items with pockets, careful of cockroaches, but turned up only old movie tickets and gas-station receipts. The walls were covered in movie posters and a corkboard with photographs of friends with red Solo cups, a scruffy orange cat, a long-lost boyfriend from whenever the last time was she was weighty enough to crush to his side while he held the camera out in front of them. The dresser drawers held dozens of bottles of disintegrating nail polish and depleted pans of eye shadow. At least fifty pairs of underwear, which I pushed aside with a clothes hanger, scraping the bottom of the drawer: nothing underneath.

I shook out each of her shoes next—cowboy boots, Toms, slip-on sneakers—turning the left and then the right upside down.

Something fell out of the right one. I'd been expecting Robin's real ID, or maybe a baggie, so the anticlimax startled me: a pair of pearl earrings, so light that they made barely any noise against the carpeted floor. For a moment I thought they must be insects, moths, alive inside Robin's shoes, and their brief bouncing trajectory across the floor was translated by my gaze as mad, frenzied flapping; then I blinked, and they resolved into dead objects.

It took me several seconds to realize why I was staring at them. When it came to me I snatched them up so quickly that my fingernails scraped the carpet. My mother's earrings. Five-pointed, like stars, each seed grasped by a minuscule gold claw. I hadn't seen them since I was a little girl. I suppose I thought they'd been buried with her, or my father had sold them. But here they were in Robin's cramped rented room in Las Vegas.

Had Daddy given them to her and never told me?

He wouldn't have done that. She didn't deserve them. I was the one who'd made his doctors' appointments, helped him swallow, taken him to the movies every Sunday. Robin had done nothing but call occasionally, after she turned sixteen and disappeared.

He hadn't given them to her. Probably she'd stolen them the night she left. She'd taken forty dollars out of my purse that night too.

I rubbed my thumb along the surface of the pearls, feeling several faint scratches on the curvature of one of the seeds, invisible to the eye but evident to the touch. Pearls were easily scratched. My grandmother had taught us to polish her pearl jewelry with olive oil and a chamois cloth, pushing our cloth-covered fingernails into the crevices where each pearl was secured. But Robin was careless.

I closed my fingers around the earrings. The backings dug into my palm like children's teeth. If I didn't call the police, Robin Voigt could stay Rachel Vreeland. Rachel Vreeland could have a crappy City of Las Vegas burial, a heroin addict with no family, the person she had chosen to be when she was sixteen. It gave me a thick, sick pleasure to think about. I wanted her to be alone in the ground.

But it wouldn't matter. Either way, I couldn't get what I needed from her.

She would have loved that.

I had been in the room with her body for almost five minutes now. The pacing on the porch had stopped; Iker was considering whether to come back upstairs for me.

There was a series of faint rusty creaks as someone else came up the second set of stairs, which clung to the siding on the rear of the house, allowing access to the upper floor from the backyard. Whoever had come in went into the second bedroom and slammed the door.

Her roommate. Yes. Iker had said there was another tenant.

I heard the muffled noises of quick movement from the second bedroom. The roommate could come into the hall at any moment and see me—see Robin's body—wonder where the police were, who I was, why Iker hadn't called—

The front door opened into the house, and Iker's voice came floating up the inner stairs. "Miss, um . . . Leslie? Did you . . . Leslie . . . ?"

I didn't reach for my phone. I slipped the earrings into my purse and walked quickly toward the back door. I was out before anyone saw me, making as little sound as I could manage on the metal stairs.

At the noise of the ignition, Iker ran back out onto the front porch, waving his arm at me to stop. He shouted something after me, something I couldn't hear as I drove away.

2

Leslie

I glanced in the rearview mirror again. The same blue sedan kept pace with me until I got on the freeway, then disappeared into the crush of cars heading into the city for Saturday night. That wasn't Iker, I told myself. He drove a different car. A black one.

Gradually my ears picked up a dull buzzing noise. Coins rattling in the cup holder. No—my phone ringing. I fished it out of my purse. Two missed calls. Iker was trying again. The screen lit up as he left a message.

Why had I left? I'd run out of there as if I'd killed her myself. Stupid—stupid—

It was the earrings. I drew in a breath and felt blindly around the car for them, trying to keep my eyes on the road. They weren't in my purse. Had I dropped them? At last I thought to pat myself down and found that I was wearing them. I didn't remember putting them in my ears.

She'd just stuffed them in her shoe. I couldn't understand why it upset me so much. I hadn't even thought about these earrings in at least fifteen years. But the idea that Robin had helped herself to my mother's jewelry box on her way out—and hadn't even taken care of them—

I touched the scratch again, compulsively, like an itch. How could she have let it happen?

I was forced to stop at a light. The image of my sister's body floated up before me, more bone than flesh.

How could she have let it happen?

The exultation of my escape began to leach out of me. All the way into the city that morning I'd felt myself pushed forward as if on a wave. I'd never driven so far alone before. The highways between New Mexico and Nevada were dwarfed periodically by mesas, and the traffic was so infrequent that the cars resembled a thin rushing stream between the lowering rocks. The whole way here I'd been thinking to myself: I'll talk to her—I'll explain—and then everything will be all right—

I pulled off the freeway at the next exit and turned in to the first open parking lot I saw. Three cars took up the only spots shaded by the single tree. The sun hung just past the visor, turning the dust on the windshield opaque, so that I could barely see beyond the confines of the car. The illusion of privacy gave me a little comfort, and I picked up the phone to call Iker back.

My hands shook. I tried to press the home button, but my fingers were stiff from gripping the steering wheel so tightly. I fumbled and dropped the phone into my lap.

I clenched my teeth and let the air escape in a hiss. Maybe it was hunger. The last time I'd eaten was breakfast. It was just past five now.

I had to strain to make out the sign on the building I'd parked in front of. GEORGE's. Some kind of steakhouse. The building wore a badly constructed stone façade, like a Macaroni Grill, and all the blinds were drawn, but the outer doors stood open.

The bottoms of my shoes warmed as I crossed the parking lot into the stuffy little vestibule and pushed through the inner set of doors. It was cooler inside, with a large exposed air vent near the ceiling whuffing away; despite that industrial fixture, the rest of the restaurant was outfitted like a midcentury men's club, with dark wood paneling and heavy curtains flanking each window. At the edges of the room were large plush booths with gold hooks for coats and hats; the rest of the dining room was taken up by free-standing tables set with white tablecloths and upended water glasses. No one was in the restaurant, not even any workers; except for the air vent, I was the only thing breathing.

I went up to the host stand, feeling underdressed in my slacks and blouse. "Hello?" I said. "Are you open?"

There was a clanking noise from the kitchen, and a rat-mustached teenager leaned out from between the swinging doors, his head suspended briefly midair. "One second."

I edged behind the host stand and took a menu. It was expensive to eat here. Vegas prices. Ordinarily I wouldn't. The red meat. But my hands wouldn't stop shaking; the menu fluttered as I held it. Didn't they say you should eat protein if you felt faint?

The teenager returned and crept around me to reach the wrapped silverware. "Just one?"

"Yes," I said, trying to fit the menu back into its stack and knocking several others to the floor. The kid scrambled to pick them up for me. "A steak. A porterhouse. And a glass of wine. No—I have to drive. Water."

"Do you want it to go?" His forehead wrinkled.

"No." I gripped the edge of the host stand. "I want to sit down."

"Okay—uh . . ." He led me to a booth and leaned across one of the seats to open the blinds for me. I blinked as the late-afternoon light hit the varnished table. "We're still firing up the grill, so it'll be a half a minute."

I nodded. He went away, his too-large oxford shirt hanging off his shoulders. I sat down and put my head in my hands.

If I had shown up even a day earlier, she would have been alive.

A different oxford shirt appeared in my peripheral vision. "One glass of water. I'm Sherrod, I'll be your server today. Can I get you anything else to drink?"

My gaze drifted to the window. Outside, a man in the parking lot got out of his SUV and went around to its rear door, where he lifted out a little white boxer puppy, which he set on the asphalt next to a water bowl. He filled the bowl from a small water bottle and squatted down next to the dog as it drank, stroking its ears.

"Ma'am?"

I jerked to face him, spilling water. "I'm sorry."

"No, I'll get it." He lifted my glass and mopped the dripping table with the rag he carried at his side. "Can I get you anything else? Your order should be out shortly."

"No. Thank you."

When I looked up again, the waiter was gone.

It had taken me two months to track Robin down. The last number I'd had for her had been picked up by someone named Andre, who said he thought Robin had moved to Las Vegas but he wasn't sure, and if I found her to tell her to go fuck herself. I'd searched *Robin Voigt* as well as the fake name she'd been using to avoid her creditors, but found nothing. At last someone had left a message on my father's answering machine regarding a new credit card registered to my father's address. The name on the card was Rachel Vreeland. I searched this new name and found an address. The property was part of the SweetHomes rental company. Iker picked up when I called. *I need to find my sister,* I'd told him. *Rachel Vreeland. Our father left her a lot of money in his will.* Iker had said, *Yes, yes, Ms. Vreeland. Yes, in Henderson.*

If I told her I was coming she would only leave town. I said, *Can you come with me to her house to wait for her tomorrow? I can't get her on the phone. I think something might be wrong.*

My brain skipped ahead to the body on the bed, the smell of the hot little room.

"All right, here we go." Sherrod had returned. He set the plate in front of me.

"Thank you," I said to his back.

The steak lay in front of me, bleeding juice onto the ceramic. Someone had arranged it so that it lay artfully over the bed of potatoes and asparagus. A bloody runnel cut its way through the mashed potatoes, pooling on the rim of the plate.

I picked up my knife and fork. It took me several tries to cut a sliver from the edge of the steak, but at the first bite my hands stopped shaking. I'd been too nervous to eat lunch. Thinking I was going to see Robin for the first time in a decade. I'd practiced talking to her: *Daddy died a few months ago. He left us both some money, but you have to come home to do the paperwork.*

Why didn't you tell me? I had imagined her saying, or maybe *How much?*

I tried to find you. It took me forever.

She was good at reading faces, especially mine. Eerie, with an animal quickness. *You weren't going to tell me at all. You're only here because you need something from me. What do you need, Leslie?*

I'd spun through conversation after conversation in my mind, trying to keep her at bay.

My purse shuddered as my phone buzzed in the outer pocket. I felt my shoulders tighten, but it was my real phone, not the prepaid I'd used to call Iker. I pulled the phone out and hesitated, my finger hovering over the caller ID. Dave.

If I rejected the call he would know I'd sent him to voicemail.

I didn't do anything. I just sat there, holding the phone, until the ringing stopped. Then I put it back in my purse.

The man with the dog was gone, giving me an unobstructed view of the Target across the street. Farther away, billboards advertising tooth-whitening gels and children's hospitals flanked the road toward the city. Las Vegas had no firm vanishing point; the heat created a kind of mirage that forced my eyes to focus and refocus. A visual vacuum. I imagined myself driving past the city, toward the Amargosas, reduced to a shimmer in the late-afternoon light.

I imagined myself not going home at all.

"No rush," Sherrod said, dropping the bill beside my plate. The steak was gone; I'd been holding the knife loosely in one hand for several minutes now, looking out the window.

I put the knife down and paid the bill.

I should go back to Henderson, I thought as I pushed open the doors and went out into the blinding day. I should get Robin's body.

But the skyline sucked me toward it.

I could have gone anywhere.

I didn't, because there was someone sitting on my car.

3

Leslie

She was sitting with her ankles crossed, digging for something in the pocket of her oversize utility jacket. As I got closer to my car I saw she was only a kid, maybe twenty-two, with the twice-burned skin that true redheads get in the desert. There were patches of freckles scattered unevenly across her chest and on top of one visible shoulder, where her jacket had fallen to her elbow. She found a lighter in her pocket and lit a cigarette, closing her eyes and leaning back on one hand to inhale. From a distance her features had seemed too large for her face; closer, as her eyelids lifted, I saw that it was an effect of her makeup, which weighted her lower lashes, giving her a gentle, drooping quality. "He-ey," she said, taking the cigarette out of her mouth as I approached. "What's up?"

I stopped ten feet away. "That's my car."

She frowned and lifted one of her hands from the hood, checking underneath it as if she might have left a print. "Your car, huh?"

"Yes," I said. "I need to go, please. Can you . . ." I hesitated, in case she got angry.

She tilted her head; her bun was loose enough to tilt with her. Then her face cleared and she laughed. "Oh my gosh," she said, scrambling down the hood and brushing herself off. "I'm so sorry. I didn't realize it was your car. I'm Mary," she added, extending a dusty hand. "I thought it was my boyfriend's car. You guys have the same one, I guess."

"Leslie," I said, shaking it quickly. She was as tall as I was, but fine-boned, with narrow shoulders and small hands, so that she seemed to take up less space than I did. "I'm just—I need to—" I headed for the driver's side, then stopped. "Can I have one of those?"

She'd stuck the cigarette back in her mouth. "One of these?" she asked through compressed lips, pointing at it.

I nodded. "I'll pay you for it." I groped inside my purse. There had been a quarter at the bottom earlier.

"Oh, you're fine," she said. She sounded like she was from Texas. "Don't worry about it. You need a light?"

"Yes. Please."

She dug in the box and handed me one, then held out her lighter.

I took it from her. It was one of the ones with the buttons. I pressed the button with my thumb, but the flame wouldn't catch. I tried another three times; on the third time I let out a noise of frustration, one that I hadn't been expecting to make, and so it came out with absolutely no modulation.

Mary flinched, and I rushed to say, "I'm sorry. Sorry. Sorry. I can't—"

She took the lighter from me. "It's okay. I'll do it. You all right?"

"I'm fine," I said. She lit the cigarette easily and handed it back to me with two delicate fingers. "Thank you." I sucked in smoke and tried not to cough. I had never smoked a cigarette before, but it seemed to calm other people.

She eyed me. "You really needed that, huh? Trying to quit?"

"I needed a drink more," I said, "but I have to drive."

"Aw, you could have one," she said. "My boyfriend comes here all the time—that's why I was sitting on his car—well, I thought it was his car. I passed by and saw it and I thought I'd surprise him." She ducked her head. "They make a real good martini here, if you're a gin drinker."

I shook my head. "I don't really drink much."

"Cheap date."

There was a pause. She didn't look like she was about to leave, and I wasn't finished with the cigarette. "Do you work around here?" I said, for lack of anything better.

"No, it's just on the way. I work over there." She tilted her cigarette in the direction of the city. The sun had dropped below the roofs of the buildings, sharpening their outlines from behind so that now the skyline seemed only feet away, like the backdrop of a stage.

"Oh," I said. Mary squatted to stub her cigarette out on the pavement. "At a casino?"

"Sort of," she said, getting to her feet. "The restaurant attached to it. I serve a lot of lobster." She made a face. "I hate waiting tables, but I don't hate it the way the other girls hate it, so I feel like I should keep doing it, you know?" She glanced at me and I nodded.

"What would you rather be doing?" I asked after a moment.

"I want to move to LA," she said, dragging out the last syllable for comic effect. "I want to act. I've been saving up to move out there for forever. I want to have enough money that at least if I end up working in the service industry again, I'll be able to pick and choose a little, you know? Not worth it to move and make less than at the Strip. I'd feel like it was for nothing."

"I think you'll make it," I said, trying to be nice. "You look like an actress."

"Stop it," Mary said, grinning. She had rippling lines bracketing her mouth, which were invisible otherwise. "What do you do? Are you in the city to gamble?"

My laugh surprised me; it sounded hoarse. "I'm actually," I said, trying to compose myself, "I'm actually in the city to see my sister."

"Oh yeah?" Mary asked. "How's that going?"

"She's dead," I said, forcing back an idiotic, nervous smile. "She just died a few hours ago."

"Oh my gosh," Mary said. "I'm sorry. Wow."

"Yeah," I said. "I was just a couple hours too late. Isn't that crazy? And I really—I really needed to see her." I tried to take a drag, but it went up my nose and I teared up. "She owes me money."

Mary took this in. At last she said again, less kindly, "Oh, well, I'm sorry."

"No, I'm sorry," I said. "I didn't mean to explain all that. Thank you for giving me this," I added, holding up what was left of the cigarette. "That was really nice of you."

"Yeah, sure. Listen, I'm going to go text Paul and see where he's actually hanging out, but if you come by Letourneau's in the city tonight, flag me down and I'll sneak you a couple of shots."

"You mean come to where you work?"

"Yeah, off Harmon. It's pink, you can't miss it. Well, you can, but don't." She patted me familiarly on the arm.

"I can't," I said. "I have to . . ." I made an inarticulate gesture.

She watched my hands. "Well, if you end up dropping by," she said, and didn't finish.

I got into the car and started it. Something touched my leg, like a finger; when I looked down, I saw that it was the cigarette butt, which had fallen from my hand.

4

Robin

Why don't more people walk away? I have always wondered this. Sunk cost, maybe. Fear of the dark. Or guilt; some families run on guilt, like gasoline.

No—men know how to walk away, even men who never do it. The instructions are right there: Go out for cigarettes and never come back. Start a second family in Florida and raise the kids on Tropicana. Make sure your grandchildren find out about each other when you die, your final gift to them, so they know love is a cat in a sealed box, that if they took the heads off their husbands and looked in, they would see nothing, a bottomless drop.

I guess what I'm asking is why don't more women walk away?

The night I left home, it had just stopped raining. Leslie was back from college for the weekend, asleep in the next room. On the other side my father was out cold in a sleeping-pill daze. It was two years until his diagnosis, but he'd already developed a wet cough that took all his energy to repress. It felt like he slept all the time; it felt like I never slept. It woke me up in the middle of the night, the feeling that I was supposed to be moving toward some prophesied future. That it was waiting for me, and that lying there in bed in a medium-size town in New Mexico was only stalling.

I was sixteen and so beautiful that taking my body into the world was like ferrying around a stolen luxury car: just the having of it implied action. *You should do something with that,* I was told again and again. It was like my body was something separate from me; even the thirties-ish men who hit on my body seemed to resent the person inside it, the way you might disapprove of an eleven-year-old driving a Beemer. *You don't deserve this,* their faces said, even as their mouths said, *Baby, come here . . .*

But this is what was actually special about me: I knew that I did deserve it. And that night, dragging my bedroom window closed behind me, leaving damp handprints on the glass like goodbye waves, I took my body out.

In the house, Leslie went on sleeping. I left her there, swaddled in the bed we used to share, thinking I was burying her. She'd take care of Daddy until he died, then find a husband and take care of him until he died, and then maybe if she was lucky somebody else would help her piss until she kicked the bucket at last. Poor Leslie, I thought as I ran through the backyard that night, through the pools of the neighbors' porch lights, toward my ordinary death.

5

Mary

I went back to my car and sat in the shadows of the parking lot's single tree. If I craned my rearview mirror to the left a little, I could see her. Leslie. She was sitting in her car, just letting it idle. Twisting one of her earrings in her ear.

Why was she just sitting there?

I took out my phone and texted Paul.

I have something to tell you . . . xx.

I tipped my phone back and forth, watching the glitter in the case drift from side to side, like the tide going in and out. Then I tried to find something good on the radio while I waited for Paul to reply. I went past a dozen commercials and Christian sermons before I finally hit on a man's voice announcing P. P. Arnold singing "Angel of the Morning," which is just about as good a song as a person can make. I knew the whole thing, including the part where she pauses right before she says *It was what I wanted now*—that's the best part.

All the glitter in my phone case had descended to the bottom. I glanced in my rearview mirror. The Honda was gone.

Ordinarily before my shifts I went to the Park 2000 shopping center off Sunset and Eastern to sit with Shea, who was forty-four years old and a busboy at Letourneau's because his parents made him get a job for tax reasons. I hung out with him because he shared his weed with me for free in exchange for being able to look at my face up close for a period of thirty minutes. Sometimes he just took a photo of me and looked at that on his phone even though I was still right there in his car with him. I never wanted to ask why. We usually got real high and watched the planes take off at McCarran from across the street. You could see the wheels retracting from where we parked. Shea called us ornithologists.

Today, though, I really had to see Paul. I picked up my phone, causing a small tsunami in the case, and texted him again.

where are you xxx. I have news :)

He hadn't replied to my last seven texts either. I thumbed up the screen until I could see his last message to me.

See you tonight sweetheart

Maybe he was at home. He worked from home sometimes, although he spent more of his time at one of those freelancer offices, where people who didn't know one another could rent desks in a big sunny warehouse and make small talk at the coffee machine, just like at a real cubicle farm. One time I'd asked Paul how come he didn't want to work in the gorgeous three-bedroom in the Lakes that he was renting at a discount from his brother, and he said it was too comfortable, so I laughed, and then he was mad that I laughed.

I fixed the rearview mirror and checked my makeup in it, using my fingernail to scrape off the eyeliner that had gathered in the corners. Then I started the car, slouching a little so that the jetstream from the air conditioner hit me right in the face, making my teeth cold as I mouthed along to P. P. Arnold. *"Just call me angel . . . of the morning, baby . . ."* I whispered to myself as I turned onto the beltway.

The Lakes is this landscaped community on the west side of the

Valley with its own zip code. The whole thing is built around a huge man-made pond that someone dyed turquoise, and all the houses are supposed to look like they're in Florida. Most of them have their own little docks and boats that are named things like the *Desert Rose* or the *Camel*. Paul's brother Bobby bought the house as a wedding present for him. Since the divorce, Paul's ex lived in Denver with the kids, and Paul paid Bobby five hundred bucks a month to not sell the house out from under him.

Paul's big-ass Honda was in the driveway. Next to it was one of those Tesla cars. Either he was trying to make up for the one by buying the other, or he'd befriended a Democrat. There was nowhere for me to pull in, so I parked across the street. Before I could even reach for my seatbelt, the front door opened and Paul stepped out. He was pink and dripping, dressed in his running clothes, with big sweat patches spreading underneath his arms. He had his base-ball cap on backward, like guys in movies from the '90s, except it wasn't the '90s anymore so it sort of made him look old. I still liked his bright blue eyes.

He leaned back into the house and I saw his mouth move. Then a woman came hurrying down the stairs after him, adjusting the headphones around her neck. She was super fit, with visible biceps, and her hair was in two French braids, starting to frizz at her hair-line. A redhead, like me. He kissed her briefly on the lips—fast, instinctive—like he could find her lips in the dark—like he already had.

For a second I was weightless, watching them. Then Paul glanced across the street as he was opening the passenger door to the Tesla, and our eyes met. I jolted back into my body. I was across the street, staring at Paul through a pane of UV-protected glass.

The radio announcer came back on. "That was P. P. Arnold sing-ing 'Angel of the Morning.' She was only twenty-one in 1967, if you can believe it. We're taking a short break, and when we come back we'll begin our commercial-free happy hour, starting with the very best of Miss Dinah Shore."

I blinked, and Paul looked away. The other woman hadn't seen me. They got into her Tesla together, and she backed the car cautiously out of the driveway onto the wide, smooth pavement. I watched the two of them all the way down the street.

After a second I checked my makeup in the rearview mirror. I ran my fingertip around the bottom edge of one eye, then the other. If you want to hear the real truth, I knew the whole time how come he wasn't answering my texts. But it's different when you see it. It always is.

Letourneau's was in the middle of a cluster of pastel-colored mid-range hotels just off the Strip, closer to the UNLV area than to the shops and bars. It was pale pink, with a neon heart on the front door and no other identification, which Freddy had told me was supposed to appeal to women. I told him it made it look like a strip club. If you glanced around the dining room it was wall-to-wall disappointed dudes from Ohio. They always came in with cash, at least.

The inside was mostly casino, but they'd added on a dining room in the early 2000s, and we did a decent business in steak and lobster. I got dressed in the staff bathroom, stuffing my jean shorts and sneakers into the duffel bag I kept in my locker and changing into a black velvet wrap dress and extra-long string of fake pearls. They looked just like real pearls. They had been my birthday present last year, from me to me. Berna told me not to wear them because they sometimes fell into people's food when I leaned over, but I always got good tips when I wore them, so I didn't think anybody really minded.

Preethi sailed up to me as soon as I got onto the floor. "Somebody threw up in the men's bathroom," she said.

"It's only, like, eight."

She shrugged. "I'm taking my thirty."

I waited for her to disappear behind the swinging doors. Then I grabbed Shea by the back of the shirt. "Somebody threw up in the men's bathroom," I told him. "Pass it on."

He hefted his tray of dishes and silverware at me and shook it to make it rattle. "Hear that?" he asked. "That's 'fuck you' in busboy."

"Aw." I stuck out my lower lip. "Shea."

"You stood me up."

"I had to see Paul." I glanced away. "He's sleeping with some girl again."

Shea's ears perked up. "That's too bad." He looked me over with almost clinical interest. "You look nice tonight."

"Thank you, Shea." I paused and added throatily, "Somebody threw up in the men's bathroom, you know."

He shook the tray at me again and headed for the kitchen.

I continued toward Jordyn at the host stand. The host stand was maybe my favorite part of the décor; it was chrome, with another neon heart on the front and a Plexiglas top that you could draw dirty things on with Jordyn's pink Sharpies. The rest of Letourneau's was sort of knockoff Cheesecake Factory, with a big marble bar top, Art Deco pillars getting in the way of everything, and round crushed-velvet booths designed for maximum inconvenience anytime anyone had to get out to go to the bathroom.

Jordyn glanced up as I leaned on the stand, looking upside down at tonight's table sections. The neon heart cast a hot-pink campfire glow on the underside of her face.

"I'm taking over for Preethi," I told her. "She went on her thirty."

Jordyn adjusted her sports bra so that the CK label stuck out more. "Okay. She's got two two-tops and a four-top. Eight, ten, fourteen. Somebody threw up in the men's."

"It wasn't me," I said.

She wrinkled her nose. "That's not what I meant."

"I know," I said, grabbing a new pad and pen off the host shelf.

A couple came up to the stand giggling and leaning on each other for support. I turned to leave Jordyn to it, but she laid a hand on my arm. "There's some woman asking for you at the bar. Well, she said the one with red hair. I'm guessing that's you."

I glanced toward the marble-topped bar, which was already crowded with men in baseball caps—casinogoers love to wear hats, especially inside at night, for whatever reason. Among the hats I saw a long pale moon face turning this way and that.

Leslie glanced up when I plopped onto the barstool next to her.

She was still in her wrinkled lavender blouse and slacks from earlier. She looked staticky and slightly sweaty, as if she'd slept in her clothes. "Hi, honey," I said.

"Oh, it's you." She tilted her head.

"You sound surprised." I grabbed a bottle of Cuervo from Heather and poured us out some shots. "I thought you were asking for me. Or did you meet some other redhead who works here?"

"I couldn't remember your name." She touched her face, which was turning pink, and shook her head when I pushed the shot toward her. "I've been drinking wine. I shouldn't—"

"Come on, it's on me," I said. "I'm real sorry about your sister."

She pressed her lips together, staring down at the shot glass. Then she picked it up and sipped at it.

"You never taken a shot before?"

"I have." She sipped at it again. "I just don't like the, you know . . ." She flapped her free hand. "When it burns your throat."

"No, I'll show you. Yoga breaths. Think about what's bothering you, breathe in, and then . . ." I threw the shot back and sighed. "See? All gone. I'm a new woman."

She laughed, then covered her mouth, like she'd surprised herself.

I leaned over the bar and pulled on Heather's ponytail. "My tab," I mouthed, pointing at Leslie's head. Heather nodded, and I turned back to Leslie. "I've got to get to my tables, but I'll come back around. I know you forgot my name. It's Mary."

"Leslie," she said, putting out her hand. She had large, squarish hands, softened by a rounded gel manicure. She opened her mouth as if she was going to say something else, then closed it again. I stood there for an extra half second, waiting for her to make up her mind, but there was only a funny silence between us.

"I have to go to the bathroom," she said abruptly, and got up and walked unsteadily toward the far hallway.

The kitchen switched to bar snacks at ten, and service slowed. I made almost a hundred dollars off a table of five middle-aged white guys from Kentucky. After they went back into the casino, I slung myself onto the barstool next to Leslie and grabbed another shot from Heather. "I'm getting drunk with you," I told Leslie, nudging her with my shoulder. "I'm having a really interesting day. Like you."

Leslie was sleepy-eyed, clutching her phone. "Nobody's called me yet," she said.

"Called you for what?"

"My sister."

"Were they supposed to?"

"I thought maybe . . ." She shook her head. "I'm not sure. You're really very kind. Thank you for . . . um. Thank you for buying me drinks, and . . ."

"Anytime."

She picked up her purse and felt around in it without pulling anything out. "I should go. I should go home."

"You live around here?"

"No, New Mexico. Albuquerque."

I raised my eyebrows. "That's a long drive."

She let out a nervous giggle. "I have a hotel room. That's what I meant. Not home-home."

"Well, I'm about to take my ten outside. Want to come with me? Have a cigarette, sober up?"

She stared at my face a little too long. "I don't really smoke," she said finally. "It was only today."

"Well, you can just keep me company." I leaned over to dig into my shoe with one finger, where the heel was getting blistered.

Leslie shook her head again. "Okay," she said, contradicting herself. "All right."

I led her through the maze of columns and booths, past the black-and-purple wallpaper and the posters of semi-famous people that hung where the windows used to be, back when Letourneau's had been an office complex. You wanted a casino windowless and dark; it kept people feeling that the night was just beginning. I'd seen guests wandering out of the casino still in full cocktail getups in the middle of brunch service. One guy tried to get his money back from

Freddy because he'd missed his flight, saying it was the casino's fault for not having any clocks in the place.

"I'm taking my ten," I said to Berna as I passed her office in the back hall. She didn't look up. Leslie dragged her fingers over the rows of metal lockers, squeezing the pink rabbit's foot attached to my combination lock.

Outside, I flopped onto the smokers' bench next to the door and patted the spot next to me. Leslie stepped carefully over the cigarette butts ringing the bench and sat down, crossing her legs. I stretched out, pointing my toes and digging into my apron for my pack and lighter. "You sure you don't want one?" I asked her, once I'd gotten the cigarette between my lips.

She shook her head. I shrugged and dropped the lighter back into my apron, glancing at her as she laced her fingers together on her lap.

"What did you mean before," I asked suddenly, "when you said your sister owed you money?"

Leslie's head jerked up. "My—my father . . ." She cleared her throat. "He left us both some money. In his will. That's why I came down here, to bring her back to Albuquerque." She unlaced her fingers. "But."

"Wow," I said.

She nodded. "He wanted us to talk to each other more. He hated that we didn't talk."

"He wanted you to come get her?"

I watched her wedding set flicker in the light from the streetlamp. The rear parking lot was mostly empty, a dozen staff members' cars clustered along the left side. "He put it in his will, that we had to be there in person, together, at the lawyer's office. To get the money. That was what he wanted. It took me so long to track her down," Leslie said quietly. "And I missed her by . . ." Her mouth hung open for half a second as she stared into space. Then she snapped it closed.

"But won't you inherit her half, if she owed you?" I said. "Now that she's, you know . . ."

She turned her odd colorless eyes on me. "I don't want to talk about it anymore," she said.

"Sorry," I said quickly. "That was a dumb thing to say. I didn't mean it like that."

She was still looking at me, that half-present blankness on her face. I wished she would stop looking at me like that.

"Do you think I'm stupid?" I blurted out.

"What?" she said, seeming to come out of her daze.

I sucked on my cigarette. "I think people think I'm dumb," I told her. "I think maybe I just look like I am. I don't know."

Leslie let out a hoarse giggle again. "No," she said, when she caught her breath. "Of course not."

I frowned. "I might be. You don't even know me."

"Everybody has talents," Leslie said, her body loosening a little.

"Does this count?" I took the cigarette out of my mouth and did cauliflower tongue. She laughed, and I put the cigarette back in my mouth. "No, but I can read palms, though. I'm really good at it. Here, I'll show you."

She curled her hand up against her chest. "No, no."

"Come on." I grabbed her hand and tugged it toward my knee. "It won't hurt."

She relented and leaned toward me, letting her palm rest on my leg. I stubbed out my cigarette and added it to the fairy ring around the bench. "Okay," I said, "you've got this really fleshy Venus mound." I squished it with my thumb. Leslie made a face. "No, it's good," I said. "It means resistance to disease. And your middle finger is the longest. That means you're an overachiever."

"Aren't you supposed to read the lines?" she asked.

"Sure." I bent her fingers in slightly, so that I could see where her palm creased. "That's the life line. Yours is really faint."

"What does that mean?" She leaned in.

"It means you don't work with your hands . . . you work in an office."

Leslie laughed. "What about my love line? That's one of them, isn't it?"

"Heart line." Hers was short and straight, like a cut. "You're married?"

"Yes," she said. "Four years."

"Beautiful. What's his name?"

"David. Dave," she said, revealing a slightly crooked canine.

I dropped her hand and took out a second cigarette. She gave me a sidelong glance, watching my hands. "What do your palms say?" she asked.

I let my fingers uncurl on the bench between us. "See that long one down the middle? That means I'm going to be famous," I told her. My voice echoed a little in the empty lot. "The psychic I went to said it's the longest one she's ever seen." I pulled my hand back and stuck it into my apron, gripping the bills I'd stuffed in there, drawing in a breath through my nose.

"I should leave soon," Leslie said. "It's getting late."

"Thanks for keeping me company." A car pulled into the lot, washing us in bright, flat light, and our heads turned briefly to look at it. When I looked back, she was already gathering her things. "I hope everything works out with her. Your sister and everything," I said.

"Robin," Leslie said. That blankness fell back over her face, like a veil. "Thank you."

She started to gather her things, but paused. I followed her gaze and saw that the car had parked, and a man was coming toward us with an odd shambling gait.

I said, "You should go—you should go inside."

"Do you know him?" Leslie asked, her hand half in her purse.

"A little."

She didn't move.

Sam was my height, bald, with a reddish goatee. His ears and cheeks were the same flushed, ruddy pink. "Who's your friend?" he said, coming up onto the curb.

I dropped my phone and scraped my fingers trying to pick it up again. The cigarette fell onto the pavement. "No one," I said, sticking my index finger in my mouth so it wouldn't bleed everywhere. "She's a customer."

Leslie glanced between us. Her lips parted.

"A customer. I see." He left off staring at Leslie and nodded at my phone. "What you looking at?"

"I'm just checking the time," I said, wiping my hand on my apron. "I have to get back inside." I stood up.

Sam wandered over to me. He was wearing a button-down shirt today, khaki, which strained over his thick middle. He smelled like strawberry candy, that factory-plastic sweetness, like he'd eaten an Airhead or something. "I heard you were over at Paul's house again today." He tugged on my earlobe. "What's wrong with you?"

"Maybe we should head back in," Leslie said. "Your break's probably up."

Sam ignored Leslie. "I told you not to see that man anymore," he said, flicking my ear.

"Stop it," I said, smacking his hand away, grinning reflexively. I could feel it on my face, a panicked, skeletal expression.

He put his arms around me. "You want me to stop?" he said. "Gimme an apology." He stuck his hand in my apron and pulled out a handful of cash. "You did good today, baby," he said, stepping back a little so that he could see the bills under the streetlight. "You got two hundred dollars in here."

I felt Leslie's eyes on me as I watched him tuck my money into his wallet. "I have to get back to work," I said.

"You have time," he said. "No one's gonna fire you. Dance with me." He held out his arms.

I didn't move for a second. Then I walked stiffly over to him and put my arms around his warm, fleshy neck.

We swayed for a minute, my face pressed against the rough fabric of his shirt. He hummed and I felt it rumble through his chest. The song wormed its way into my ear, vaguely familiar. The words crept in after a minute: *Going to the chapel and we're . . . gonna get married . . .* He was making fun of me. I started to draw away.

He coughed and squeezed my waist, coming to a halt. "Okay, say you're sorry. I want to hear it."

I glanced at Leslie, still sitting on the bench, clutching her purse. "I'm sorry," I whispered, turning back to Sam.

"And you won't go back there again."

I shook my head.

"This is a good little gig you have here," Sam said. "You look nice in that dress. I'm gonna come visit you. You work most Saturdays?"

"Yeah," I said.

"All right. Have a good night, baby." He smiled at me. I was still smiling back, like I'd been frozen that way. I knew what it looked like from the outside.

He squeezed me one last time and turned away, heading back toward his car. I sat down heavily on the bench, listening to his footsteps, and then to the throat-clearing noise of the start of his engine.

"Are you okay?" Leslie asked, leaning toward me. Headlights swept over us again as Sam pulled out of the parking lot. "Who was that?"

The door to the restaurant thumped open and Berna put her head through the doorway. "Have you been out there this whole time?" she called.

"What?" I said.

"Breaks are ten minutes," she said. "I know you have a clock on your phone. Who's this? Is this a customer?"

"I'm about to head to my car," Leslie said.

Berna turned her gaze back on me. "You need to learn to budget your time," she said, her short nose twitching. "I have to write you up, unfortunately. Last chance train."

"Okay," I said.

"Follow me in here. I'm going to get the form. You need to sign it to show you understand this is your third strike." She retreated into the hallway and I got up to follow her.

"I shouldn't have come out here," Leslie said quietly as I slipped back into the building.

Inside, Berna clacked toward her office. I paused at the bank of lockers. Under the fluorescent lights everything seemed hyperreal. I could almost believe that I'd imagined what had happened outside.

I dialed my locker combination and took out my duffel bag as quietly as I could, slipping my hand into it and feeling around for the lucky veladora where I kept my saved-up cash.

Sam hadn't gotten everything.

I slung the duffel bag over my shoulder and hurried back down the hallway, pushing open the door as quietly as I could.

Leslie was still there, leaning against the wall by the jamb. We were barely a foot away from each other. She turned her head in surprise.

"Mary," she said, straightening, her dirty-blond hair slipping behind her shoulders. "Is everything okay?"

"I quit," I said, stepping on her last word.

"Don't you have—"

"That guy who showed up—Sam—that's my ex. He knows where I work now. I tried to make sure . . . Those were my tips that he stole just now. He—Leslie—"

Leslie took my hand and pulled me along the building wall, toward the corner.

"Thank you," I breathed. I rattled along beside her in my heels as well as I could on the asphalt.

We reached the front parking lot. She clicked the button on her keys and I fell into her Honda. It smelled good inside, like Pine-Sol or something. I pulled off my shoes and held them awkwardly on my lap. "I don't know what I'm going to do."

Behind me, in the rearview mirror, I could see Berna pushing open the front door, the neon heart swinging wildly.

"You can stay with me tonight," Leslie said, reversing out of her space. "I have two beds. It's no trouble." She pulled onto Harmon. Taillights from the car in front of us turned her pale skin a deep red. "I'm sorry about your ex," she said into the quiet car.

"Sorry about Robin," I said. Then we didn't say anything for a while.

6

Leslie

"*Sheboygan, Wisconsin, is the self-proclaimed capital of this German sausage,*" Alex Trebek said.

"Frankfurter," Mary called. "Frankwurst."

"Frankwurst is not a sausage," I told her, just as one of the contestants said, "*Uh, what is bratwurst?*"

"See, I knew it." Mary raised an eyebrow at me. "I knew the end part. I forgot about the front part."

"The ending doesn't count. Every German sausage is a -*wurst*. It literally translates to *sausage*."

Mary slapped another miniature bottle of schnapps into my palm. "Drink this. Stop talking in German."

"*This fruit-and-nut-filled sweet bread sounds like it was . . . pilfered,*" Alex Trebek went on. The contestants stared at him, slack-jawed. "*It's called stollen,*" he explained, when the buzzer went off. "*Stollen.*"

I laughed. Mary glanced at me. She was back in her leggings, cross-legged on one of the double beds, holding a pillow in her lap. The room seemed more stable with her in it. Alone, I'd felt almost disembodied; the thick green felt curtains and the industrial air-conditioning unit absorbed all the ambient noise, even my own breathing. After George's, I'd come back here and tried to sleep, lying motionless on the bed, trying to think of ways to explain my absence to Iker.

I'm so sorry. I was overcome by grief. I hope you understand.

I was shocked. I needed a few moments alone.

I couldn't look at her anymore—I couldn't be in that room—

"Did you know this is the first time I've ever gone anywhere by myself?" I said, as *Jeopardy!* went to commercial.

Mary thumped off the bed and went to get another bottle of vodka, weaving slightly. "I feel like my mouth is making, you know, more than the amount of spit it's supposed to make," she said, talking over me. "Do you ever get that? Wait, what were you saying?"

"Are you drooling?" I took the vodka bottle out of her hands as she struggled to open it and tossed it onto the opposite bed. "That's not a good sign."

"I didn't mean drooling. That's not what I meant. I'm going to wash my face. You keep telling me what you were telling me."

I fell back against the pillows. "I've never been on a trip alone before."

Mary stuck her head out from the bathroom. "How old are you? Like thirty?" she asked around a toothbrush.

"Thirty-one."

She disappeared, and I heard her spit into the sink. "That's crazy."

"I've never been anywhere, really. Dave got his job right before our wedding, so we couldn't take a honeymoon, and before I met him my dad was sick, so we never traveled. I don't even remember traveling when I was a kid. We went to the Grand Canyon once, I guess." I wiped my nose.

The water ran briefly, and then Mary exited the bathroom. She looked different barefaced; despite her bronzed, freckled sternum, the skin on her face under all the contour was like marble, and her unpainted eyebrows were girlishly curved, without the harsh arch she gave them with the pencil. "I got your towel all black," she said. "I couldn't find the Kleenexes."

"They're not my towels," I said.

She shrugged.

Jeopardy! came back on as she flopped down next to me on the bed, humming along with the theme. "How come your husband didn't come with you, then?" she asked. "If you're scared to be here by yourself?"

I stared at the screen as DAILY DOUBLE appeared, accompanied by air horns. "I didn't want him to meet her," I said laconically.

Mary chewed peanuts. "Your sister?"

I nodded.

She waited for me to say something else. When I didn't, she said, "How come?"

The *Jeopardy!* contestant paused; the air conditioner rushed in to fill the silence. "She did a lot of drugs," I said over its heaving breaths. "Heroin, lately. That's how she died."

"Oh." Mary stuffed more peanuts in her mouth.

I shifted on the pillow, pulling my blouse down over the roll of flesh above my waistband. "You look like her, kind of. Without your makeup on. She had hair like mine, though."

"'Return to Sender'!" Mary yelped, spraying peanut dust. "I knew it. Was she pretty?"

She hadn't turned to me; it took me a few seconds to catch up. "Robin?"

"Yeah, your sister. Was she pretty?"

"Yes." At least when I'd known her she had been.

"All pretty people kind of look alike," Mary said, unblushing, still watching TV. "At least that's what I think. I get told I look like people all the time. Daughters . . . nieces . . . Amy Adams . . ." She grinned at me. "A young Melanie Griffith."

"The group of painters known as 'the Eight' established this 'sooty' school of art," Alex Trebek intoned.

"I wish I had something. Like falafel. Or a gyro," I said.

Mary silently offered me the packet of peanuts.

"Peanuts aren't falafel."

"They're all we have."

I screwed up my face as she pushed them at my cheek. After a few seconds she gave up and fell back next to me on the bed, sending peanuts scattering across the floor. "Leslie," she started, and then seemed to forget she had been about to say anything.

"Have you been a lot of places by yourself?" I asked after it became clear she was lost in her own thoughts.

"Um . . . here. Texas. One time I got flown out to Florida to be in a short film about a dog. But then it never aired anywhere." She yawned. Her teeth were white and perfectly aligned, like a toothpaste advertisement.

"Did you use my toothbrush before?" I mumbled.

She ignored me. "Paul told me he could introduce me to people. His brother used to be a PA for James Cameron. Paul's the one I was waiting for today, outside the restaurant. But he never introduced me to anybody, and today I found out he's got some new girlfriend."

"I'm sorry."

She nodded. "I just don't know how else you do it. Like if I don't know anybody important, how am I ever supposed to get started?"

"Build up savings?" I guessed, pulling the sateen coverlet over my feet. "Find an agent?"

Mary shook her head as much as she could, pressed against the pillow. "Something always happens. I think I was born under a dark star, Leslie. I really do."

I put my hand up to cover my smile. "Because you haven't gotten to act yet?"

Her eyes were big and solemn; behind her, on the television, a Corona commercial cast blue light across the pin-striped wallpaper. "Things don't work out for me."

"They will," I said. "You just have to wait."

"No." The corner of her mouth lifted. "Some people are lucky. It's just in them. Like they were good in a past life, and now God wants to reward them. I'm not like that. Paul cheats on me. I got this job I'm actually doing okay at, and Sam tracks me down, and I gotta . . . That's how I lost the last one too. I know how he is. He'll show up every day now that he knows where I am."

I didn't know what to say. She wrapped a loose thread around her finger, then unwrapped it slowly. "Hey," she said suddenly, "how did you know your husband was the right one?"

The change of subject caught me off guard. "Um, I just knew."

Mary smacked me on the arm, letting the thread fall to the bed. "Ugh. I hate that."

The atmosphere had shifted so suddenly that I couldn't help laughing. "I mean, I don't know how else to say it." The truth was one of those things it was impossible to say aloud: I knew because it terrified me. I had never been in love before, so I didn't understand what it meant until it happened to me. Early in our relationship, I'd gone through a phase of dreaming that he was dead, then waking in a cold horror, my face soaked. I dreamed it a dozen times or more, all in the middle of a courtship so intense that it had made me feel crazy. I did things with Dave I never would have done with anyone else: skipping classes to stay in bed all day, moving in with him after only two weeks. I didn't sleep in my own apartment once after meeting him—at the time that had seemed absolutely sensible.

Mad, funny, beautiful days, and then at night, his corpse, again and again. As if, having encountered happiness, my brain had instantly learned to fear its loss.

I would have done anything for him. That was how I knew.

"He keeps calling me," I said. "Wanting to know how things are going with my sister."

"You haven't told him?" Mary frowned.

"I didn't know how. It's ruined everything. I needed—we needed that money."

Mary nodded. "But you'll get it anyway, won't you? I mean, eventually."

I shook my head. "I needed it right away. Contesting the will, going back and forth with Vegas, it'll take months. A year, maybe. I can't—I thought I was going to get it before then. I thought I was going to get it this week."

Mary's mouth had fallen open a little listening to this. "I could help you pawn your ring."

"That's not what I mean."

"I'm just saying. I've pawned a lot of stuff. It works."

I turned the stone toward my palm. "No. Thanks, though."

"Maybe we should pray," Mary said inexplicably, sitting up and crossing her legs.

"We're drunk," I said. "You can't pray when you're drunk."

She fixed me with a reproving look. "Sure you can. I have a friend who does the whole rosary whenever she thinks she's going to throw up, and then she never does."

"What are you going to pray for?"

"For whatever we want." She got up and scrambled over to the other bed, lifting a jagged pink piece of quartz out of her backpack.

"What's that?" I asked, pointing at it as she arranged it on the nightstand between us, right in front of the alarm clock.

"His name is Pop Rock 'cause he's the biggest one, the daddy. I've got littler ones at my apartment, but he's the best of the bunch. Okay, come down here with me."

She pulled one of the decorative pillows off the bed and patted it. I stumbled around the bed and knelt next to her, imitating her solemn pose.

"All right. Here we go. Are your eyes closed? Leslie, close your eyes. Dear God and spirits, thank you for all the good things that happened to us today. We are truly grateful." Mary elbowed me. "Name some good things."

"Um . . ." I tried not to laugh. "Quitting jobs. Schnapps. Game shows."

"Yeah. Now I usually use this next part to focus on what I want out of life. Like really try to envision it. So for me I'm going to say I see myself not being poor anymore and getting out of Las Vegas and finding somebody who loves me, really loves me, and helps me with my goals."

"That's a good vision," I said, nudging her gently with my shoulder. "This is nice. I see why you do this."

"Okay, now you."

I closed my eyes again. It took me too long to come up with something. I could feel Mary fidgeting on the decorative pillow next to me. "I want to know what to do when I wake up tomorrow," I said finally. "I want to have a plan."

"Perfect," Mary said. "Now don't you feel better?" She picked up Pop Rock and shuffled over to her backpack to tuck him away again. I lifted myself off the decorative cushion, slipping a little, and replaced myself on the bed.

Mary wandered back over to me and sat down, then seemed to change her mind and stood up again. "I have to pee," she said, and headed placidly toward the bathroom.

She paused as she crossed in front of the television, brushing pieces of crushed peanut off the sole of her foot. The light from the TV turned her two-dimensional, silhouetted like a child's portrait. There was something familiar about the curve of her forehead. For a moment she really could have been Robin. A more perfect Robin, a Robin the way she should have looked, in another life.

The idea filtered through my disordered thoughts, spreading itself across my vision. A solution. A way out.

7

Mary

"Do you still want to watch this?" I said over my shoulder, picking bits of peanut out from between my toes. "We could find something else."

"Whatever you want." Leslie's eyes looked half-unfocused in the dim light of the bedside lamp. I'd expected sharing a room with her to be sort of chummy, like a sleepover, and for a while it had been, but now the booze was burning off, leaving a sheen of grade-school sweat on her. I was still a stranger, and now we were alone in a hotel room. The intimacy of it was creeping in. I saw her fingers seize and release the coverlet, kneading it like a stress toy.

I picked up the remote and clicked through a football game and two channels of cartoons. *American Graffiti* was on the next channel, just at the part with Toad and Candy Clark where they play that song, the "I Only Have Eyes For You" song. "Oh, this is good," I said, faking cheer, turning toward the bathroom.

I stumbled backward. Leslie had appeared in front of me. I hadn't heard her leave the bed. We were practically nose to nose.

"Mary," she said, grabbing my arm. A sour smell rose off her, liquor and something stale, like when you've slept too long. "Do you want to come to New Mexico with me?"

Even drunk, I still had my waitress's reflexes; I reacted to her invading my space by letting my muscles go gluey under her fingers. "What?" I said, laughing, letting the drunkenness carry me along.

"Nobody knows Robin's dead yet," she said. "You could pretend to be her."

I stared at her, a leftover smile on my face. *American Graffiti* went on playing in the background.

She released my arm. "It's acting, right?" she said. "You want to be an actress. It'll be like practice. You'd only have to do it for a few days. She just needs to be there, at the lawyer's office. That's all that's in the will. And then you could have her half of the—"

"What?" I repeated, interrupting her.

"Fifty thousand dollars," Leslie breathed. "That's Robin's inheritance. She's dead. She can't use it. It's yours. You can have it all. Cash. That could give you a good start in LA, right?" She tilted her head. "And your ex . . . He'd never find you again."

I giggled, shrieky. "You're so drunk," I said. "You need to go lie down."

Leslie followed me as I retreated toward the bathroom. Her skin reddened as she spoke. Strands of hair were stuck to her cheek. "You look like her, Mary. At least, you look enough like her, and nobody in Albuquerque has seen her since she left ten years ago. All you have to do is show up and sign the papers with me. I've got her old passport if anyone asks for ID."

I didn't want to antagonize her, so I said something like "Hmm" or maybe "Okay," and I stroked her lank hair a little bit, the way you stroke a nervous dog.

Leslie grabbed my stroking hand. "Mary, Robin was using a fake name to avoid her creditors. Rachel Vreeland. She died under that name. The only person who has my contact information is the landlord, and he doesn't have my real name."

"He doesn't have your real name?" I was getting drawn in.

"I told him it was Leslie Vreeland when I was looking for her." Her gray eyes protruded slightly above puffy lower lids. "He let me in to see her. I was going to call him tomorrow, but if I don't call him . . . if she just stays Rachel Vreeland to him and to everybody else . . . it's like Robin Voigt is still alive. Legally."

"Until they, like, investigate, and send you to jail." I scrunched my toes against the carpet.

"No one's going to investigate. It was an overdose. She was an addict. And anyway, if they did, you'd be long gone with the money by then. All they'd find in Albuquerque is me. And I don't know your last name."

I opened my mouth and she put her hand over it. "Don't *tell* me your last name," she said, as if I were the idiotic one.

"Ih dosen mar becah I'm nagana do ih," I said into her fleshy palm.

"What?"

I pulled her hand off my face and wiped my mouth. "It doesn't matter, because I'm not going to pretend to be your sister." An absurd smile crept over my face again at the idea.

"You need the money," Leslie said, following me. "And—and I need the money. I can't wait for them to contest the will. I lost my job. We're going to lose the house. Dave can't accept it, he won't—he thinks he can fix it all himself, but . . ." She flexed her fingers, as if they'd lost feeling. "Fifty thousand dollars would fix everything for me," she whispered. "Wouldn't it fix everything for you?"

Sam's song licked at my ear: *Going to the chapel and we're . . . gonna get married . . .* His ruddy hands grasped at my waist.

"It's just a few days," Leslie said. "A week, maybe."

I stared at her, the smile falling off my lips.

"Please, Mary," she said. "Just think about it."

She left this long quivering silence between us. It was uncomfortable on purpose; it was uncomfortable so I'd say something, so I'd say *Yes!* and fling myself into her arms.

Instead I just enunciated, "I have to pee," went over to the bed, grabbed my duffel bag, pushed past her into the bathroom, and shut the door in her face.

8

Mary

I did have to pee, anyway, but then once I was done I didn't want to go back out there. The door closing had given me instant relief. There was something funny about Leslie's body language, a nearly infectious panic. I wished she would go back to normal. It had felt like we were friends, sort of, until the last few minutes.

It would have been nice if she'd just wanted to be my friend.

I turned on the shower so Leslie would think I was doing something in the bathroom, but instead of showering I squatted on the nasty tiled floor in front of the full-length mirror and took the veladora from my duffel. I counted the money, quickly at first, then again slowly to be sure I'd gotten it right. My life savings was in here—I never left it at home because my roommate was a kleptomaniac. Five hundred forty-five dollars. I sat there in front of the mirror, holding the money.

I'm gonna come visit you, Sam had said to me. *You work most Saturdays?*

The glass slowly fogged as I stared at myself. At first under the fluorescent lights I only saw my reflection in familiar bits and pieces, the hairpin lines beside my mouth that never went away anymore, the slightly asymmetrical eyebrows. Eventually my features blurred, and blurred again.

I could have been anyone in there, underneath the condensation. Just a smudge with hair.

I stayed in the bathroom until I was almost sober again, looking at myself.

When I came out finally, the room felt like it was freezing. Leslie was lying sideways on one of the beds, watching the credits roll over *American Graffiti* and jiggling her feet, first one, then the other, so the bed creaked in an annoying little rhythm. I came closer and startled her into a sitting position, her back against the pin-striped wallpaper. "Hi," she said, too loudly. "How are you feeling?"

"I'm okay." I sat down on the other bed and pointed myself toward the television. The credits finished rolling. *Next up on TNT: Transformers.*

Leslie kept glancing at me and opening her mouth like she was going to say something, then shutting it again.

"What?" I said, after the fourth time.

"Nothing," she said. "Are you okay?"

"I said I was fine." I picked at my nails. There was peanut gunk under one of them.

"Mary—" she started.

I thumped my head back on the pillows. "Oh my God," I told her, "I just want to watch *Transformers*. Okay?"

I flung an arm into the narrow canyon between the bed and the wall and groped for my backpack, which had my cigarettes in it.

"You can't smoke in here," Leslie said meekly from the other side of the room as I pulled out a Spirit.

"Well, maybe I'll just head out, then," I snapped.

"No—you don't have to—"

I glanced at her. Leslie closed her mouth and crawled over to wrestle with the window, pulling the blinds to one side, but it wouldn't open. She groped her way over to the door and yanked it open. The noise of car horns and descending airplanes rushed in.

"I feel sick," Leslie said suddenly, as I lit up. She tried to sit down on the bed and almost missed, scooching her torso up until the rest of her made it onto the mattress.

"You're just drunk. You'll be fine."

She shut her eyes. "I don't think so."

I looked at her lying on the bed. Half of her tow-colored hair had fallen over her face, and her makeup in the lamplight highlighted the ruts and creases on her skin where it had begun to age. She was a mess. Part of me wanted her to pass out.

If she did, would I leave?

Across the room, the door hung open.

"Leslie," I said, reaching across the empty space between our beds and poking her in the shoulder. "Leslie?"

She sighed. "It's almost four in the morning," she said, opening her eyes. "We should go to sleep."

I nodded, lifting my cigarette.

"Do you want me to turn off the television?"

"That's okay," I said. "I like it on." I went over to the gaping door, taking a few last pulls, then tossed the cigarette onto the walkway outside and shut it. In the freezing room I pulled off my leggings, letting them puddle on the floor, and yanked up the covers. Leslie got into bed and reached for the light. Then she rolled over in the other bed, still fully clothed, her back a lump in the dark.

I listened to the noise of the television for a long while, my brain feeling too sharp, buzzing.

At last, unable to sleep, I said, "What was she like?"

Leslie's body under the covers was still, and I thought maybe she hadn't heard me. Then she said, "She was . . . you know, she was the baby of the family." She rolled onto her back, eyes closed, speaking to the ceiling. "She liked attention. She had my dad wrapped around her finger. She ran away when she was a teenager, but she used to call him up for years after that. Tell him lies about her life, how she was getting a business degree, ask him for money, then spend it on drugs. She was pretty and charming and everybody who knew her thought she was going to grow up and do something big. She would get these—I don't know if they were crushes, these things about other people that she admired, and then she would try to be just like them, then forget about it the next week. She would take my things and deny she'd done it. She could be really sweet sometimes, though. Really thoughtful. Mostly not toward me, though."

"Do you miss her?" I asked. When she didn't answer right away, I added, "I've never known anyone who died before. I can't imagine it being, like, my sister. Is it weird for you that she's dead?"

Her chest rose and fell in the dim light. "I haven't talked to her in ten years," she said. "It doesn't feel like much has changed."

9

Robin

It was April. Plastic luminarias and string lights persisted here and there despite the Easter crosses in the yards below, from which Jesus lolled woodenly. That night it snowed, shockingly late in the year for Albuquerque. Leslie and I dragged blankets over to the window and watched it come down. From beneath the snow, the lights in the neighbors' bushes gave off an unearthly pink-and-green glow.

In the morning the television said school had been canceled for the day. My father had left for work already; my mother was asleep, stretched facedown across the bed in the silk nightie I coveted and stole to dress up in whenever she left it on the floor. Leslie and I carted our snow boots out of the closet and wandered outside. It was forty-eight degrees already and climbing; the sun gave the snow a permanent glare. We tramped all the way across the packed-down sidewalks to the arroyo by Indian School Road. There were barely any cars out, and no other people. It felt like we were the only ones alive, which was how I liked it.

The runoff from the Sandia Mountains was enough to fill the arroyos in any ordinary April. With the snow melting, the water reached nearly to the concrete rim of the gully. A Styrofoam Wendy's cup bobbed on the current, its straw flopping out like a tongue.

We clung to the railing, watching the cup go by, boots slipping on the rungs. Leslie had to yell over the sound of the water. She told me a kid my age had died here, right here. He'd fallen in and been sucked underneath the current before he could call for help. His body surfaced all the way in Los Lunas. That was twenty years ago now. They said that every twenty years the water took a six-year-old just like him. A sacrifice.

Leslie waited until I was looking wide-eyed at the water before she poked me in the ribs. I shrieked and fell backward off the railing, pinwheeling my arms as I went, and landed in the snow with my arms spread like Jesus Christ. She dissolved into giggles.

I don't want to die, I told her when I stopped crying.

You won't, she said. *I'm sorry.*

I savored it. What she meant was *I love you.* She never said it to me, so I always said it twice for her.

I love you. I love you, Leslie.

She held my mittened hand on the way home.

10

Mary

I woke up just as the sun began to press in at the edges of the blinds, casting long hot stripes across Leslie's face. She was completely passed out, mouth open, arm hanging off the mattress. I lay there across from her, staring at her face. Prickles of sweat rose on my skin underneath the covers, like ants crawling up my stomach.

When my brain came back online I got this thick jolt of adrenaline. I sat up, sending the springs wild, *creak creak creak,* and froze in place as Leslie frowned in her sleep at the sound.

There had been something not right about her. That strong, sick smell she'd given off last night, clutching my arm. I could still taste it in the back of my throat.

It was gone now, whatever it was. Asleep, Leslie was just another drunk upper-middle-class lady on her Vegas weekend, crashed out in her wrinkled Ann Taylorwear. Her throat rattled as she drew in a dry breath through her mouth, and her chest rose and fell slowly.

She wasn't my friend. Not really.

I thought suddenly: I could pick up her purse. Put it over my shoulder, walk right out to her car. I'd be halfway to LA before she noticed I was gone.

Leslie kept sleeping as I got slowly out of bed, dressed, and went

over to her purse, which she'd left slouched against the wall. I un-
zipped it and drew out her wallet, one of those Vera Bradley paisley
wristlets. She had at least six or seven credit cards in there along
with her ID and insurance stuff. I remembered how she'd said she'd
lost her job. Maybe she was maxing them out, one by one. The
pouch had a lot of cash, though. Four twenties, a five, and a few
ones.

I thought about her big fancy wedding set and her nice new-
smelling car and how she was probably going to get her fifty grand
even if it was after a lot of legal shit instead of right away like she
wanted. I thought about how she probably deserved to wait for it,
the way she'd talked about her sister yesterday. *She owes me money,*
sucking on one of my cigarettes.

Then I took all the cash, stuffed it in my duffel, and closed the
door on her as gently as I possibly could.

Outside, standing in the thin shade under the awning of the entrance to the motel, I sent another text.

baby?
we have a lot to talk about 😬 😬 😬
can you pick me up?
im at

I glanced around. The motel was on the corner of some street
adjacent to Boulder Highway, but I couldn't find the street sign. Farther away, on the edge of the highway proper, I spotted a Blueberry
Hill next to the Walgreens on the corner and realized I was totally
starving.

im at the blueberry hill on boulder hwy. breakfast on me

The restaurant was already crowded, and I started to feel good
about myself after a few minutes sitting on one of the drugstore-
style stools at the counter slurping my Diet Coke. I'd ordered one

of their half-ton platters of chilaquiles and the restaurant was playing the underrated Canadian folk anthem "You Were On My Mind,"
which felt like it was telling me something about me and Paul. I
took out my phone and started playing Fruit Ninja.

I felt somebody at my elbow and twisted around, the thank-you
halfway out of my mouth before I realized it wasn't a server with
my chilaquiles.

Sam tapped the man beside me on the shoulder. "Could you
scoot down, please, sir? I want to sit next to my girlfriend."

The man shifted over one stool, and Sam hefted himself onto the
pre-crushed vinyl. "That's what I told my friend you were," I said to
him, eyeing the other man over his shoulder before I let my eyes rest
on him. "My abusive boyfriend. I said you stalked me and hit me."

Sam chuckled. "Is that so? Well, wouldn't I be flattered."

"Maybe I wasn't lying. Seems like you're stalking me now." I
sniffed. "I'm feeling kind of emotional about it, actually. Like I could
start crying to some strangers in this restaurant about the scary man
following me. If you don't leave me alone."

The waitress appeared behind the counter and set down my chilaquiles, her face lighting up as she saw Sam. "Been a while, Sammy!
We missed you around here. You want anything? Something to
drink?"

"Maisie! How you doing? If I could get a . . ." Sam craned his neck
to see the edge of my plastic menu underneath the chilaquiles. "A
buttercream waffle, and a cup of coffee, please. Thanks very much."
He winked at me. "Breakfast on you, right?"

I slumped in my seat. "Fine. Do you want more money? Is that
what this is about?"

"It's about you still talking to Paul," Sam answered, filching a
chilaquile. "Honey, you got to cut it out." He rested his chin in his
hand and looked at me for a few seconds without speaking. I stared
back, trying to keep my face neutral. "You're not getting back together with him," Sam said finally. "I don't know if you get that, you
know, in here." He tapped my breastbone with two thick fingers
uncomfortably hard.

I regarded him, his little round blue eyes, his round pink face, and tried to figure out the best way to get myself out of there alone. Finally I put on a wide, warm smile, showing all my teeth. "Don't you have better things to do than worry about me, Sam?" I asked, resting my hand on his arm.

"To be honest, I do," he said, crunching on another one of my chilaquiles. He nodded to himself. "Yes, I do. But I have a soft spot for you. You got that pretty face, you got legs for days. You deserve more than this Paul guy, honey. You deserve to never have to work again. You could really set yourself up, you know? You could have more than this." The waitress dropped off a mug of coffee and he paused to smile at her. Then he looked at me and the smile disappeared into his puffy face. "But unfortunately, I think you are *intent* on wasting your potential on guys like Paul. Rich guys who tell you they're gonna take you to the Maldives while they run around behind your back telling all the other pretty dummies the same thing. You're that kind of girl. You'll just pine, and moan, and work your good looks right off. Maybe you'll do some meth to stay skinny. Eventually, you'll be a little wasted shell of yourself, forty years old. And then," he said, stirring sugar into his coffee, "maybe you'll finally lower yourself to be my lady friend for real, huh?"

I barely breathed for a few long seconds, feeling my jaw tense and relax in a compulsive rhythm. When I could speak, I said, "Oh, Sam. I wouldn't fuck you if your dick would cure my cancer." I stood up, grabbed my duffel bag, and extended two fingers to tap his khaki-covered chest. "I don't know if you get that. In here."

He laughed and caught my hand. "I'm just telling you the truth. I know you don't hear it that often."

I wrenched my hand out of his grip.

"See you next Saturday," he said. "Get your tips ready."

I leaned in and said into his ear, "You'll never see me again."

He snickered and turned back to his coffee as I headed for the exit.

11

Leslie

Someone had pulled the plug, or maybe there had been a power outage; the bedside clock read —:—. Next to me, my phone went *fbbbbbb* against the mattress. I swiped green. "Hello?" I whispered.

"Oh, shit, I woke you up," Dave said in my ear. He sounded so close, like he was in bed with me. "I'm sorry."

I sat up. "No, no. I'm fine." I yawned a little, feeling my jaw pop, and glanced over at the other bed.

It was empty.

My heart began to pound. "What time is it?"

"It's a little past ten. Wait, is Las Vegas Pacific time? It's nine for you, then."

"Nine already?" The room still smelled sour. Me, maybe—I'd slept in my clothes—or Mary's cigarettes from last night.

Her duffel bag was gone.

"You didn't pick up last night," Dave said. I could hear rattling in the background. "Have you been out for like ten hours?"

"I guess so." I crawled out of my bed and leaned over hers to look in the gap between the bed and the wall. No duffel. "It was a long day."

I stepped away from the beds and stumbled toward the bath-

room. My mouth was sticky. Bits of peanuts littered the carpet between the beds and the door to the bathroom. I pushed it open and
turned on the light.

"Did you find her?"

It took me too long to answer, standing there in my wrinkled
clothes staring at myself in the bathroom mirror.

I was alone.

It was over.

Finally I said, "Yes."

"Well, that's great! She's in Henderson, then, right?"

I put Dave on speakerphone on the nightstand and went over to
my purse and pawed through it. I'd left my wallet unbuttoned last
night; it was lying half-open on top of everything else. I tossed it on
the floor and pulled out the iron-free dress and pair of underwear
I'd packed. "No."

Television in the background. Dave's voice was tinnier on speaker.
"What do you mean? She wasn't at the address?"

I took my wrinkled clothes off, my fingers clumsy on the buttons. "I—"

There was a rattling noise and a knock on the motel-room door.
I yanked the dress over my head and hurried to open the door.

Mary was standing there, makeup-free, in cutoffs and that utility
jacket from yesterday. She held up a Walgreens bag. "You said she
was blond, right?"

"Is that her?" Dave asked from the nightstand.

All the breath went out of me in a rush. I snatched up the phone
and switched speakerphone off. "Yeah. I think she's going to, um,
come with me," I said, voice wobbling. "We might be back late tonight. I'll text you." I looked at Mary as I said it, but she only pushed
past me into the musty room, rummaging in the Walgreens bag.

"Good." A pause. "I'm missing you, baby."

"Me too," I said automatically. "Dave, I—"

The television in the background shut off, and Dave laughed. "Eli
says—"

"What?"

"Eli says—"

Mary finished tugging on her tank top and turned to face me as she sat on the bed, crossing her legs. She opened her mouth, then closed it again. There was something uncertain about her expression, a slackness to the muscles there. "Can I call you back?" I said into the phone. "I need to talk to . . ."

"Robin?" Dave asked.

"Yes," I breathed.

12

Mary

"Was that your husband?"

Leslie nodded. She was in a shapeless navy shift dress now, still wearing those pearl earrings. The skin around the earrings was red and irritated from where they'd dragged against the mattress in her sleep.

She was just standing there, clutching her phone. I held up the box dye and wiggled it. There was a picture of a frowning woman on the cover with a platinum Cleopatra bob. "Didn't you say Robin was blond?"

Leslie let out a breath. "You mean it?"

I shrugged my jacket off and hung it over the chair. "It's just a week, right?"

"Yes," Leslie said almost before I stopped talking.

"And we never see each other again."

"Yes," Leslie said, "yes—I'll get you a burner phone, you can toss it as soon as you leave." She shut her mouth on whatever else she was going to say. Her eyes were red-rimmed, makeup caked in the corners.

"I want to get out of here," I confessed. "I need to not be where—where Sam is."

"What about your parents?" Leslie asked. "And your car? Will anyone come looking for you if you're gone for a whole week?"

"Wow, Leslie," I said.

She blanched. "I didn't mean it like that."

"I know you didn't." I glanced down. "No. No one will come looking. I don't have . . . people like that, people who would worry." I shrugged. "It's just me. And you now."

For a second we were motionless, staring at each other, linked invisibly by our ridiculous partnership. Then she stumbled across the room toward me. I could have brought my arms up to defend myself, but I didn't. I let her fall against me. She clung to me, smelling of yesterday's schnapps and Lancôme powder and sweat. She hugged me, like I was saving her from something.

I slipped the cash back into Leslie's wallet when she went to take a shower. When she came out, I was watching an infomercial about a food processor, with the bits and pieces of the hair-dye kit scattered around me on the mattress.

"I can't open this," I said, holding out the bottle of developer. "Hey, have you ever used one of these things? The chopper thing? Does it work?"

Leslie took the bottle from me and pulled at it. "They don't chop things evenly," she said. "So some stuff cooks all the way through, some gets burned . . . It's a—let's go into the bathroom, I feel like this is going to explode—it's a scam."

I gathered up the rest of the kit and followed her meekly into the stuffy motel bathroom. "Am I going to have to watch videos?" I blurted suddenly, watching her wrench at the cap.

"What?" Leslie glanced up, her ears peeking through her wet hair.

"Like of Robin," I said, the name feeling foreign in my mouth. "Do I need to, like, watch videos of her so I can pretend to be her?"

She frowned and pulled again at the developer bottle. The cap came free at last and Leslie sighed in relief. "We never made home videos or anything. There's a few photos of us in old albums and things, but . . . it's really just signing her name. I guess you could practice her signature, but I doubt anyone's going to be looking that closely at it." She swallowed and handed the bottle back to me. "You just have to act normal. You don't even have to act like you like me. She definitely didn't."

"What if I get caught?" I asked. The bathroom lights were bright blue fluorescent, washing us both out in the mirror. "What if they find out I'm not her?"

"Albert—the lawyer—he's met her maybe twice, more than ten years ago," she said. "If I say you're her, I'm the one who would know. I don't have any other close relatives. Dave's never met her. There's almost zero chance that you'll get caught. But there is a risk. It's fifty thousand dollars and it's not really your money."

I poured the developer into the dye and shook the bottle. "And no one knows she's dead? She'll be in the city records as Rachel Vawhatever?"

"Rachel Vreeland," she said. "Yes. No one knows except me, I'm pretty sure. She was living under the other name since she moved to Las Vegas, I think."

I put on the plastic gloves and lifted the bottle to my hairline.

"How did you end up in Vegas?" Leslie asked, watching me spread the dye along my scalp.

I hesitated. "A boy," I said at last, dragging out the second word. "He lived out here. A little older than me. He helped me move and everything, set me up in his apartment. It didn't work out, but it sure was nice while it lasted." I made it sound more romantic than it was so that Leslie wouldn't think I was a sucker.

"Where were you from before?"

"My folks are in Texas. Outside Dallas. I don't talk to them now. They didn't much like me running off to Vegas for a guy." I sucked in air through my teeth as I spread more dye across the back of my head. "Gosh, this stings! I didn't know it was gonna hurt." I looked in the mirror, at Leslie behind me, her broad shoulders and long pale face. There was a funny flat spot just at the bridge of her nose. "Come on, distract me," I said. "Tell me something about you. Something Robin would know."

Her forehead twitched, and she leaned against the damp sand-colored tiles, folding her arms. "My middle name's Elizabeth. After my grandmother."

"Aww," I said, scrunching my fingers in my hair. "Were y'all close?"

Leslie shook her head.

"How about you and Robin?" I said. "You made it seem like she didn't like you much. You were the older one, right?"

"Four years," Leslie said, seeming to shrink against the wall. "When we were really little, I guess we were close. We shared a room and everything. Then when I was in middle school she got her own room and suddenly she hated me."

"Wow," I said. "Like, for no reason?"

Leslie lifted a shoulder. "I never really thought about it. She was just a kid. You can't blame kids for things."

I finished scrunching dye into my hair and came over to crouch on the tile floor. After a minute, Leslie slid down the wall next to me. "I gotta wait on this stuff," I said. "Twenty minutes. Tell me more. How did your parents meet?"

Leslie's shoulder brushed against mine, and a little more color came into her voice. "He was older. He was forty-four when they met and she was twenty-six. He was a lawyer, so he didn't really have time to date. He met my mom at a restaurant where the department store she worked at was having a Christmas party. He said when she used to tell the story, she said she almost didn't go to the party because she was getting over the flu. She sat in the corner and coughed and coughed, and he brought her a glass of water, and then he asked her out. She said she would go out with him if she was well by New Year's. He had a care package of cough medicine and Kleenex and soup delivered to her store. So then she had to go out with him." She smiled, crooked tooth on display.

"That's adorable."

"Yeah."

"What happened to your mom?"

The smile disappeared. "She died," Leslie said. "When I was twelve."

"I'm sorry."

"Yeah."

"When did your dad die?"

"A few months ago. It wasn't a surprise. He had thyroid cancer. He couldn't do much for the last seven years or so."

I itched at my scalp. Leslie watched me do it. She had pale eyes, as unsaturated as the rest of her coloring, so that against the vanilla tiles she could have been part of the motel décor.

After a while she said, "I think that was part of why Robin ran away. She didn't want to deal with it."

I stayed quiet, squatting next to her.

"Daddy and I, we didn't know where she was for the first few years. We kept thinking she'd come back . . . Then we thought we'd never see her again. When she was nineteen she called and asked for money to go to business school in Florida. Daddy was thrilled. He sent her the money right away. Then we didn't hear from her for a couple months, so I called the school and asked them to check on her. They said she'd never been enrolled. After a while a creditor in Louisiana got in touch with us about some debt she'd run up. She called from New Orleans a few times after that, asking for money, which he gave to her, of course. Then saying she was thinking about getting married and wanted his blessing. She was planning to bring the guy home to meet us. But she never showed up. When I got married she left a message for me with Daddy's home nurse. It didn't make any sense. The nurse said she sounded drunk. Then we didn't hear anything from her anymore."

I picked through my hair, moving locks aside so I could make sure I hadn't missed a spot. "You don't sound mad at her."

Leslie was silent, hands braced on her knees. Finally she said, "She's dead. It's useless to be mad at her now." She looked over at me. "I should let you rinse that out."

It took almost ten minutes before the water was clear of dye, and even after the second round of chemicals it still felt like sticks. Leslie peered around the door just as I started finger-combing the ends in the mirror.

Her expression went all funny when she saw me.

"What do you think?" I said. "It's kind of yellowy, but maybe that'll go away when it's dry."

She blinked. "Mary, you . . . It really looks like her."

"Robin," I said. "You should call me Robin."

"You're right," she said, but she didn't correct herself, just hung there in the half-open doorway. "We should . . . practice, I guess."

"Go ahead," I said, making eye contact with her in the mirror. "I don't want to slip up later."

Leslie's face was pale. "You mean start right now?"

"Hi, Leslie," I replied, imitating her flat New Mexican accent. "It's me, Robin."

She flinched.

"Good?" I asked her, turning around to look at her in person, but she was already disappearing behind the door again.

"Yeah, good," she said, muffled. "I'm going to pack up. I'll be ready to go in a minute."

I turned back to my reflection in the mirror and practiced smiling. Then I stopped. It felt strange to be smiling alone.

13

Robin

We were obsessed with the car, a '78 Pinto, painted what I called in my head Nineteen-Seventies Orange, straight off the muddy color palette of the decade, so that only a few years into my parents' marriage it started to look dusty next to the '80s models on the road, whose yellows and reds had been calibrated for television commercials instead of magazine ads. The interiors were cognac leather, same as my father's briefcase. It was his commuter car; I imagined him speeding off to work, cradled in his Pinto like an important file.

Mostly we loved the back windshield, which stretched from roof to license plate in a single sheet of reinforced glass as big as a picture window. Had we ever been rear-ended we would have been ribboned, which never occurred to us as we stood backward on the seat to look out at the billboards and gas stations disappearing in our wake. They shrank almost faster than I could fix my eye on them, the way things did when you tried to remember them on purpose.

Before the Grand Canyon we had ridden in the Pinto only a few times each—four times for me, six for Leslie, an injustice—and never on the highway. At sixty miles per hour I thought I might grow wings. That was the year I was four and Leslie was eight; whatever I was, she was double it. I regretted my babyishness bitterly, feeling that I was letting her down. Had I been even two years older I could have been everything to her, as she was everything to me; but as it stood I knew I was too shallow a receptacle for her secret thoughts. It was torture to be aware of these separate chambers of her personality yet too short to access them.

Later, Leslie would say, *Do you remember our vacation?* and I'd pretend I did, nod along as she told her favorite story from it: Daddy in the Hawaiian shirt and rolled-up khakis, beltless, deck-shoed, as if the edge of the canyon were a prow; his bare ankles were as white as the skin under a cast. Next to him my mother, just after she'd cut her hair, wearing her old shirtdress with the wooden buttons. *Let me have your camera, Warren,* she said to my father. *I want to take a picture of this*—motioning at the sunset, whose striations echoed the layers of sediment. He handed it over and she stood on the bars of the lookout point for half an hour getting tan, pointing the camera this way and that, while Leslie and I complained. At last the light faded and she agreed it was time for dinner and held the camera out to Daddy, who didn't grasp it quickly enough; it cracked to the ground and skittered under the safety fence, slipping over the edge of the canyon with an anticlimactic *chhup!*

Leslie and I went survivalistically silent. My mother began to apologize. His expensive camera! But he was bare-ankled, in high spirits. *Who cares about the camera,* he said, and took her in his arms. He bent her over backward, like a ballroom dancer, kissing her against the magic backdrop. Like all good vacations, it convinced us that these versions of ourselves were truer than the others, that the workaday shell of my mother could at any moment spring open to reveal her more buoyant, romantic insides.

I didn't remember any of that. Leslie could have made it up and I would have believed her. I don't think she did; she clung to it for years after, never bothering to change it out for a better story. For her it represented a kind of perfect happiness. I wanted to share her happiness, so I lied: *Yes, I remember!* When my only memory of the trip was of Leslie gifting me her Honey Bun, which I ate facing the enormous picture window, smearing sugar grease on my father's beloved briefcase seats, licking my fingers one by one as the Pinto lifted off like a plane. Leslie beside me, my mother in front of her, Daddy in the driver's seat, cameraless: each of us experiencing exactly as much happiness as we could successfully contain.

14

Leslie

Even with stops for gas, a new phone for Mary, and brown-sugar cinnamon Pop-Tarts (traditional on road trips, she told me), the trip home seemed half as long as my drive to Vegas. I kept swallowing nervous spit as we crossed into Albuquerque. "Birthdate," I said.

"May . . . twenty-second?" Mary said. "Um, 1992," she added, more confidently.

"Good," I said. "What's your father's name?"

"Walter Voigt."

"Warren." I gripped the steering wheel.

"Warren. That's right." She leaned down to unzip her duffel and took out a tube of strawberry Chapstick. "Want some?" she asked as she rubbed it over her lower lip.

I shook my head. "What's your mother's maiden name?"

"You didn't tell me that." She capped the Chapstick and put it back in the bag.

"It's Stetson," I said, feeling sick.

"Like the hats?"

I smiled perfunctorily.

It was the worst time to drive. The sun blinded me in one eye as we entered the foothills. Every so often it gained the perfect angle and turned the dust on the windshield totally opaque.

"What have you been doing in Vegas?" I asked.

She looked blank. "Waitressing. You know that."

"No—Robin-you. Dave will ask."

Mary shrugged. "She could be waitressing too."

"I guess that's true."

Mary turned her head to stare out at the trickle of the Embudo arroyo. "I'm good, you know. I'm not going to freak out."

"Okay." I blew out a breath. "I guess we'll see when we get there."

She gave me that smile she'd practiced in the mirror, the Robin smile, then turned back to the window.

I turned the radio on. "You Light Up My Life" immediately oppressed the car.

Every time I glanced over to check on Mary, the color of her hair startled me a little—that and the slight pink fleshiness of her arm resting against the divider. She was real, meaty in a way that Robin's body hadn't been. With her hair lighter, closer to the color I remembered from childhood, she seemed more like my sister than my sister had.

"What's that?"

"Lynnewood? Just a park."

"It looks like it was air-dropped in from Connecticut."

We went slowly north, following the mountains, the sun sinking over the tops of the adobe roofs.

"You live way out here, huh?" Mary asked.

"Kind of," I said. "It's a nice community."

"I thought you said your husband was a firefighter."

"Fire safety engineer," I said. "It's different."

"Must be." She stuck her finger in her mouth and ran her nail along one of her molars.

I turned in to our neighborhood and drove down High Canyon Trail. Mary rolled down her window and lit a cigarette. It was twilight now and cool. The hairs on my arms rose. "Please don't smoke in the car."

She looked at me and ashed into the wind. "We're almost there, right?"

I didn't answer. Eventually the silence made her put the cigarette out.

We pulled up to the house a few minutes later, the grit on the driveway crunching beneath the tires. My ears felt stuffed with cotton after eight hours of engine noise. I paused in the driver's seat as Mary put her shoes back on and glanced up at the house. For a moment we were both staring at it. When we'd first bought it I'd felt exultant every time I looked at it. Mine, ours: the superclean, near-white stucco façade; the arched, shining window over the reclaimed-wood front door; the long, lazy concrete walkway, which wound like a stream from the front door to the driveway, suggesting that the people who lived there had eons of time on their hands.

The porch light flickered on. After a moment, Dave opened the door and came hurrying out. He was in his new jeans, the effect of which was ruined by the combination of his old thin Tweety Bird T-shirt and flap-soled sneakers, and the familiar warmth at seeing him crept into my fingertips. He was still beautiful, the porch light separating the lines of his face into smooth, rounded planes. Just behind that, equally familiar, I felt the flood of nausea as he approached.

I can't do it, I thought suddenly. He'll know right away.

I couldn't get out of the car.

"Lights," Mary said nonsensically beside me. I looked wide-eyed at her. "Camera. Action!" She gave me a smile. At some point she'd put lipstick on. When had she done that?

Dave had reached the driver's-side door. He pulled on the handle, then knocked on the window and waved at me. I fumbled to unlock it. "Hi," he said when he'd gotten it open, giving me a quick kiss on the lips. "How are you?"

I tried to focus on what I'd say if I were coming home alone. "Tired," I said, touching his cheek. His stubble scraped my palm. "Hungry."

"Good. I made chili. You must be Robin," he added, coming around the car to take Mary's duffel bag from her.

"Oh, you don't have to do that," she said. She was doing the same accentless voice she'd used earlier, in the mirror. It sounded fake to me, but Dave seemed undisturbed. "Are you Dave? It's so nice to meet Leslie's husband."

"Yeah, you too," Dave said, heaving the duffel on his shoulder. "Come in, you can get something to eat. How was the trip?" he asked over his shoulder as he led the way to the front door.

I tensed.

"Nothing to tell," Mary said. "I ate a lot of Pop-Tarts. Your house is so fancy," she exclaimed as she stepped over the threshold.

"Thanks," Dave said. "We like it."

I followed them into the house, glancing up at the wrought-iron chandelier in the entryway as I almost never did. I hadn't thought of it as being fancy in a long time.

"So Leslie said it took her a while to find you," Dave said, coming back down the stairs and heading for the kitchen. His tone was casual, but I could read the sliver of his face visible over his shoulder as he opened one of the cabinet doors.

"Oh, do you have wine?" Mary asked.

There was a brief pause before Dave followed her gaze to the cabinet, which held a line of Viognier glasses. "Yeah," he said. "Oh, sure. White okay?"

"That's fine."

He went to the refrigerator as she sat down at the breakfast nook. I leaned against the island countertop. "Yeah, she was kind of in the middle of nowhere outside of Vegas," I said. "No cellphone or anything. I had to call the landlord."

"Oh, but it was so funny," Mary broke in, accepting her glass of wine and grabbing Dave by the arm. "She had been hanging out at my place all day waiting for me, and when she finally got tired and went to get a bite to eat, guess which place she chose."

"Your restaurant," Dave said, going to the counter for two more glasses and brushing against me.

"Yes! Well, not exactly, but it's the one my boyfriend works at, and I was just there keeping him company. We ran into each other outside. You should have seen her face." Mary re-created the face for him.

Dave glanced at me and I tried to smile. "You guys had a good time, huh? You went out drinking?"

"Oh my gosh, you should have seen her," Mary told him. "Does she drink a lot at home? No, right? You guys have glasses for wine and everything. Well, she matched me shot for shot." She gave a hoarse chuckle that was nothing like her ordinary laugh; it was carefully unfeminine, designed to contrast with her lipsticked exterior. I realized all at once that she wasn't doing an impression of Robin. She was waitressing. It was that simple.

The tension seeped out of my shoulders.

Dave was grinning as he handed me my glass of wine and took a sip himself, settling into the breakfast nook next to Mary. "Nah," he said. "I've only seen Leslie do a shot once. And I knew her in college."

"You knew me in grad school," I protested, coming over to join them.

"Oh, were you the tequila champ of '09? I just missed your partying days?"

I laughed. Mary glanced between us. When she caught my gaze, I saw a triumphant flicker in hers, which disappeared as Dave spoke again.

"No phone, huh? Are you against technology?"

"Technology is against me," Mary pronounced, pressing her free hand to her chest. "I cannot hold on to a mobile device. I've dropped them, put them in the washer, flushed them . . . I mean." She sipped her wine. "Leslie bought me a new one," she added, as if it had just occurred to her. "On the trip. It was really sweet."

"Not a smart one," I said, as Dave looked at me. "Just an old flip one. It wasn't much."

"Yes it was!" Mary exclaimed. "It was really—Oh, sorry!" She interrupted herself as Dave shushed her. "Is someone else here?"

"Just Eli," Dave said, lowering his voice. "We don't want to wake him up."

"Who's Eli?" Mary asked, looking from me to Dave.

Dave laughed. "No—Eli! Didn't Leslie . . ."

Mary frowned.

"You didn't tell her about Eli?" Dave asked me.

"I didn't have time," I said.

"Who's Eli?" Mary asked again.

"He's our kid," Dave said. "It's past his bedtime, so . . ."

Mary was quiet for once.

I took a long sip.

"You have a baby?" she said at last.

I nodded.

"How old is he?"

"A year," I said. "It was his birthday a couple of weeks ago."

"Wow." Mary sat back in her chair. "Wow. I didn't know." She looked at me, her face a little pink. "I mean, I guess I just didn't think."

"You're an auntie," Dave put in. "Bet you didn't think of that." He was being a little forceful. I touched his knee.

"It's okay," I said. "I mean, you had to find out sometime."

"Wow," Mary said again. "I mean, congratulations. What's he like?"

Dave relaxed. "Well, he just learned 'Yikes,' which I didn't even know he knew. I was going to tell you about this on the phone," he said, turning to me. "You must have taught him that, or Ma. I was making the chili earlier today and I put some red chile in it, and he was in the kitchen playing pots and pans and just demanding to have a piece. He was losing his shit. So I gave him one, and he goes—" Dave imitated Eli's squeak, making Mary stifle her laughter behind her hand.

"He's not going to ask for that again," Mary said.

"Sure he will. His first word'll be *chile* if I have my way." Dave stretched, and stopped in the middle. "Hey, do you guys want some of it? The chili? I forgot all about it, I'm sorry."

"Oh my God," I said, realizing as I said it. "Yes. I'm starving."

"Okay," Dave said, getting up. "Robin, you want some?"

The sound of her name still startled me, but Mary answered to it easily. "Yes, please," she said.

"Two bowls. Actually, I want seconds. Three bowls," Dave said, crossing the room.

"How am I doing?" she asked me quietly. Her hair had dried in a staticky, fluffy halo around her face.

I put my hand over hers on the placemat and squeezed it, once. She grinned.

"I want sour cream on mine," I said to Dave, whisper-shouting across the room.

15

Mary

It was the easiest job I'd ever had.

Warren.

Stetson.

May twenty-second.

He didn't ask me any of those things.

"Why Vegas?" he said, leaning back in his chair. It was past eleven and Leslie was slipping, wine-drowsy. She excused herself to the bathroom.

I could've made up something. I wanted to. Something good, to make me seem more interesting, more specific. That's what I would have done at Letourneau's, so he'd remember me and come back next time. Or so he'd feel sorry for me, tip me extra. But liars are always specific. People who are telling the truth don't bother to try to convince you.

"I was bored," I said instead, picking at a loose stitch at the cuff of my denim jacket.

"In Louisiana?" He was poking for information. Leslie seemed to have told him very little about her sister. He liked me, but he didn't want to. He was scruffy and loyal, like a dog. He wanted to be on Leslie's side. Any reason I gave him to dislike me would relieve him.

I smiled. "Yeah, I was there for a little while."

"Yeah? What'd you do?"

"You mean, like, job-wise?"

"Sure." He watched me.

"Bunch of restaurants, mostly," I said. "I got fired a lot."

"I waited tables too," he said. "That's mostly what I did during college. You really get a feel for humanity doing that shit."

"Yeah," I said. "That's why I got fired a lot."

He laughed.

"So you have a kid," I said, seizing the opportunity to redirect his attention. "You know, I didn't think Leslie was the mom type."

"Leslie's a great mom," he said.

I had hit a nerve. "That wasn't what I was trying to—"

"It's fine," he said. "No, we've always wanted to be parents. That was always in the cards."

"Does she stay home with him?"

"With Eli? No." He took a sip of his wine. "We have a daycare for weekdays."

I frowned. "I thought—"

Leslie came back and flopped carefully into the seat next to Dave. Her cheeks were pink as she leaned forward to kiss Dave's eyebrow. He made a face, then smiled. "Hey, baby," he said. "You look ready for bed."

"I am," Leslie said.

"Me too," I said. "Leslie, can you show me where the guest room is?"

"Oh—sure." She got up, gathering the bowls and glasses and taking them to the sink.

"Dave, thank you so much for dinner," I said, standing. "You don't even know how glad I am to finally meet you."

"Yeah, same," Dave said. His smile flashed across his face so quickly I nearly missed it.

"Mary," Leslie said, as we went into the hallway, just outside Dave's earshot, "thank you. You are doing such a good job," she added, lowering her voice.

I waited as she led me through the white stucco hallway and up the stairs. When we were in the guest bedroom (unnaturally clean, framed photographs of the New Mexican landscape lined up on the bureau), I shut the door and pressed the lock on the knob.

"So there's a luggage rack in the closet," Leslie said, pointing at my duffel bag, which Dave had leaned against the closet door.

"You didn't tell your husband you got fired," I said flatly.

She didn't answer me right away. I could see her face in the mirror. Her ears, sticking through her lank hair, were mottled red. "Not your business," she said. "There are fresh towels in the bathroom closet." She turned to leave.

"How was I supposed to know that?" I hissed, reaching for her shoulder. "What if I fucked it up for you?"

"Did you?"

"No."

"Well, just keep not fucking it up, then," she said. "Okay?"

"Does he know you're going to lose the house?"

"If we get the money, we won't lose the house," she said, jaw tight. "So it's not an issue."

I stared at her. Finally I sat down on the bed, which gave slowly underneath me. Memory foam. "How come you didn't tell me you had a baby?" I asked.

"I told you everything you need to know," Leslie said. "All you need to do is stick to small talk, sign the papers, collect your money, and disappear. At no point do you need to discuss my personal life with my husband."

"Not telling me was stupid," I said, my voice pitched low. "I want to make sure there's nothing else that's going to get me in trouble. If you don't want your husband to find out about your *personal life*, you should think about that."

Leslie's lips thinned. She didn't look drunk anymore. "You're doing a great job," she said. "Focus on that." She came over to the bed, and I felt her long, cold fingers tuck the tag on my jacket back into my collar.

I just looked at her. She exhaled through her nose and left the room. The door clicked shut behind her.

16

Leslie

Alone in the master bedroom, I stepped out of my clothes and gathered up the pile for the hamper. Then I padded into the bathroom to wash my face. I was almost out of retinoid cream. I put a thin ring around each eye, rubbed a stripe into the paper-crease lines on my forehead. Dave had left his shaving things out on the counter. I examined his razor and dropped it into the trash can; he always forgot to switch. I dug out a new one from the package under the sink and left it next to his shaving cream in the cabinet.

When I went back into the bedroom, Dave was in his underwear with his reading glasses on, holding his tablet. I admired the way the long, hard line of his calf muscle shone a little in the reflected light from the lamp, and wondered why it was that the things I liked best about his body were natural, genetic, whereas the things I liked best about mine were artificial: my carefully maintained skin, my gel-protected fingernails.

It took him a moment to notice me. He dropped his tablet into the blankets and held his arms out to me. "Come here, you makeupless kid," he said.

I got into bed and draped myself naked over him, pressing my face into his neck. He smelled like cumin and wine. "I missed you," I said.

I felt his laugh. "You were only gone for, like, two days."

"Yeah, but the whole thing was . . ." I sat up. "I don't know. It was weird."

"Seeing your sister again?"

I nodded. Seeing her body had been awful, but also a relief: I'd never have to worry about her again. If she needed money. What kind of upsetting message she'd left on my machine.

"You never talk about her." Dave was trying hard to sound casual, incurious.

"Because she's not a part of my life." I stopped, and tried a softer tone. "Because her life is not easy on the people around her. I don't want you to be sucked into that part of my family."

"I appreciate that." He rubbed his hand over my back. I sank into the blankets. "Do you think you'd ever forgive her?" he asked after a minute. "I mean, she seems . . . she seems like she's cleaned herself up a little, right?"

He likes her, I thought. "No," I said flatly.

Dave studied my face. "Okay."

I rolled off him. "What did you do? While I was gone."

He made a creaky groan, stretching a little. "Shot the shit with our incredibly charismatic baby, mostly," he said. "Saw my mom for a little while. Took Eli to Elaine's for a playdate with Brody."

"Another one?"

"Yeah, they seem to get along pretty well, although Brody is definitely the one in charge. Our son may be beautiful, but he is a follower by nature. Not a future president. Maybe a future personal assistant. He was all ready to hand Brody his sucker. Not even a peep of protest. Natural philanthropist."

I made myself smile. "How's Elaine?"

"Oh, you know. The Internet's star mommy." Elaine was Dave's coworker, the first one he'd made friends with when he'd started four years ago. Back then her older son, Tanner, was a year old. Elaine had run a semi-popular blog chronicling Tanner's firsts—first steps, first words. Two years ago, when she was seven months pregnant with Brody, her husband left her. A few similar blogs picked up on the story, and Elaine gathered more and more followers. She moved most of her blogging to Instagram, where she posted professional-quality photos of herself and her kids several times a day. She had a funny, dry tone to her writing, undercut by the dream-like, idyllic photography. Dave said she had enough followers now to do ads.

He picked up his phone and scrolled through Instagram. "Look, she posted a picture of Eli. Doesn't he look great?"

Eli was sitting on a tiled floor, staring at one of Elaine's cats, who skulked blurrily in the background. His face was turned away from the camera, which emphasized the length of his thick dark eye-lashes, and his mouth hung open in fascination, the edge of a small pink tongue poking out. He looked just like Dave when he was con-centrating. He looked just like the baby I'd dreamed we would have.

3 seconds before he tried to kiss Misty, Elaine had captioned the pic-ture. *Disappointing results. #ladieshesacatlover #cutebaby #thesmallest-flores #brodyspals #playdate.* It had 654 likes.

"She's a good photographer," I said. "Wow."

"I think she's thrilled I have spawn now, so she can change it up for the 'gram," Dave said. "You can only take so many pictures of the same kids before people are like, *Call me when they cure can-cer.*"

"I mean, she probably just wants more adults to hang out with," I said. "She must be lonely."

Dave laughed. "I doubt it. She's got people over at that house day and night. She could be on *Martha Stewart* or whatever. Handed me a glass of homemade lemonade as soon as I walked in."

"Still." I pressed my cheek into the pillow. "It's different, not hav-ing a husband."

"Yeah, probably." He set the phone back on the nightstand. "Eli had a good time over there. I think he needs more friends. I feel like now that you're getting things wrapped up with your father's house, you'll have some extra time to hang with him. There's a birthday party for one of the other kids at daycare next week. Friday the thirty-first. Maybe you could take him."

I didn't move. "I don't know how long this thing with her is going to take. With Robin."

"Well, if you're free." The mattress tilted as he shifted his weight. "You want to watch something?"

I let him touch my hair, too gently. It felt apologetic. "Do you think Netflix has Anthony Bourdain?"

"Baby, we are gonna find out," Dave said, and clicked the TV on.

Dave fell asleep barely fifteen minutes into "Hanoi." I waited until the episode was over to get up and pull on my T-shirt and boxers and shut the light off. Then I crawled in next to him once more, trying to will myself into sleep.

I pulled his arm over my shoulders and pressed his wrist to my face. His heartbeat, like a live worm, moved against my cheek. His pulse had always been quicker than mine, reminding me every time I was in bed with him of his more subcutaneous functions. It was as if, as the night blinded me, I became more able to see the beauty of his insides: the violet thermal glow of his chest cavity, the electric-blue slosh of his stomach, the red pulsing veins embroidering his skin. He bled heat into the covers, into the mattress, his living so aggressive it kept me alive by proximity. I clutched him to me.

I'd expected to dream about Robin last night, but instead I had dreamed about Dave. The camping trip we took, up in Abiquiú, a few months before we got married. He'd borrowed his sister's wife's old gear, which included a clear-topped tent, and we lay in bed under an enormous glittering canopy as Dave tried to convince me of the existence of various types of desert predators I'd never heard of, complete with sound effects. *That one's the conejillo,* he'd said. *You don't know it because it's a Spanish name. Can you hear it?*

And then later: *Wake up. I miss you.*

I'm right here, I'd said sleepily, opening my eyes to the still-bright stars.

How long had I been lying awake now? An hour? I looked at the bedside alarm but couldn't remember when Anthony Bourdain had ended.

Dave's heartbeat pounded in my ear.

I gave in and sat up.

Down the hallway, lit a little to my dilated pupils. Mary's door across the hall, shut tight. The next door, propped open. I pushed it farther and slipped inside.

There he was, asleep in the crib. He slept facedown, knees tucked underneath him—a position that suggested sleep had caught him standing up, crumpling him thoughtlessly. I stared at him, Eli, our baby, listened to his tiny, rapid breathing.

I don't know how long I stood there, thinking, One more week. Then everything will be fixed.

One more week.

17

Robin

Am I making Leslie sound like a saint? To me she was, at least back then. She taught me how to tie my shoes, how to heat up soup on the stove. She taught me how to read, in between school lessons, sat at home with one of the old *Sassy* magazines she stole from the hairdresser's, helping me follow along the lines of "Ben Stiller: Cute Boy Director" with my fat pointer finger.

She taught me how to lie.

My mother was away again, although her purse still hung on its usual peg by the front door, and Grandma Betty had come to take care of us. We were unused to the surveillance. When it was just my mother around, I went to bed at nine, at Leslie's provocation (she stayed up later, hours that I deeply begrudged her, plagued by visions of Leslie having dozens of friends over, all of them dancing madly around the bonfire without me or eating my personal Cheez-Its). But Grandma Betty believed that children should go to bed at eight, and sometimes barged into our shared room without knocking, hoping to catch us awake.

That night, having gone to bed earlier than I ordinarily did, I'd woken up alone at half midnight. The other bed was empty, Leslie off doing whatever it was she did without me. Instantly I was filled with outrage. Probably she was watching television on the tiny screen in the garage, or was in my parents' bedroom, trying on my mother's things. I jiggled the doorknob, but it was locked from the outside, something Leslie often did when she wanted me to stay out of her business.

I resolved to wait up for her. I thought about folding myself into a ball of blankets at the bottom of her bed and seizing her toes as soon as she got into bed, but I had done that once already, so the sheen had come off. Instead I rolled under her bed, which was taller than mine and could fit a broad-shouldered five-year-old. I'd let her discover my empty bed and fear the worst. I'd come out when she was good and sorry she'd left me out of her surreptitious adventure.

Arms reached out and grabbed me as soon as I rolled under the dust ruffle. I screamed. Leslie clutched me to her and put her hand over my mouth, and I sagged into her embrace.

"What are you doing under the bed?" I said into her fingers, drooling not a little. I hoped she wouldn't ask me what I was doing there.

She nodded at an overturned water glass on the carpet. Inside it, something went *tink, tink, tink,* as if about to make a speech at a wedding. Its shape stretched and shrank as it moved around, bent this way and that by the curvature of the glass. I reached for it and she slapped my hand away.

"What is it?" I whispered, annoyed.

Her eyes didn't leave the glass. "A mouse."

"Oh." I twisted around to look at her. "What are you going to do with it?"

"I'm waiting."

"For what?"

"For it to die."

"Why?"

"I kept hearing it under my bed at night. I thought I would trap it, and then . . ." My body was propping the dust ruffle open, letting the light from the nightlight under the bed. I could see the flutter of her lashes as she blinked rapidly, and her body against mine was as hot as a coal.

The doorknob rattled and the door burst open. I froze in place.

"Robin?" Grandma Betty said, flicking on the light. "Leslie? What are you doing under there?"

The dust ruffle had given me away. I rolled out resignedly. Leslie followed, mouseless.

"Why were you out of bed? What was all the noise about?"

"It was a mouse!" I blurted.

"A mouse game," Leslie said. "Robin pretends to be a mouse and crawls under my bed, and I have to catch her."

Grandma Betty seemed to swell. "Your father has to get up for work in the morning."

"I know. It was all my fault," Leslie said. "I couldn't sleep. I wanted to play the game."

Grandma Betty adjusted her translucent nightgown. Through it I could see her cotton underwear with the lace stitching around the waistband. "Kitchen floors tomorrow, and silverware, Leslie. Don't make another noise."

She shut the door and locked it behind her, plunging us into nightlight-gloom again.

"Leslie?" I whispered.

Leslie got out of her bed and climbed into mine, stroking my hair. I fell asleep before I could remember what I had wanted to say, listening to the *tink, tink, tink* from underneath Leslie's bed.

In the morning she was already in the shower before I woke up. I got on my hands and knees and crawled under the bed. The overturned glass was still there; I supposed Leslie had been too scared to do anything about it. I gave the glass a sharp poke and it tipped over onto the carpet. The mouse was revealed. A girl mouse, gray and cream, with long silver whiskers. It was too exhausted to run; it only dug its claws into the carpet and twitched. I picked it up by its tail and put it in my backpack to take to school with me.

"What did you do with it?" she asked that night, when we were again in bed.

"With what?" I said.

She closed her mouth. I never caught her under the bed again.

18

Mary

The crazy thing is that I woke up with a big smile on my face. I couldn't help it. I'd slept so good in Leslie's ginormous memory-foam bed, and there were wooden hangers for my five articles of clothing in the closet, and rose-scented tissues on the nightstand . . . and I was free. I didn't have work in the morning. I didn't have a boyfriend. I didn't even have to answer to my own name.

Leslie's voice filtered into my consciousness as I squirmed around in the bed, testing how it was possible that I could be comfortable in literally every position. She was on the landing, talking to someone. Dave's voice, low. "Are you sure?"

"Yeah, I'm sure. Go on, go to work." A kiss, then his shoes on the stairs. Her voice again: "Hi, Diego. Just calling to say I'm not feeling well today. I'm going to stay home for now." A beat. "Yeah. I'm going to try to work on it this afternoon if the medicine kicks in . . . Okay. See you."

I frowned. The front door had shut halfway through her conversation, and she'd still faked the whole thing, like Dave might be able to hear her through the wall.

In the other room, the baby began to cry. I rolled over, giving up on going back to sleep. Also, I hadn't bothered to take a shower last night and I was sort of grossing myself out.

I got up and padded over to my duffel bag to get my cigarettes. I thought Leslie probably wouldn't appreciate me smoking in the room, but I didn't want to negate the air-conditioning by opening the window, so I went into the closet and hotboxed myself for a couple minutes until my body assured me it had been satisfactorily saturated in nicotine.

After that I went into the adjoining bathroom and sat down on the toilet. Leslie had mini cruelty-free toiletries lined up on the sink. There was a basket behind them, containing folded hand towels and what looked like inflated macaron cookies.

BOMB, the middle one read.

Oh. Perfect. I ran a bath (built-in, with its own set of wooden stairs leading up to the edge) and dropped the macaron into it. It fizzed happily, turning the water into a dense purple mirror flecked with blue and pink stars.

I climbed into the galaxy and stared down.

There was a faint banging. "Mary?"

Don't you mean Robin? I thought. What if your husband hears from all the way at the firehouse?

"Mary?"

"Come in," I called.

The bedroom door clicked open, then the door to the bathroom. "Oh!" Leslie backed into the doorframe, as if she had entered the bathroom expecting to see me filing my taxes.

"It's okay." I smiled. "Could you hand me the conditioner? Actually, don't worry about it, I'll get it."

I stood up, dripping stars and glitter, and descended the little wooden stairs while Leslie covered her eyes and turned her back.

"Are you—decent?"

I sloshed back into the tub and slouched low enough to cover my chest with stars. "I love your bath products."

Leslie stared at the glittery puddle on the hardwood floor, then made a visible effort to refocus. Was she angry? "I made an appointment with Albert. The trustee, I mean. He couldn't get us in today, though."

More time for me to spend in Leslie's luxury bathtub. "That's too bad," I said.

"I thought you could come with me to my dad's place. I'm packing up his stuff." She waited, adding, when I didn't respond, "You don't have to do anything. You just have to hang out there for the day."

"You don't want me to be here alone," I said, half questioning.

There was a silence. "Be downstairs in half an hour," Leslie said.

"I'm not going to run away or anything," I said, sliding lower in the water and squeezing my eyes shut. "Is that what you're worried about?"

But I was talking to nobody. Past the open doorway, I could hear Leslie's steps echoing on the stairs.

19

Leslie

"How come you don't want to take him with us?" Mary asked through a bite of egg-and-cheese biscuit. She had insisted we stop at McDonald's on the way.

I was unbuckling Eli from his car seat. "Ah. Ah. Ah!" he insisted. I stuck his pacifier in his mouth and hefted him onto my hip.

"I need to focus on getting my dad's things put away," I said.

"I could babysit him." Mary took another bite. "He's cute," she said after swallowing, eyes following Eli's attempt to grab my earring.

"Have you ever taken care of a baby before?" I slammed the car door and lifted the bag of baby items onto my other shoulder.

She leaned over into the driver's seat, cooing at Eli from the rolled-down window. "Aunt Robin. Come on, baby. Say 'Aunt Robin.'"

"That's not funny." I tried to control the tremor in my voice.

She was instantly remorseful. "Sorry, Leslie. I was just joking."

I stared at her, then turned and took Eli into the daycare.

When I came back out, she was licking her fingers, crumpling the tinfoil in her other hand. "I'm really sorry," she said.

"It's fine." I put the car into drive and turned onto Comanche, heading west.

Mary stared out the window as we pulled into the driveway on Riviera a few minutes later. "This it?" she asked, chewing on her lip.

"Yeah." It was a single-story adobe in the style popular in the 1920s, with exposed vigas striping the wall over the garage and a painted teal gate standing slightly open. The latch was broken and I hadn't bothered to fix it yet. There were a few succulents lining the front walk among the multicolored stones that took the place of a lawn, and the neighbor's desert willow cast rippling shadows over them. I thought, as I always did, how much Albuquerque yards looked like aquariums waiting to be filled with water. I remembered being twelve, lying on the ground outside, covering my ears while above, an airplane passed through the clouds like a far-off nurse shark. I'd watched it, listening to the tidal noise of my own breath passing through my nose.

Mary kept quiet as we passed through the gate and into the front hallway. It smelled musty inside, like all dark houses in the desert, cut with a chemical lemon scent from when I'd scrubbed the tiles a month ago. No one had been here; it hadn't faded.

I dropped the boxes next to my dad's La-Z-Boy in the sunken living room and went to hang my purse on the hook by the door. I remembered my mother hanging her purse on this hook years ago, and how elegant I'd thought she looked, lifting it with two fingers just as she left the house. "I thought we'd go through his records and books and give them away," I said. "There's a used bookstore not too far down the road."

"You're not going to keep any of them?" she asked.

I shook my head. "I don't even know what's in here," I said. "He never played any of it, just collected."

"You know, there's, like, a vinyl resurgence," she said, sitting on the carpet in front of the pinewood bookcases and running her hands along the faded album spines. "You could probably sell some of these on the Internet or something."

"I mean, feel free to take one if you like it," I said, crouching next to her. I tilted my head. These books were so familiar to me, and yet I'd never read them the entire time they'd been here—some of them longer than I'd been alive. The tattered red-and-green capitals of

The Recognitions; the pale blue of *Red Sky at Morning;* the ugly off-white of *Wanda Hickey's Night of Golden Memories.* I took out *Myra Breckinridge* and paged through it.

"Your dad sure liked to read, huh?"

I glanced at her. "I don't know. I think he liked to have them there for people to see more than he liked to read them. I never saw him open most of these."

"Did you read any of them?" She was picking through the records too carefully, dropping them in the box one by one.

"No," I said. "I never did. I don't read that much." Dave bought me audiobooks for the car. Otherwise I read mostly magazine articles and the news and Facebook. Opening a real book—holding it up in bed—felt farcically virtuous. I could never tell if I liked it or if I only liked the picture I made. I remembered my manners and cleared my throat. "Do you? Read much?"

She smiled, her eyes locked on the album in her hands. "Sure. I read sometimes."

"What kind of stuff do you like?"

Mary pursed her lips. "I like to challenge myself to read five important books a year. For self-improvement. Last year I read *Middlesex.* And I was reading a book this month by a woman named Mary Carson. No. Mary Karr. But I left it behind."

"You can take whatever you want from here." I grabbed a handful of books and fitted them into one of the cardboard boxes. "I'm dropping them all off at Menaul otherwise."

"I don't think they'll fit in my duffel," she said, running her fingers over the spines. "I'm gonna have one of these someday. A big old shelf to show I'm not just looks." She grinned at me and went back to adding records to her own box, one at a time. After a minute she said, "What was your daddy like?"

"Um," I said. "He was a decent guy." One of the books clipped my fingernail and I winced and stuck it in my mouth, continuing, muffled, "It was hard to be really close to him, you know, because he was already pushing sixty when I was a teenager, and he got sick right after that. I spent a lot of time taking care of him." I went back to adding books, heaviest at the bottom, more carefully this time.

"What did he look like?"

"Hang on." I unfolded my legs and stood up, going over to my dad's study opposite the living room. On top of the old secretary was a photograph of him and my mom on their wedding day. He had an enormous blond mustache and no hair on top. Her hair was a feathered, backcombed pageboy in the Princess Diana style, and she wore a high-necked powder-blue nightgown of a wedding dress. She looked so young next to him, like it was her first dance.

I brought the photo to Mary. She laughed as I put it in her hands. "He looks like Ron Burgundy."

"Who's that?"

She shook her head at me. "It's from a movie. Never mind. Your mom was cute. How old was she here?"

"Twenty-six." Something about her silence made me keep talking. "She was pregnant with me in this picture."

Mary looked up in surprise. "Really? Wow. Shotgun wedding?"

"I'm not sure," I said, telling the truth. "She was only one or two months along, so maybe she didn't know until after."

"You look like her," Mary said, setting the photograph on the carpet.

"My dad used to say that." After his first surgery, he was on pain medication almost all the time. It helped give him some respite from the open wound in his neck and the persistent, wracking cough that made it hard for him to swallow food, but it also sent him swimming out into a kaleidoscopic half reality. He called me Chrissy a lot. It made me sad, and then a little angry; he spoke to me-as-Christine in the absent imperative: *Get me my chair, Chrissy. Leave me with my nurse, if you please, Chrissy.* I hadn't even remembered he'd talked to my mother that way until he got sick and mixed us up. Then it came creeping back: what a tight ship he'd run then, how silent we all were.

I looked around at the room. The long thin bars of light coming through the blinds had slid toward the wall, signaling noon's approach.

"We should get back to work," I said. "I'm almost done with this shelf. I'll go through his study next. You can help me when you're done with the albums." I dropped the last few books into the box haphazardly, bending a few of the pages.

"'Kay," Mary said, still looking at the photo on the floor. I snatched it up and went into the study to unfold another box.

The study was cramped and dark, full of floating dust motes that flurried every time I picked up one of Daddy's clothbound 1960s textbooks and heaved it into the box. I was wondering what to do with the cigar box that held his class ring when there was a rustling sound from the other room and then music began to filter into the hallway.

"Mary?" I called.

I went back into the living room. Mary wasn't there. I followed the music down the hall, feeling sicker and sicker the closer I got to the open doorway.

She was standing in the middle of Robin's old bedroom, facing away from me toward the record player propped up on a chair. When she heard me push the door farther open, she turned around and grinned. "Look what I found!" she said over the noise, holding up the record sleeve with both arms like Vanna White. "He's got so much ancient stuff here. I love it. Have you ever heard of Laura Nyro?"

"No." The photo on the cover of the album was of a long-faced, heavy-browed woman pulling on her own dark hair. She looked like my mother the way I remembered her, with the thin, round bangs. "Come back out to the living room."

"You barely got to this room at all," Mary said. "Wow, I feel like I'm being stared at."

She didn't mean me. She meant the posters.

Robin's room was covered in faces. Photographs lined the walls and ceiling. Iggy Pop approximating Munch's scream, Grace Jones snarling, Britney Spears ducking her head, Kate Hudson as Penny Lane, Ava Gardner as herself, Lincoln, Kahlo, Courbet's desperate man. From behind, bits of the pale blue wallpaper peeked out, the prim white wainscoting. Two mirrors faced each other at either end of the room. In between, an enormous bureau and a third, smaller mirror, garlanded with dusty plastic hibiscus flowers. The comforter was a dull black, incongruous, strewn with clothes, which were scattered over the rug and hung from the open drawers of the bureau. The mess was a teenage girl's, in medias; she might have returned at any moment. Daddy had never touched it.

Now Mary was standing in her room, wearing her face.

"You don't want me to be in here, huh?" she asked with Robin's mouth, wrinkling Robin's forehead.

I felt dizzy. "We need to pack."

"Okay, but you gotta listen to the song first. I'll start it again." Mary gathered up the record player and carried it out into the hallway. I shut Robin's door firmly behind her.

"You look stressed out, Leslie," Mary said, setting the needle and lying down in the middle of the sunken living room, closing her eyes, spreading her arms and legs like a snow angel. "Come rest with me. I'm sorry I went in Robin's room. I didn't know it was hers."

I sat down next to her. "It's all right." After a second I said, "Oh. I do know this song. I recognize this song."

"Lie down," she said, without opening her eyes.

"Why?"

She didn't answer. After a moment I lay down next to her.

Laura Nyro sang fuzzily, *"In your voice I hear a choir of carousels. Oh, but am I ever gonna hear my wedding bells?"*

The carpet smelled like the rest of the house used to. No antiseptic lemon, just cigarettes and Brut and old lasagna.

"Bill! I love you so, I always will . . ."

20

Robin

That photograph was the only one he displayed of her. *Do you see those earrings?* Leslie asked me once when we were children, pointing to the little bride, my mother. *He gave them to her as a wedding present.* Five pearls in each, five-pointed stars. He used to refuse to kiss her if she didn't have them on. It was a romantic joke between them, full of affection, *To the moon, Alice!* She kept them in a bowl on the night table, but sometimes she forgot and slept in them. The next morning her earlobes would look red and sore, and he would pinch them, telling her he was giving her a massage as she winced. Leslie used to watch with that curled-lip look on her face, an expression like she'd been caught in a sneeze, the disgust trying to disguise the satisfaction.

I was never angry with my mother like Leslie was, maybe because I had never expected anything of her. It seemed natural to me that Leslie should be responsible for the day-to-day ablutions while Christine came and went. Three times during our childhood she disappeared for months at a time, which meant she had gone on a trip, according to my father. He always gave her yellow roses when she came back, so we knew he had missed her. I assumed these vacations were much like Daddy's business trips; it was only later that I realized she had no job, so they couldn't be business trips at all. At the time I viewed them just as I did her occasional all-day errands—it was as if she exited the house directly into a void, and I didn't think about her again until she returned.

I think it was this attitude that earned me, not Leslie, the prize of accompanying her into the void one day. I was six, halfway through first grade, Christine freshly returned home after months away. I was called to the office to meet my mother just before school ended, but when I got there I hardly knew her. She had curled her hair so tightly it resembled a perm, and wore hot streaks of blush across the tops of her cheeks. Instead of her loose, soft cardigan, she wore a light blue skirt suit with matching vest and white chiffon blouse that tied at her neck and wrists. The makeup gave her face that blurry Vaseline-lens effect that I recognized from television. "It's you!" I said.

She smiled, revealing the same crooked canine that Leslie had only recently inherited with her adult teeth. "It's me. Do you want to come with me to a party?"

Had her errands been parties all along? I was electrified by being entrusted with such a worthy secret. I imagined her sneaking off to dozens and dozens of formal affairs, like the twelve dancing princesses. "Does Daddy know?" I asked her in the car, trying to get a look at her shoes.

"No," she said, coming to a stop so slowly that the car behind her honked. She was not a frequent driver. I don't even remember if she had her license. She looked over at me, blinking her lengthened eyelashes. "Don't tell him, okay? This is just for you and me."

I was a practiced sidekick; I gave her a wink. She laughed.

We drove for what seemed like a long time. I expected that we were going to a ballroom, or maybe somebody's enormous house, so I was surprised when she pulled into the Monroe's parking lot near Arroyo del Oso and began touching her hair in the rearview mirror, as if she were about to get out of the car. "Are we here?" I asked.

She glanced at me. "Yeah, of course. Here, fix your skirt." She pulled on the belt loops of my denim skirt until the side seams were again at my sides.

Inside the restaurant, she took my hand and guided me to a corner, where several tables had been pushed together to accommodate a lot of people I had never seen before. "Chrissy!" a gray-haired woman called out. "Over here!"

I glanced up at my mother, who was wearing an open, cheerful expression that was almost as jarring as the clothes. "Hi, hi, hello," she said, kissing the woman on the cheek, embracing other strangers as if she'd known them for years. "Merry Christmas!"

"Merry Christmas!" the table chorused.

"And who are you?" the gray-haired woman asked me.

"My name is Robin Voigt," I said, offering her a hand.

Instead of taking it, she turned to my mother and said, "She's so *cute*! Did you teach her to do that?"

My mother glanced at me, slightly puzzled, and said, "No, but I love it!"

"Who are you?" I asked.

"Oh!" the woman exclaimed. "You can call me Miss Susan. I used to work with your mother at Macy's—how long has it been now, Chrissy?"

"I don't even want to think about it," my mother said. "Too long!" They laughed together, and I stared between them, amazed.

"You work at Macy's?" I said.

"I used to," my mother said, barely looking at me. "I worked there for years before I got married. You know that."

I hadn't known it at all. For the next forty-five minutes, I watched my mother drink two glasses of wine and eat from a community basket of chips and salsa and say things that sounded like lines from a TV show, like "Tell me everything, don't leave out a detail!" and "How did I guess . . ." and "Well, she's a handful!" She knew my grades in school and had a picture of Leslie in her wallet—I'd never seen her carry a wallet before, only her old pink purse. She talked about Daddy's job and our trip to the Grand Canyon, and threw back her head and laughed until she choked when Miss Susan brought up a story about her hiding from a customer for three hours in the employee bathrooms.

On our way home, we stopped and bought KFC chicken, which she paid for with money from the wallet I'd never seen. "Do you always go to the Christmas party when you go away?" I asked.

"I go every year," my mother said absently, sorting her change by size in her palm.

I selected a penny from her hand and put it in my shoe, startling her. "Leslie always lets me have a penny," I explained.

"I see," she said.

"How come you're so dressed up?" I asked, hoping to press my advantage before her Christmas-party chattiness died away.

She glanced down at herself. "I used to dress like this every day," she told me. "You had to wear hose or they wouldn't let you work."

Leslie was watching TV in the living room; she jumped up as soon as we came in the front door and watched with her mouth hanging open as my mother put the chicken on the table and arranged napkins on everyone's placemat. I strutted in behind her, being sure to make eye contact with Leslie: *Yes, that's right, she chose me to go with her on her secret excursion.* As we sat down to eat, my mother went to bed. She stayed in her bedroom for the next two days, and when she came out again she was back to herself, soft clothing, soft voice, that shuttered expression that meant we weren't to upset her by asking too many questions. Leslie was too proud to bug me for details, and I was too busy trying to understand it myself: whether once a year our mother became a stranger, or whether she was a stranger for the rest of the year and only once a year became herself.

21

Mary

I couldn't wait to get out of the house. Cramped and dark, a little hump of clay in the middle of the desert. Like some kind of burrow. The old man hadn't read his own books or listened to his own music or opened the blinds in his study. He'd just stayed in, dying, as if it were an activity. That kind of sadness leaves something behind. It was all over the house, a blue film, spots on your vision that stuck around.

I'd tried to cheer us up with the record, but the feeling only lasted for the length of the song. Then the dimness set back in, infecting us both. I had this horrible idea that anybody who stayed in that house too long would turn ghost.

In a way I already was one. I was walking around a dead girl's house, wearing her face. Sometimes I could see it in Leslie's expression when she looked at me. For that moment I wasn't Mary to her—I was Robin.

That night after the Floreses had gone to bed I went out on the back porch, dying for a cigarette and some anonymity. It was eerily quiet for a neighborhood with children; noise ordinances, maybe, or rich-people thick walls. And the outdoors itself was free of that heavy, ambient buzz you got in other states, states with trees.

I hadn't been out here before, and my window faced the street, so

I was shocked when I saw they had grass in their backyard. Thick, fresh-cut green grass that must cost a fortune to maintain, even though it wasn't a full lawn, just a curvy patch bordered by a rock garden and a line of rattleweed bushes. I squatted to touch it. It was cool and slightly damp, as if they had just watered it.

I glanced back at the empty yellow-lit door and took off my shoes. The grass was probably full of mosquitos, but it felt so good on my feet. I hadn't walked on grass in ages. You don't get much in Vegas outside of the golf courses. I probably looked like a moron doing mini laps in the backyard, holding my sneakers in one hand and grinning my face off, but I didn't stop, happy to be unobserved.

Except I wasn't unobserved. At the edge of the house, near the neighbor's property line, I saw a slow orange blink in the darkness, like a firefly, and then I realized what it was.

"I thought you were asleep," I said.

"Shit," said Dave, nearly dropping his joint.

I laughed. "That's not a ciggie . . . David."

His dark face was unreadable until his teeth flashed suddenly. "Forgot my manners," he said. "I won't tell Leslie if you don't." He held out the joint to me between his thumb and finger.

"I do *not* mind if I do," I said, setting down my shoes and taking it from him. "So, what, do you stand at the side of your house at ten at night every Monday? And Leslie thinks you're just, like, taking extra long in the bathroom?"

"Watering the lawn," he said, retrieving the joint from me. "What are you doing out here?"

There was a little singsong lilt in his voice; automatically I replied, "Looking for you," as if he were a customer. I leaned back against the wall, next to him. "You know, I usually don't go to sleep until three in the morning where I live."

"How old are you? Twenty-something? I used to be able to do that."

"Around here?" I made a show of looking around the corner at the quiet driveways.

He chuckled. "The nightlife scene is more in the UNM area, not so much out here."

"If by *nightlife* you mean 'doing exactly what we're doing now, except with Solo cups,' sure."

"Vegas really spoiled you, huh?" Dave said, inhaling. "Too good to climb a mountain and drop acid like a real Burqueña?"

"I hate it here," I said truthfully. "I don't know why you live here. I mean, why not at least move to Colorado and smoke whenever you want?"

He tilted his head back and seemed to consider. "My mom is here, for one thing. Eli's abuelita, she'd be pissed if we moved away. And the food, I always miss it. But mostly it's because for the last ten years Leslie's been taking care of her pops."

He glanced at me. I thought he didn't intend it as a guilt trip, but he didn't not intend it either. He was waiting for my reaction. I didn't give him one.

After a minute of silence, he went on. "He had a home aide, you know, but Leslie was over there all the time. Real sad thing, the way he went."

"How come you don't tell Leslie you smoke?" I said abruptly.

"Ah, come on, Robin." He flicked the end of the joint, examined it, then stepped on it.

"I'm serious," I said, eyes following him as he deposited the butt behind the rattleweed. "You put the baby to bed and get stoned in your backyard—why should she care?"

He gave me a flat-eyed look, the first negative expression I'd seen cross his face. I felt a small thrill at getting a rise out of him. "You seem real smart," he said. "You figure it out."

He started to walk back across the grass. "Night, David," I called after him.

He looked back at me. The light from the doorway was a bright rectangle behind him, flattening him into silhouette. His black eyelashes flickered in profile as he blinked. "Night."

22

Mary

Tuesday morning I woke up to a piece of paper on the floor in front of my door.

Appointment is Wednesday 4:30 p.m.
There are leftovers in the fridge.
Please be ready for dinner at 7 tonight!

So I was trapped in their house until they got home. Fuck. I smoked my morning cigarette in the closet, hugging my knees to my chest. Where had Leslie gone? She didn't have a job—and the baby was at daycare—why had she left me here alone? Had I done something to upset her yesterday? I went back through yesterday's mental file. I'd been super nice to her, I thought. I'd offered to baby-sit and I'd helped her pack up real neat. We'd gotten through almost a whole bookshelf together. And I'd wanted to poke around for way longer in the room full of faces, but Leslie had looked like she was gonna throw up, so I'd made sure to head right out and help her calm down.

I could just leave. But I had no car, and what if the door locked behind me? I'd be stuck outside all day.

For a second, sitting there among the extra coats and dry cleaners' bags, trying not to light anything on fire, I imagined myself getting on a bus, going to LA or Utah with my five hundred fifty in cash. Leslie and Dave had a ton of nice things lying around. I could find something good to pawn. That might buy me the first few nights there, and then . . . The fantasy fell apart. I put out my cigarette on the baseboard and fumbled for the door.

There had to be a spare key. Everybody had a spare key lying around somewhere. And if Leslie was going to lock me up in her enormous fancy house, I was going to snoop. It was basically my right.

Downstairs first, into the kitchen. I went through all the drawers, looking for the junk drawer, but there *was* no junk drawer. Each one had its own custom-shaped plastic organizer. Silverware, nicer silverware, spatulas, pizza cutters—it was like looking through Patrick Bateman's kitchen. So then I went through the cabinets, but those were just as neat, pots and pans grouped by set (she had *three* separate matching sets of cookware, including one of those shiny copper kinds that I'd only ever seen in magazines). The only messy part of the kitchen was the baby cabinet, which was a shambles of cartoon-printed plastic cups and spoons. I poked through those, mostly just out of surprise that Leslie had allowed a single area of her kitchen to be less than spotless.

In the corner of the kitchen, beside the entrance to the hallway, there was a nook for a desk, with a wine rack and a tiny hanging lamp built into the wall above it. Below, on the desk, the family Mac sat, draped attractively with real ivy from a real ivy plant, which took up one of the wine-bottle nooks above. I jiggled the mouse and the screen woke up, prompting me for a password. *flores,* I typed. The password box shook itself no. *floreshouse. Flores. password. password123.* The computer informed me that I had two more tries before it would lock itself. I found the power button on the back of the screen and held it down until the computer shut itself off.

Off to the side of the kitchen was a narrow wood-paneled laundry room, which contained a washer and dryer, a rack for clothes, and a hanging organizer with detergent, dryer sheets, a fabric tape measure, shoe inserts, and a couple of Dave's baseball caps. The only evidence of mess was a piece of twine shoved into the corner of one of the pockets and a loose silica gel DO NOT EAT packet.

The living room had no place to hide things except in the giant walnut entertainment cabinet. It had two wrought-iron doors beneath the TV that matched the style of the chandelier in the entryway—like, who even knew they sold matching chandeliers and entertainment cabinets? I searched through the shelves on my hands and knees, but it was only wires and a lot of DVDs and video games, along with one of those big yellow phone books and a couple of the baby's things, a blue plush kitten and a play piano. I sat back, red-faced, then thought, You dummy, and went to the front door.

I kept it carefully propped open as I searched the mat and the little pots containing succulents on either side of the door. The neighbor, a curly-haired mother with her kindergartner, saw me standing on my toes to run my fingers over the doorframe. She waved and I waved back, keeping a smile on my face as my fingers discovered nothing.

I went inside again and hustled over to the rear door. No key there either. It finally hit me what was so strange about my search: there were no hiding places in this house. Everything was so perfectly organized, each surface cleared of stray items, that there was nowhere to stuff any of the little indiscretions that occurred in any normal house—the stash of Ding Dongs, the Christmas-gift receipts. And Leslie and Dave had more than the ordinary number of indiscretions. She was lying to him about their finances, about her sister. He disappeared every few nights around the corner of the house. Where were the corners, the space behind the bookshelves, the lockbox on top of the refrigerator?

Then I thought: I'm the secret. Her house is my lockbox.

I closed the back door and sat against it, breathing in the air-conditioning.

When the house phone rang, I startled so badly I hit my head against the glass. It rang again, deafening in the empty house. I unfolded myself slowly and went to the phone, which sat on the desk in the kitchen nook, next to the computer.

I picked it up in the middle of the third ring. "Hello?" I said, then remembered to add, "Flores residence."

I could hear breathing on the other end. No one spoke.

"Hello?" I said again.

The other person hung up before I could say, *Sam?*

I set the phone back in its cradle. It couldn't be Sam. How would he know where I was? He'd left with my money—he hadn't seen me go with Leslie. And even if he had followed me to the hotel, would he have followed me all the way to Albuquerque?

There was no way. I was safe here. I did my pranayama breaths, one nostril, then the other.

I hadn't checked upstairs yet.

Leslie and Dave's bedroom was bright, even with the gauzy white curtains drawn. A huge soft bed dominated the room, with the bathroom to the right; light filtered in from the bathroom too, via midcentury-style glass blocks. The bedding matched the curtains except for the red Chimayo blanket covering the foot of the bed. On the walls hung framed paintings, one a modern-art bloody splash of orange, and the other a reproduction of Van Gogh's sunflowers. Their wedding portrait rested on one side table, a black-and-white shot of their first dance in a roomful of blurry faces and fairy lights. They had a huge flat-screen television angled on top of their dresser across from the bed.

I squatted to look under the bed. Nothing—not even dust bunnies. I lifted the pillows.

There—my first secret. A flat silver tablet. The screen was dark, but the tablet hadn't shut down. It was still running, overheating; the bottom nearly burned my palm as I picked it up and pressed the power button. The screen lit up immediately, no password needed.

Dave's tablet. He'd been logged in to Facebook, and now he was logged in from his work computer, so that everything he did showed up on the tablet in my hands. Dave was messaging with someone named Elaine Campbell, whose profile picture showed a tiny figure on a snowboard. Goggles covered the top half of her face, leaving only her smile visible. She had dental-assistant teeth.

They'd started chatting just a few minutes ago. I scrolled upward to the timestamp, and started reading even as the chat spooled out below.

9:53 A.M.

me: Joanna's eyes are following you around like you a steak girl
Elaine: She can't do anything about it ;)
me: No but I guarantee you we're about 5 minutes from another email
"Just a reminder, the employee dress code applies to everyone!!!"
Elaine: Maybe she has a crush on me
me: I'd attend that wedding
Elaine: It'd just be me and her, bare knuckle boxing in a field
Whoever knocks out the most teeth gets to take home the registry gifts
me: lololol
Elaine: You're lookin fly today too btw
me: It's that dress code chic, I know you don't know about it
Elaine: Haha
I do like your hair though, it's all soft today
me: Ran late this morning
Elaine: Are you bringing the smallest Flores over this week?
me: Not sure yet.
Elaine: Last week was fun :)
me: Yeah :) I'll think about it

Elaine's icon showed ellipses for a few seconds, then went blank. The chat was over. I scrolled up again, this time to their earlier conversations. Last Thursday, 2:55 P.M.:

Elaine: I got a lil sloppy
me: Uh-uh it was amazing
You serenaded us
Elaine: You loved it
me: Who wouldn't
Elaine: I'm ugly pink in the face right now
me: Let me see

Before that, a conversation about some project, small talk about the coffee machine, an exchange of Beyoncé gifs . . . I got bored and clicked on Elaine's profile. Jesus! Sixteen thousand friends . . . All of the most recent items on her wall were autoposts from her Instagram. She'd posted a photo of herself that morning in the car with a Cheerio stuck to her cheek. It was captioned, *Literally did not notice Brody's "decoration" until I went to take a picture of my makeup today . . . #toddlergifts #realglamour #ifeelpretty #ohsopretty #momlife.*

I scrolled down. Shiny hair, pretty house . . . smaller than the Floreses', but nicer-looking inside, with bright colors accenting every corner and professional frames for her children's drawings hanging on the walls. Elaine had two kids, one maybe kindergarten age and the other a little older than Eli. No husband in any of the pictures.

Halfway down her wall, Eli appeared, his face turned away from the camera, toward a funny-faced cat in the distance. She'd posted it this weekend, when Leslie had been away.

Last week was fun :)

I thought about the way Dave had singsonged to me in the dark last night, flirting almost reflexively, just as I did. I felt the same tone in his messages to Elaine. Was it just something he did with everyone, or was it serious? I couldn't tell.

If Leslie knew . . . if she'd been through his Facebook as well . . .

Maybe to Leslie, fifty thousand dollars was divorce-lawyer money.

That gave me a certain relief to imagine. The Flores house, with its real grass and kitchen-drawer organizers and matchy chandelier, creeped me out. Walking around in it alone was like being a mannequin in a showroom. If Leslie and Dave were falling apart, maybe that was the only reason it felt so strange to be a guest here. Maybe there was nothing more sinister to it than a rotten marriage.

It was almost a perfect theory. I closed the lid and replaced the laptop under the pillow, smoothing the comforter where I'd left an ass print. Then I let myself think it: if the money was for a divorce and not to save the house, then Leslie hadn't only been lying to Dave. She'd lied to me.

23

Leslie

I pulled into the daycare parking lot and shut off the car. I meant to go in right away, but the late-afternoon sun filled up the car with warm mushy air so quickly that I felt as if I'd been plunged into a hot tub. I sat back against the seat, momentarily paralyzed, as my face heated.

Get up, I said into my own skull.

I didn't move.

Get fucking get up.

Inside the daycare, a sheaf of kids sat along the duct-taped line on the floor—the "quiet line." Miss Alma sat in front of them on a small beanbag chair, reading aloud from *I Want My Hat Back*.

Eli wasn't among them.

Miss Alma saw me enter and raised her eyebrows at me over the kids' heads, pointing toward the back door.

"What do you guys think?" she said as I headed for the door. "Where is his hat?"

"*There!*" chorused the toddlers.

Outside, Miss Gloria held Eli draped halfway over her shoulder. He sobbed snot into her T-shirt. I watched them for a while as she did a funny little jiggling walk that made his teakettle screams wobble in pitch, Auto-Tunelike. She had flat, wide feet and square hips; her low center of gravity gave her the air of a sphinx.

"Oh, Mrs. Flores." Miss Gloria grinned, holding the still-whistling Eli out to me. "We're teething this afternoon. Third top tooth!"

I took him and set him against my shoulder, just as she had. He screamed against my cheek, and I imagined my ear fluttering in the breeze from the sound waves like in a Bugs Bunny cartoon.

"Thanks for walking with him," I said.

"Oh, no problem. He's been very good about learning his sign language. He signed 'Up!' during story time, and he didn't cry until we made it outside."

I nodded and smiled. "Well, thank you," I said. "Have a good night."

She tilted her head. "Sure, honey," she said. "You too."

In the hot-tub car, Eli shrieked as if I were cutting him as I buckled his seatbelt and handed him his gummy key ring. He flung it away, and I replaced it in his lap. He flung it away again, and I abandoned the effort and shut the door, heading for the front seat.

"Hurts, huh?" I said over the noise of his screams and "Cheap Thrills" on the radio.

He sent another wave of sound up toward the driver's seat.

I hummed along with it tunelessly.

He tried to drown me out.

I pulled onto the main road toward the Sprouts.

"Ahhhhhhhhh," I said into the din. Slowly, I got louder and louder to match him, until we were both screaming in the car.

He fell asleep in the parking lot of the Sprouts, wheezing a little with exhaustion.

I wish Dave were here, I thought, looking in the rearview mirror. I wish Miss Gloria were here.

For the first time since I'd become a mother, it occurred to me to wish my mother were here. Robin—Mary—had put her into my head, played me that record.

But I didn't want her with me. Not really.

I thought about what Eli might look like as a grown-up. Babies were so featureless, like tadpoles. I pictured him looking like his older cousin, Maria's kid, curly-haired, broad-shouldered. Would Eli ever sit in a parking lot with his kid in the backseat, both of them screaming at each other? Would he think about me then? Wish for me to be next to him? Or would he take after his mother, as my mother had taken after hers, and be grateful he'd escaped me?

Back in the driveway at home, I lifted Eli's limp form out of the car seat and pressed him into my shoulder, hefting the grocery bag with the other. He stirred but didn't wake as I made my way up the walkway.

"Mary?" I called as I opened the front door, then thought better of it—Dave could have come home early, been dropped off by someone else . . . "Robin?"

My voice echoed in the front hallway. I dropped the grocery bag in the kitchen, then spun slowly. All the cabinet doors stood open. "Robin?"

She wasn't on the patio or in the living room. I went upstairs. The guest room door was open, and her bed was unmade, half her few clothes strewn across the floor.

"Mary?"

Against my shoulder, Eli woke up and began to sob in the empty house.

24

Mary

It was brighter outside in the afternoon than it had been when I'd crawled onto the porch in the morning, and I shaded my eyes as I made my way through Leslie's neighborhood. I'd run out of cigarettes around four in the afternoon, and I'd figured that wasn't too long to be locked out. Besides, I wanted to send a message to Leslie: I wasn't her pet. She couldn't just lock me in her house and expect me to be there when she got back.

There was a surprising number of people out, despite the hour and the heat—women, mostly, in sleek gray-and-neon athletic wear, jogging or biking down the wide white sidewalks. Like the women, the houses matched, although each one boasted some unusual feature: timber accents, Spanish tile, lime-green Nikes. It was impossible to look into any of the houses, or any of the women's eyes; the latter wore shiny mirrored sunglasses, and the sun turned the former's plate-glass windows into mirrors themselves.

After fifteen minutes or so I came upon the entrance to the neighborhood. The sidewalks turned grubby along the edge of the main road, broken here and there by creosote and yucca. The road was flat and straight, so that I could see a long way in either direction. To the right lay the mountains. To the left was another residential pocket, this one patterned with single-story adobe houses, and beyond that I could see a sign for a Shell station.

I was gathering sweat underneath my tits and shoulder blades by the time I made it to the station, and the cold air from the refrigerated drinks was a relief. "Two packs of Spirits," I said to the woman behind the counter.

"Yellows, blues?"

"Blues."

She blinked slowly and got up to get them. "Thanks," I said when she handed me my change, and turned to leave.

"Oh—hi," the woman behind me in line said as she saw my face. Her expression was sheepish, like a student running into her teacher outside of class, except she was at least thirty.

"Hi, uh . . ." I said, stuffing my change in my pocket.

"Lindy," she supplied, shifting her purse straps on her shoulder. "Serrano, now. Sorry, it's so weird to run into you."

I tried not to let my confusion show on my face. An old customer? A friend? I couldn't place her; she was Asian, with a wide, apple-cheeked face, an upturned nose, long soft bangs.

"Lindy," I repeated, going for a smile.

She didn't like that. "You don't remember me," she said, her nose wrinkling a bit.

The cashier interrupted. "Ladies."

"Oh—just these," Lindy said, pushing a couple of Cokes toward the register. She turned her attention back to me. "I'm Nancy Courtenay's sister. I didn't think we would see you around Albuquerque again, Robin."

Understanding broke over me like an egg.

"Oh, right," I said. "Sorry, I didn't recognize you at first. How are you?"

She opened her wallet to pay the cashier, then looked back at me a bit warily. I tilted my head, and she answered in a rush, "I'm good. I'm good. How are you?"

I felt strangely elated.

"I didn't think I would come back," I said, leaning on the counter. "How's Nancy doing these days?"

Lindy's face tightened. "She's a police officer," she said. "She's married, so." There was a defensive tinge to her tone.

"Married!" I echoed. "Wow. To who?"

"That's not . . ." Lindy paused and collected her change, scooped up the Cokes, and headed for the door. "It happened a while ago. Are you married?"

"Me?" I hurried after her. "No, no. I guess I never met the right one."

We were outside now. I felt my face heat up. Lindy said, "How come you're in town?"

"Oh, um, my sister had a baby," I told her.

"Congratulations," Lindy said, thin-lipped. I watched her face avidly; it was like playing a game of hot and cold. She had relaxed a little as we left the store. I decided to reverse course.

"So, I'd love to see Nancy while I'm here," I said, walking with her toward her SUV. "Catch up, you know."

"Well," Lindy said, trailing off while she stuck her arm in her purse and fished for her keys. *Getting hotter.*

"Could you give me her number, maybe?" I pressed.

Lindy found her keys and pressed the button too many times, making her car honk. A voice yelled in delight from the backseat. "I don't think that's a good idea," she said, not looking at me. "Nancy lives her life the way she's going to, and I don't think you need to go around shaking her up again."

I could tell she was struggling to remain polite. "It was ten *years* ago," I said, leaning on Lindy's car. "Wasn't it?"

"I have kids in the car," Lindy said stiffly.

I didn't know what that had to do with anything. "I just want to see how she's doing," I said, smiling. "Since we used to be really close."

Lindy blinked several times, too fast, then yanked the driver's-side door open, pressed the button to roll up all the windows, and stepped back, slamming the door. The sound of her kids' chatter disappeared. She leaned toward me and said in a rapid-fire mumble, "I have accepted what Nancy wants to do because she is my sister. But don't think I have forgotten that this all started when you began hanging out with Nancy and telling her she was your little girl-friend. You treated her like shit. She doesn't need to see you again, and I certainly won't be telling her that you're back in town. Go find somebody else's family to screw up, please, Robin."

She got into her car and drove away in a determinedly sedate fashion, not making eye contact through the windshield. I stood where she had left me for a few seconds and then a great big smile crept over my face, and I laughed too hard and had to sit down on the curb.

I hadn't expected to run into anyone like that. Leslie had kept me locked up in the house, and maybe this was why: so I would play the version of Robin she wanted me to be, and not the one Lindy had known, the kind of person you hoped never to run into at the gas station.

But if Lindy didn't want me to talk to Nancy, she shouldn't have told me so much about her. Thanks to our surprise conversation, I knew that Nancy Courtenay still lived in Albuquerque, and that she was a police officer.

My burner phone didn't have Internet, only call and text, and I couldn't return to Leslie's yet. I went back out to the curb and finger-combed my hair, rubbed underneath my eyes to smear my makeup—only a little, just enough to suggest tears. Then I waited, smoking.

An old man passed me, then another. The second one stopped. "You need help, sweetheart?"

I could see his phone hanging from a holster on his belt. Old-fashioned, flip top. "No," I said flatly, and looked away until he went inside.

A family with two toddlers passed through, and a couple of middle-aged women. Finally a teenage boy walked up on foot. He had his phone out already, a smartphone in a bright orange case. I stubbed out my cigarette and arranged myself on the curb, knock-kneed. "Hi," I said when he got close enough to hear me.

He glanced up, then at me. "Hello?"

"I'm so sorry," I said, "but I kind of got stranded here and I don't think my ride knows she's supposed to pick me up. Can I please use your phone for a quick call? It'll only take a second."

"Yeah, yeah, sure," he said. "I'm Vincent."

"Oh, wow," I said, pushing my hair back and sticking my hand out. "I'm Mary."

He was too young to shake hands; he put the phone in my hand instead. "Nice to meet you," he said. "Where you from?"

I was already on the phone. I googled *albuquerque county police station phone number*. "I'm from Texas," I said absently.

"Oh, damn," Vincent said, then trailed off into nothing.

The first number was for the Sandoval County sheriff's department. I called it, smiling quickly at Vincent. "Hi, I'm looking for Officer Courtenay?" I said.

"Officer who?"

"Nancy Courtenay?"

Typing noises. "We don't have anyone by that name," the voice said after a minute.

I hung up. "Sorry, I guess I called the wrong thing. I'll try her other number."

Vincent capitulated, but he was getting restless, shuffling rocks with the toe of his shoe.

The next number was for Bernalillo County. I called that one. "Hi, I'm looking for Officer Nancy Courtenay," I said.

"Officer Courtenay?" the man on the line said. "Okay, can I tell her what it's regarding?"

"It's, um, it's Robin Voigt. I mean, that's the name to give her."

"Fine," he said, and there was a brief rustling silence. Then I heard the click of the line transfer and more ringing.

"This is Officer Courtenay."

"It's Robin," I said. "Robin Voigt? I just ran into your sister Lindy. She wouldn't give me your phone number, but I had to look you up now that I'm in town."

"Robin?" She sounded young.

"Yeah, it's me." Too late I thought: She's a police officer. What if she looks the name up in her system, or . . .

But there was a sudden exhale on the line, and Nancy said, "Oh my God. I thought I'd never hear from you again."

"Me neither," I said. Vincent was staring at me now, trying to make me uncomfortable. "Listen, I can't talk much now. Can you call me on my other number and we can meet up?"

"Today?" Nancy said.

I hadn't been expecting that, but what else did I have to do? "Yeah, today," I said, putting a little extra enthusiasm into my voice, and I gave her my new number.

"Okay. I'll call you," she said. I smiled and took the phone away from my ear to hang up. At the last second I heard her say tinnily: "I can't believe it's really you."

25

Robin

She didn't even know she wanted me. That was what was so appealing about Nancy. I'd lost Leslie—Grandma Betty died—my father turned further inward, like a snail—but in those absences boys started offering themselves to me, one after another, and I accepted, again and again. I felt voracious, like I could eat a dozen and it wouldn't be enough. I liked the way they died to touch me, suffering tremors down their skinny, ropy arms, giving off that hothouse smell. But the look in their eyes was all wrong, a brief startled yop, like when you turn the flashlight on the raccoon. I thought there had to be something more to it than that.

It was there in Nancy's eyes the first time she saw me, outside the schoolyard. A little pained grimace, totally involuntary, she wasn't even aware she'd done it; she saw me, wanted me, denied herself immediately. The next second it was gone, replaced by confusion: *Why are you staring at me?* I couldn't help myself: I smiled, completely charmed. In a single glance she'd given more of herself to me than any of the boys I'd slept with. A stranger one second, and the next, I knew more about her than her own family.

Now I understood what the problem had been with the boys I'd slept with before. They were too aware of their own desires; their knowledge made them feel entitled to me, as if, having seen me, they already owned me. When I gave in, it was nothing more than what they had expected. Giving myself to Nancy was so much more rewarding. She had never allowed herself to want any girl, so I could not be just any girl. To her I was the only girl, or the only one who mattered.

This was how easy it was with Nancy: a few weeks later, I saw her in the girls' bathroom, washing her hands. "Hi," I said, going over to her, leaning on the next-door sink.

"Hi." Nancy shrank a little as she reached for a paper towel, too conscious of our reflections in the mirror above the sink. She was barely five feet, bony, with a boyish quality that caused her church-issue khaki skirt to sink oddly on her slim hips. Beside her I looked titanic. Even my teeth were bigger.

"I'm Robin." I stuck out my hand.

"Nancy," she said, trying to shake, but I only held her hand in mine, looking at our fingers wrapped around each other as if it were the nicest thing that I had ever seen. The air changed around us. When I looked up, I saw that Nancy's face had changed too. She wasn't afraid of me any longer. She was afraid for me—for us. In half a second we had become conspirators, keepers of the same secret.

Nancy gave me everything I wanted. We kissed in the girls' bathroom at lunch, shoved into a single stall. I stopped her in the middle, brushed her bangs back from her face. "Wait," I said. She froze, her eyes focused on mine, tracking every minuscule change in expression. I thought: If I blink, she'll cry. I imagined myself licking off her tears.

Her sisters didn't know at first. No one knew. We fucked with our hands over each other's mouths. She called me almost every night, compulsively. For my part I couldn't get enough of how badly Nancy wanted me—*me,* specifically—not the girlness of me, the headless story I became in boys' mouths. In Nancy's mouth I only ever tasted myself.

I was the first person Nancy had ever slept with, but she was the first partner I'd ever fought with—really fought. In a way it was the same thing, a means to stick your fingers in. You never knew exactly what someone was like in bed or in a fight until you were in it with them, and once you had the feel of them, they were yours forever, yours in a deep secret way. They kept their peace of mind at your pleasure; you had only to stroke them correctly and they became your little animal again, purring or scratching.

After a while I think she hated me for knowing her like that. I wasn't careful with her, I can see that now. Still—she made herself naked for me, again and again, told me she loved me, let me lick the salt from her. There was something insubstantial to me; I felt I didn't exist until I could see my effect on her. Did she know that?

Maybe it's only my memory. I'm getting dimmer, as ghosts do.

26

Mary

Nancy agreed to meet me at the Pop-Pop's around the corner. I was sitting cross-legged on the wooden bench outside, burning the insides of my thighs in the sun, when she pulled up in an old green Nissan.

For some reason I hadn't expected her to look like she did. Maybe it was the way she sounded on the phone, or her sister's round-cheeked face and button nose. She wasn't especially tall, but she swung out of the car like a cop in her collared shirt and flat-fronts. Her black hair was almost crew cut short, and dimples appeared in her tanned cheeks when she smiled nervously. She came up to the bench and did an awkward little dance as she tried to figure out whether to shake my hand or hug me.

Ten years and she was still nervous. I decided to experiment: I leapt up and threw myself at her like I was still her girlfriend, Italian ice dripping off one of my hands. When I touched her a jolt rippled through her body into mine. We fit together too familiarly, her hands sliding around my waist, then slipping away just as quickly. Like she still expected to know my body.

"Oh, wow," Nancy said, laughing a little as we separated.

"Robin . . . I mean . . . this is a trip, isn't it? What are you doing here?"

"I'm visiting my sister," I said. "She had a baby. Isn't that wild?"

"Is it? I thought everybody we knew had babies now."

I widened my eyes. "You had a baby?"

"No, no," she said. "You?"

"I'm the baby," I told her.

She smiled. "I mean, you still look the same."

"You look like a cop," I told her. I wondered how good of a cop she was.

She scrubbed a hand over the back of her neck. "You like it? I cut it not too long after you left, actually."

My Italian ice sloshed red onto my hand. "Oh, fuck," I said, licking it off.

"What flavor is that?" Nancy asked.

I grinned. "Tiger's blood."

"Oh, you got the good stuff. Hold on, I'm going to get one of those."

I finished off the syrup-soup while she was inside. A breath of chilled air hit me as she came back out. I didn't move over when she sat down on the bench, and my bare thigh pressed against her slacks. "So, um . . ." I said, shifting my weight so that our legs rubbed together. "How did you get into that?" I gestured at the cop car.

She dug her spoon into the ice. "I, uh, did a couple tours in the army. I wanted to get out, after . . . I spent some time in California with my cousins, which should have been perfect, like this great Taiwanese community I could be part of . . . But my roots were here. I came back and ended up staying."

"Yeah, I met your roots in the gas station." I pointed over my shoulder. "I don't think she likes me."

"Lindy?" Nancy snorted. "No."

"Because we dated?"

She cast a short look at me. "Because I dated anyone, probably."

"But it was me who gave you the idea to date girls."

Nancy laughed. "Is that what she said?"

"I was really flattered." I tipped my head from side to side. "I never converted someone before."

"I don't believe you," she answered, meeting my eyes. Hers had faint cheerful crow's feet at the corners. I loved them immediately.

"Well," I said, looking away, feigning demure.

Nancy went back to her tiger's blood, but there was a certain agreeability to her posture now; I was getting somewhere. "What about you, what do you do?" she asked after a minute.

"I don't do anything right now," I said, mirroring her body language, lowering my shoulders. "I'm still kind of figuring things out. I was a waitress until this week."

"What happened?"

"I had to leave my job," I said. "Leslie offered to let me stay with her, and I needed a change of scenery, so . . . here we are again."

"I'm sorry," Nancy told me, sounding sincere.

I hadn't meant to make myself seem pathetic. I lost track of my attempt to mirror her and couldn't think what to do with my hands. "It's just for a week," I said. "Did you know you have pink teeth?"

Nancy ran her tongue over her teeth. "Is it gone?"

"No." I grinned.

"You're pink too," she said, peering at me.

I bared my teeth at her. "It looks sort of ghoulish."

"Not on you." She brought her napkin to her mouth to try to scrub the stains off.

A family came out of the Pop-Pop's, ringing the bell on the door. The two children were babbling loudly to each other about somebody's birthday.

"How come you could come meet me?" I asked. "Aren't you supposed to be working?"

"I'm only doing paperwork today. I took a break." Red crept up her neck. "Why are you free? Is your sister working?"

"Yeah. She left me at home. I got creeped out stuck in their big old house. Have you been down there since I left?"

Nancy licked her spoon. "To Leslie's house? No. I don't even know what neighborhood she's in these days."

"Is there . . . Do you hear anything about her? About how she's doing?" I tried not to seem like I was digging.

Nancy frowned. "What do you mean?"

I shifted on the bench. "I just think there's something weird going on with her. Maybe it has to do with Dave. Her husband. I think maybe he's having an affair."

"Well, I mean, you would know better than I would," Nancy said, crumpling up her plastic cup and tossing it in a perfect overhand arc into the trash can nearby. "I've only run into her a few times at the grocery store, places like that. We don't really talk." She gave me a sidelong look. "I thought you guys didn't really talk either. After you took off. You told me you weren't going to come back here."

"I wasn't," I said, my heart pounding. "But it's been a long time. People get over things, don't they?"

"Sometimes," Nancy said. "But I didn't think you would."

"Yeah?" I rested my head against my arm on the back of the bench, giving her space, so she wouldn't feel pressured. "How come?"

"Those stories you told me about her," she said. "About how awful she was to you. But she was just a kid then. And after everything with your guys' mom . . . Anyway, you talked to Lindy, you saw. Sisters can be assholes." She smiled. "I think Leslie knew about us. Just from the way she's acted when I've seen her around. Did you tell her, or did she actually see me sneaking in?"

I laughed. "You snuck in?"

She blinked. "Of course. All the time. You don't . . . ?"

"No, I do. I only . . ." I waved a hand at her, at her button-down open at the neck, her flat chest, her tanned hands. "It's hard to picture it now."

She glanced down at herself and smiled. "I guess. But I did. I used to climb in your window."

"You did." I grinned.

"Yeah," she said. "I was always so scared."

"You, scared?" I said. "The law enforcement officer?"

"Terrified," she told me, returning my gaze seriously. "You used to play jokes on me, you know. The first time I came in, do you re-member?"

I shook my head.

Nancy cleared her throat. She smelled good—even her breath smelled good, sugary. "You barely knew me. You said, 'Come here,' and when I got in bed with you, you were naked. I thought you were trying to embarrass me."

"I didn't," I said, surprised.

"Yeah. You grabbed my arm." Nancy took my hand. "You said, 'Don't you want to?'"

I stared at our intertwined fingers. We sat facing outward, toward a parking-lot audience, like actors in a stage play. Slowly I brought her hand up to my face. The next line appeared in my head, scroll-ing out in front of me as if it had been scripted. "Let me guess," I said, tilting my head back as she cupped my cheek. "You did want to. Right?"

"I did," she said, watching me.

Neither of us moved for a second. Then she drew her hand back. "I have to tell you something," she said.

"I know." I looked at my thighs.

"I should have said something," she went on anyway. "I'm with someone."

"It's okay." I moved back on the bench. "You don't have to—"

"It only happened last year," she said. "I mean . . . we got married so quickly."

"Nancy. It's fine."

There was an awkward pause. "I should get going," Nancy said at last. I still had my head down; I could feel her eyes on me. "I was only supposed to be out for a break."

I waited as she got up, patting herself for her keys, and turned toward her car. The right moment was almost there, pressing on my chest. When she touched her car door I called, "Nancy!"

She turned around immediately, like she'd wanted me to stop her.

I'd gotten it right, the way the play was supposed to go. A last glance, a final exchange—the part of the scene where people talked about secrets.

"Do you think Leslie's still upset? About what happened?" I swallowed.

Twin vertical lines appeared between her eyebrows. For a moment I thought she could tell I had pushed the conversation here, that all the rest had been scaffolding. "Oh. I mean, it's a hard thing, when somebody does that. Everyone wants to think they could have done something to prevent it. And when it's a parent . . . But I don't think Leslie blames you." Nancy shook her head. "It's no one's fault."

"Okay," I said. "I just—I don't know that many people who knew both of us. So I thought you might . . . I'm sorry." I lifted the corner of my mouth. "I just wanted to see you again."

Nancy gripped the top of the car. Her eyes were dark, and I felt she took all of me in at a single glance, as if she might not have the opportunity again. "Yeah. Bye, Robin."

"Bye," I said, standing up.

I watched the cop car disappear into traffic. *She died when I was twelve,* Leslie had said back in the motel bathroom. As if it had just happened. As if it had been an accident.

The longer I stayed in Albuquerque, the more I understood how death ruptured its setting, leaving a kind of black hole where the person had been that the survivors had to take care not to be sucked into. There were a lot of black holes around Leslie now. There was a stickiness to being Robin. I didn't know if it would be as easy as I'd thought it would to pull myself free when all this was over.

27

Leslie

When Dave got home Eli was in his bouncer on the kitchen floor as I made boeuf bourguignon. "Hello, my favorite Winona," he said as I was pouring red wine into the sauce. He kissed me and I closed my eyes, dropping the spoon, setting down the wine bottle to hold his face with my hands.

"I love you," I said, not pulling away.

"I love you too," he mumbled against my mouth. He slid one hand inside my shirt and felt me up a little, out of habit. Then he froze. "Is your sister home?"

"No," I said, certain he could feel my heartbeat against his palm. I twitched away from him and he withdrew his hand. "She wasn't here when I got home. I left her a dozen messages. She's not picking up."

"Oh. Good." He caught the look on my face and amended that with "Not that she's not answering your calls, just that she didn't catch me getting to second base with you in the kitchen." Dave went over and lifted Eli out of his bouncer, inhaling the smell of his smudgy hair. "Our baby's head is delicious to me. Is that normal?"

When I grabbed the spoon and went back to stirring the pot, he added, "I'm sure she'll be back soon."

I didn't look up. "You know, the last time someone said that to me about Robin, I didn't see her for ten years."

He paused mid-lift, leaving Eli stranded in midair, giggling. "Okay. That's fair." Eli shrieked and Dave resumed doing the Simba dance. "Let's just worry about it later. I invited Elaine and the kids over for dinner, is that cool?"

"What?"

Dave's expression dimmed. It was an old argument between us. My parents had never had anyone over to the house when I was growing up. When we'd started dating, I was happy to be invited to his family events, which happened at least once a month, with at least fifteen people squashed into his parents' backyard every time. *We want enough space to have everybody over for dinner,* Dave said to the realtor when we bought this house. But when it was our house, it was different somehow; I went around the housewarming party making everybody nervous. Dave's sister Cadence told me I looked like I thought people would spill things. I hadn't known you could see it on my face. *We'll get better at it,* Dave told me, meaning, *You'll get better at it,* only I hadn't, and people still gathered at his parents' house instead of ours, and although Dave didn't bring it up, I knew he could tell I preferred it that way.

"I don't know if we have enough food," I said, trying to sound neutral.

"We have enough. You used the army pot," Dave said. "I didn't think it was a big deal. She'll be here at eight."

"Next time you have to warn me," I said. "This could get cold by the time she—"

"Then put it in the oven," he said. "That's what the oven's for."

"I don't—"

He put Eli down. "I'm sorry," he said, touching my shoulder. "I should have warned you. I'll warn you next time. It's just when Eli and I went for a playdate last time I told her we'd have her over to say thank you. I mean, do you not want her here?"

"No," I said, hating the pitch of my own voice. "It's fine. I'm just . . . I'm worried about Robin. I don't know where she went. What if she comes back while we're eating?"

Dave stared at me. "Then she can join us."

I went to the refrigerator. "I don't want Elaine to meet her."

"Why not? She seems—Eli, come back here—she seems fine." Dave imprisoned Eli in his bouncer and gave him a couple of noodles from the pot to munch on.

The noise of a car driving up made us pause, except for Eli, who was occupied with the strands of pasta. I stood motionless in front of the refrigerator as the car shut off and the doors slammed. Dave disappeared into the front hallway, throwing open the door before Elaine had the chance to knock. "You're early," I heard him say.

"I know, I thought it would take longer, but I made margarita mix—and virgin, for the kids—"

"For the kids?"

"They love to be included." Her voice got louder as they entered the kitchen. "Brody, Tanner, say hi to Dave."

Tanner shouted hello; Brody huddled silently behind him. They were each dressed in tiny denim jeans with plaid button-down shirts, Brody's red, Tanner's blue. Elaine stood over them, carrying two glass pitchers. She had her hair in twin fishtail braids tied off with what looked like twine, and she wore a brightly embroidered tunic and leggings. I was still holding the spoon I'd been using to stir the pot.

I went back to the stove, dropped the spoon in the pot, and moved toward her. She handed the pitchers to Dave and hugged me with her purse still on her shoulder; it slipped down onto her elbow, dragging her tunic over her shoulder. "Leslie, hi," she breathed in my ear. "*So* happy to see you. How long's it been?"

I nodded. "Dave, can you put those in the fridge? For later?"

Elaine released me and grabbed Brody before he could take Eli's last remaining noodle, swinging him up over her shoulder. "Honey, you're in your going-out shirt. Can't get food on it before we've even been here five minutes." She glanced down at the half-chewed noodle on Eli's front and smiled, turning toward me. "I think you've got a little emergency on your hands."

"I got him," Dave said, letting the refrigerator door slam and whisking Eli into the laundry room.

"Sit down," I said as Elaine got Tanner set up with a pop-up book in one of the kitchen chairs and let Brody sit on her lap, poking at her phone. "Can I get you anything to drink?"

"Well, one of those margaritas," Elaine said. "The purple lid is virgin. For the kids. Brody, do you want one?"

Brody shook his head, absorbed in some sort of game involving bubbles with faces.

"Tanner?"

He held out his hand and made a grabby motion. Elaine laughed. "Tanner! Say please to Leslie."

"Please, Leslie?" Tanner said, baring his baby teeth. Elaine rolled her eyes at me as I put the virgin mix in a plastic cup from the baby cabinet and handed it to him, making sure he didn't spill.

I didn't have any margarita salt for Elaine's glass. She told me not to worry about it. Lowering light from the kitchen windows picked out a few strands of early silver in her left braid. "Dave said your sister is in town. Am I going to get to meet her?"

"Robin," I said. "She's just in town to do some paperwork. For my dad's estate. I couldn't— She won't be here, most likely. She's out tonight." I made myself smile back at her. "How are you?"

"I'm so grateful not to be cooking tonight. You're an *angel*." She rummaged in her purse, jostling Brody, and took out a camera, a real one, the kind with a vertical viewfinder, for shooting from the waist. "Would you mind if I took a picture of you? I have so many pictures of Eli, I thought maybe people would like to see where he gets his looks."

"He looks just like Dave," I said. "Everyone says so."

"Oh, just one." She slipped the strap over her head. "This light suits you."

I watched as she transferred the camera from one hand to the other, twisting off the lens cap and craning her neck to see through the viewfinder. I was still looking at her when she snapped the first photo.

"How'd you get her to pose for a photo?" Dave asked, coming back into the room with Eli tucked under his arm. "I got her to do it for our wedding, but I think that's just because we'd already paid the photographer."

"I didn't say you could take the picture," I said, half under my breath.

Elaine looked stricken. From her lap, Brody gave a pleased yelp when he saw Eli being placed back into his bouncer. "I'm sorry . . ." Elaine started.

Dave glanced at me. "Don't be sorry. You've got to catch her unawares. That's the only way to do it. She's like Nessie. How's cooking?"

It had almost burned; I turned down the heat. "Done," I said. "Just a second. I'll get plates."

"They're so cute together," Elaine said, watching Eli give his spatula to Brody of his own accord. "And your house is so beautiful. Anytime you need a babysitter, Leslie—"

"When do you have time to babysit?" Dave took his plate from me. "You have a playdate every other day."

"I'd make time." Elaine smiled up at me as I set her plate in front of her. "It's part of the mommy code. The mommy brigade."

"There's a code? Is there a code for dads?" Dave asked.

A dimple appeared in her cheek. "How would I know? But the mommy code is real. I didn't need it so much with Tanner—he was my real quiet boy . . ." Tanner looked up from his book and Elaine patted the seat next to her. "But with Brody, I relied on other moms so much. The network I found online was incredibly important to me, just to know that it was hard for everybody sometimes, and not to freak out if there was ever a day where I couldn't get everybody to brush their teeth."

"I always brush my teeth," Tanner broke in, climbing onto the chair.

Elaine laughed. "We had to get him cinnamon-flavored toothpaste so he'd stop eating it straight. He likes mint too much. Brody hates all the flavors."

"Does Brody like noodles?" I hesitated. "I was going to feed Eli some of the noodles with carrots . . ."

"Oh, Brody eats what we eat," Elaine said. "We're not picky in our house. We try everything, right?"

Tanner nodded. "I tried squids."

"You did not," Dave said.

"I did," Tanner rejoined. "Alive ones."

"Pics or it didn't happen," Dave told him. Tanner was chastised.

"You're one year in now," Elaine said to me. "How are you doing, Leslie?"

"I'm fine," I said, bringing Eli to the table and watching his face wrinkle up when I gave him his bowl of noodles and carrots and brought his plastic spoon to his lips. I felt Dave's eyes on me. "I think next year will be even better," I said, as Eli took a bite.

I stood in the kitchen washing dishes. Dave and Elaine were black shapes in the glass patio door, outlined against the purplish shrubs. Eli, Brody, and Tanner darted through the grass at their feet. I set a pot in the drying rack and shut off the water.

"His back is getting so bad." Dave's voice spilled through the crack in the door. "He sleeps in that old La-Z-Boy. He says it's the only thing that doesn't hurt him."

"He should get a million dollars for what they did to him," Elaine murmured back. They were talking about Dave's father, I realized.

Eli began to cry in the grass. I watched as Dave made to stand and Elaine waved him back into his seat. She picked Eli up, their shapes merging, and stroked his hair. "Almost bedtime," she said, or I thought she said, over his screams.

"No, he's teething." Dave pushed the patio door farther open with a finger. "Leslie?" he called. "Do you know where Eli's gummy key ring is?"

"He didn't want it today," I said, startled at being included. "In the car. He threw it away."

"It's still in the car?" Dave asked. "Can you go get it?"

"He won't want it," I said.

"You're a very important man with a lot of responsibility," Dave was already saying to Eli in Elaine's arms. "You have to keep better track of your keys. You can't keep locking them in the car." Eli whimpered.

"We should go, anyway," Elaine said, noticing I hadn't moved. "You can walk me out and grab the gummy while you're there. Tanner, time to pack it up," she called, as Tanner abandoned his attempt to climb the stone fencing.

Elaine induced Tanner to hug me before he left, Brody too shy to join, and Dave showed them to the front door, leaving it open as he went into the driveway still holding Eli. "Thank you, Leslie!" Tanner called into the echoing foyer, and then they were gone. I was still standing in front of the glass patio door when a shape walked up and knocked on it.

Mary grinned at me when I let her in. She was sweaty and her makeup was smeared a little underneath her bottom lashes, but it only made her look intentionally disheveled, her tangled hair backlit by the porch light in the dim hallway. There was something shocking about each new time I saw her. I kept forgetting what she looked like.

"Where the fuck have you been?" I whispered as Eli's wails filled the house and Dave shut the front door behind him.

She gave me a puzzled look. "Sounds like someone's a little cranky."

I couldn't tell whether she meant me or the baby. "I came home and you weren't here."

"I got caught up."

"In what?"

"I just met some people and hung out. I didn't know I wasn't supposed to leave the house."

"What people?" I could feel my ears getting hot.

Mary's eyebrows drew together. "Where were *you* all day?" she countered. "I'll tell you mine if you tell me yours."

"Stop fucking around." I took a deep breath. "I need you to stay here tomorrow. It's just one day. Then you can go wherever you want." I turned and headed for the kitchen. Mary followed me, and I stopped. "Go upstairs," I said.

"It smells good in here," she said. "Did you guys eat already? Can I have some?"

"You were right, he hates the gummy key ring," Dave said, reentering the kitchen with Eli on his hip. "I don't know what's up with that. He loved it yesterday. Robin, hi, I hope you didn't plan on sleeping tonight."

"I don't sleep," Mary said. "I just kind of hang upside down by my feet." She gave me a wide smile. "You guys look tired. Want me to hold him for a while?"

"How did you know?" Dave said, handing Eli over as I opened my mouth to protest. He quieted immediately. "Did you see that?" Dave asked me, twisting around. Then to Mary: "What the hell are you?"

Mary shrugged. "Babies love me."

"Don't put your finger in his mouth," I said as Mary let Eli chew on her knuckle.

"Leslie, babies need exposure to all kinds of germs and stuff. That's how they build up their little immune systems," Mary told me, wiggling her finger.

"Well, let's not stop there," Dave said, catching my expression. "Let's go roll him in the mud right now. We'll bring his blanket outside and he can sleep out there, snack on some worms if he gets hungry in the middle of the night."

Eli stared into Mary's eyes. He had a small confused expression on his face. "Did you torment your daddy all day?" she asked him in a baby voice. "Did you scream right in his ear? I bet you did. You're the worst."

Eli laughed.

My throat went dry. I watched as she disappeared around the corner with him, asking him if he wanted to watch *My Big Fat Greek Wedding*. "Leslie, can you bring me, like, a bowl of whatever that was?" Mary called from the other room. "I can't move with him on my lap, but I'm starving."

"I'm glad your sister's home," Dave said, coming to put his arms around me.

"I know," I said, thinking of the body on the bed.

I waited until he went into the other room to bring Mary her dinner, and then I sat down at the kitchen table alone. There was a notification on my phone. I'd been tagged in a photo. Elaine had been right. The light suited me.

28

Mary

That night I waited until Dave and Leslie's bedroom went dark. Then I lugged the Floreses' phone book upstairs to the guest room, called a taxi, and slipped out the back door into the sleeping neighborhood.

The real-grass back lawn was summer-warm during the day, but cooled to numbing after midnight. I wanted to take my shoes off again, drag my feet through it, but instead I just squatted to touch it. It was like a dozen buzz cuts against my palms.

I went around the house and sat on the curb under a streetlight, waiting for the cab. The houses all had their lights off except one, farther down the block. A husband and wife drifted across the lighted upstairs window, getting ready for bed. They looked fuzzy, tricolor, like old television.

A car went by, playing "Get Up 10" at top volume. The sound washed up against the houses and faded again as the driver steered past, his head turning to look at me on the curb. I pictured myself briefly through his eyes, the halo the streetlamp would make on my red hair. No—I'd forgotten I was blond now. With my pale arms I would only register as the white shape of a girl.

I imagined Robin like this, a bright, flaring afterimage, leaving behind a bedroom full of faces and a ghost waiting for a taxi.

The cab pulled up after half an hour or so, and I jumped up to keep the driver from hitting the horn. He was an old man, with the ruddy, broken-capillaried skin that you saw all over Vegas, Irish people who'd been under the desert sun too long.

"You going to the airport, you said?" he asked as I swung open the back door.

"Yeah, the Hertz rental."

"You got any bags?"

"No."

He started to turn around in the Floreses' driveway. "You going to the airport and don't have any bags?"

"I'm just going to rent a car."

He looked at me in the rearview mirror. "Yeah? Kind of late to be renting. You going on some kind of trip?"

"I just need to get out of my sister's house for a while," I said. "I'm in town to visit her and she keeps taking the car and leaving me in the house by myself."

"She take the car overnight?"

"No, I just . . . If she knew I was renting a car she'd want to know why, and it'd be a whole argument, and I don't . . ." I shrugged. "Can I smoke in here?"

He tapped his thick fingers on the steering wheel. "Tell you what," he said, after a few seconds, "you can come sit up here with me and open the window if I can play my music."

"Deal," I said immediately.

He pulled over on the neighborhood street and put his hazards on. I got out onto the sidewalk and shuffled over to the passenger-side door, sliding in beside him and pressing the button for the window.

"I'm Billy," he said when I'd lit up, sticking his hand out.

I hesitated, then shook it. "I'm Alice," I said, making up the name on the spot.

Billy shifted the car into gear. "You like Wanda Jackson, Alice?"

"I don't know who that is," I said truthfully.

"She invented rockabilly," he said, taking out a CD case and prying it open one-handed. The woman on the cover had blue eye shadow up to her eyebrows and helmetlike ratted hair. He slid the CD into the dashboard's mouth and turned up the volume.

"Please love me forever . . ."

"I met her once," he told me over the sound of her voice. "In 1965. I didn't know who she was then. I didn't use to listen to popular music. Saw her again at the show she did in Tucumcari a few years back. She's just as pretty as she ever was." He gave me a sidelong glance. "How long you been in Albuquerque?"

"A few days." I sucked on my cigarette. "I'm from Washington State. You?"

"I grew up here," he said as I stuck my head out the open window. "Lived here all my life."

The music swelled, and Wanda Jackson went into a final crescendo. The Nashville vibrato was impossible to talk over; it was almost operatic. I stared at the irregular shapes of darkened condos sliding past as Billy sped up on Tramway. A mini-storage building loomed like a boulder, widened as we met it, and shrank again in the side mirror. The movement of my face caught my attention, and I pursed my lips as the song ended. "Billy, what do you think about ghosts?" I said into the brief silence.

"About ghosts?" Billy repeated, keeping his eyes on the road. He had a long, straight wrinkle down his cheek, the only angular element in his otherwise lumpen face.

"Yeah." I leaned back against the seat, loosening my shoulders to show that I wasn't serious.

"I try not to think about them." Billy came to a stop at a red light, jostling us.

"Have you ever met one?"

I watched him peel a sliver of his thumbnail away; it went too easily, with the consistency of bar soap. "I don't know," he said, putting his hands back on the wheel as the light turned green.

"You don't know? That sounds like maybe you did." I exhaled a long, pretty plume of smoke out of the window.

"Well, it was my grandmother," Billy said. "She died when I was young. But for years after she died, I used to think she'd come sing to me, you know, just as I was falling asleep. Not any song I'd heard on the radio. It was in German. My parents figured I'd made it up—they'd never heard it either. But when I was a teenager we heard a recording of Elvis singing my song. *'Can't you see, I love you, please don't break my heart in two . . .'* And I knew the words in German, I could sing right along with him. *'Muß i' denn, muß i' denn, zum Städtele hinaus, Städtele hinaus . . ."* That's the name of the song in German, *'Muß I Denn.'* I don't even speak German. My grandmother never spoke it around my mother. She thought it would keep her from learning English, you see."

I clasped my hands. "But she sang it to you. That's so sweet."

"That's what you think, huh?" Billy said.

"You don't think so? She sang you to sleep."

"Well, let me just say: I believe when we die, we go to heaven. Or we go to hell. And my grandmother was a good person. I believe that too. How can I imagine that a loving God would confine her to half an existence here on Earth? I can't believe that, Miss Alice. I have to believe that she is truly gone. So what was the thing that sang to me? I think it was the devil, or one of his emissaries."

I rolled up the window and folded my hands in my lap. "Maybe you were just remembering. From when you were a baby. That's nicer, isn't it?"

Billy smiled. "If I could choose what to believe, I sure would choose that."

"You can choose. I do it all the time. You can think exactly what you want to think. The thoughts make the person, you know." I tapped him on the shoulder. "Ask me what I do."

We were pulling up to the Hertz lot, and Billy distractedly searched the signs. "Well, I would if I could figure out where to go. There's no entrance that I can see . . . Oh, there we go." He looked over at me, recovering the conversation. "What do you do, Miss Alice?"

"I'm an actress," I said, fooling myself even as I said it. "Now ask me where I'm from."

"You're not from Washington State?"

"Not if I don't want to be." I beamed at him, and he chuckled.

"All right, where are you really from?"

"Los Angeles, California," I breathed. "Am I lucky?"

"I don't know," Billy said, the long deep wrinkle pressing into his cheek as he parked in front of the Hertz rental office. "Are you?"

I handed him the fare, and dug out a penny to put on top of it, Lincoln face up. "I'm your lucky sign," I said.

Billy laughed outright, picking up the penny and putting it in his cupholder. "I'll hang on to that," he said. "Why don't you hang on to this?" He gave me twenty dollars of the fare back. "For keeping me company."

I pictured him younger, with yellow hair and the same blue eyes; the specter of his charm was still upon him. "Oh, Billy," I said. "That's really kind of you. Really, really kind."

"Have a wonderful trip, sweetheart," he said. "Give me a kiss before you go." He tapped his cheek.

I kissed his melting cheek and hung there for a moment, gripping the roof of the car. The Hertz sign backlit me, setting the stray hairs in my peripheral vision on fire. I wondered if you could possess someone for a good reason; if maybe it was an angel who had visited him after all.

I drove back to the Floreses' in a little white coupe that smelled like someone else's perfume. The streets had been sparse at midnight, but they were empty nearing two A.M. Cop cars sat with their headlights off in the dusty shoulders of the road. I switched the heater on and shivered at the change in temperature.

Back in Leslie's neighborhood, I parked around the corner, in a no-man's-land stretch of road between two large houses. I walked back slowly, listening to the wind pick up. The neighbors' window was dark now. I lit another cigarette, wanting the warmth in my lungs.

The back door was still unlocked, and I let myself in, making my way half-blind through the house. I blew smoke out as I went up the stairs, wondering if it would set off the smoke alarm, but the house didn't react.

I had to pass the master bedroom to get to the guest room. The door was open tonight, and I could see the shape of Dave's body underneath the covers. Next to him, the bed was empty.

Had Leslie heard me sneak out?

I went into the guest bedroom. There was nobody waiting for me on the bed. I exhaled and locked the door behind me, going into the bathroom to wash my face.

When I came out of the bathroom I saw that there was a shadow in the dim crack of light between the bottom of the locked door and the carpet. It moved as I watched, just a little.

Someone was standing outside the door.

I stopped. *Leslie.* She'd come in and ask me where I'd been. My mind spun. I'd been buying cigarettes. I'd met a man and he'd invited me to . . .

But the shadow remained where it was. The doorknob didn't turn.

It was so quiet I could hear the breathing on the other side.

Was that Leslie breathing? Or someone else?

We stayed there like that, on either side of the door, motionless, for what seemed like hours. Then the shadow moved away and I heard soft footsteps fading as whoever it was went down the hallway.

I got into bed, but I couldn't lie down. I just sat there, eyes open, looking at nothing, for a long time.

29

Mary

I woke up slumped half-upright against the headboard with a killer pain in my shoulder. The Floreses were awake; I listened to them move around as I got dressed and put makeup on. Dave left first, taking Eli to daycare. Leslie thumped around in the master bedroom, getting ready. I heard her shuffle toward the guest room, and then a note slid under the door:

I'll pick you up at 4 for the appointment. Please be ready.

She'd pressed down hard on the second sentence.

I waited until I heard her go back into her bedroom, and then I went downstairs and left the house as quietly as I could, sticking a little gum into the back-door lock for good measure. My rental car was where I had left it around the corner. I pulled it up to the intersection and idled, waiting for Leslie.

A green pickup slowed down behind me, then honked. I waved at the driver to go around me.

I tilted my head to see myself in the side mirror. I'd put my hair in a bun and pulled my hoodie loosely over it. Leslie's bug-eyed sunglasses covered most of my face.

Another car pulled up behind me, and I waved it through. Leslie was taking forever. Maybe she was looking for her sunglasses.

I fiddled with the radio, flipping through channels until the college radio station surprised me with the Stone Roses.

There. Leslie's big silver Honda trundled down the street past me and turned left toward the neighborhood exit. I waited until she had completed the turn and then followed her, keeping a car between us.

It was sort of exciting to be playing detective like this. The adrenaline cut my exhaustion from a night spent driving to and from the car rental.

The craziest thing was it wasn't the first time I'd tailed someone like a cop. Paul had cheated on me before. I never thought he'd do it. The first time we'd slept together he'd made me turn in a circle so that he could look at me. He took my clothes off and folded them for me, touching each item sentimentally. I'd made him tell me over and over that he was in love with me. Every time he'd sounded sincere. *I can't believe you're not famous yet,* he'd told me once, stroking down the line on my palm. I hadn't even told him what it meant yet. His thumb reached my wrist, and I felt the heartbeat in my vein twitch against it.

And then he'd stopped calling me.

I couldn't believe I'd read him wrong. Most people are easy to read, especially when they're naked. I would've sworn to you I had him wrapped around my finger. This time next year, I'd thought, me and him, a house in the Hills . . .

I'd given him a week to come to his senses and try to win me back. But at the end of the week, I was still alone in my apartment, and he was still nowhere to be seen.

So then I'd driven to his house, turned off my headlights, and waited. It was a Saturday night and he didn't stay home on Saturday nights. I watched his big lifted truck turn in to the driveway, watched the bathroom light switch on behind the frosted glass. He came back out showered, dressed in nicer jeans and a blue polo that I'd bought him a couple of weeks ago for his birthday.

I followed him through twenty minutes of evening traffic. It was difficult to keep enough space between the cars that he wouldn't notice me but stay close enough to remain on his tail. Paul never signaled, either; he'd once told me it kept the other drivers on their toes.

He parked on the street and went into a Thai restaurant. I stood on the street, watching the windows. A girl who looked like a teenager stood up when he walked in, and he kissed her, picking up her hand, stroking her palm. She glanced out the window, as if she could feel my stare against her cheek.

I was only twenty-five. Twenty-seven—but Paul hadn't known that. Nobody knew that. To him, and to everyone else, I was twenty-five. And he'd traded me in.

She was twenty-two, I found out later.

That was the first time.

Anyway, unlike Paul, Leslie used her turn signal religiously.

She turned in to the parking lot of a three-story building that looked like a bank. HARGRAVE RESIDENTIAL, LLC was written on the shoppe-style wrought-iron sign outside. I turned in to the Dunkin' Donuts drive-thru across the street and ordered an iced latte as Leslie went through the big glass doors. Then I found a space and shut off the engine, watching the building across the street.

I stuck the straw in my mouth. Ten minutes passed. Leslie didn't emerge. After half an hour, I started the engine again and pulled into the Hargrave lot.

Inside, the lobby was designed to look like a home, full of squashy furniture and lined with floral wallpaper. In the center of the room a woman sat behind a huge mahogany desk outfitted with a Mac and a stained-glass lamp. "Hi, how can I help you?" she said as I made my way across the too-thick carpet, leaving little tufty footprints behind.

"Hi, I'm looking for Leslie Flores? Does she work here?"

"Yes, Ms. Flores is on the third floor. Do you have an appointment?"

"I have a job interview at ten. I'm supposed to meet with the person in charge of . . ." I groped. "HR? Is that her?"

The receptionist glanced at my jeans. "No, Ms. Flores is the director of accounting. HR would be second floor. May I take your name?"

"Oh—I'm Alice." I gave her a big smile. "I'm a little early, though. I'll go get my purse and be right back."

"'K," the receptionist said, her eyes already back on her screen.

In the car, I sucked down the last of the melted whipped cream and glanced up at the Hargrave building.

So it was true. Leslie hadn't lost her job. She'd been lying to me. Now I had to find out why.

30

Mary

I got back on the freeway to Leslie's house. I couldn't stop thinking about the way Leslie had talked last night, the panic in her voice. *Stop fucking around.*

What did Leslie need fifty thousand dollars for? I was pretty sure at this point that it wasn't for her house. I was equally sure that she was desperate for that money.

I pulled into the neighborhood and parked the car on the same adjacent street. A woman in running gear passed me and waved, as if she'd seen me parking in that spot every day of her life. I could barely summon the energy to wave back.

The Flores house was echoey with nobody in it. The noise of the back door shutting clattered around the kitchen. I could have gone to bed again, waited for Leslie to come pick me up. Trusted that we were in this together.

Anyway, you know what I did instead.

I tried the tablet in the master bedroom again first. Dave had left it on top of the bed this time, in sleep mode. I opened the lid and found that it was password-protected. *password*, I typed. *eli*. The Mac informed me that if I entered another incorrect password, the computer would be locked. Fuck. I went downstairs.

The desktop computer in the kitchen had been shut off, its screen black. I started it back up. I was about to try *password* again when something occurred to me. This was the house computer, in a house that had no place to hide things.

I pressed ENTER.

The screen loaded, just like that.

I should have known. It was obvious to me at this point that Leslie loved to pretend she didn't have any secrets.

I scanned the icons on the desktop. Outlook. Yes. Email. I clicked on that, but it prompted me for a password. I tried pressing ENTER again, but nothing happened. I searched the underside of the keyboard and the back of the monitor, but she wasn't one of those people who wrote her passwords down, or at least not anywhere I could find them. The drawer to the desk that held the computer itself was full of carefully organized receipts from Target and Sprouts and White House Black Market. A little pouch held coupons, and the rest was loose rubber bands, twist-ties, ballpoint pens, and one of the baby's dusty old binkies.

I went to Facebook. Success—she'd set it to autofill her password. Her feed was all onlooker, passive, no interaction, just friends from high school promoting their multilevel marketing schemes and friends from college "Five Years Ago Today"–ing their lush honeymoons. I clicked on Messenger. She didn't use Messenger to chat, apparently—it was only invitations to public events and messages from Babs at Planet Fitness reminding her to renew her membership.

I started going through her bookmarked sites. No access to any of the bank-account websites that autoloaded in the search bar. Weather reports, a yoga exercise video, some clothing sites with shoes and blouses. I moved on to the desktop. Leslie had a ton of illegible, apparently work-related Excel spreadsheets and Word documents scattered across her background. I went back to the browser history. Children's YouTube videos, a "lullaby baby" playlist on Spotify. Somebody had searched how to get vegetable-oil stains out of clothing.

I pulled up Gmail—davetherover was automatically logged in. Finally, something useful.

I scrolled through. He didn't sort any of his email except insofar as Gmail did it for him; his header read "Inbox (1,891)." The unread emails were mostly reminders—from himself and from innumerable mailing lists. *Pick up Eli 4:30 pm. Your credit card statement is now available. Join us at Albuquerque's annual beer and wine tasting event!*

I clicked on one of the emails he had already read, from a woman named Cadence.

OK, we're doing it this way because its easier and none of u text back >:/ Pls fill in your availability n reply with what you wanna bring :) me n sonya are bringing sangriaaa surveymonkey.com/poll/938882220

Dave had replied:

wd like to bring 1 wife 1 baby and 1 gallon posole. is joa bringing karaoke? I want to make mama sing gasolina

Joachim replied:

imma tell her u said that

Cadence replied:

u both uninvited bye

I clicked back through his inbox. His sisters, Cadence and Maria, emailed him a lot, and he had a dull intermittent correspondence with several friends who sent him pictures of their lives in other countries. Scattered throughout were people emailing him links to Clickhole articles or YouTube videos.

Six hundred emails back, it finally occurred to me to click Chats, and suddenly I found an avalanche of archived conversations between Dave and people who appeared to be women he worked with. He used Hangouts even more than Messenger. "Erin" was mostly trading HuffPo-style news articles and occasional snickering about coworkers who didn't show up in the chats. "Sarah" was the next most frequent name, chatting him several times a week about her boyfriend and her rescue dog—the stuff about the boyfriend was coyly sexual in an attempt to shock Dave, but he only ever replied with "lol" or earnest advice, which made me laugh.

There weren't any chats with that woman, Elaine. Finally I searched her name. A few mentions of her in the chats with Erin and Sarah, but nothing else. A tiny line of text at the bottom of the search read: *Some messages in Trash match your search.*

I clicked *View messages.*

Sixteen deleted messages with Elaine's name in them. They were mostly confirmation emails from something called Shekel. I clicked on the first one.

Congratulations! You've successfully paid Elaine Campbell $355.00. She will be able to redeem your payment in 3–5 business days.

Three hundred fifty-five dollars? I clicked on the next email.

Congratulations! You've successfully paid Elaine Campbell $320.00. She will be able to redeem your payment in 3–5 business days.

What the fuck?

I went through the rest of the Shekel confirmations. They stretched back a little over a year. A hundred here, two hundred there. Three hundred or more for the past three months.

There were two Hangouts conversations in the Trash as well. I clicked on the first one.

me: did messenger send you a gif 5 times in a row
Elaine: haha I didn't see this earlier
No why?
me: it's freaking out for me imma try it again

That was the end of the conversation. I clicked on the other one.

Elaine: I left my phone at home today I'm so bored

me: haha you've gotta revert to gtalk like the rest of us Olds

We don't have fancy emojis here u must express your feelings in the form of ugly yellow blobs

Elaine: 😦 —this one's a sad face

me: 😏

Elaine: that's work inappropriate

Can you keep a secret?

me: Absolutely not

Elaine: no im serious

Come here

I sat back in the chair.

Had Leslie gone through Dave's email? Had she looked in the Trash folder?

Why the fuck was he sending Elaine so much money?

I searched the rest of the computer, then the rest of the house. Nothing in the bathroom, in the closet, in the underwear drawers, in the bedside drawers, in any of Leslie's jewelry boxes. The baby's room had toys, diapers, gift receipts from friends, and a stained UNM sweatshirt. I went back downstairs and looked in the garage, but the only thing I found was Dave's weed in an old tin can behind the toolbox. I gave up, rolled myself a joint, and ordered a pizza.

I was on my third slice of tomato-and-olive, high as shit (whoever Dave was buying from was not fucking around) when it occurred to me that Leslie had another place she could be keeping her secrets.

Somewhere Dave never went.

Robin

The first time I ever got high: Marisol Borrego's birthday party in the year 2004. My father was working and Leslie had no car, so I walked from school to the Borregos' house, sweaty and red-faced by the time I arrived. I wasn't there to see Marisol—she was one of those children who clung to childhood even into puberty, dragging dolls onto the playground and covering her ears when the older girls talked about sex. Her birthday party was more of the same: pin the tail, Barbie napkins, cupcakes with plastic animal figurines baked in.

I took an extra cupcake and put it in my purse, then asked Mrs. Borrego where the bathroom was. She pointed. I went into the hallway and began pushing doors. A bathroom, a closet, Marisol's bedroom, and finally, near the end, her brother's. Kevin was lying on the bed with headphones on, eating Bugles.

I slipped into the room and tapped him on the shoulder. His leg jerked in surprise and he opened his eyes.

"I brought you a cupcake," I said, pulling it out of my purse and offering it to him. It was slightly crushed.

He struggled to sit up. "I know you," he said. "You're that chick Robin. You're friends with Marisol?"

I crossed my arms. "I feel so famous. How do you know about me?"

Kevin snorted. "I'm sure you're fuckin' mystified," he said as he unwrapped the cupcake. "You don't like the party?"

I shrugged. "It's not to my taste," I said, trying to sound older.

"*Hagh.*" Kevin doubled over; he'd bitten into a plastic pig. "Ow, fuck! What the fuck!" He pressed his fist to his mouth and came away with bloody cake crumbs.

"Oh, the ears got you," I said, watching him interestedly. "I forgot to tell you there were animals in the cupcakes. It's good otherwise, though, right?"

"Jesus," he said, wiping his hand on his black jeans and licking his lips. "What do you want?"

He was fourteen, already barrel-chested, with long thin limbs and a wide, melancholic face. I sat on his lap.

It took barely anything after that to convince him to share his weed with me. Nicky Chiklis, my recent first boyfriend, had told me Kevin's older brother who lived in Bernalillo sold weed, so Kevin always had some. It was true; Kevin said, reclining on the bed, "It's shush money, basically. I don't tell our mama what he's doing on the weekends, and he gives me dimes whenever he visits."

"Hush," I said. He cocked his head. "Hush money."

"Oh, right," he said, nodding. "How are you feeling? Is it like what you thought?"

"I feel like I'm in a movie," I said. "Like I'm echoing."

He laughed too loudly. "I'm high, like, all the time in school," he said. "I can't stand it otherwise. I think I'm not cut out for it, you know?"

"Sure you are," I said, touching his ankle with mine. It was thrilling, like passing a finger through a flame. Kevin drew his leg back and wrapped his hands around it protectively. "Don't you want to feel close to me?" I said.

"I don't know anything about you," he answered, but his eyes crinkled. "You got any older brothers?"

"An older sister," I said. "Leslie."

"Oh, with the . . ." Kevin held his hand to his chin.

"Pageboy," I said. "Yeah."

"I knew her. She was an upperclassman in the junior high when I started. Looked like a kid." He eyed me. "You don't look like a kid."

"She's not a kid," I said, inhaling. "She used to lock me up, you know."

"Lock you up where?" He leaned forward to take the joint from me.

"In the guest bedroom." I closed my eyes. "She stole the key out of Daddy's desk. Whenever she didn't want to watch me anymore . . . or didn't want to talk to me . . . I'd spend hours in there. Looking at the ceiling."

"My brother locked me in a closet one time," Kevin said. "It's like a rite of passage."

"No," I said dreamily. "It wasn't to mess with me. It was over and over. Like I wasn't really human to her." I opened my eyes. "She pretends to be a good person. But she locked me in there like a dog."

"Jesus," Kevin said.

I patted his hand. "Do you feel closer to me now?"

I think he did; Kevin's brother went to prison the next year, and by the time I was in high school Kevin was dealing. Discounts for me, because I was his first. We never had sex, but he liked to watch me get high, lying beside me, his face next to mine. I fed him stories that way, like putting my tongue in his mouth; as intimate, if not more. Should I call him a boyfriend? I'd rather call him my priest. I only ever told him the truth.

Mary

The house on Riviera squatted by the road, dull-eyed. I'd seen the big pink stone next to the door when Leslie had taken me here to pack boxes, and I'd been right about it: when I nudged it with the toe of my sneaker, the spare key lay underneath, grimy with dirt.

Inside, the old man's smell still clung to everything. Spoiled vegetables and cigarettes underneath a hospital varnish of antiseptic gel. I wrinkled my nose and started searching.

Leslie's room first; why wouldn't she hide her secrets in among the rest of her stuff? It was the first room down the hall, painted a sunny, virtuous yellow. But it was empty save for a white bed frame and several sealed cardboard boxes. I examined the boxes. TOYS, two boxes of BOOKS, and VINTAGE CLOTHES. Were '00s clothes vintage? Who was going to buy Leslie's old low-riders and bedazzled tees?

I scratched at the carpet where it met the baseboards, but each corner was stapled down tight, no way to access the flooring underneath. Whatever it was, she wasn't keeping it under the floor. Crawling on my hands and knees, I checked the underside of the bed frame—dead spiders and dust balls.

I shuffled back out into the main part of the house and turned toward the old man's study. There was an ancient IBM desktop, from the time when powered-off computer screens were gray, not black. At the very least, I bet I could play *King's Quest* on it, no problem. I pressed the power button and the modem wheezed, rousing itself into a gradually increasing pitch, like an airplane taking off. The screen remained gray. I poked at the mouse and pressed a few sticky keys. Nothing. I felt around the back of it for the cord and followed it with my fingers down to the modem. It was plugged in, the computer was running, and yet nothing showed on the screen. I held down the power button and tried again. The monitor was dead.

Okay. I glanced around the study. Dust motes drifted in the faint light from the blinds. Bookcases, mostly empty. Boxes here and there. A closed door on the opposite side of the room, maybe leading to the second hallway. An outdated globe, scattered office detritus: plastic in- and outboxes, chunks of Post-its. The wedding photograph was back on the desk.

There were a lot of little drawers in the desk—maybe in there. I opened them one at a time. Mostly they were badly organized documents, things that should have been in the filing cabinet across the room—mail from the bank, tax documents, the carbon copies of dozens of checks. Here and there I found household things like packs of playing cards and pencils and old spare keys, and one little drawer held nothing but a fragile-looking glass-blown Christmas ornament still attached to its gold hook. Another held a few childish construction-paper drawings of houses and cats. The longest drawer had a lock on it, and it wouldn't open when I tugged. I looked closer.

The handle had no dust on it. No—one side had a wad of gray, as if someone's thumb had dragged all the way across the handle, gathering up the dust as it went. And it was recent enough that I could still see the track.

That was it.

I tried the spare keys in the lock, but they were all too big. I stuffed them in my pocket in case I needed them in the rest of the house. There weren't any other keys lying around the rest of the study that I could see, and most of the books were in boxes, so I doubted the drawer's key had been in any of those. I crawled underneath the desk and craned my neck, but there wasn't anything taped to the underside of the wood, and pushing on the bottom of the drawer from below did nothing but rattle whatever was inside.

I stood up and opened the little drawer with the Christmas ornament, carefully removing the gold hook. I'd picked a couple of locks before, but I wasn't an expert by any means, and I had no idea whether the hook would work. I fitted it into the lock and tried to feel for tumblers, jiggling it up and down.

There was a click. My breath caught.

The drawer slid open. What a shitty lock. I could have opened the drawer by yanking it hard enough, I thought—but then Leslie would be able to tell someone had broken in. This way was better.

Inside were more documents, crumby Hostess wrappers, a very nice Montblanc, and—

A cellphone.

My heart was pounding. I took out my own phone charger and plugged the phone in, waiting as the screen came slowly to life. It was a BlackBerry-style cell with a physical keypad, one of the ones you paid twenty bucks for at Best Buy. No password. I used the navigator arrows to select the text-message icon.

There was only one exchange in the phone, between the user and a number that hadn't been added to Contacts. A 505 area code, local. I clicked on it.

It was definitely Leslie's phone, not the old man's. The last text message had been sent in late February, after he'd died. Leslie had said:

We met earlier this afternoon. Please use this number to contact me from now on.

The reply came several hours later:

OK to come by Sunday with the cash. If Ed is at front desk ask for me.

After that, the other person never responded again. Leslie had texted over the next several weeks:

Please confirm one more time so I can be sure.

Please confirm.

I need to hear back from you.

No one answering door. Please reply.

I need an answer.

Reply.

The store has been closed all week. What's going on?

I want my money back.

I want my money back.

Give me my fcking money back.

I clicked slowly through the rest of the phone. No email. Nothing in the trash. When I clicked on the navigator, the navigation history loaded below the search bar. Just one address: 31 Piedra Roja Rd, Corrales, NM, 87048.

I copied the address and went back to the phone's main screen to paste it into the Google search bar.

Google said it was a Curves—one of a chain of gyms that only allowed women and were decorated like the set of an infomercial.

But Leslie didn't go to Curves. She went to Planet Fitness—I'd seen the messages on Facebook only this morning reminding her to re-up her membership. I thumbed through the reviews, of which there were three. One of them began, *I've been going to this gym since it opened in April, and I've lost twelve pounds with the help of their lovely trainers!*

Thank you, Carol Fernandez. I gave her review an anonymous thumbs-up.

So Leslie had gone to the Curves before it was a Curves. I scrolled through all the Google results for the address, but I couldn't find the name of the business it had been before it went up for sale.

how to find out what building used to be, I searched.

The National Archives, Find a Historic Building, Cyndi's List, How to Find Out If a Building Is Being Demolished Near You! Zoopla, Zillow, Reddit threads, Google Maps. I tried Zillow and a couple of records-of-sale sites. None of them listed the sale to Curves—maybe it was too recent to have been entered into the archives online. I clicked on a Quora question that more or less matched mine. The respondent listed several of the links I'd already seen on Google and finished up with, *But if you're looking for a privately owned residence that's not a historic building, and there are no records of sale available online, there's not much you can do unless you're buddies with a P.I.!*

I blinked. I wasn't buddies with a P.I., but I did know a police officer.

33

Mary

The phone rang six times before Nancy picked up. "Hello?" I tried. "Nancy? It's me."

A long few seconds of silence. Then Nancy said, "Okay, hang on," far away, as if to somebody else. The line went dead.

I blinked and jabbed at the phone to redial. It went straight to voicemail this time.

I paced out of the study and into the living room, opening my texts app. For some reason I had expected her to pick up right away. I could've sworn that was exactly what she would do. The way we had tilted toward each other—how easily it had happened, as if the muscle memory was still there.

As I was staring at the texts app, my phone buzzed in my palm. I swiped to answer.

"Hi, sorry," Nancy said. "I was inside, I don't have good reception in the building."

My mouth hung open for a moment. "It's Robin," I said experimentally.

"I know." I heard her make a little glottal noise; she'd almost said something else.

"I wanted to talk to you again," I said, hoping to draw it out of her.

She cleared her throat. "I was thinking about calling you," she said quietly. "But then I thought . . . I didn't know when you were leaving again."

A funny feeling stole through me. Nancy is in love with me, I thought. That's what this is about. I pictured her wrapped around her wife, staring at the phone on the bedside table. My face in her mind now. For ten years, she'd wanted to see Robin one last time.

And then I'd arrived.

It was sort of beautiful. Romantic, almost. And if Nancy could help me with Leslie, that was a win-win, wasn't it?

I let the silence spool out before I said, "I was supposed to leave today. But I didn't."

Nancy exhaled, sounding like she was trying not to let me hear her relief. "Okay," she said.

"I'm scared." My throat felt tight. "I've never . . . You're just . . . I don't know."

"What do you mean?"

"I don't want to get in the way of you and—I don't want to get in the way of anything," I said. "I don't even know what I want."

"I don't know what I want either." She sounded like she was echoing me just to soothe me.

"Things are so crazy right now," I said. "With my family. I found out—I mean, I can't tell it to a cop. But I wasn't even thinking about it with you. It felt like ten years hadn't even passed." I put the phone close to my mouth and drew in a quick breath so she could hear it. "Did it feel like that to you?"

"Maybe," she said. "Are you in trouble? What's going on?"

"It's nothing. I just—This is crazy, but I canceled my flight home."

"You canceled?"

"I want to see you again," I said, letting the words spill out like I couldn't help myself.

"I don't know."

She was so ready to give in. I could hear it in her voice. "Please, Nancy," I said.

"I'm on a shift."

I squeezed the phone. "I could meet you somewhere?"

She didn't reply for a minute. Then she said, "Do you remember where we used to meet at the lookout off La Cueva?"

"Yeah, of course," I said quickly.

"We could talk there. I have to go," she said. "Wait there for me."

"I will," I breathed into the phone. "I'll wait for you." I picked my words carefully. Nancy had waited for a decade. She'd like it, me waiting for her this time. I envisioned myself leaning against Nancy's cop car with the hazy, dusty city spread out below me. Where was my lipstick? I rummaged in my purse.

"Bye," Nancy said, unable to prevent a hint of shy conspiracy from edging into her tone. Like we were the last two girls awake at the sleepover.

"Bye," I said softly, and let her hang up first. Then I went back into the study to unplug Leslie's phone and clear the history. As I set the phone back in the desk, the papers underneath it shifted slightly, and a wrinkled envelope peeked out from behind the rest. I drew it out. It was lumpy, that's why it was wrinkled. The flap hadn't been sealed, only tucked into the rest of the envelope like a Chinese take-out carton. I opened it curiously.

Inside was a pair of earrings.

Those were the earrings Leslie had been wearing that first night, when we'd met in the parking lot. She'd put them in the desk some-time between then and now. I glanced up at that wedding photo-graph. There were the earrings I was holding. On Christine's ears this time, as she looked timidly into the camera, clutching her new husband's arm. In a dozen years she would be dead. In a few decades, Leslie would be the only one left in this house, laboring on her knees to pack her family's things into each labeled cardboard box.

I shoved the earrings back into the envelope and replaced them underneath the phone in the drawer. It took me three tries to get the lock to catch. Leslie should have picked a better place to hide the phone. But I knew why she'd been drawn to this one. The kids' drawings, the Christmas ornament. It was where her father had stored the private objects of his life.

I got slowly to my feet. I needed to get out of this fucking house. It was as full of secrets as Leslie's house was bare.

34

Mary

Back in my rented coupe, I checked my reflection in the rearview mirror. My eyelids felt puffy and heavy, but I didn't look any different. I studied my face for a moment, thinking about what Nancy would see in it, and then I got my lipstick out of my bag and applied it carefully. It was too dark a color for daytime, but that was all right. I'd look like I was trying to impress her.

La Cueva was a winding road that peaked right before the valley drop-off into the foot of the mountains. The government had marked a portion of the land just off the road as a picnic site. I pulled into the bare-dirt lot and got out. It was a clear, sunny day, and I could see for miles, until the roofs blurred together into the purple band of the horizon. In the other direction, the mountaintops were still white here and there with snow, although it was nearly gone, drained into the arroyos below.

I leaned against my car for almost ten minutes, sunning myself like a lizard. It was bad for my skin, but I didn't care. After the close, dark interior of the house on Riviera, I felt like I needed to be covered in sunlight.

The cop car pulled up beside me, crunching pebbles under its tires. A Crown Victoria. I hadn't seen one of those in years. All the cop cars in Vegas were SUVs or those ugly, round-nosed Camaros. I half expected Nancy to get out looking like Officer Krupke, but her uniform was modern and close-cut, black trousers and black collared shirt with a patch on the sleeve. She looked slim-hipped and serious in it, like those old photographs of young men in khaki. I saw her throat move as she swallowed, and suddenly I couldn't tell if I was pretending to want her or not.

"Nancy," I said. In two steps she had crossed the distance between our cars and pushed me up against the coupe, her hands tipping my head back, lips on my neck. I let out an inadvertent breath as she kissed me and slid her hands down my body, pulling my hips toward hers. "Is this okay?" she mumbled, not looking at me.

"Yes—yes," I breathed, flattered by her impatience.

"We should get in the car," she said, glancing at the road. I nodded.

The back of the Victoria was easy-scrub leather, scalding after half a day's trapped sunlight, and I instantly broke into a sweat despite the air-conditioning as Nancy pushed me inside. "You canceled your flight," she said, biting me on the shoulder hard enough to hurt.

I added a little extra to my gasp, and fumbled for the buttons of her uniform. "Please, Nancy," I said, and then she was crushing me onto the seat, mouth hot against mine.

"You missed me," she said, pulling my shirt off.

"Uh-huh." I glanced up at her. She was wearing a sports bra under her uniform shirt, and I pushed my hands underneath it, groping, until she yanked it over her head. "I'll show you."

It was cramped and hot in the Victoria, and Nancy laughed a little hysterically as I sank down into the well of the seat. It was easy to make Nancy come—she was so sensitive that I had to pin her hips in place with one arm—and I did it over and over again until she was half sobbing, covering her face with her hands.

I climbed up into her lap, straddling her, waiting for her heart to slow. After a while she opened her eyes and tilted her face up, and I kissed her, slacker this time than the last.

"I want to fuck you," she said. "Not with my hands. I feel like you'd like it."

"I'd like it," I said, realizing as I said it that I was telling the truth. Realizing it probably wouldn't happen. I'd disappear, and then Robin would disappear too. A funny sinking feeling entered me.

"Next time, then." She touched me gently, running her nails down my back. I leaned into it—it felt hypnotic, like she could tell exactly where I needed it—and she trailed her lips across my chest. "You're so beautiful," she said, resting her cheek against my breast. "I feel nervous to even look at you."

"I know," I said, leaning forward again and grazing her cheek with my nose. But I didn't know—not really. I was fascinated by the people who fell in love with me. It came over them like a fever, turning them sweaty and desperate, ready to fall to their knees at a moment's notice. In return what I felt was a kind of hunger. Was it love if you only consumed it? I thought about how I'd made Paul say *I love you, I love you, I love you,* like a child writing lines on the blackboard.

It felt stranger with Nancy, too easy. I should have felt guilty, but I liked it, the closeness, the way she looked at me, like she was seeing a real person. When Paul looked at me it was more like he saw my demographic, and approved. Twentysomething, redheaded, aspiring actress. Check. I thought about that other woman, the one with the Tesla.

"Do you know anyone named Sam?" I asked. "Sam Driscoll?"

Nancy shook her head a little too slowly. "Who's that?"

I could have swallowed my tongue. "Nobody. Never mind."

"Are you okay?" she asked, stroking my face. "On the phone, you said something was going on with your family."

"I can't talk about it to you," I mumbled. "I wish I could."

"What?" Nancy's eyes sharpened. "It's something illegal? Are you in trouble?"

"It's not me." I slid off her lap and started pulling on my underwear. "It's my sister. Anyway, I don't even know for sure, so . . ."

"What is it?"

I rubbed my face. "I'm scared you're going to arrest her or something!"

"Robin." Nancy reached for my hands and caught them up like a high schooler, fingers laced awkwardly in midair. When she was moving deliberately, she was so elegant in her motions, but moments of distraction revealed her natural hesitancy. "She's your sister. I swear I'm not going to arrest her. I just want to know what's going on."

"Maybe you should arrest her." I sighed. "She has another phone. I found it. It's her talking to some guy about how she gave him all this cash and she wants her money back. I looked up the address where she met him, but it was sold recently and I can't find out who owned it before, or what the guy's name is."

"What's the address?"

"It's a Curves gym in Corrales. Why, do you think you could look up what it used to be?"

She shrugged and leaned over to grab her shirt. "It's not a lot of trouble to look up an address in the system, if it'll make you feel better. I'm sure it's just money she loaned a friend. Your sister doesn't strike me as a criminal mastermind. Isn't she an accountant?"

"But why keep it on a separate phone?" I widened my eyes. "You know? The Leslie I knew would *never* keep a phone hidden from her husband. They share all their computers. She leaves her Facebook logged in."

"Are they having problems or something?"

I shook my head. "I don't know. I think maybe—maybe yes. Maybe it's something to do with trying to get a divorce. Dave's been—But if she's into something shady, I have to know. I mean, we've only just started talking. I don't want her to mess up her life like—like I did." I closed my eyes, and when I opened them Nancy was biting her lip.

"You didn't mess up your life," she said. "You're still here, aren't you?"

"Yeah," I said, visibly shoring myself up.

"Here." She passed me her phone to type the address and phone number in.

"This is so sweet of you." I finished typing and crawled closer to her, putting my arms around her neck.

She batted me away. "I have to go back to work. Everybody's going to know." Her face was pink.

"Then you should probably get rid of all the lipstick on your mouth," I said, wanting to rub my face against hers.

"What, really?" She sat up and leaned forward to look in her rear-view mirror. "Fuck," she said, scrubbing at it.

"I've got it. Come to my car." She followed me out into the dusty lot, the horizon looming. No other cars were on the road this time of day, and it felt like we were in an atmospheric pocket so high up, where no one could see me get my lotion from my purse and dab it on Nancy's face. She screwed up her eyes as I swept the Kleenex over her skin. It was covered in raspberry stains when I was done, and I held it up to show her.

"Magic," she said. "Thank you, baby."

Baby. I let my eyes light up. "I can't kiss you again," I said. "I'll ruin all my hard work."

She laughed and kissed me on each corner of my mouth, just where it began to curve upward. It was so intimate, like something married people would do. "Don't worry about your sister. It's probably nothing."

"When can you get away?" I breathed, pressing my cheek into her uniform. "Tonight?"

"I don't know." Her face shuttered. "Maybe. I'll text you."

"Don't go."

"I have to." She stepped back, and I pulled myself away from her as if we were magnetized. I leaned on the Nissan, knowing I'd be silhouetted against the white paint, and when Nancy glanced over her shoulder I was touching my lips, letting out a shaky breath.

I could have been in love with her in another life. In another life, I had been, maybe.

Nancy got in her cop car and shut the door. I waited for her to round the bend, and then I scrubbed the rest of my face with the Kleenex. Leslie would be home soon, and I wanted to look like I'd been on the couch all afternoon.

35

Leslie

The back wall of my office was a single plate-glass window. The heat was making me sleepy. I had my desk fan turned on full-blast, with makeshift paperweights holding down all my files—stapler, pair of scissors, pencil sharpener. Their edges fluttered as the fan swept across my desk. I rubbed my temples and stood up to get water.

Justin was sitting at his cubicle just outside my door. I leaned over. "I'm leaving a little early today, so if you finish after four o'clock, send it to Paige, not me."

Justin looked up. "Oh, is Eli okay?"

"What?" I said, turning back.

He pursed his lips. "Is Eli okay? Are you picking him up?"

"He's fine, why?" I frowned. "I have some things to do about my dad's estate."

"Oh, thank God." Justin laughed. "Not about your dad, obviously. But you're at Haven too, right? My two-year-old came down with the worst stomach virus and it's going around. I hope you guys are spared."

"Oh, how fun," I said. "I hope so too. And—sorry, I'm completely blanking on her name—"

"Catherine," Justin supplied.

"Catherine! I hope she feels better soon."

"Me too. She's miserable." He grimaced. "But at least she's improving her Spanish. We've been watching a lot of *Pocoyo* while she rides it out."

I tried to look sympathetic, and turned to head toward the office kitchen.

"Are you guys raising Eli bilingual? Your husband speaks Spanish, right?"

"Yeah." I turned back and folded my arms. "He does."

"So how's Eli doing with that?" Justin grinned.

"I mean . . ." I shrugged. "He's only a year, so he's not very verbal yet."

Justin tilted his head. "Does he use sign language? I know they taught Catherine some signs at Haven, although she was starting to make sentences by the time Ben went back to work. We found it really useful."

I didn't know how much sign language Eli used. "He does enough."

"Well, if you're worried about his language acquisition, reading picture books really did wonders for Catherine. They make the connection much quicker and it's supposed to speed up their reading. We have some old ones from last year if you want to take them off our hands!"

I gave him a vague smile. "That's really nice of you. We've got too much baby stuff already, though. You really have to let them set their own pace."

"That's so true." Justin smiled at me. "Okay, well, I'll let you go. Sorry for all the baby talk, but this office is so baby-free, I just need to talk to somebody who understands sometimes. I was so thrilled when you said you were going on maternity leave last year!"

I laughed and turned toward the kitchen. I'd spent enough time talking with Justin that it was almost time to leave. In my office, I closed the blinds—something I never did until the end of the day; the striped light from the closed blinds made my office feel cagelike— and gathered my things into my purse.

The appointment with Albert was in an hour. My neck itched as I got into the elevator.

I couldn't listen to the radio on the way home. The noise set my teeth on edge. I drove in silence, hearing other people's music wash over from their open windows.

What if she wasn't there again?

I could feel my pulse in the hollows of my jaw as I pulled into the neighborhood.

She wasn't on the lawn.

I parked and went inside.

"Robin?" I called, just in case Dave had come home early.

There was no reply.

I wandered through the hall into the kitchen. Two chairs had been pulled out, but she wasn't there.

"Robin?"

I heard the television click on. I went into the living room.

"Leslie," Mary said. "You're home!"

She was stretched out on the couch in cutoffs and a lacy white top, sneakers still on. Bits and pieces of a pizza littered the empty box and the floor around it, and she'd left a wadded-up napkin on the coffee table. I looked at the TV. A tennis game. The room smelled like weed.

"You're not dressed," I said. "Did you bring drugs here? Why didn't you answer me before?"

She adjusted her top. "You know what's funny?"

"What?"

"You know what's funny?" she repeated. "I found out why you weren't that worried about me blowing it for you with Dave about your job." She shuffled her dirty sneakers on my couch thoughtfully. "I guess it doesn't matter if there's nothing to find out. Since you weren't fired."

I swallowed. "I asked you to stop prying into my personal life."

She sat up. "I came out here because I felt sorry for you, Leslie. Because you said you were about to lose your house. But it turns out you guys are fine. You actually don't need fifty grand. So why did you tell me all that crap?"

"Did you call my work?" I asked. "Did you give them a name?"

Mary's face darkened. "Is it because I'm so cute, is that why everyone assumes I'm a fucking dumbass? I didn't give them any name. I just wanted to know where you were going all day." She flopped back on the couch and folded her arms. "Because you don't tell me shit, Leslie. I went with you out of the goodness of my heart and you are making me question that."

I blinked hard as my eyes watered. "You went with me because you were failing in Vegas," I said, hearing the edge in it. "So don't pretend it was because you care about my problems. I need the money, and so do you. It doesn't matter why."

Mary studied my eyes dispassionately, as if trying to determine whether the tears were real. Finally she said, "I thought we were kinda getting along, you know. I don't know what you want from me."

"I want you to get dressed," I said flatly.

Mary raised her eyebrows, but got up off the couch and went upstairs. I shut the TV off and gathered up the pizza detritus.

When she came back down, she had left the white Adidas on, but changed into a polo dress. Not ideal, but it was enough. We got into the car in silence. Mary looked out the window as I started the car and pulled us onto the main road.

After a minute I dug Robin's passport out of my purse and tossed it into her lap. "Found that in the safety deposit box. It's got three months left on it. You can use it if they ask you for ID."

She thumbed through it. "There's no country stamps in here."

"We didn't travel much."

Mary flipped back to the photo. I could see her examining it out of the corner of my eye.

"I'm sorry for lying to you," I said finally. "I didn't know what else to say to explain why I need the will to go through."

"You could tell me what's really going on," she said timidly.

I shook my head. "I can't tell anyone. It's not personal. And it won't affect you." I looked over at her. "I promise."

Mary's hair had fallen into her face. The light turned green as we stared at each other, and I hit the gas. Mary glanced back down at the passport in her hands. "She takes a good photo," she said.

I knew the photo she was looking at. My dad had been talking about a trip to Europe as a reward if Robin stayed out of trouble. But Robin never stayed out of trouble. They'd told us not to smile in the picture, but she'd smiled anyway, looking into the camera as if it were her conspirator, the light turning her pale skin pink at the edges. Like she really had thought we were going to Europe.

"She ran away right after that." I didn't know why I said it. To stop Mary looking at the photo that way, maybe. "I saw her leaving, you know."

Mary flipped the passport shut. "You didn't stop her?"

"She left all the time." I glanced over my shoulder and switched lanes. "She always thought she was quiet about it, but my bedroom window was right next to hers. I heard it every time she opened it."

"And you saw her that night?"

"Yeah." I pulled the visor down. "She just walked straight across the backyard and climbed the fence, and then she was gone. She barely took anything with her. I figured she'd be back in a few days."

"But she wasn't."

"No."

Mary rolled her window down and adjusted the side mirror so that she could put on lipstick. "Do you ever wish you had stopped her?"

I shook my head. "I was angry at her. For making everything so hard. She was failing school, lying about where she was. And she wouldn't have listened to me. We were really close when we were kids, but after our mom died, she was different."

Mary rolled the window back up and snapped the cap back on her lipstick. "Different how?"

"I don't know." I flipped on the radio. "Anything you need to know before we go inside?"

"How'd your mom die?"

Vintage radio, Tino Rossi. *Besame, besame mucho . . .*

"She drowned."

"Huh." Mary rubbed her lips together.

"I meant anything about Robin. So you won't slip up."

"I won't slip up." She gave me a facetious glance that did in fact look exactly like Robin, and I thought maybe she had forgiven me.

We were in the parking lot. I felt strangely buoyed by Mary as we got out of the car. I had been alone with my secret for a long time. Now I had somebody in this with me, even if she was a stranger. I reached for her hand impulsively as we approached the building, and she let me take it, the surprise showing on her face, which was so much like my sister's face. We looked mirrored in the mirrored doors, two of a kind, side by side.

36

Robin

After the funeral, Leslie was allowed to stay in the living room with the adults, while my four-year-old cousin Tad and I were shut in the rec room. In *Family Plot* there was singing. I didn't hear any singing.

Tad rolled underneath one of the plastic chairs and began lifting it with his feet, like a parent playing airplane with a baby.

I draped myself across the beanbag and decided to sing anyway. I didn't really know the hymns so I sang "Un-Break My Heart" instead.

In the middle of my song, my father's friend Albert walked in. He was wearing a brown suit. I looked at him from upside down on the beanbag chair and kept singing. Albert folded his arms and waited for me to finish.

"Very good," he said when I'd run out of lyrics.

"Oh, thank you," I said, still upside down.

"I didn't see you around, so I thought I'd come check on you," he told me. "How are you feeling?"

I bounced up to face him. "My heart is broken."

He sucked his lips in and out. "I see."

"Can you reach the tapes? Tad wanted to watch *Look Who's Talking Too,* but I didn't want to stand on the beanbag."

"Probably wise," Albert said, going to the cabinet and pulling out the VHS. I took it from him and loaded it into the player.

"Yes, yes, yes, yes!" Tad said as soon as he recognized the music. He sat down on the rug in front of the TV so quickly that it was more like an incredibly confident fall.

Albert regarded him. "It's nice to see somebody cheerful today."

"Right?" I said conspiratorially, going back over to sit on the beanbag chair by the sunny window.

Albert didn't like that for some reason. He knelt beside me and took my hand. For a minute it seemed like he would say something. The longer this went on, the more horrible I thought the thing had to be.

Over his shoulder, I saw that a car had slowed down in front of the neighbors' house. A man in a Hawaiian shirt got out carrying a white box, the kind that store cakes came in. As I watched, he sat down on the curb and took out a large turtle. The turtle was at least the size of my head.

"Your father will need help," Albert said at last under the noise of *Look Who's Talking Too.*

The turtle's legs windmilled as the man held it up by its shell, which I knew you were not supposed to do. He set the turtle down at the base of a kids' slide that someone had left out in the yard. The door to the neighbors' house opened and a woman stepped out. She called to the man and he got up to go talk to her, looking irritated.

"Are you listening to me?" Albert asked.

The turtle made its way painstakingly up the slide. The neighbors argued on the porch steps. I couldn't hear their conversation, but I could tell from the set of his back that he was yelling. The woman slammed the door in the middle of his yell and he stomped back over to the slide, where the turtle had nearly made it to the top. The man picked the turtle up by its shell again and placed it at the bottom of the slide.

"My father will need help," I repeated.

———

That night, back at our house, I climbed into Leslie's bed and kneaded her belly. "Leslie, I have to tell you something," I said.

She was stiff as a board. Even her hair was cold.

"I saw a man outside," I whispered. "He had this turtle. A huge turtle. He let it climb the slide in his—"

Leslie twisted a hand in my hair, sat up, and got out of bed. I went with her—I couldn't help it. Boy did I make a lot of noise, though.

She dragged me into the guest bedroom and loaded me in between the sheets. A really violent tucking-in. Then she said, her voice as good as a face in the dark, "I don't want to speak to you again."

"Because of our secret?" I whispered.

"What secret?"

She waited for an answer, or seemed to. Then my understanding changed. She was waiting for me to realize that she'd already given me the answer: What secret?

I lay there, straitjacketed in the bedclothes, as Leslie went out of the room and closed the door, shutting me in.

37

Leslie

We took an elevator to the fifth floor. In a fit of coincidence that made me unaccountably nervous, "Bésame Mucho" was playing in the elevator too. It was a jazz version.

The doors opened onto a hallway lined with confetti-print carpeting. Plain wooden doors marked each twenty-foot stretch. I led Mary down the hall until we reached the little plaque for GRUNDMAN, JAMES & RODRIGUEZ.

"Are you okay?" I asked.

She patted my cheek. I flinched.

"Let's go inside, sis," she said, sounding Texan again.

I pushed open the door. The firm was fairly small, just a tiny front room preceding a series of cubelike offices assembled with floor-to-ceiling room dividers. At the front desk, presiding over a truly astonishing number of framed family photographs, sat Mrs. Guzmán.

"Mrs. Flores!" she said. "Nice to see you again."

"Nice to see you too," I said, and was about to check in when Mary came up to the desk.

"I'm Robin, Leslie's sister," she said, holding out her hand. Mrs. Guzmán shook it, showing off clawlike red nails. "Are these your children?" Mary asked, pointing at the photographs with her other hand.

"They are," Mrs. Guzmán said, smiling.

"Oh my God, you all must be raising the average height of the state of New Mexico all by yourselves," Mary exclaimed. "I love it."

"That's my husband's influence," Mrs. Guzmán said. "If I stood up, you'd see."

Mary laughed. "Your grandkids are super cute."

"Well, thank you." Mrs. Guzmán pointed at one in particular that showed a little girl with her hair in box braids, folding her arms on a pedestal for the school photo. "This one's twelve now. But I like to keep the photos of them as babies. Makes me feel younger." She tapped the frame with a nail and turned back to us. "How can I help you ladies?"

"We have an appointment with Albert," Mary said before I could open my mouth.

"Perfect. I'll let Mr. Grundman know you're here. You can take a seat just over there." She picked up the receiver on the desk phone and pressed a button with the flat of her thumb.

"You remembered his name?" I asked Mary in an undertone as we sat down in the wooden chairs.

She made a face at me. "It's like you have no confidence in me, Leslie. I swear." Then she took out the burner phone I'd bought her and stared at it. "I miss Fruit Ninja."

I shifted position several times, listening to Mrs. Guzmán talk to someone on the phone about the weather. "Put that away."

"I was on level two hundred twenty-three," she said, stuffing phone in her bag.

"Leslie!" Albert walked out from behind one of the room dividers, his arms outspread, one holding a black wooden cane. I got up to hug him. "I see you brought Robin," he said over my shoulder.

"I did, finally," I said as he moved to hug her as well. Mary threw her arms around him with the abandon of a toddler, which annoyed me. It wasn't as if she actually knew him.

"Long time no see," he said, patting her on the back. "You are *beautiful*," he added as they pulled away. "Just lovely. Leslie never said."

I pulled my lips into a smile. "She's hard to warn people about."

Mary's eyebrows pinched together for a second. "Wow, thank you, Albert. It's so nice to see you again."

"Come on back." Albert began his slow hustle to his office. He'd told me last time we visited that the doctor wanted him to use a walker, but he didn't want any clients to see him looking like an old man, so he stuck to the cane at work. It shortened his steps to a few inches at a time so that he didn't fall over. "Inner ear problems," he'd said, tapping his head. "Vertigo and bad knees at the same time. A NASA scientist said, 'We can lick gravity, but the paperwork is overwhelming.' That's me, I'm at the doctor every other week these days."

He held the door open for us despite his cane. Mary went in first, and I heard her little noise of surprise.

Plants covered Albert's office on every available surface. One bookshelf held, on top of all the casebooks, a series of bonsai trees, like a well-ordered miniature forest. From the ceiling near the window hung three shallow silver basins bursting with snowball plants, like beaded hair. The desk, a mess of paper in the middle, was bordered with tiny pots labeled BASIL, PARSLEY, THYME, and so on.

Albert shuffled in behind us and shut the door. A corner of his mouth lifted. "You like my little garden?"

"It's amazing," Mary breathed. "How did you do all this?"

"Well, I get a nice bit of sun through the window, and I keep it open when it's not too chilly," Albert said. "Those are real herbs, you know. You want to taste?"

"Oh, no," she said.

"Oh, come on." He plucked a leaf from one plant and held it out in thick-knuckled fingers. "It's mint. Just like toothpaste."

"It's hairy," she said, wrinkling her nose as she took it from him and chewed. I laughed and she shook her head at me.

"I can't believe he got you to eat his plants in less than ten seconds," I said.

She spat the leaf into her hand. "Are you not supposed to eat it? It really did taste like mint!"

"No, no, you can eat it," Albert insisted. "You can swallow it. It won't hurt you."

"He tries to make everyone eat his plants," I said. "Most people don't do it."

She dropped the chewed leaf into the trash can. "I guess I'm politer than you, Leslie."

"No, Leslie ate it too," Albert said. "Don't you remember? I used to bring her mint leaves when I came over. You were probably too young."

"Probably," Mary muttered, looking discomfited for the first time since we'd arrived.

"How's your son, Leslie?" Albert asked. "Doing okay?"

"He's fine," I said. "How are your daughters?"

"I think I've finally persuaded Ruth to move," he said. "She'll have to retake the bar, but her husband's found a position in Santa Fe that will give them a little boost."

"That's great." I smiled and scooted my chair forward slightly.

"I have to tell you, I'm glad to see you after all this time, Robin," Albert said, leaning forward to cover her hand with his. "I know this business with the will is a pain in the behind, but Warren just wanted to get both of you girls in a room together again. It killed him when you moved so far away. Where'd you go anyway? Leslie said she was looking for you in Louisiana."

Mary stroked his hand with her thumb. "I was there for a while, but I moved to Nevada a little while back."

"Nevada," he said, shifting away. "Las Vegas?"

"Restaurant work," she said, affecting a sheepish shrug.

"I worked in restaurants many years myself," Albert said, smiling at her. "When I was working my way through law school, I washed dishes and helped around the kitchen at a place that's since been closed. El Cerdito Rojo. The Little Red Pig. The busboys used to watch for pretty girls, and when one came in they'd yell "Corazón!" into the back of house. We'd make sopapillas in the shape of hearts and send them out, complimentary."

"Did that work?"

"It never worked." He chuckled. "But it gave us hope."

I crossed and uncrossed my fingers beneath the chair, a nervous habit. "So today's the day, huh?" I said, trying not to speak too fast. "Signing checks?"

"Yes. Well, not *today* today." He thumbed through the papers at his desk, humming to himself.

Mary and I both froze.

I shifted into a more natural pose, consciously relaxing my shoulders. "What do you mean? Is there some other step? Because"—I nearly said "Mary," and saved it with a cough—"my sister has to go home soon."

Albert glanced up. "Oh, I thought I'd explained this. Before I can give you a check, we need to file a release and refunding bond with the county and pay the fee."

Mary's fingers twitched on the arm of her chair. "What's a release and refunding bond?"

He pulled out a manila folder from underneath a pot labeled CILANTRO and slid it toward us. "You can see there, it's all in the language, but essentially it releases me of my duties as executor, and refunds any unpaid debts if there are no other assets to pay them. You don't have to worry about that, since your father had us take the cost of probate out of his remaining savings, whereas your inheritance was held in a separate account. For your purposes, it states the amount you are both to receive—in this case, fifty thousand dollars each—and it requires you to sign in front of an attorney, saying you accept."

I stared at the paper. "How long does it take to file?"

"Well, I can have Angela file it as soon as you leave. But they won't acknowledge receipt until tomorrow morning at the earliest. My next available appointment is"—he squinted at his calendar—"Monday. You girls could come back in then and we'll have the checks ready for you."

My stomach dropped. "I thought—I mean, is there any way we could do it faster than that?"

"What's the rush?" Albert turned back to me and frowned. "You had plans for the slots this weekend?"

Mary interceded. "I have a flight on Friday, that's all. I thought this would be a one-appointment kind of thing."

Albert sat back, his stomach rising and falling above his battered silver-buckled belt. "Well, I think that goes against the spirit of Warren's will, if you want to know my opinion. He wanted you two to spend a bit of time together."

Mary touched my shoulder and assumed an expression of beatific concern on dramatic par with the Pietà. "We have been. Leslie drove me back, let me stay with her and her family. If you'd told me a year ago that that would happen, I'd never have believed it. But she's been amazing." She glanced down. "I've been here since Monday, though, and a whole week—" She gave a little laugh. "Well, I'll be surprised if I'm not fired by the time I'm back. Jessica's been covering my shifts, but . . . And without this I can't—I can't afford the plane ticket."

"You don't have to tell him that," I said quietly, picking up her thread. Her eyes flicked to me, startled, but then her face resettled.

"It's fine," she said. "I don't care if people know I'm poor. There's nothing wrong with that."

Albert regarded us. The room had heated as soon as he closed the door, and it was as humid as a greenhouse in his office. I was sweating at my hairline and the places where my back met the chair.

"What if we met for dinner," I said, unable to stand the silence. Mary's fingers whitened on her chair, and I saw a tilt of displeasure in her profile, but I couldn't stop talking. "Since you don't have any appointments available until Monday. It would be a little more time for Robin and me to spend together, and you could tell us about Dad when he was younger and hand us the checks at dinner. We'll go somewhere nice. My treat. How about Blue Roof?"

"Well," Albert said, then paused. I glanced at Mary and saw that she was giving me a wide-eyed look. "I think that would be very nice," he said at last. "Very nice. I haven't been to the Blue Roof in many years. They used to have a pretty good salmon dish there. I wonder if they still do that."

"They do," I said, the words coming out in a relieved rush. "They do! Dave and I were just there a couple of months ago. He thought about getting it."

"Well, then, we'll go ahead and get dinner," Albert said.

"Tomorrow night would be wonderful," Mary said smoothly. "Then I'd have a little time to pack before my flight, if you don't mind."

"Well, it is rushing things, but if the county notifies us of receipt, I could have Angela make the checks before the bank closes in the afternoon," he said. "That's an if, obviously."

"We understand," I said. "Give me a call. I'll make the reservation, just in case."

"I hope you can get a reservation," he said. "That place used to be pretty stuffed."

"I don't think it should be too hard for a Thursday. Not like a Friday or a—"

Mary plucked a mint leaf from the plant and handed it to me. "Want some gum?" she said.

I took it from her and, resigned, put it in my mouth and stopped talking.

"Who knew I'd have fancy plans this week?" Albert said. "Ain't I a lucky bastard. The James & Rodriguez will be gnashing their teeth in jealousy. Well, go ahead, since we're in a rush; sign the form and I'll get out of your hair."

"We really appreciate it," Mary said, taking the pen.

"Yes, we—" I began, and Mary tapped me on the underside of the chin.

"Don't talk and chew at the same time, sis," she said. "You'll spray me."

She was about to sign when I thought suddenly, I've never spelled out our last name for her, and I seized the pen from her in a panic.

"Ow!" she said, glaring at me. "What's your problem?"

I made a heroic effort and swallowed the hairy, half-chewed leaf in my mouth. "I think I'm supposed to sign first, because I'm older. Right?"

Albert scratched his head, a tic that caused his shoulders to hunch as if he were embarrassed for me. "Honey, it doesn't matter. Just sign on any of the beneficiary lines."

I nodded seriously and wrote in schoolmarm cursive *Leslie Voigt Flores*. When I handed the pen back to her I tapped once on *Voigt*, hoping she'd understand.

Mary scowled at me and scribbled underneath my name. It was almost illegible; no one would have been able to identify a misspelling in the first place. The only clear letters were the *R* and the *V*, inscribed in huge narcissistic loops.

Albert glanced briefly at the paper and put it back inside the manila envelope. "Perfect," he said. "I'll take this out to Angela."

"Oh, we can do that on our way out if you like," I put in. "Since we're going past her desk. It wouldn't be a bother."

Mary gave me a slack-faced look of exhaustion.

"No, no," Albert said, his sparse eyebrows drawing together. "I can do it, Leslie. Do you need me to show you out?"

"No," Mary said, cutting me off. "Don't worry about getting up. Thank you so much for seeing us, Albert. I'm thrilled we'll have more time to visit together before I go. You're so sweet for making time."

Albert sat up a little straighter in his leather chair. "You're just as I remember, Robin. Your father would be proud of you."

They shared a warm moment. My face heated; I was drowning in this greenhouse air. I had to get out.

"I'll go call the restaurant right now," I said, standing up too quickly, making the chair wobble on its legs. "Nice to see you again."

"You too, Leslie," Albert said absently, turning back to his papers. Mary patted his hand. I jerked the door open and walked dizzily into the hallway, sucking in a lungful of dry air.

Mary passed me, moving with the lazy satisfaction of a big cat, and said, "Bye, Mrs. Guzmán!"

"Goodbye, sugar," Mrs. Guzmán said as I passed her.

I followed Robin in silence to the elevator. It wasn't until I got in that I realized my mistake and corrected myself mentally: Mary, not Robin.

She straightened her polo dress and ran a hand through her blond hair. It was still rootless, natural-looking. "What's wrong with you?" she said pleasantly.

I looked away. "What do you mean?"

"You acted like a crazy person in there. You were pushing too hard."

My throat burned. I swallowed. "I panicked," I said, fighting to sound normal. "I thought we were going to get the checks today."

"What's a few more days?" Mary said, pulling out a tube of lip balm. "You said it was for your house, right? Are they gonna foreclose this weekend, or what?"

The elevator slid open and I hurried out toward the lobby doors. The light of the late afternoon was nearly blinding through the glass. I blinked hard.

"Leslie?" Mary called from behind me.

I pushed through the doors.

38

Mary

My phone had buzzed in my purse during the meeting with Albert. Now Nancy's text floated up to meet me as I glanced at the screen. *Can you meet me at the Frontier in an hour and a half?*

Yes I'll be there, I texted back as we turned into the Floreses' driveway. "I'm going for a walk," I said to Leslie.

She gave me a startled look. "Well, I have to go pick up Eli," she said, pulling the parking brake and glancing at the car seat in the garage. "There won't be anyone to let you in."

"I'll just wait for you, then." I smiled sweetly at her.

Her phone started ringing; she wasn't looking at me. "Fine." She got out and headed for the car seat. "Just be back for dinner."

I didn't have any intention of waiting around for her to get home, but she took the call before I could tell her that I wouldn't be back in time for dinner. She could wait around for me tonight. I had things to do. As I made my way across the lawn, I heard her say quietly into the phone, "Yeah, of course. Everything went well."

I did walk for a while, bored and killing time. No one passed me, and I considered taking the too-white sidewalk all the way to the

edge of the neighborhood, where a sandstone wall kept the less en-
terprising bobcats and coyotes out. If I wanted to, I could scale the
wall, or follow the main road out and around to the mountains. I
could walk from spring desert to snow, still in my shirtdress.

Instead I went back to my car. The air was still smarting from the
heat of the day, and a scent of ozone rolled in from the west, where
the clouds occasionally flickered like a flashbulb going off. It would
rain soon.

The Frontier was a restaurant across from UNM, open almost
twenty-four/seven except for a few hours in the early morning, just
long enough to clean everything and start again before dawn. Parking consisted of a vaguely L-shaped strip of pavement behind the
restaurant, crowded with the protruding backs of pickup trucks and
SUVs, that created a meandering path just large enough for one car
to pass, going forward or shamefacedly backward when they
reached the end without finding a space. Inside, it seemed to go on
forever, one roomful of red vinyl booths giving way to another
hung with patterned rugs, until you reached the main room, dominated at the far end by a long low counter whose upper wall disappeared under a row of at least ten signs containing the restaurant's
hundreds of menu items.

I got a carne adovada burrito and waited in one of the slatted
wooden booths under a chandelier made out of a wagon wheel. It
was crowded in the main room, the noise of the busboys and the
diners occasionally interrupted by the order-up bell, like the triangle in a kindergarten orchestra. I amused myself by smiling at a boy
waiting to order. He looked like a student at UNM, with curly black
hair and thick glasses, and he was horrified at being caught staring.
He pulled his hoodie up, then looked back at me a dozen times in
several minutes. I met his eyes serenely each time. When he got to
the front, I heard him stammer, having forgotten his order. Three
people passed him in line as he studied the menu boards, cheeks
burning.

Nancy walked in just then. Her hair was wet from a shower,
pushed back from her forehead, and she was wearing gray sweats
and a sleeveless jersey slung over a sports bra. Her arms were thick

with muscle, unevenly tanned from her short-sleeved uniform, and her body was tense. She scanned the room for me, and I waved.

"Robin," she said, throwing herself into the booth across from me. "Hi."

"Hi, baby," I said, echoing her from earlier. "You look tired. Are you okay?"

She waved a hand in front of her face. "I'm fine. Just . . ."

I tilted my head.

Nancy checked her watch, abandoning her train of thought. "Sorry for asking you to meet me again right away, but I looked up the address you gave me."

I didn't want to appear too eager. "Do you want any food? I could get you a plate of something." I pushed the remains of my burrito to the edge of the table.

A bit of warmth crept over her face. "I'm not hungry."

I waited, but I couldn't hold out long. "What did you find?"

Nancy sighed. "Look, I don't want to scare you. It could be nothing."

My pulse jumped. "What is it?"

She glanced at my hands, inches away from her own on the table, and her fingers twitched. "The place—it's a gym now . . . It used to belong to a guy named Francis Clery. Frank Clery. It was a pawnshop for a while, but I guess they sold it after he went to jail."

"He went to jail? For what?"

"Pretty recently. Aggravated assault against a household member, one of the DV laws. He hit his wife across the face with a gun, cracked her eye socket. She's fine, but he's doing eight months. That's a third-degree felony." She blew out a breath. "Assuming she doesn't lose her nerve. It's hard to make DV cases stick."

I frowned. "I don't . . ." I caught her eye and added quickly, "I mean, that's awful. But what does it have to do with Leslie?"

Nancy laced her fingers together, gripping until the knuckles turned white. "We . . . keep track of this guy. Not officially. There's been no cause to arrest him, and I think everyone thought he'd go down for tax evasion, but you live for moments of stupidity like this. She ran to the neighbors' house and called us. We'd gotten complaints before about disturbances, but she'd always sworn he never hit her. This time, we took care of it before he could get to her. Had an officer on the corner already, got him booked for the assault practically as soon as she hung up." She shook her head.

"You guys keep someone on the corner at all times because he beats his wife?" I said, thinking it through. "Or . . . you keep a guy on the corner because . . ."

Nancy's dark eyes met mine. "Because people hire him to kill other people sometimes."

I didn't say anything for a long time. "How do you know?" I said at last.

"We don't." She shrugged. "If we knew for sure, he'd be in jail for that instead of for assault. But there are guys you hear things about, even if you never have enough to arrest them. Look, maybe Leslie just went to the pawnshop."

"But you don't think so, do you." I watched as Nancy cast her eyes down. "Why not?"

Nancy spoke to the table. "If it was just the address, sure. But you gave me his phone number. That's not the store's phone. That's a personal cell. Maybe he bought it just to talk with customers. But why give them another avenue to bother him at all hours of the day and night?"

"Some businesses do that," I said absently. "If he's posting online and wants people to be able to text in offers."

"That's true," Nancy replied. She pressed her lips together, then said measuredly, "He doesn't post online."

"You guys track that too?"

"Like I said, we figured he'd go down for taxes. His business doesn't make enough for him to drive a '67 Camaro. He had it restored and repainted within the last year."

I raised my eyebrows. "What's that, twenty grand?"

"More. No pawnshop in Corrales is moving enough to throw that much money away on a single car. He takes in people's grandma's jewelry, guns, art pieces from Santa Fe where the frame is worth more than the canvas. There's no way."

"Maybe he's a drug dealer."

She tapped her fingers on the table. "The thing is, if you're pulling down enough to move out of your mom's basement and start restoring classic cars, I'm probably going to hear about it. It's a hazard of the trade when your customers regularly get pulled over with your merchandise in their car."

"But, I mean, how can it be profitable? There aren't that many murders per year, right? It's Albuquerque, it's not, you know, Los Cabos."

Nancy shook her head. "We get lectured on it every fucking month at the station. Violent crime here is more than twice what it is on average in the rest of the country. Most of it's opioids. People assaulting one another because of drug money. I'm not surprised you don't think it's dangerous here, though. It's not really dangerous for you."

I looked up. "Because I'm white?"

Nancy lifted her shoulder. "And you don't do drugs. Your biggest risk is what happened to Jennifer Clery."

I pressed the name into my mind. "His wife."

"Yeah." She slid her hand across the table to cover mine, then withdrew it just as quickly. She'd remembered we were in public.

"Then Leslie has to be even safer. You should see their house. They have a lawn in the backyard, a real lawn, with real grass. And she doesn't do drugs. Dave—her husband—he smokes a joint from time to time, and he hides it from her—that's how much of a teetotaler she is."

"What else do you know about Dave? Is he an angry person?"

I let my hands fall into my lap and glanced down. "Dave would never. He loves her." But my mind was going a mile a minute. Had Leslie found out about the money to Elaine Campbell? Had she confronted him and—?

The lines around Nancy's mouth deepened. "If you listen to those guys when they get arrested, that's why they do it. Because they love their wives."

"No way," I said. "He's got this big family, older sisters, loves his mom. They have a baby—he loves the baby."

"How about Leslie?" Nancy asked. "I don't mean to be—you know. But while you were gone, did she have a big support system like that? Or did he isolate her?"

I fell silent.

"If he controls the finances, it can be very difficult to leave. Some women say they feel like there's no way out."

We gazed at each other for a few moments.

"I have to know," I breathed at last. "Because when I think about it, I want to say Leslie doesn't have it in her. But I can't say that. Because I know she does."

"If it makes you feel better . . ." Nancy trailed off, then swallowed and started again. "Most people do. When they feel trapped, most people do have it in them."

She was so beautiful, even under the fluorescent lights. Her body was marked by strong, clean lines connecting one element to the next. It made her appear more sharply present than everyone else in the room, the way the cowboys looked in old Westerns. I couldn't imagine her killing anybody, although I knew she'd been in the army.

"Can I talk to him? Frank Clery?" I asked.

Nancy leaned back. "I can't bring you in. And anyway, he wouldn't tell you if it's true. He's smart enough to keep his mouth shut most of the time."

"I have to try." I put a catch in my voice. "I have to know."

"Why don't you ask Leslie?" Nancy said. "If it's true, she needs you right now."

It was a good question. It took me several seconds to come up with an answer. "You don't know how messed up our relationship was until last week. She hated me. She's allowing me back into her life on a very, very temporary basis." True. "If I start accusing her of—of crazy shit like this, she'll throw me out immediately. And if she does that . . ." I took a deep breath. "I don't think she'll ever let me back in. She could die, Nancy. If Dave is really doing . . . what you think he's doing—if she's that far gone . . . I could be her last chance at getting help."

Nancy ran her hand through her hair. "Clery is not a nice guy, Robin. I don't know what you think you're going to say to him to make him talk to you."

I was getting somewhere. "I'm an actress. I'm great at getting people on my side. I can see into his psychology."

She smiled reluctantly. "An actress, huh?" Like she thought I was being cute.

"I know it probably won't work," I said, pressing my advantage. "But it would mean a lot to me if you'd let me try. This could be my last chance too, at—at having a family." At staying in New Mexico. At staying with Nancy.

I let my eyes fall to Nancy's mouth, her hands.

She bit her lip. "I could let you in for five minutes tomorrow. Visiting hours at the jail start at twelve-thirty."

The man in the paper hat at the register yelled out, "Next up, next up!"

"Nancy," I said, leaning forward in the booth, tilting my chin up. "Thank you."

A flush saturated her face. "It's only five minutes," she said. "You know where the station is?"

"Yeah." I got up from the booth, stretching my sore limbs. "We should go."

Nancy dropped her eyes. "You're right."

As we passed the rows of booths and hanging plants, I saw the student from before. I winked at him behind Nancy's back, high on my victory. He stared after me, his expression panicked, as if I'd threatened him.

In the dark outside, among the newly sparse cars, Nancy stuck her hands in her pockets. It was raining now, a soft patter turning the dust on the asphalt to rivulets of mud. I couldn't see her features clearly, but I could feel her eyes on me. "You seem different," she said. "Than you were in high school, I mean."

"I grew a couple inches," I said. "Can't you tell?"

She didn't laugh. "I just meant you seem . . . I don't know."

I swayed toward her, letting her wrap her arm around my waist and pull me the rest of the way in. When our lips separated, I said, "I have to go soon. Leslie will wonder where I am."

Nancy's gaze stuttered. Someone was expecting her too. I waited for her to pull away, but instead she kissed me again, harder, pushing me against the wet car. I wondered if she ever thought about leaving her, if she had thought about what could have been, all these years. If there was some way I could stay in New Mexico. If there was some way she could come to Los Angeles. As long as I was Robin, someone would be in love with me.

My skin against the metal started to feel too hot. Like I was getting sick. A fever, maybe. I put my damp hands over my face and Nancy moved to pull them away.

"Robin?" she said.

I didn't know what my face was showing her. "I have to go," I said again. "I'll see you tomorrow. At the jail. Okay?"

39

Leslie

On the way to pick up Eli I found myself thinking inexplicably of my wedding. Dave and I had gotten married at the Loretto Chapel in Santa Fe in midwinter. It had snowed that year, enough to make driving difficult, and his cousin Dani had almost spun out on the highway. But inside the chapel it was cloyingly hot from the candles and the body heat of so many people packed into the wooden pews. My face was red, and I felt my dress sticking to me as I went down the aisle.

I wasn't afraid at all. Why wasn't I afraid?

We'd known each other just over a year at that point. Now, after having been married for nearly five years, I could see that we had been strangers—but it didn't feel that way at the time.

We had hidden ourselves away from each other for twenty-four hours before the wedding, the longest we'd spent apart since meeting, and when I saw him in the stuffy little chapel my only feeling was relief. I strained toward his observation like a houseplant toward a window. Without him I was tethered to my father, who now addressed me just as he addressed the home aides, with a kind of detached finality; and to my mother and sister, whose memories I dragged with me in our neighbors' eyes. Dave's family wasn't like that; his parents treated him and his sisters like local celebrities, cheering them on and heckling them in equal measure. To him, my tethers were invisible. I was Leslie Voigt, local celebrity; he sought out my opinion as if it were an autograph.

That night we'd gone upstairs to our room at the inn at two in the morning. We were drunk and it was freezing in the room. I remember struggling to get out of my dress as Dave frowned at the thermostat. "I'm turning it, but the needle's not moving," he said.

"Just get in bed," I said, rubbing my face against the pillow like a cat.

"I'm not going to be bested by a—by a temperature thing," he said, groping for the word. "Is that the kind of husband you want? A husband who can be humiliated by a . . ." He paused while I laughed. "A heat device," he tried. "A dialed instrument—"

I got out of bed, dragging the comforter along with me as a cape, and pressed the power button, then turned the dial. The needle moved. "You idiot," I said, and licked his cheek.

"I see," Dave said. "You'd rather humiliate him on your own."

"Yes." I wrapped the blanket around both of us, like a cocoon, and we shuffled four-footedly back to the bed, where we collapsed.

He slipped the comforter over our heads. "I love you," he said, his breath making the air inside the blanket taste like beer. "Are you my wife now?"

I nodded solemnly. He kissed my mouth, then leaned back and examined my face as if to check his work. Then he kissed my cheek, just as gently. Next both my eyelids, my eyebrows, my chin, my ear, directly into my eardrum.

"Loud!" I exclaimed, pushing him away.

He ignored me and kissed my neck, my shoulder, my elbow.

I began laughing, and so did he. We were half-asleep by the time we were finished having sex. I remember him twitching inside me as he softened, his body heavier than usual on top of mine. I let him crush me, feeling that otherwise I might float up to the ceiling. I had the spins and I couldn't quite focus my eyes. "Baby," Dave said into my neck, and I thought: I don't deserve this. This should have belonged to some other woman, and I've taken it from her.

I didn't want to give it back, though. He pressed me down into the mattress and I thought: Mine, mine now, mine forever.

The next morning I went over to see Daddy as usual—we didn't have a honeymoon because I felt sure my father could die any second. He was always telling me how much he needed me, how he was afraid to be alone very long with the home aides. *They don't respect me,* he said once. *They steal things.* And things did go missing in the house every now and then, so I believed him.

The aide—Stephanie—told me that my sister had called for me. She played me the message on the machine. It was the last time I heard my sister speak. The message started with several long seconds of static, and then Robin said, "Oh . . . getting married!" She laughed. "Hi . . . getting married! Leslie said to tell you—I mean, I said to tell Leslie. Why? You need to consider that, honey. What happens at the end of it? Are you gonna wear a big . . . a big dress? I looked up this person you're getting married to. David Flores. I don't know which picture is his but I'm sure he's a real kind of . . . a real type of guy. I almost went tonight, did you know that? I have a friend who was going that way and she could have driven me, but I thought . . . no . . . Leslie wants to feel pretty. Don't you? And you don't want to have to tell me what to do. You hate that. So I'm not there." She paused and there was a crackling noise. "I love you," she sang into the phone. "I love you, Leslie—" The message cut off.

The way she said it dug itself into my brain afterward. I couldn't get it out. It was like a horrible, creepy jingle. *I love you. I love you, Leslie.*

The last thing Daddy said to me was that he was going to take a nap and not to leave the house.

I didn't remember the last thing my mother said to me. I didn't remember anything about her death. It was as if I had gouged it out. Why had I done that?

She drowned, I'd told Mary.

I twisted the volume dial. The radio was still on. "Esta tarde vi llover" filled the car, a big melodramatic Hollywood crescendo. It drove out the jingle—that's how big it was.

———

Dave's parents lived in the North Valley, one of the neighborhoods clustered underneath the curving arm of the Rio Grande. Their house was a single-story ranch-style with a basketball hoop at the foot of the driveway that had belonged to Dave and his sisters as children and now was collectively owned by the MacGregor and Da Silva kids from down the street. When I pulled into their particular cul-de-sac, Dave's mom, Teri, and his sister Cadence were squatting in the wide flat driveway with Eli and Cadence's twin daughters, Riley and Jessa. Teri was painting an overalls-clad Riley's face with glitter paint while Jessa looked on, and Cadence had Eli in her lap, rubbing him down with white-cast sunscreen.

My windows were down. I heard Teri say, "Look, it's Aunt Leslie." Riley kept her eyes closed. Jessa turned to squint at me as I parked next to the mailbox.

"Hi," I called, popping the door open. "I'm a little late, sorry."

"Oh, don't worry," Teri said, dabbing purple dots across Riley's nose. "We're doing slow cooker, there's no rush. Are you hungry? Do you want to just stay?"

"Oh, you don't have to do that," I said. "I've made you do too much work already today."

"Eli's not work," Cadence said from the steps. "He's a quiet boy, huh?"

Eli just looked at her, cow-eyed.

"Anyway, we're making carnitas . . ." Teri singsonged.

"Carnitaaaas . . ." Jessa echoed. "Riley, don't move!"

Riley had opened her mouth to join in just as Teri drew the body of the butterfly down her mouth.

"Oh, Riley, you look like the Joker," Jessa lamented.

"No-o." Riley giggled and tried to wipe at her face.

"Not your shirt—" Teri warned, then gave up. "Okay, you can wear one of mine for dinner and we'll put yours in the wash."

"We should probably head out pretty soon," I interjected from the end of the driveway. "It's getting late."

"Yeah, Mom," Cadence said. "Leslie has to head out."

Teri made a face. "Well, I promised Eli I'd paint him as a tiger."

"He doesn't remember," I said.

"Sure he does." Teri made grabby hands at Eli, who lunged out of Cadence's arms and toddled toward her. "See? You just sit over there with Cadence and we'll make you a tiger to take home."

Riley leapt up from the concrete and dashed toward the front door. "I want to see what I look like!"

"You're not gonna like it," Jessa opined, following her.

"Don't get paint on anything!" Cadence called after them. "If you want to take it off, use paper towels, not the real towels." She brushed grit off her palms. "I should go in with them."

"No, stay with us," Teri said. "We never have Leslie here."

"That's true," Cadence said, eyeing me. "Why don't you come over more often, Leslie?"

I was trying to sit down on the concrete while keeping my knees together and avoiding scraping my heels; I fumbled.

"She's busy," Teri said, dipping her paintbrush into the Eeyore cup next to her. "She's still getting back into her job after taking the time for this tiger. Don't bug her."

Cadence looked away. "What noise does a tiger make, Eli?" she asked.

Eli craned his neck toward Cadence when he heard his name.

"Hold still, honey," Teri told him, grabbing his chin.

"Eli," Cadence persisted. "What sound does a tiger make? Is it *quack*? Quack, quack?"

Eli laughed.

"I don't think he knows his sounds, Mom," Cadence murmured. "Does he do it at home, Leslie?" She still wasn't looking at me.

"I think Dave does the sounds with him," I said.

"Okay, go like this," Teri told Eli. She pushed her lips out. Eli laughed and laughed. "No, you do it too," she said. "Do just like me." After a minute she got him to push his lips out and she colored them both black. "Now I'm going to put fangs on you," she said. "Ready?"

Eli cheered.

"We used to have a tiger mask at home," Cadence said. "David was terrified of it. Maria was absolutely merciless. She would put it on and wake him up with it. One time he wet the bed."

"In front of you?" I said.

She nodded. "I think it's still a fond memory for Maria."

"Well, she had to wash all the sheets herself," Teri said placidly, "so I'm glad she treasures that moment."

"Okay, it's hella quiet in there," Cadence remarked. "I'm gonna go break up whatever's going on. Mom, should I wake up Dad?"

"He's not sleeping," Teri said. "He's just resting in the living room. You can tell him we're going to start making plates as soon as Sonya gets here."

"I think he needs a David visit," Cadence said.

Teri frowned at her. "He's getting one this weekend. Go inside."

Cadence went into the house, wiping her gray-soled feet on the mat. Teri turned back to Eli, who'd gotten bored and was trying to lick the paint off his lips.

"Don't eat that," I said, prying his fingers away from his mouth.

"No, no, it's fine," Teri told me. "It's a set just for little kids. I mean, don't let him eat the whole thing, but it won't poison him."

"Oh." I sat back. She dipped her paintbrush in the orange and painted careful stripes across Eli's forehead and cheeks. "He's really looking like a tiger," I said after a minute. "You're good at that."

She smiled, wrinkles lifting her cheeks. "I used to paint sets for the Little Theatre," she said. "For a while in the seventies."

There was a sudden shriek from inside the house, then the thundering of two pairs of feet down the hallway as the twins chased each other.

"Do you think Eli should have siblings?" I said, as Teri switched to white.

Teri shifted Eli in her lap. "Is that something you're thinking about?"

"I know Dave wants it," I said. "A lot of kids. He's always wanted that."

"That's true." Teri smiled at me. "Well, I'm ready for another one too. Sonya and Cadence are done after twins, and you never know with Maria, she could get bored in another couple years, but I think she's done too. I had kids mostly so I could be a grandma, you know. I felt it call to my soul. I love hard candy and fanny packs."

"And glitter face paint."

"And glitter face paint," she agreed, turning Eli around. "Want to go look in the mirror?"

He patted his own face and made a questioning noise.

"Mhmm, the mirror." She stood up, holding Eli a little apart from her body so he couldn't smear paint on her. "Leslie, will you grab the palette and the cup and stick those in the sink?"

I followed her in, holding the paint set, as she stopped in the guest bathroom to show Eli his own face. He gave a yell of pure terror as soon as he saw his reflection. Cadence appeared from the kitchen and hurried over to them with her phone.

"Leslie, you're welcome, I'm capturing this on video," she said. "It's genetic. Oh my God, I'm sending this to Maria and David right now." She cackled, and I heard Eli screaming on the playback as she hit SEND.

"Are you sure you're not staying for dinner?" Teri asked over Eli's sobs.

"No, I should take him—" I snatched Eli out of her hands. "Thank you for handling him all day."

"I love you, my darling," Teri told him, kissing him on the head. "I'm sorry I am so good an artist that I scared you right out your pants."

Eli whimpered, while Cadence laughed.

"He's a good baby, Leslie," Teri told me. "You should think about making more of him."

I didn't go home. I went the opposite way, crossing the river toward Taylor Ranch. I followed the streets, thinking how much this neighborhood looked like the one I grew up in. I could imagine high school romance here, small weddings, babies in the kiddie pool out back.

The house I was looking for was on Flor Del Rey. It was absolutely ordinary, a single-story adobe with a big picture window in the front, a couple of evergreens shading the right side of the house. In the short tiled driveway, I could see Dave's car. There was an old OBAMA BIDEN 2012 sticker on the bumper, and the Steve Nash bobblehead Cadence had given him wobbled in the rear windshield.

I didn't know why I still checked. I knew he would be here. I'd known for a long time. Before, I used to call him. I wanted to hear him lie to me. Now I just drove by. It was enough to see his car in her driveway.

In a way it was almost a relief, knowing what I was about to do.

Eli was asleep in the back with the ring of keys in his mouth. His breathing grew labored, and I reached around to pull the keys out. "You ready to go home?" I whispered.

40

Robin

I make her sound so cruel, but Leslie wasn't only cruel. I really loved her, you know; that's the thing people get wrong about love. They think the closer you are to someone, the more they narrow; that love shears you down to the slimmest core, as if people contained seeds you could fish out and keep, saying, *That's the real you; all the rest is just flesh.*

But it's the other way around. The more you know someone, the more someones you know. They kaleidoscope outward before your eyes. If you feel you're finally getting a handle on someone's true self, you haven't got a clue. Once you've met forty versions of them, then you can comfort yourself you're getting closer.

I've seen a hundred Leslies, at least.

Here's another Leslie:

Winter, late nineties. Eleven years old, with long sloppy bangs like Meg Ryan. She comes scrambling over the wall behind the abandoned gas station. "Tommy said you were back here," she pants. "What are you—"

Her eyes flick between me and Placky, who's lying on the ground. "Did he bite you?" she asks at last.

I shake my head.

"But he tried to bite you."

I nod.

"Okay," she tells me. "Okay. You didn't mean to do it. Did Tommy see you? Is that why he was freaking out?"

"Yes," I say. I hadn't known he was there until he started yelping, and then he was running too fast for me to catch him.

"That's not good," Leslie says, almost to herself. "Did anybody else see?"

"No."

"At least there's that." She stares at Placky. "I'm going to get a garbage bag."

She disappears back over the wall. I sit down on the ground, dragging the pipe through the patches of dirt and snow to write my initials. It's heavy and my arms ache.

Only one of Placky's eyes is still intact. A blood vessel burst in it, so there's a pink blob settled in the bottom of his eye, nearly obscuring the iris.

Finally Leslie returns from the other side of the gas station, pushing her bike and carrying a black plastic garbage bag. She turns the bag inside-out and puts it over her hand, just the way you do when you're cleaning up shit, except she's cleaning up the dog itself. It takes her a minute of struggling to get all of Placky inside the garbage bag, but then she's pulling the ties tight and loading him into the metal basket on her handlebars.

"Give me the pipe," she says.

I hand it over. She uses it to scrape through the bloody dirt and snow on the ground, until it's just a messy pile of weeds and mud.

"Where are you taking him?" I ask.

"West. Candelaria goes almost to the river." She stands up and peers at her handiwork, clapping her mittens together. "It'll look like a coyote got him."

"Why can't we just put it in the trash?"

"Because someone might recognize him and tell the Schwartzes." Leslie squints at me. "It's a crime."

"It is?"

"You didn't know. But you can't do it again."

"I know." I knew even when I was doing it.

"Okay." She sighs. "You're lucky it was just Tommy. But he's going to tell people. You're going to say that he's lying."

"I will."

"Good." She carries the pipe over to the broken back window of the gas station and drops it in. I hear the clatter as it hits the tile. "I have to leave now if I'm going to get back before dark. It's your turn to make dinner."

"Thank you," I mumble.

She wipes her nose. "Wash your hands. Before you make dinner."

I nod.

Leslie gets on her bike, wobbling a little from the weight of the bag, and turns onto the sidewalk. I watch her puffy silhouette disappear past the rows of storefronts with electric luminarias lining their roofs.

Like the person, the event is never static. You could say this one is about love, about Leslie rescuing me, and that would be true.

You could say she shouldn't have rescued me at all. That it's about the blood in the snow. And that would be true too.

41

Leslie

I stood over the sink. The dishes were soaking. I put my hands in, turning the skin pink, and then I went to the refrigerator and poured out the last of the wine with wet fingers. When I came back into the living room, Eli looked up at me. "Euh," he said, and reached for my glass. I sat back on the couch and closed my eyes. Mary hadn't answered my last three texts.

Where are you?

We're having omelets for dinner

You said you would be home by now

I picked up my phone again.

Are you still on your walk?

I drank the rest of my wine as *StoryBots* ended, and then I picked Eli up and carried him to his room. In his crib, he chewed on his gummy key ring, looking up at me. I shut off the light and went into the bedroom and lay on the bed. After a minute, I heard Eli start to cry. I didn't move. I imagined him dropping his key ring through the rungs of his crib, leaning over and crying when he couldn't see it; he did it all the time.

Footsteps on the stairs. Eli's door clicked open and shut, and his cries grew louder as he was carried down the stairs, then tapered off again. After what seemed like ages, the bedroom door opened and Dave came in alone, yawning. I didn't turn my head, but I could feel him standing at the foot of the bed, watching me.

"What?" I said.

The mattress dipped as he climbed onto the bed. He knee-walked toward me and seized one of my feet. "Remember how you used to wear a toe ring?"

I was surprised into laughing and it turned out more like a cough. "It was trendy!"

"Not when you were doing it." He stroked the toe in question, causing me to yank my leg into the air and shriek. "It was 2014. Everyone else was done with that by 2007 except, like, Renaissance-fair chicks."

"That's not true," I said, although I suspected that it was. "I'm just sentimental. I like to hang on to my jewelry."

He moved up to curl himself around me. "You had a little tan line on your toe," he whispered into my ear. I laughed harder, and tears sprang to my eyes. "Whoa," he said, brushing his thumb over my eyelashes. "You okay?"

I nodded, not trusting myself to speak.

"I won't make fun of your toe ring anymore. I can see I've really hurt you."

I pinched his earlobe and he smiled.

"You got Eli to sleep?" I asked after a minute.

"Mhmm," Dave said, stretching. "What was all that stuff on his face? I thought he was a goblin when I looked in the crib."

"Your mom painted him like a tiger," I said. "Cadence sent a video. You didn't see it?"

"Oh, that," he said. "I didn't open it. I was driving."

I glanced at him, wishing I could press the shape of him into my memory exactly, so I could return to it when I couldn't look at him anymore. His curly hair, slightly uneven teeth, the places on his skin the sun had textured. Sometimes I wanted to crawl inside him, touch him from the inside out. Sometimes I felt like that was what he did to me.

"Are we watching TV? We're now two weeks behind on *Naked and Afraid*, just so you know."

I shifted to get under the blanket with him. "I hate that show."

Dave shook his head confidently. "You only think you hate it until you watch it, and then you're telling me how you could survive in the wilderness because you read *My Side of the Mountain* and you know how to identify mushrooms."

"I don't want to watch TV." I rolled over and rubbed my cheek against his shoulder. "I want to kiss you."

Dave raised his eyebrows. "What kind of kiss?"

"A full-on high-school make-out session," I said. "I want to put a hickey on your neck."

He laughed. "Everyone at work will make fun of me for being fourteen."

My heart seized. "Too bad." I climbed into his lap and put my arms around his neck. "I'm your wife, and that's what I want."

He tilted his chin up, and I leaned down to press my lips to his. He tasted like rum, and something else, slightly tangy.

"We need to be doing this in a movie theater," he mumbled against my mouth. "For realism. Go get your toe ring and chew some bubble gum."

I wrinkled my nose. "What do you do with the gum? Do you pass it back and forth?"

Dave snorted. "What a goody-goody. You were studying while I was gaining all this knowledge. No, you stick it on your finger so you can chew it after you're done."

"That's disgusting," I breathed.

"It's conserving resources." He pulled me back in. We kissed until I forgot about the bubble gum and reached for him, stroking his face.

"I love you," I said without meaning to.

Something about my expression must have been off. He tilted his head. "I love you too, baby," he said. "What's wrong?"

I opened my mouth and said nothing, as I always did, as I'd been doing for months and months. I took a deep breath. "Sorry. I'm just tired. Robin's not home yet. I don't know where she went." I untangled myself from Dave and reached for my phone. *Where are you?* I texted again.

Sunset grille & bar makin lots of friendsss, she texted back instantly.

"Is that her?" Dave peered over my shoulder.

"She always does this," I said. "I have to—I have to go get her. I'll be back soon."

"Are you okay?"

"Yeah." I pushed my hair off my face and got out of bed. "I'm fine. She just needs a ride. She's all the way across town. Stay here with the monitor, okay?" She was going to fuck everything up.

"I could go get her if you want," Dave offered. "You're tired."

"No," I said. "You've been out all evening. You don't need to go out again."

He didn't answer. I watched him reach for the remote.

I'd never been to Sunset before. It was on Lomas, near the Downs, with one of those plain white signs on the façade. $2.50 Michelob. There was an older bald man in a denim jacket standing beside the front door, thumbing through his phone. He gave me a once-over as I passed him.

The Sunset's ceiling hung low over a collection of red vinyl seats and tabletops. The middle of the room had been cleared for dancing, but no one danced. A carpeted stage, full of amps and wires, with a screen and a mic for karaoke, overlooked the bar, and a woman with round-brush bangs presided, belting "Last Night I Didn't Get to Sleep at All" to a group of friends leaning against the pool table. I scanned the room for Mary's blond head and spotted her down by the L-shaped bar at the far end of the room, where several old men in ball caps shifted on their black barstools. She and a man with broad shoulders and a ponytail were bent over one of the nearby tabletops, holding hands.

I had to walk across the dance floor to reach them, and my heeled loafers made it sound like there were a dozen of me. The women by the pool table stared, but Mary didn't seem to notice me.

"Okay, so see this joint, and how long it is? That means you're really logical, and you need to be careful to listen to your emotions more." She said this last part gravely. She was reading the man's palm, I realized.

"Mary?"

They looked up. Mary was still holding his hand, and she squeezed it when she saw me. "Leslie! You got my text!"

"I sent you a dozen texts," I said as calmly as I could. "You weren't answering. You said you'd be back for dinner."

"Oh, I ate," she told me. "You don't have to worry about me. Come sit with us! Amos, Leslie. Leslie, Amos. Amos, can you get my sister a drink too?"

Amos's shoulder jerked, and then he grinned. "Nice to meet you, Leslie. What'll it be?"

Mary jumped in. "She wants what I got. Two more."

"I need my hand back for that," Amos said.

Mary laughed and released him to the bar, then patted the vinyl seat beside her as the woman on the makeshift stage fitted the microphone back in its stand with a crackle of feedback.

I shook my head. "Let's just go home."

"Aw, you don't want to go home." Mary shook her head at me. "I can see it in your face. You want to stay here with me and have a gin and tonic on Amos. Rough day?"

The bar was briefly quiet while the next woman got up on the stage and adjusted the karaoke screen. I hesitated, then pulled out the chair with a scrape, and sat down. Mary gave a little hoot of approval. "What are you doing here? With . . . Amos?" I asked quietly, my gaze drifting toward the ponytail bending over the bar, trying to get the bartender's attention.

"He paid me to read his palm," Mary said. "I charge twenty bucks per. Guess how much I made today." She grabbed my wrist and pushed my hand into her purse, sitting on the chair beside me. My fingers felt a crumpled nest of bills. I pulled my hand away.

"I—" The next song started, something I didn't know, classic rock. Mary looked at me. She was red-cheeked, her light hair fluffy at the ends, lips chapped and free of lipstick. She smelled a little sour, like she'd been out in the rain. "I don't know if I can do this," I said, instead of telling her she shouldn't read people's palms at a bar, which had been my first instinct. It seemed like such an intimate thing to do for a stranger. But she had read my palm too, when we'd met. And I had been a stranger then. It wasn't even what I had come here to be upset about.

"Do what?" Mary asked, sucking on the dregs of her old gin and tonic. Several soggy citrus slices sagged at the bottom of the drink. She dug one out and picked off a little string of lime flesh.

"The whole thing," I said. "Dinner with Albert . . . I didn't know it would take this long."

Mary slipped the lime flesh into her mouth and licked her lips. "It was your idea."

"I know. But not like this. I didn't know where you were today."

"So are you—"

Amos set two highball glasses in front of us. "That took forever."

Mary grinned at him. "Amos, you owe me twenty dollars, please."

"I thought the reading came free with the purchase of drinks," he suggested.

She shook her head. "I figured that was just your generous nature, right?"

He stared at her, and then decided to laugh, digging a couple of tens out of his wallet. "I'm trying to keep listening to my emotions," he told her. "Like you said." He leaned across the table as Mary stuffed the bills into her purse and zipped it up.

"Oh, I'm so glad you heard me, Amos," she told him, leaning back in her seat. "I could feel it when we were holding hands, that you were really listening to me. Now I need to talk to my sister. She's having a personal moment. Could you give us some time?"

"We weren't done," Amos said. "You only did one of my hands."

"They match, honey," she said. "We're bilaterally symmetric, like moths."

"I want my drink back, then," he said, and reached for the high-ball glass. Mary leaned over and spat in it.

"What are you—?"

Mary slid my glass over to her and spat in that one too.

"I'm leaving," Amos said, and scraped his chair back, adjusted his ponytail, and flung himself toward the bar.

Mary pushed my gin and tonic back across the table and motioned for me to drink it. I stared at her. "I'm not sick," she said. "Don't worry."

I left the glass where it was. "What was that for?"

She stuck the straw in her mouth. "I got you a drink. For free. He's a drip, he won't be back." She chewed her straw and regarded me cautiously. "I did it all the time when I used to go out in Vegas."

"Albuquerque isn't Vegas."

Mary seemed to relax. "I know. I've barely even thought about Sam or Paul since I came here."

"You don't think Sam would come after you, do you?" I asked, feeling myself soften. I remembered Mary's face as she'd been crushed to his chest outside the restaurant.

"He misses this," she said, unzipping her purse and pulling out a handful of cash, then letting it flutter back inside. A few men at the bar, including a red-faced Amos, watched her do it. Mary propped her chin on her palm. "Otherwise, there's nobody in the world who would notice if I disappeared right now. Except you. You came all the way out to the bar to look for me. You could have just texted me 'Get your ass back home, young lady.' "

"I was worried about you," I said. "You never tell me where you're going."

Mary gave me a brilliant smile and downed the rest of her drink in one long effort. "Last week no one was worried about me. And last week no one knew you were deep in some shit you couldn't talk about. So we're both a little better off than we were, huh?"

"Don't disappear," I said. "Not until after the dinner."

Mary reached for my gin and tonic. "Then don't chicken out. Deal?"

I nodded.

She rested her slightly damp head on my shoulder and reached up to touch my earlobe. "What happened to those earrings you had on?"

I opened my mouth to reply but was drowned out by the bartender's voice over the sound system saying, "Uh, 'Careless Whisper'?"

"That's me!" Mary announced, and bounced up from the table, jostling the remaining glasses with a clatter. "I'll be right back." I touched my ear uncomfortably.

She crossed the blond-wood dance floor, shuffling a little in her Adidas. When she got onstage, the knot of women by the pool table stopped their game to watch her adjust her polo dress and bend to tie her fluffy hair up into a topknot. "Okay, I'm ready," she said into the mic, over the opening saxophone.

She caught on to the beat a little late, closing her eyes and swaying, forgetting to open them again until the second line had scrolled over the karaoke screen, throwing blue-and-white light across the planes of her face. The woman who'd been singing when I arrived shouted the first line to her, too late; Mary laughed and started in the middle, stumbling until she caught up with the verse. She had a decent voice, a little scratchy, higher than I would have predicted. But her face was the reason to watch her. I'd never seen her on a stage before, and even the weak light of the karaoke screen picked out her features in a way that seemed to spotlight her on purpose. She wanted my attention, leaned toward it; when the chorus hit she opened her eyes wide and pointed at me, motioning for me to sing along.

I thought: *She reminds me of . . .* , groping for an actress, and then recalled what she'd told me in the hotel room, how people always did that to her, comparing her to all the other beautiful people whose faces began to run together. I never reminded people of anybody but myself. I wondered if it was better to look like what you were. I felt glass-faced, transparent; it was only because nobody looked at me that no one had seen through me yet.

I didn't sing along. I couldn't. The rest of the room joined in, and Mary turned away from me, soaking it up, pink spreading across her cheekbones. She opened her arms as if to embrace them.

A door opened and closed behind me, barely audible over George Michael. I glanced over my shoulder and saw the man in the denim jacket from outside talking with an older man behind the bar who must have been the manager. Amos hovered at his elbow. We made brief eye contact.

As Mary hit the second chorus, the man in the denim jacket strode across the dance floor and onto the stage. "Hi there," Mary said into the mic.

He ducked his head and tried to speak into her ear, but she shimmied away from him, pulling the mic from its stand. *"Guilty feet have got no rhythm,"* she sang to him playfully.

I clenched my jaw as his face darkened, reaching for my phone instinctively. But who did I think I was going to call? Amos approached the stage, brushing past me. Mary saw him coming and dragged the mic down the stage steps, darting behind one of the women at the pool table. She motioned for me to leave in the split second that Amos and the bouncer couldn't see her. Her purse with the money in it was still sitting on the table in front of me, and I stumbled to my feet, trying to zip it closed.

"The way I danced with you!" Mary sang through laughter, coming to the end of the microphone's cord and twisting past Amos.

"Turn off the music," the manager was saying, loudly enough for me to hear. I slung both our purses over my shoulder and wove through the chairs and tables under his gaze.

"You don't have to kick me out," Mary said, her voice echoing over the backing vocals. "I wasn't hurting anybody. Sheesh."

I pushed the door open and stepped out into the night. Stubby cigarettes littered the asphalt around the entrance.

"I don't even have it anymore," I could hear Mary saying inside, still into the mic. "I could get you guys arrested."

I waited, tucking Mary's purse under my arm and checking the time on my phone.

After a few seconds, Mary appeared in the doorway, giggling. "I lied about your heart line," she said to Amos before shutting the door behind her and stumbling over to me.

"You're drunk," I said.

"So are you."

"No, I'm not. You spat in my drink."

"Oh, right." Mary braced one palm against her thigh and flapped the other at me. "Sorry about that. Can I get my purse back?"

"I thought you wanted to be in this together," I said, still clutching my phone. It was colder outside in the evening. My jaw clenched.

Mary straightened. "I do. What are you even talking about?"

"You almost got arrested," I whispered. "What if you'd gotten arrested?"

She frowned. "They wouldn't have arrested me," she said. "Just for doing palm readings? Come on. They only kicked me out. Now I'm banned from the"—she tipped her head as far back as it would go and read the sign upside down—"Sunset Grille and Bar in Albuquerque, New Mexico. Probably for good. Whatever will I do?"

"You were sharking," I snapped. "And you're not taking things seriously."

Her face dropped. "I'm taking things very seriously, Leslie," she said, overenunciating to make up for the soft slur that had entered her voice somewhere around the third G&T. "You don't even know how seriously I am taking it. Now give me my fucking purse."

I let her take it from my shoulder. "But you—"

"But it's just a little *stressful*," she continued, hoisting the purse onto her own shoulder and feeling around for the money inside, "that my partner doesn't trust me at all. So why don't you go home to your giant house, and your nice husband, and your baby, and I'll find somebody else to have fun with."

I turned away from her on the pretense of digging for my keys. "Just get in the car," I said, when I found them. I unlocked it and had my hand on the driver's-side door when I realized she wasn't beside me anymore.

"See you tomorrow, Leslie," Mary called from the far end of the parking lot. I watched as she disappeared around the side of the building.

Maybe she can use all that money for a cab, I thought. I got in my car and pulled out of the lot. As soon as I made it to the light I thought better of it and turned around, but she was already gone.

42

Mary

I walked in circles until I felt sober enough that I probably wouldn't die in the car and then I drove home mostly fine, except I had an awful time trying to remember which back street I was using to park the rental. I found the spot again after having to do a three-point turn and almost knocking somebody's garbage cans over, and trudged around the corner down the sidewalk feeling pretty low.

When I saw him outside I thought he was a bobcat, maybe; the blanket he wore over his shoulders had distorted his shape so that he resembled only a black mass with flat, reflective eyes.

"You're home late."

"Sh— You scared me." I laughed, but it was more like a series of exhalations. Dave shifted under the blanket. "What are you doing on the porch?"

He shrugged. "Couldn't sleep. What are you doing in the street? Did you walk here?"

"Took the bus," I said, because I didn't want him to get mad at me. I sat down next to him, and he let the blanket slip down his shoulders, so he wore it as a kind of fuzzy evening wrap.

"Leslie's worried about you," he told me. "She went out looking for you for hours. She only got back like forty minutes ago."

I cocked my head. "I didn't tell her I needed a ride. She decided to go look for me. I didn't ask."

"You're not telling her where you're going, sneaking out . . ." He let his head fall forward and rolled it gently from shoulder to shoulder, stretching the muscles in his neck. "You couldn't call her from time to time?"

I shrugged. "Does she call me?"

He chewed on the inside of his cheek for a second, then grinned, looking over at me. "That's immature."

There was something infectious about his smile. I meant to give him an insincere one back, but a tiny bit of real amusement crept in. "Sisters," I said.

"Yeah, sure. Sisters." He stuck his thumbnail in his mouth and worked at it with his teeth. "Is something wrong with Leslie?"

A muscle in my thigh twitched, as if something had bitten me. "What?"

"You know . . ." He sighed. "Did you say anything to her, did you . . ."

"Did I tell her about your disgusting habit?" I asked. I thought about rocking my knee sideways to touch his, to show I was joking, and then I remembered what Nancy had said at the Frontier, about men who wanted to be in control.

He shook his head. "I don't mean that. Just if you guys fought, or you told her—I don't know." He shifted his weight onto the edge of the step, jostling the blanket, which slipped off his back onto the porch steps.

"I didn't tell her anything," I said. "If there's something wrong with Leslie, it was wrong before I got here."

"Yeah, whatever," he said, putting his hands on his knees like he was about to stand.

"Dave?" I said. "Are you ever scared?"

He cocked his head. "Of what?"

"Of her?" I said, unable to stop my voice from ticking up at the end.

Dave laughed, and just like before it warmed me against my will. I found myself unable to really believe it could be like Nancy had

said. He didn't seem like the kind of man who could hurt anybody.
But neither did Sam, with his round belly and pink ears. "Sure," he
said. "She's, you know, five foot ten, wicked serve. Play volleyball
against Leslie, fear for your testicles."

"Oh," I said. "Right." He stood up, and I reached for him. My
fingers brushed against one of his knees, where the bone protruded
knobbily; it made me feel sort of tender toward him, as if I knew
him, maybe because I could imagine him as a teenager, all that stark
bony flesh. "Hey, do you have another joint?" I asked, wanting to
keep him with me a second or two longer.

He stared at me. I thought about Leslie finding his messages with
Elaine, all that money gone to some other woman. I thought about
Paul and the girl at his house, that girl who'd looked like me, my
replacement. For a second they almost looked the same to me, Dave
and Paul; I could have wanted to kill him too, if I'd loved him more.
If I'd loved him as much as Leslie did. "I don't do it that often," he
said finally, moving toward the door.

My hand stayed in the air where his knee had been, hovering un-
certainly, so that it looked like I was saying, over and over again,
Hello, or maybe *So-so.* "Could you put me in touch, then?"

"With my dealer?" His hand closed over the doorknob. "I guess
so."

"What's his number?"

"Hers," he said, fumbling in his pocket for his phone. "Um . . ."
He read me the number, then added, "Elaine. Tell her you're my
sister-in-law, it'll be fine."

"Elaine," I repeated, my fingers pausing against my own phone
screen, which lit me sickly from below.

"Don't tell Leslie, okay?" he added, opening the door.

"Right," I said, tapping Elaine Campbell's name into my phone.
"I won't tell Leslie."

He went inside, pressing his fingertips against the glass door to
keep it from slamming. I stayed seated on the porch, staring at the
way the streetlight picked out the small downy hairs on my thighs.

43

Mary

The inside of the Bernalillo County jail was so ordinary—a little tan lobby with linoleum floors and plastic plants. I don't know what I expected. Bars over everything, maybe, or a big hefty guard at the door. The only guard was the clerk sitting at a desk protected by Plexiglas, chewing on the nubby end of a pen cap.

Nancy had walked in ahead of me and she went up to the clerk. "I'm here to see one of the prisoners, Francis Clery." She slid her badge into the well beneath the glass.

The clerk studied it briefly, then glanced up at me. "Who's that?"

"This is Robin Voigt. She's going to sit in."

I held my breath. He pursed his lips. "Okay," he said at last. "ID."

I fumbled in my purse.

After the clerk was done taking my information, Nancy and I went to sit in the plastic chairs lining the far wall. They were textured to feel like sand, and my hands started sweating as soon as I gripped the edges. I let go, trying to relax. My body drifted toward Nancy—close, too close—and I whispered, "How long until we can go in?"

Nancy was straight-backed. "Depends on whether he's in the middle of a structured block of time. Could be five minutes, could be an hour. He can refuse to talk if he wants. Then they'll come out and tell us to go."

I didn't know what I'd do if that happened. I ran my tongue over my teeth, thinking.

There was no television in the lobby, no reading material—which was the only thing that distinguished it from a dentist's office. I stared at the peach-colored metal door. It had a little window cut into the top, crisscrossed by thin metal bars. Almost the only thing.

It was nearly an hour before an officer came to the door and nodded at us. I had been watching Nancy play Words With Friends on her phone. She was a terrible speller, which she tried to hide from me by tilting the screen away, but I could tell. I watched her laboriously assemble D-A-C-K-E-R-Y and frown when the game kicked it back to her.

"Officer Courtenay," the other officer said as we passed. She nodded and we went in.

Past the door lay a short industrial hallway lined with more peach-colored metal doors. At the end of the hallway was a plate-glass door left ajar. Nancy and I followed the officer into this new room. It was small and cramped, with walls made of cinder block and tables shoved cafeteria-style along the perimeter of the room. Someone had painted a decorative stripe on the walls in a dark, burnt orange, which gave me the feeling of passing through chambers in a conch shell, where the peachy accents of the outer rooms gave way to a deeper shade nearer to the heart.

The focus of the room was a long squat set of windows, each outfitted with telephones and bolted-down wooden stools. Sitting in the second window was Frank Clery.

He was white, blue-eyed, with a long face and weak chin that undercut the effect of his well-muscled torso. He wore glasses, plastic Buddy Holly frames that he'd propped up on his fleshy, lined forehead. His tongue crept out to wet his lips as he caught sight of us—he was one of those men who had permanently red, shiny lips.

"Here you are," the officer who had led us in said. "You have until one-thirty."

"Thank you," Nancy said. She crossed the room quickly and cast herself down onto the wooden stool. The windows weren't de-signed for two-on-one conversations; I sat awkwardly off to the side, leaning into her space in order to see.

Clery eyed Nancy, then me. I couldn't read on his face what he thought of us.

Nancy picked up the phone and motioned for him to pick up his end. He lifted the receiver with two fingers.

"Mr. Clery," Nancy said. "I'm Officer Courtenay. This is Robin. We'd like to ask you a couple of questions about your relationship with a woman named Leslie Flores. We're investigating her possible criminal conduct."

Clery looked from Nancy to me. His odd oblong face remained flat, although his watery eyes gave him a persecuted air, like a man caught in a permanent windstorm. "Not talking," he said, after some time had passed.

"Do you remember anyone by that name?" Nancy pressed.

He set the telephone gingerly back in its cradle, then met Nan-cy's eyes through the glass. Not talking.

"Did she ever try to pawn anything at your store?" Nancy contin-ued, speaking loudly and enunciating. The glass was thick, but not soundproof. We both saw him take in her question. "Did she ever hire you to perform any services?"

Clery turned in his seat toward the officer lurking on his side of the glass. His mouth moved, but he was facing away and I only caught the timbre of his speech. A question—*Can I go yet,* probably.

"Nancy, let me try," I said, reaching for her hand under the stool, out of Clery's sightline. "Please," I said. "I have to. For Leslie. It'll be different if he knows she's my sister."

Nancy's face said that she didn't believe it would be different at all, in fact, but she found it endearing that I did. She paused, then tapped the glass twice with her knuckles. Clery turned around. She pointed at me.

"Can you get me a coffee?" I said, glancing at the digital clock on the wall. "I saw a break room on the way here—I bet they would let you in."

"I don't want to leave you alone with this guy." Nancy was at her most heroic. If the room had had windows, a beam of light would have hit her right on her square jawline.

"I think it's the only way," I said. "Besides, there's not enough room for both of us to talk." I adjusted my weight on the stool, crossing my legs.

She rubbed her neck. "I'll come right back," she said finally. "Call if he says anything to you that you don't like."

"I will." I gave her a tremulous smile.

Nancy left and I spun to face Clery. The officer behind him was bored, face aimed away from us.

I was almost always smiling when I was around other people. Even when I was only walking down the street, I'd trained myself to keep the corners of my lips curved up. Now, in front of Clery, I let the smile drop. He eyed me, startled.

Clery picked up the phone—full-handed, not like a germaphobe this time, so I supposed I had already exceeded Nancy in his estimation—and I picked up my end.

"What's up, sweetheart?" he said into the line. He had a strangely adolescent intonation combined with the gravel of a habitual smoker.

"I don't have a lot of time," I said. "I'm here to bargain with you."

He laughed. "Bargain? Sure. Pack of cigarettes for a presidential pardon."

"I want to know what Leslie Flores paid you to do. You want to avoid prison. Sound fair?"

His watery eyes fixed on me. "You a lawyer?"

"Nah," I said. I let Robin fall off me, like a skin. Mary fell away just as quickly. Underneath I was nothing; teeth and holes. "I'm just like you."

He looked me up and down, or as much of me as he could see. "Scrawny. Stupid. Not seeing any similarities."

The teeth showed. "Jennifer's your wife, right?"

He gripped the receiver. "Did she say something to you?"

"Nancy—Officer Courtenay—she told me the whole case rests on getting Jennifer to testify against you. If she swears it was an accident, you've got a much better shot, right?"

He swallowed. I watched him consciously stop himself from twisting to see what the officer behind him was doing. "What do you care?"

"I have my own reasons for wanting to know what Leslie Flores paid you to do. In exchange, I'll go to your wife's address—1515 Los Alamos, right?—and I'll beat the shit out of her until she tells the police it was an accident."

He laughed again, this one more like a burp. "That's funny. You almost got me."

I leaned closer. "When I said I was just like you, what I meant was I will beat the shit out of your wife, and I will do it like I was painting my nails. Do you understand me now?" For a second I imagined us as twins, mirrors facing each other, reflecting nothing. A long black socket where violence might go.

Then he believed me. I saw when it happened.

"Talk fast," I said. "Nancy will be back any second."

He licked his lips. "Why do you want to know about that chick? Leslie?"

"She's my sister," I said. "If she hired you for what I think she hired you for, I'm going to ruin her fucking life."

He smiled, an involuntary twitch. "If you don't do it," he said, "you know I'll track you down. Don't you?" He tilted his head. "Robin, sister of Leslie Flores."

"I know." I smiled back.

"No broken bones," he said after a minute. "No scars. Nothing on her face." His long cheeks sagged.

"I'm not an idiot," I said. "She'll be fine."

He nodded, licked his lips again. Then he sucked in a breath and opened his mouth.

Nancy returned as I was still working through what Clery had told me. I looked up at her. "He wouldn't tell me anything about Leslie," I said clearly into the receiver, summoning tears.

Clery hung up the phone and mumbled something to the officer behind him, who finally nodded and began to unlock the door to the prisoners' section of the jail. I kept my head down and pinched both cheeks hard. There. I was splotchy and weeping.

"Crap," Nancy said, setting the coffee down too hard, so that it sloshed a little. "Clery! I have a few more questions."

He didn't turn around. The door shut behind him, a muffled thump.

"We can't bring 'em back," the officer who'd led us in said from the doorway. "Visiting hours are voluntary."

Nancy clasped my shoulder. I took a fortifying sip of coffee. "Did he say anything to you? I saw he had the phone up."

"He called me a bitch," I said. "I tried really hard to make him—make him see . . ."

"It's not your fault." Nancy rubbed my shoulder. "Look, you saw him, you talked to him. Do you think your sister would have anything to do with him? She probably sold him your dad's antiques and he screwed her. There's nothing you can do but just ask her for the truth or decide to let it go."

I trembled. "You're right. Nancy—"

"Let's go," she said. "We can talk outside."

The officer at the door led us back into the lobby. Nancy and I signed out with the clerk. She held the door for me, guiding me through with a hand on the small of my back.

It was hot outside, leaning into summer. Nancy shaded her eyes. "Are you sure you're okay?"

I nodded. "You have to go back to work, right?"

"Yeah." She gazed down at me, at my mouth, at the tears still clumping my eyelashes. "I wish I didn't."

"I wish you didn't either."

She squeezed my hand. "I'll call you later. You should talk to your sister. I really think it'll all be fine."

I held on to her hand. It was solid and sticky in mine, our fingers interlaced, like we'd done it a thousand times before. "You think so?"

She nodded. "See you later, Robin."

I watched her get into the police car and start it up, and then I went around to the driver's side of my own little Nissan. The heat had stolen all the oxygen in the car, and the breath went out of my lungs as I pressed my forehead to the burning steering wheel and let my heart rate pick up again.

What a fucking moron, I thought. All it had taken was a promise from a stranger, and he'd spilled his guts. He deserved to be in prison; no one who killed people for a living should be allowed to go on being so naïve. But he'd learn, once he realized I hadn't held up my end of the bargain. Why should I find Jennifer Clery? He'd already given me everything I asked for. And he'd done it in less time than it took for Nancy to get a cup of coffee.

He'd try to track me down once he was out. I had no doubt about that. But I'd be long gone by then.

44

Leslie

At five-thirty I shut my computer off by unplugging it. I walked as quickly as I could from my office to the elevator, to avoid having to make conversation with Justin. "Have a good night, Leslie!" he said energetically at my back anyway. I didn't reply. Mary was waiting for me.

Stretches of the drive home disappeared from my memory. I was in the parking lot, then the intersection near the Target. Then I was sitting in my car in the driveway, thinking: I forgot to stop by the daycare.

No—it was Dave's turn. I opened my car door. Taryn, who lived next door, waved at me from her yard. She was barefoot, aiming a kid's lime-green squirt gun at the succulents. "Hi, Leslie!"

I lifted my head, and there was a brief moment before I remembered to reply. "Oh, hi, Taryn," I said, running a hand through my hair.

"This is Austin's." She laughed. "Couldn't find my spray bottle."

I didn't know what she meant, and it showed on my face.

The gun. Right. The squirt gun.

I laughed back.

Taryn cocked her head. "Have a good night!" she said after a second.

"Oh, thanks." It wasn't quite the right thing to say. I went into the house.

The stairs were strewn with fresh socks. A stack of mail sat on the floor next to the door. From the back of the house, muffled laughter issued. I took off my shoes and followed the noise into the kitchen.

It was brighter than the rest of the house, full of sun, and it smelled like someone had been cooking—curry, maybe. Pots and bowls crowded the sink, and the counter was covered in yellow splotches and fat, soggy grains of rice. The back door was open and the air from outside hung in the house. I stepped out onto the back patio.

Neither of them saw me at first: Mary in a blue-and-white-striped bikini top, the strings trailing into the waistband of her cutoff jeans. She was cross-legged on the grass, my sunglasses propped on top of her head, laughing, holding out her hands. The garden hose snaked over the ground beside her, parting the grass. Dave, his back to me in a lawn chair, sprawled out, still in his office clothes, tie missing.

"Come on," Mary said, and Eli, wearing Dave's tie around his neck, came hurtling across the lawn toward her, his legs so rubbery that his entire body was jostled from side to side with every step. He fell into her arms giggling, and Dave clapped.

"Five point four seconds," Dave called. "Necesitas trabajar más, mijo."

Mary rocked Eli from side to side and said into his ear, "Ready? Three . . . two . . ." She pushed him out of her arms so that he had a nearly airborne head start into his next dash toward the edge of the lawn.

"Leslie," Dave said, twisting around. "You're home."

Mary looked up and pulled my sunglasses onto her face.

"You're not ready," I said. "We have to go to dinner."

"You can stay out here and play for a second," Dave told me. "Eli, look, Mommy's home."

Eli, distracted, tripped over Dave's tie and fell hard. He let out a wail, coming up grass-stained.

"Oh, no," Mary said. "Party's over. You want to take him, Leslie?"

Dave glanced up at me. "I can do it," he said. "She just got home." He heaved himself off the lawn chair and went over to scoop Eli off the grass.

"Guess it's time," Mary said, raising her eyebrows at me over the sunglasses.

I shut the door to the patio behind us when we were inside. "You have to take this seriously," I said.

"I am taking it seriously," Mary replied. I couldn't see her eyes.

"You're wearing cutoffs," I said. "You're playing with the baby. Where's the dress I left for you?"

She sighed. "It's upstairs. It doesn't fit. I got another one."

"Another dress? From where?"

"Does it matter?" She took off my sunglasses and set them on the counter. I snatched them up. "I'm going to get ready," she said. "You should have a glass of wine or something."

When she turned around I saw that the backs of her thighs were pink and crazily patterned where she'd been sitting on the grass holding my baby, pretending to be his aunt. I stood there for a second, listening to Eli and Dave chattering on the back porch. Then I went to the sink and put on my yellow dish gloves.

I scrubbed every bowl, waiting for her, and then I wiped down the countertops. Dave was back on the lawn chair now, Eli draped over his chest, both of them asleep. I went to the bottom of the stairs and called, "M—Robin?"

No answer.

I climbed the stairs, picking up socks as I went. "Robin?" I said, once I'd reached the landing. The guest bedroom door stood open. I went inside with my handful of socks.

She'd made a mess of the room. Covers and sheets strewn across the floor, clothes hanging from the bedposts, dirty plates and glasses on the bedside table. The dress I'd left hanging neatly from her doorknob that morning was lying in an inside-out heap on the bare bed. The door to the bathroom was ajar, and I could see her moving around in front of the mirror.

"What's taking so long?" I asked, sitting gingerly on the bed, next to the rejected dress. I made a neat pile beside me of the socks.

She pushed the door open farther and leaned out. Her mouth was a bright vermilion, matching her painted nails, and she'd curled her hair, except for a long limp hank that hung down behind her ear.

"You're still in, aren't you?" I said. "I mean, everything is still . . ." I stopped speaking.

Mary let the door fall open farther, and I saw that she was in a neon-yellow cocktail dress, strapless, her feet bare. Against the wood and ceramic of the bathroom she looked hyperreal, like a cutout from a magazine. I could see myself in the mirror behind her, almost a shadow in the dim bedroom. "Yeah," she said, white teeth showing. "Everything's good. What's up?"

"I—" I shifted on the bed. "It's fine. I just wanted to check."

Mary turned back to the mirror and took up the last lock of hair, twisting it around the curling iron. "Hey, can I ask you something?"

I hadn't sat in a bedroom watching another woman get ready in a long time. It smelled like hot hair and perfume, like the dressing room at prom. A memory floated past. My mother in the bathroom with Robin, me at the door. She'd told Robin to smile as wide as she could, and Robin had. *You put it on the apples of your cheeks,* my mother had said, patting her with the powder puff. She used loose powder and too much of it, like a lot of the women I remembered from my childhood. Pink circles, fever spots. Robin grinning. It wasn't a happy memory. Why wasn't it happy?

I'd been watching my mother in the mirror. It was her face that was wrong. A half smile, like a grimace. My father used to tell us it was her nerves. We wore on her nerves. We weren't supposed to be in our parents' bathroom. It was her private space. Us being there was wearing on her nerves. That was why she looked that way.

Had I called Robin away, told her to stop bothering our mother? I couldn't remember. The rest of it had faded.

"How did you meet Dave?" Mary said, jarring me. "I don't think you ever told me."

I shook my head. "It's not an exciting story."

She smiled into the mirror. "Sure it is."

"No." I couldn't see myself behind her anymore. "Just in school. Business school for me. He was getting his MS."

I had been about to leave the party when we saw each other. I just went over to him. I never did things like that, bold things. But I'd had three beers and I went over to him and I said, *I'm Leslie. I love your face*, which I almost hated to remember. I did love his face, though; I'd loved it immediately, his wide, funny, flat-lipped mouth and faded pockmarks on his cheeks. The outside corners of his eyes tilted up a little, making him look permanently good-humored. His dark brown eyes, nearly the same color as his pupils.

He'd laughed, but not at me; he'd laughed and turned away from the woman he'd been talking to and said, *I'm Dave. I love your face too.*

I believed him when he said it. I didn't even have a moment of doubt, the way I did when other men complimented me, their expressions expectant rather than admiring, waiting for the compliment to kick in, the way you waited for a faulty engine to turn over.

"How long ago was that?" Mary asked.

"Six years."

She nodded. I watched her put in earrings, one after another. "Do you love him?" she said.

"Do I love my husband?" I repeated. "Of course I do."

She padded back into the bedroom and kicked the sheets on the floor aside until she found a high heel. She put it on, then went around looking for the other one. "I just wondered if it, like, fades as you get older. I feel like everything kind of dries up, you know, eventually."

"Not for me," I said.

She found the other heel and straightened, several inches taller. "Okay. I'm ready. How about you?"

I couldn't answer.

Mary came over and sat on the pile of socks next to me. The memory foam pressed us together. "If you need me to," she said finally, "I'd help you, you know."

I tried not to move next to her. "You are helping me," I said.

She turned to me, her face half-lit by the bathroom. "With whatever it is you can't tell me," she said. "If it's important, I'd help you. Like you helped me with Sam."

I stared straight ahead. After a second, she got up. I heard her heels clicking down the stairs.

I stood stiffly and turned around, looking for my purse. The dress she'd discarded was still lying on the mattress, and I picked it up to turn it right side out again.

Downstairs, the porch door opened and I heard Dave and Mary speaking in murmurs. She laughed, then stifled herself, as if she was afraid of waking Eli up.

I stepped back to fold the dress and my foot landed on something sharp inside the rumpled sheet on the floor. I stumbled and dropped the dress. Then I lifted the sheet and shook it.

A key fell out, black plastic at the top, with a Hertz sticker. A rental car.

She had a car somewhere.

Mary's footsteps grew louder again. "Leslie? Are you coming?" she called up the stairs.

I dropped the sheet back over the key.

How had she gotten the money to rent it? Had she done it under her own name?

I'd almost told her when we were sitting on the bed together— almost trusted her. But she was a stranger. I had forgotten for a second that she was a stranger.

"I'm coming," I called back, voice stronger now.

She was nobody.

Mary was at the foot of the stairs, holding out my purse. "Can I drive this time?" she said, as if she really were my sister, as if she asked for the keys every week. As if she didn't have her own car hidden somewhere, so she could leave me whenever she felt like it.

"Not this time," I said, as if I believed her. When had she started talking to me like that?

Her eyes were clear and guileless as she handed me my purse. "Well, come on, lady," she said, pushing open the door. "Let's go get your money."

45

Leslie

The Blue Roof had once been alone on its lot, but in the past several years it had sold the surrounding land to dentists' offices and realty businesses, and so the parking lot had had a face-lift as well, with too-white curbs and obsessively tended shrubbery. In the middle of all this the restaurant itself was incongruously shabby, the rest of the world having rejected its particular kind of tackiness in favor of the Colonial Revival brickwork and pillars meant to remind you of the buildings of yesteryear—a New England yesteryear that had never existed in the desert. The Albuquerque of my youth had looked more like the Blue Roof. Stucco, exposed beams. Strings of Christmas lights all year round.

I crossed the parking lot with Mary, several steps behind her. From this vantage point I could watch the little flickers that passed over the faces of almost everyone who saw her, as if she were famous, but she was only beautiful. I wondered if it was uncomfortable, to walk in the middle of so many gazes, skewered by them, or if she did it on purpose—drew them all in, searched for their eyes. Like a mirror made of faces, reflecting her wherever she went.

But when we reached the front doors, she didn't appear to have noticed anything. A short middle-aged man held the door for her, and her face lifted as if no one had ever thought to be so kind to her before. "Thank you!" she said, her puffy Texas vowels back again. I realized that this too was an act—an old act, one I should have recognized a long time ago. Beauty was untrustworthy, so she added naïveté, a country accent. Like Marilyn Monroe, with the breathy little-girl voice. I remembered her back at Letourneau's: *I think people think I'm dumb.*

Had I seen any part of her real personality? Or had she just shown me whatever she thought I wanted to see?

Wasn't that what I'd hired her to do?

Some parts had to be real, I thought. It was impossible to be disingenuous every second. When she'd dripped across my bathroom floor on purpose—that had been the real Mary, maybe. And when we'd lain on the carpet in my father's old house, listening to the Laura Nyro record. I hadn't been alone then.

Inside, the restaurant was designed to look like an Old World courtyard, with murals of people leaning from painted balconies, their arms full of real ivy, which snaked down the walls along decades-old cracks. Wicker fans hung motionless from the ceiling, a holdover from when the restaurant hadn't had air-conditioning, and each table had a miniature chain-pull lamp and a built-in ashtray, which could be emptied from below. No one was allowed to smoke in restaurants anymore, but the ashtrays suggested a sort of bitterness about this rule on the part of the management that was soothing to the many elderly smokers who were regulars there.

"We're with Albert," Mary said to the man at the host station, leaning familiarly on his podium. "I don't know if he's—Albert! Hi!"

Albert was at a table at the far end of the courtyard, underneath a painting of a red-cheeked woman leaning out of a window, clutching a bottle of wine in one hand and a dripping glass in the other. Next to the painting, he looked dour in his brown sport coat, napkin in lap and walker propped against the wall. He didn't hear Mary call out for him, but his head turned as she approached, a bright bit of yellow against the fake Spanish tile. "Girls," he said, rising from his seat. "Nice to see you again. Robin, I'm speechless."

Mary seemed to blush. I watched curiously as I saw that she only performed the body language of it, or maybe it was just that her makeup was thick enough to hide any extra color in her face. "Thank you! Oh my gosh. No, don't get up—we're too fast for you, we're already sitting down. How are you?"

He tilted his hand: *comme ci, comme ça*. "I shall wear the bottoms of my trousers rolled. Look." He stuck out his leg; there was a cuff sewn into the bottom, a bit too high, so that his translucent leg hairs showed just above the tops of his socks. "How are you? No trouble with traffic?"

"No, no. It was fine."

He squinted at me. "And your husband? Your son—what's his name? Eli?"

"Yes, Eli," I said. Mary twitched in my direction and I added, "They're fine."

A potbellied man in plain clothes came to our table. I thought he might be the owner; he wore an expression that suggested both that he was ready to murder the incompetents around him and that he hoped we had a pleasant evening. "Can I get you something to drink? A bottle of wine for the table?"

"What do you think?" Albert asked us. "We could have a bottle, couldn't we? Is red all right with you?"

"That would be amazing," Mary said, smiling between Albert and the owner.

"How about you, Robin?" Albert asked when he'd finished ordering. "Have you been around to see old friends this week?"

"Oh, yeah," Mary said, clasping his hand. "I looked up a couple of people I used to know. It's been pretty interesting seeing what's changed and what hasn't."

I stared at her. Had she really been talking to people Robin had known? Was that where she was going when she left the house, in the car she'd hidden from me?

"You found some who hadn't moved away, then? It seems like it's a rite of passage now, to leave home as soon as possible. I don't know too many parents whose children stayed in one place." Albert patted my leg. "Except for Leslie, of course."

"Do you ever think about moving away, Leslie?" Mary chimed in.

"No." I glanced around for the owner.

"No? Not even as a thought?" Albert smoothed his napkin. "You know, I always thought maybe I'd move to Vermont. I knew a family with a cabin out there. They used to invite me up for grouse season. It's an interesting sport, although I might not be limber enough anymore."

"Yeah, Leslie," Mary said. "You could move to Vermont and shoot grouse."

I shook my head.

"What's your dream location, then?" she asked. "Where would Leslie go, if she could go anywhere?"

"I've never thought about it," I said. "Maybe I'd live in Santa Fe."

She laughed. "That's an hour away! That's the dinkiest dream move I've ever heard of."

A waitress appeared at her shoulder, holding the bottle of wine. She poured it for Albert first, then paused. Albert glanced at her, brow wrinkled, and then said, "Oh, I see. No, I'm sure it's fine, no need for all that," so the waitress moved on to Mary's glass.

"And where would you live, Robin?" Albert asked, when we had all placed our orders and the waitress had gone away again. "Would you stay in Las Vegas?"

"She'd go to LA," I said without meaning to.

Mary's eyes fixed on me. "Yes," she said to Albert. "I would. I love it there," she added, sinking back into her cheerful attitude. "It's always seventy-five degrees and everyone has a tan and a therapist. I'm going to buy a long scarf and drive around in a convertible, like Grace Kelly in *To Catch a Thief.*"

"A film buff! Do you like Hitchcock?"

"I hate Hitchcock. I love Grace Kelly," Mary said.

Albert laughed. "Hate Hitchcock? How?"

"His movies are all so slow, and all the people in them are like little cutouts in a dollhouse." She propped her chin on her hand.

"I think he'd say that's what he wanted from his films," Albert suggested. "He called actors cattle, you know."

"I knew it!" Mary declared. "You can just tell from watching those movies that Hitchcock was a big old dick."

"Ma—Robin!" I said.

"Well, he was."

Albert chuckled. "Robin isn't wrong. Tippi Hedren might agree with her. But of course you can be a real jerk and still make great art."

"Sure. But I think it creeps into your art. Art is intentionally show-ing your ass." Mary fiddled with the built-in ashtray, sticking her finger in it from the underside. "If you've got poison in you, the art will show it, eventually."

There was a pause as Albert pursed his lips, considering this. Fi-nally he said, "Well, I suppose every generation must hate the previ-ous generation. It's a measure of growth."

She smacked him gently on the arm. "Aw, Albert, we don't hate you! We just want you to tip your waitresses nicer."

The owner reappeared, followed by the waitress from before, bearing mustard-yellow plates with salmon covered in sliced lemons and parsley for Albert and Mary, and a Cobb salad for me.

"You know," Albert said, pointing his fork at Mary, "you remind me of your father."

I made a little noise, like a sneeze. Mary kicked me harshly under the table and I exhaled in surprise.

"Thank you," she said at the same time. "Wow, that really means a lot. Is it my chin? I feel like he had a really distinctive chin."

Albert pulled his fork out of his mouth; I heard the tines against his teeth. "Not that. Your sense of humor. He was a funny man."

"No, he wasn't," I said, jerking my chair back several inches to avoid Mary's shoe. Robbed of a target, she was forced by momen-tum down into her seat, as if several vertebrae had liquefied. Then she had to drag herself back up again, pretending nonchalance.

"You don't think so?" Albert squinted at me. "I guess not so much when he was sick. But before that, he was like Robin. Quick, you know."

"What a compliment," Mary said, adjusting the top of her dress, which had lost its grip during her abrupt descent into her chair. "I really appreciate hearing that from someone who knew him so well."

"He wasn't like that," I said. "Not with us. Not at home."

Mary glared at me; Albert patted his mouth with a napkin. "I'm sorry to hear that," Albert said at last. "It's too bad you only had so many years with him when he was well. I knew him for almost thirty years. We were very good friends, your dad and I."

I didn't reply.

"Tell me more about him," Mary said, leaning toward Albert. "How did you meet him?"

"How did I meet him?" He took a sip of his wine and coughed. "Actually, we were coworkers. At Hogarth and Wyeth."

"When was that?"

"The late seventies, I think. I hated him at first—he stole my girl."

"He didn't!"

Albert shook his head. "Of course he did. You knew him. He was competitive. I was dating one of the secretaries. A nice girl—a little meek, I thought. Well, not too meek, because she two-timed us for a while. All at the same office! We were in meetings together and we didn't know about it. She let slip to him eventually, or he got it out of her that she was seeing other men, and she came to me one evening and said, 'Warren told me that I must choose between you two, and I'm afraid our time together has come to an end.' So formal. So I didn't like him very much for a little while. But I figured I couldn't hold a grudge, because the guy married her. I certainly hadn't had any intention of marrying her. I thought, Good on her!"

"Wait, when did he marry her?" Mary asked. "That wasn't how he met Mom."

"No, this was Yvonne. They were together for five years or so, and then they got divorced. I don't know what it was all about, exactly. He never liked to talk of it. But my personal thinking is that it was about you two."

"But we didn't exist," I said.

Albert took another bite of fish and said through it, "He wanted children. I think that's part of why he married Yvonne. She was very young when they married, twenty-one or so. But they never had any. I didn't ask, but . . ." He shrugged. "Five years seems about right. You can't try much harder than that."

I stared at my plate. I hadn't eaten any of my salad.

I felt Mary's eyes on me. "Did you know?" she asked. "About Yvonne?"

I shook my head.

I'd spent years with him in that house as he died. I was the only person who'd stuck around—the only one who'd showed up for him. Illness had given us time together that we'd never had before, long stretches of boredom that invited conversation. One night *Rocky* was on TV. He'd muted it, looked over at me—said, *I should have married someone like you, Leslie. I was in love with your mother, but she was too fragile. I should have seen that. Should've looked for someone with a spine.*

But he'd looked before. It wasn't just Christine who had failed him. Yvonne had failed too.

Why hadn't he told me that?

Albert and Mary had gone back to eating while I'd been lost in thought. They were almost done, wearing identical expressions of polite regret: how sad your father never told you, but you can't change the past, what's done is done, etc. I picked up my wineglass and set it back down again.

"Why didn't he just leave everything to me?" I felt weightless again, as I had this morning. My ears ached.

Mary swallowed quickly and said, "Let's talk about that some other time. Leslie, will you come to the bathroom with me?"

Albert wouldn't look at me.

"I was the one who was there. She ran away." I watched the top of his head as he examined the edge of the table. "Why would he put this clause in there, that we had to be here together to receive the money? Why wouldn't he just leave it all to me?"

Albert sighed and put down his fork. "It's not an unusual situation for a decedent to leave his estate in the hands of his attorney, rather than burden a family member with the role of executor. You have a baby, a full-time job . . . it was a good thing he did, not to put this all on your shoulders."

"That's not what I asked." My tongue felt swollen. "Why did we both have to be here? Why not just mail her the check and be done with it?"

Mary put her hand over mine. I felt her fingernails dig into my palm. "He was sick, Leslie."

"I know he was sick." I jerked my hand away and sat on it, flexing my fingers uncomfortably beneath my thigh. "I took care of him. He could barely eat. He could barely move or speak. He slept all the time. It spread to his lungs. He coughed up solids. I cleaned it out of the carpet. I helped him go to the bathroom and shower and brush his teeth. So . . ." I turned to Albert. "So I am just . . . just *asking* you. Why did he want her here now?"

His mouth trembled, and I thought he was close to giving me a real answer. Then, on the other side of me, I heard Mary say, "Thank God you're here," laughingly, and the waitress leaned over the table to take our plates, breaking the spell.

"Are you sure you're finished?" the waitress asked me, glancing down at my barely disturbed plate.

I sat back in my chair and closed my eyes. After a second, I felt her take the plate away.

"I'm very sorry for your loss," Albert said to me, touching my shoulder. "I really am. The truth is, I think Warren wanted you girls to spend some time together after so long apart. That's all it was. Of course he trusted you and loved you both. Of course he did."

I opened my eyes. Albert looked smaller, sitting there in his crumpled button-down, the collar gaping at his neck. Like my father's shirts had, near the end.

Mary smiled at him. "Thank you so much for saying that. You have no idea how much that means, coming from such a close friend of his."

Albert cleared his throat. "What a nice meal that was. I haven't been here in a long while. I need to start coming back more often." He patted his belly. "Well, all right. I suppose you've got to get home."

"It's past Eli's bedtime," Mary said. "If you want any time with him, Leslie, we do need to start getting ready."

I stared back at her. She was still perfectly cheerful. Her lipstick was fresh, and there was a faint red stain on one of her front teeth. Had she put on a fresh coat just now? When?

Albert leaned down and shuffled through the papers in his brief-case. "Aha! Well, here we go. You were in luck after all. The county notified us of receipt in time, and Angela made out your checks this afternoon." He pulled out two envelopes, each stamped with the GRUNDMAN, JAMES & RODRIGUEZ letterhead. On the other side, his as-sistant had written our names in blue bubble letters: *Leslie Flores* and *Robin Voigt.*

I exhaled.

Albert pushed the envelopes across the table toward us. "Oh, here's the check," he said, turning his attention away immediately. "I didn't even see it arrive." He took out his wallet.

"Oh, no, we should pay," Mary said. "We invited you. Leslie?"

"Yes," I said after a moment. "Sorry. Yes." I fumbled in my purse and found my credit card; Albert sat back and folded his knobby hands as I tucked it into the bill.

"So that's it, right?" Mary added as the waitress came back to take the bill. "We don't need to do anything else?"

Albert patted her arm. "We're all finished. Thank you, dear. And thank you for dinner, Leslie."

I picked the envelope up off the table and stared at my name on the front. It was sealed. I slid my thumb under the flap.

"Well, don't open it now, honey!" Mary exclaimed.

But I'd torn the flap open far enough that I could see it: PAY TO THE ORDER OF LESLIE VOIGT FLORES. FIFTY THOUSAND DOLLARS AND ZERO CENTS.

There it was: the finish line.

46

Mary

Leslie started the car. I held my check on my lap, between my thighs, running the sharp edge under my fingernail. The ragged flap of her own check stuck out of the top of her purse. "We can't go to the bank until tomorrow morning," I said.

"You've got your passport," she answered distractedly. "We shouldn't go together. Have I given you Robin's Social Security number?"

I looked at her long, sharp profile. "I did good, right? I did Robin right?"

The light turned red, and Leslie slowed to a stop. "Yeah," she said, glancing over at me. "You were perfect."

I grinned. The seconds ticked by, the car so quiet that we could hear the muffled sounds of someone else's music from the next lane.

The light turned green. It took Leslie a moment to press the gas. "Hey," she said. "Do you want to go somewhere?"

"Like where?" I tugged on the top of my dress.

"It's a surprise." Leslie reached a long stretch of avenue and sped up. Her features flickered in the intermittent light from streetlamps and passing cars, the shadows of her nose and brow slipping over her face like liquid.

I bit my lip.

"You're leaving in the morning," she said. "So tonight's the last night for us."

I thought about Dave on the lawn chair, timing Eli in the three-meter dash. "You don't want to go home?" I said.

Leslie shook her head, but she kept going east, toward the mountains. I shifted in my seat when we passed the sign for her neighborhood, its silver metal lettering gleaming. "I just have to stop to get something," she said at last, pulling into her own driveway. She didn't turn the car off. The headlights against the closed garage door created a stagelike effect; Leslie's shadow was enormous in the spotlight, moving silently beside her as she crossed the driveway and disappeared into the dark.

I slumped into the passenger seat and waited for her. The sound of my own breaths seemed to gain volume.

A tap on the window startled me. Leslie was just outside, her face flushed. I opened the passenger door an inch. "Turn off the car," Leslie whispered.

I crawled across the console and pulled the keys out of the ignition, shutting off the headlights. "I thought you just had to get something," I said when I was out of the car.

"Shh," Leslie said. "People are sleeping." I saw that she was holding a bottle of wine.

She saw me looking and the corner of her mouth lifted. Then she motioned for me to follow her. She didn't go back into the house; instead we set off down the sidewalk, past the dioramic windows of her neighbors.

I stopped in front of the third house, where long, thin windows clustered around a breakfast nook. The family sat at the table with plastic cups, a longer, more formal table abandoned in the dimmer room beside them. I watched as the little girl leaned down to confer with the dog. "See, it's not even that late," I said. "They're not sleeping."

Leslie, ahead of me, kept walking.

I followed her around a corner to a cul-de-sac, where the house on the left was half-hidden by an enormous six-foot fence. The gate was chained shut, and a plastic lock with a keypad hung from the chain. Leslie crunched over the landscaping to the lock and pressed the keys quickly. The chain came free and the gate swung open. Leslie glanced over her shoulder. Something behind the fence lit her face with an eerie greenish glow. "You ready?" she whispered. Then she disappeared into a stranger's yard.

I glanced around the empty street behind us. Wind swept across the ground, rattling the dry-leaved bushes like chandeliers.

Then I stepped through the gate, the chain clanking as I closed it behind me.

"Oh—" I began, and Leslie clamped a hand over my mouth. I started to laugh behind her palm.

"Shh," she said. "We're not supposed to be here."

It was a swimming pool, taking up almost the entire length of the yard. Lights were set into the sides of the pool where shallow steps led into the water, sending a wavering glow over the dark perimeter. A wooden deck near the house held a wrought-iron table and two chairs, the bistro umbrella that shaded them during the day flapping wildly in the sudden wind. The surface of the pool rippled.

Leslie took her hand away. "You got lipstick on me," she said, studying her palm.

"Are we breaking in right now?"

She wiped her hand against her arm and carried the bottle of wine over to the table. "Not exactly."

"Not exactly?" I raised my eyebrows, trailing after her.

"Dave knows the homeowner," Leslie said, pulling out a chair as soundlessly as possible. The wind had pulled strands of hair from her bun, which lifted in unison around her face as she sat and pulled the cork out of the lip of the bottle. "She rents this place out for Airbnb, which is against the neighborhood bylaws, but Dave agreed to let people in and out occasionally in exchange for her letting him use the pool when the place is unoccupied in the summer." Leslie shrugged and took a sip directly from the bottle. "I don't think any-one's here right now, but let's not draw attention."

I sat down beside her. "Do you come here by yourself?"

"No." Leslie passed me the bottle, and eyed me as I tipped it back. "You know, I hadn't had a drink in more than a year before I met you in Vegas."

"Why not?" I said, feeling my accent start to come back with the wine.

She shook her head. "I don't know. I could have. I couldn't— I didn't breastfeed, so. I didn't produce enough—enough milk? So we gave him formula." She took the bottle back and picked at the label. "I could have gotten drunk anytime after he was born, but I didn't."

"Well, Vegas is the best place to break your sobriety," I said.

She smiled. "Maybe." She looked out across the pool. "Thanks for coming out here with me."

"To the pool? Or to New Mexico?"

"Both," she said, lifting the bottle again. "It's funny," she went on, once she'd finished swigging. "I feel like I'm going to miss you."

"Aw, Leslie—" I said.

She laughed, stifling herself, and pushed the wine bottle across the table at me. "Isn't that crazy? I don't even know you. Not really." She put her hands in her lap. "Tell me something about you. Since you're leaving tomorrow."

I thought about it. "I'll trade you. One for one. Since I'm leaving tomorrow."

Leslie snorted. "You're so mercenary."

I picked up the wine bottle and winked at her. "AMA."

She pulled her knees up to her chest. There was a long silence; someone's dog barked over and over somewhere down the street. Finally she lifted her head. "Where do you go during the day?"

My fingers twitched toward my hip, but I hadn't brought my purse. No cigarettes. I took a deep chlorine-scented breath instead. "I met somebody. A police officer. We've been sleeping together. That's what I've been doing when I leave the house."

Leslie's mouth fell open. "A police officer? While we're—while this—" She twisted in her chair. "Why would you do that?"

I handed her the bottle. "I don't know. It was fun. I didn't have anything to do during the day. You left me while you went to work."

"I had to go to work," Leslie hissed.

I nodded. "I know."

I waited while she took another swig. Finally, her cheeks darker in the green light, she said, "He's not suspicious, is he? I mean, does he think he's sleeping with Mary or with Robin?"

"She doesn't know anything," I said. "She's more worried I'm going to tell her wife."

"Her wife?" Leslie set the bottle down hard enough that it made a sloshing noise. "I just— Mary, I just— It's too dangerous. You have to stop."

"I am stopping," I said. "I'm leaving tomorrow. I'll ditch my phone. She'll never hear from me again."

"Oh." Leslie paused and sat back. She frowned. "Did you really like her, this, um, woman?"

A breeze stirred my hair. I pushed it over one shoulder. "I don't know." I thought about making Paul tell me he loved me again and again. As if repetition would make it true. Nancy only had to look at me for me to know what she felt. It had satisfied something bone-deep in me to be looked at that way.

Leslie sighed and watched a ripple drift over the surface of the pool. "It's too cold to swim. I wish we could get in."

I took another long slug from the wine. "This is pretty good," I told her. "Dave has good taste." I slipped one foot out of its shoe and nudged her in the thigh with my toes. "Okay. Your turn."

She shut her eyes. "I'm not telling you about why I need the money. I can't."

I touched her again with my foot. "I know. I'll ask something else."

She hunched forward. "Okay. What do you want to know?"

"What were you thinking about, on the bed earlier?"

I saw her shoulders tighten. "My mom. Christine." She twitched, like a shrug. "I never thought much about her until I had the baby. I keep thinking what it must have been like for her. Getting pregnant right away. Getting married. I guess that's why he married her. She wasn't like the other one. Yvonne."

I sipped from the bottle and handed it back to her. "Do you think they were in love, though?"

She leaned from side to side, bending her elbows, like a full-body weighing of the scales. "I used to think so. Now . . . Maybe it was because of us. He thought he should have kids. He was so much older than her. And she'd never been in a relationship with anybody else. When I was a little girl I thought that was so romantic. Like they'd been waiting years and years for each other."

"Let's go down to the water," I said. "Let's put our feet in, at least."

Leslie looked over her shoulder and picked up the bottle. "All right."

I stood up, my head a little lighter than it had been, and took off my heels. Leslie slipped her shoes off too, and the deck creaked under our bare feet as we left it to sit on the concrete next to the pool steps. "This is going to make my dress get those, like, little pills," I said. "I can feel it already. It's like I'm sitting on Velcro."

"Just on your rear end," Leslie said, craning her neck to look at it. "You can shave those off, you know. With a razor."

"I'd rather throw this dress away than have to shave its ass."

Her cheeks bulged as she tried to swallow her wine while she laughed.

I stuck my feet in the pool and had to bite my own arm to keep from shrieking. "Oh, fuck, that's cold," I whispered, sliding backward and ruining my dress for good.

"It's May," Leslie said. "What did you expect?"

"It's the desert! It was hot yesterday."

She stretched her own legs out, skimming the water with the soles of her feet. "It's not that bad. You're a wimp."

I crossed my legs and put the wine bottle in my lap, watching her profile. "Tell me more stuff about your mom."

"Why do you care?"

"Because you don't like to talk about her. Feels like a secret."

Leslie shook her head and hunched her shoulders. "There's no secret. She was my mom. She was tiny, like five two. She got a perm when I was ten or so. She liked music and cooking. She taught me how to make apricot pie and coq au vin. She could swim. I remember she smoked Gauloises because it was cool when she was a kid in the seventies, to be the kind of girl who smoked French cigarettes. She wouldn't let me wear any eye shadow and I hated that. She was gone a lot, though, and I wore it whenever she was gone because Daddy couldn't tell that I had it on. And then she died. And so I don't like talking about her. It makes me uncomfortable."

"Why was she gone a lot?"

Leslie took the bottle from my lap and tipped it back again. At last she said, "I guess it doesn't matter to tell you. Daddy didn't want me to tell people, but he's dead now." She pulled her feet out of the water and crossed her legs, matching me. "She was in and out of hospitals. She was sad—depressed."

"How come?"

The wine bottle was empty; Leslie rested her head drunkenly on her own shoulder. "You know, I thought it was just me blaming myself for the longest time? Because kids always blame themselves? But I— After hearing Albert today, I really do think—it was me. I think it was because she didn't want me."

"What do you mean?"

Leslie sighed. "She got pregnant so fast, and he wanted the baby, and so they got married, but . . ." She shrugged. "I always felt like she didn't really like me. Like we were so distant from each other. And maybe it was true. Maybe she just . . . didn't want me." She shook her hands out. "Is that good? Is that enough? No more secrets?"

"Yeah," I said. "That's good. Thanks."

"You're welcome," she said, and took my hand, holding it in both of hers. "I hope you have a good life," she said, slurring a little. "I hope you make it as—as an actress. You're a good actress."

"You're drunk," I said.

"Am I?" She shook her head. As if prompted by her movement, a square of yellow light fell over both of us. We started, scrambling to our feet, the wine bottle rolling off Leslie's lap into the shallow end of the pool. "Fuck," she whispered. We both watched as it hit the bottom of the pool with a hard, sharp sound. Somehow, it didn't break. Leslie exhaled and turned around to look at the house. "Somebody's home," she said.

I could see a figure in a white T-shirt moving around in the upstairs bedroom. "I don't think they saw us," I whispered back. "Let's go."

She pointed at the pool. "We have to get that."

The wine bottle stared up at us from under the waves. "You first," I said.

Leslie's face was pink. "They'll see me if I get in."

I retrieved our shoes from under the bistro table. "Let's go," I said.

She followed me, and took her shoes from me blankly when I handed them to her. Above us, in the house, another person joined the first in the bathroom. "But they'll see it," she hissed. "In the morning. They'll know we were here."

The two people in the house shuffled out of the bathroom, and the light shut off again. The pool lost its yellow square. I looked at Leslie, and she looked back, and then I watched her burst into silent laughter. She took my hand and we ducked through the gate together in the dark.

47

Robin

I roll over in bed and Nancy's there, long black hair, bangs cut sharply over her forehead. I'd forgotten she was in bed with me.

She stares up at my ceiling, at the only poster I have that isn't a face. Another Courbet. "I can't believe your dad let you put that up."

"He never looks up." I inch over to tilt my head next to hers, so our ears are pressed together, seashell to seashell. "It's great, right?"

"It's gross."

"Beautiful and gross and beautiful." I grab her shoulders and wrestle her under the comforter. "Don't you love it?"

"You're disgusting," she mumbles into my thigh.

I twist my fingers in her hair, enjoying feeling like I could suffocate her in me. "You're breathing in."

She struggles, and I press back for a second, just to fuck with her. I feel her throat move against my leg, about to make too loud a noise, and so I let her up. "Why did you do that?" she whispers when she's out from under the comforter.

She's red-faced, stiff with irritation. "I don't know," I say. "Don't be cross." I've started saying *cross* now instead of *mad*. That's what Bette Davis says in *Jezebel*.

Nancy's quiet for a minute. "Are you really running away?" she says finally. "I'll miss you," she adds, when I don't answer.

She's a child.

"Soon," I say. "After that I'm never coming back."

"Why?" She rolls toward me, tucking her face into my neck. "I want you to stay."

"Because I want to be a ghost," I say, eyes wide, staring at the ceiling. "Ghosts never get old. Everybody remembers them exactly as they were." I stroke her dark hair. "Like you. You'll remember me forever, won't you, Nancy?"

She doesn't reply. I feel her chest rising and falling against mine.

"Nancy?"

48

Mary

I woke up with a start.

The room was full of light, but Leslie's voice was still in my ears, muffled through the door.

What was she saying?

"I love you—I love you."

To Dave. I twisted to look at the bedside clock—8:35.

Footsteps on the stairs, his and hers.

I levered myself out of bed and pulled the yellow dress down, stepping out of it. The strapless bodice had left wrinkled red lines across my chest. I found my leggings and jacket, and combed my hair with my fingers.

I heard the jingle of her keys. The front door shut. Leaning closer to the mirror, I studied my face. I'd slept in my makeup; there was a red pimple forming next to my nose. I wiped the black from under my eyes and left the rest as it was.

I opened the door to the guest room and stepped on something crumpled. ROBIN. Leslie had left me a note. I folded it twice more and put it in my pocket.

Out the back door, around the corner. I sat in my rented car at the stop sign, waiting for Leslie's car to cross the intersection. Dave's car was first, the Jeep. I watched as he disappeared around the corner, heading for the highway. Leslie's silver Honda arrived half a second later. I waited until the car behind her passed, then turned to follow.

She was speeding a little, not using her turn signal enough. I fell three and then four car lengths behind, and lost her halfway through downtown. Which bank did she use? I'd thought she was heading toward BOA. Yes—there was her car, a quarter mile ahead, turning in to the lot for the largest branch in the city.

I pulled in and sat in the car, slouching so that she wouldn't see my face. But she wasn't looking around. She walked quickly through the glass doors, clutching the envelope.

It took her nearly an hour to emerge. I decided to watch her car instead of the doors, so that I wouldn't miss her in the stream of people going in and out. At last she appeared again, divested of the check, carrying instead a thick manila envelope sealed with white-and-green tape. She was pale-cheeked, expressionless. I watched her start the car and glance over her shoulder as she backed out of her parking space.

She followed the main boulevard for a few miles, and then she turned east. Now I knew where we were going. I settled back into the driver's seat and angled the rearview mirror so that I could see my own face. I scraped flecks of mascara off my cheeks with a fingernail and reached into my duffel in the passenger seat, fishing until I found a tube of lipstick in the veladora.

The Honda turned onto Riviera. I coasted in its wake. The sun turned the dust on the windshield solid, striping the landscape with sepia. Familiar houses slid past, one after another, as if counting down to our arrival.

There it was: the painted gate. Leslie's tires crunched over the gravel in the driveway. I stopped a few houses down, pulling up against the empty curb.

I could only see the shape of her head beyond the headrest. She was still. Why wasn't she getting out?

I stared into my own eyes in the rearview mirror. I could start the car right now. Pull out, go to a different bank with my passport, sweat through the paperwork. I'd leave fifty thousand dollars richer, in a rented car on the way to LA. Wouldn't that be enough for me?

Leslie hadn't moved.

I shifted in my seat and felt the crackle of notebook paper in my pocket. Leslie's note. I drew it out and smoothed it against the steering wheel, careful not to press the horn. ROBIN, said the front. The rest was in Leslie's neat handwriting in black ink. The words were chosen deliberately, so that if Dave came across the note in the guest room, it wouldn't raise any alarm.

I'm heading out now. I didn't want
to wake you up to say goodbye.
I hope you find your way on your own.
I'm glad our time together is over.
I can't feel any other way.
But I'll think about you.
　　　　　　　　　—Leslie

At the bottom of the note was a string of numbers. Robin's Social Security number.

I looked up. Leslie's silhouette had disappeared from the Honda. The cracked teal gate hung open, drifting on its hinges.

I thought about what Clery had told me about what Leslie had hired him to do. About Dave on the porch, telling me he only went over to Elaine's house to buy weed, that he didn't want to worry Leslie, Leslie with the junkie sister who had died alone in her bedroom. Leslie who had taken care of her father by herself, nursing him into his decline. And the way Dave looked at her when she was turned away from him, how it had never occurred to him to be afraid of her. I thought about Leslie leaning into me last night, slurring into my face, *I hope you have a good life.*

I got out of my car, slammed the door, and headed toward the house on Riviera.

49

Leslie

The house was almost packed up, except for Robin's room. Before her death, I'd been putting it off; Daddy had kept it just the way it was, as if she'd return at any moment and want her things back. After, it was like I was afraid of it. I'd ditched her there, hollowed-out and ugly, a City of Las Vegas burial under someone else's name, and I'd brought back a stranger to stand in her place. If she knew, she'd be furious with me. So I left her room alone. A silent apology.

And now it was too late. I wouldn't have time to pack her things. Someone else—Dave, maybe—would be the one to put away her old belongings, clear the nail polish off the bureau, untack the posters from the walls.

I hung my purse on the hook by the door and went into Daddy's study. The blinds were down and it was dark. I walked to the secretary desk and searched through the keys on the ring. The little copper one. I slid it into the lock and it popped open.

The burner cell was inside, on top of the old mail and candy wrappers. I reached for it and froze as I heard the front door open.

Someone stepped inside.

My heart pounded. I had no weapon. I grabbed the phone and moved around the desk into the far corner of the study. Maybe whoever it was wouldn't see me in the shadow.

The manila envelope with the fifty thousand was still in my purse by the door. My eyes flicked toward the front hall. I couldn't go out to get it without giving myself away.

The house was silent. I couldn't hear the intruder anymore. Where were they?

I watched the doorway into the hall.

"Hi," said a figure from across the room.

I screamed.

Mary laughed, coming through the second door. "Aren't you happy to see me?"

I sat down heavily on the carpet, putting my forehead on my knees. "Why the fuck did you scare me like that?"

She shrugged. "I didn't mean to. What are you doing in here?"

"I thought you were leaving." I pushed my hair out of my face.

"I figured I'd stop by and see if you were smart enough to come back for the burner. Good for you. A lot of folks would have forgotten it after three months."

I held the phone to my chest. "What?"

She tilted her head at me. "Don't play possum. I know what you've got planned."

"I don't know what you're talking about." I held still, trying to read her face.

Mary walked over to me and flopped down on the carpet, cross-legged. "Sure you do, Leslie. Who's Frank Clery?"

My heart pounded so loudly I could hear it in my ears. I felt color flood my face. "I don't know."

She poked me in the side and I flinched. "Come on, give it up. Blue eyes, no chin, does that disgusting lizard thing with his tongue?" She imitated this, flicking her tongue out like a snake. "Nasty."

"I have to go," I heard myself say.

Mary shook her head a bit sadly. "No, you don't. You're staying right here until you tell me who Frank Clery is. Or if you want, we could wait for the burner to charge and I'll show you the texts you sent to him in February."

"What are you, a cop?" My voice was hoarse. "Are you going to call your married police officer friend, tell her what I did? What we did?"

Mary set her hand on my knee. I flinched away. "I don't want to hurt you, Leslie. I just want you to tell the truth for once. It costs you nothing."

"Why do you care?"

"Because I've been trying to figure out what you were up to since I saw you in Henderson," she said patiently.

"What I was up to?" I felt dizzy. "You mean in Vegas?"

"In a minute," she said. "First, Clery."

There was barely any light coming in through the blinds. There wouldn't be until noon. Mary's face blurred in front of me in the half dark, her features seeming to shape-shift.

"He's a pawnshop owner," I whispered.

She smiled and patted me on the leg. "What else is he?"

I swallowed. "He does things. For money."

"You have to be more specific." She leaned back on her palms.

"He kills people."

"Right." Mary observed me in silence for a second. "I thought at first maybe you'd hired him to kill Dave. But I was wrong, wasn't I?"

I felt the idea like a blow to the chest. "No! No, I'd never— I love Dave."

"You do, don't you? It took me a while to figure that out. You love him so much."

"Yeah." My mouth was dry.

"He's a good man. I tried real hard to find something on him, some reason you might want him dead. For a while I thought he was cheating on you."

"He . . ." I didn't finish.

"Oh, so you thought so too?" Mary nodded. "He sure did talk to Elaine a lot. And sent her quite a bit of money. Was that what made you think so?"

"Not just that." I bit my lip.

"Well, it turned out that wasn't it." She smiled. "Elaine's his dealer."

She phrased this carefully and with a kind of glee; I recognized that she thought it was some sort of bomb. But—"Dave doesn't do any drugs," I told her.

"Dave might as well not do any drugs." Mary snorted. "He smokes weed around the back of the house when you're in bed sometimes. And he buys it for his dad's back pain and his sister, who's too square to know any drug dealers."

"No . . ." I thought of Cadence saying *Dad needs a Dave visit,* and Teri's quelling look. They knew.

"He's terrified you'll find out about his little vice," Mary said, "on account of how your sister is a junkie. He begged me not to tell you."

I'd told him on our first date that I didn't tolerate drugs; that I'd never marry anybody who did. He'd promised to give it up. For me.

"He loves her," I said. "He lied to me, to go over there."

"To buy weed," Mary said. "He loves *you.*"

"She's better than me," I said, my voice cracking.

She laced her fingers together. "Well. After talking to Clery, talking to you . . . the picture's really coming together."

My mouth fell open.

She grinned. "Nice to have a, uh, what did you call it? A little married police officer friend? She took me down to county. Frank and I had a good chat while she got herself some coffee."

"You spoke to him?"

She rolled her eyes. "The fact that he talked to me at all is proof that you should have picked someone else. Even if he's the only dude who whacks people professionally in all of New Mexico, I mean, drive to Vegas. It's not that far and at least those guys'll go away for ten years before they say shit to a stranger. But I promised him a favor, and suddenly he was a big ol' chatterbox. Can you believe it?"

I didn't move.

Mary pushed her hair over one shoulder. "Anyway, you already know what he said. It wasn't Dave you wanted dead, was it?"

"No," I said quietly.

"No," she repeated. "It was you."

There it was. I felt the truth bore down on me.

"You didn't hire him to do anyone else. You hired him to do you."

I couldn't meet her eyes.

"So I thought about that for a while. It didn't sit right with me at first. You have this husband you're so in love with that you won't even leave him when you think he's cheating on you. You have a baby. You have that beautiful house. Neither of you were fired; in fact, you both have cushy office jobs where you get to use your master's degrees every single day. Was it that you were just so depressed that Daddy died that you wanted to follow him out? I batted that one around, but it didn't really stick for me. But clearly something was rotten, because you were *desperate* to shed the coil. I thought, what could it be? And then I realized—it wasn't Daddy. It was Mommy, wasn't it?"

"No," I said again. "It has nothing to do with her—I just wanted—"

"Nah," she said. "I think it does. I think you're just like her. How did she wind up in those hospitals over and over again? It wasn't just because she was depressed."

I couldn't speak.

"She tried to kill herself too," Mary said. "She tried more than once."

"I'm not like her," I bit out.

Mary giggled and sent up a cloud of dust as she clutched the bookshelf again for support. "You're right! I mean, that's the part that gets me the most. You hired a professional wetworker to *leave you alone*."

"What?"

"Well, he wasn't supposed to really kill you, right? He was supposed to smack you around, get a few blood spatters on the Honda, and take it for a joyride. Ditch it in one of the arroyos, am I right? Carjacking gone wrong. And then you're free to start your new life." She paused. "You *wanted* your husband to be in love with Elaine. You thought Eli would have a new mommy built right in. You thought you'd be Yvonne." Mary tilted her head. "Clery said all that cost you forty thousand dollars in cash. Must have taken you all year to get that much cash out of your accounts slowly enough that Dave wouldn't notice. No wonder you were so pissed when Clery got sent to prison."

"The pawnshop closed." I cleared my throat. "I didn't know what to do."

"It must have been horrible for you," Mary said sympathetically. "Now you had to start all over again. By the time I got to this point, I started thinking, wouldn't it have been easier just to off yourself and be done with it?"

I looked at my hands.

"Oh, so you thought about it," Mary said. "I figured. Why didn't you do it?"

It took a long time for me to say, "Dave."

Mary's voice warmed. "You didn't want to break his heart?" She paused. "That's the part I didn't understand, I guess. That's nice of you, Leslie. Okay, so you had one last light at the end of the tunnel. The estate was finally getting settled. That money was just your money, not Dave's. Maybe you didn't even tell him about it. You could use it to take off by yourself. Make it look like a carjacking, make sure Dave would never know you'd left him on *purpose*. But Daddy knew you a little bit better than you thought. He didn't trust you to give your sister her share. He left instructions to make sure Albert would hand the check to her in person. You were good. You tracked her down. You made it all the way to the house in Henderson. And then you made a mistake."

"You said you saw me in Henderson," I whispered. "How?"

"I lived there, silly," Mary told me.

My head was spinning. "What do you mean?"

"Rachel Vreeland was my roommate."

I stood up and stumbled away from her. "You mean Robin was your roommate."

"No, honey," Mary said. "Come on, step away from the door. You know what I'm saying." She paused. "I almost thought you saw me in the house, but you were out of there like a shot! Couldn't wait to leave your sister's body behind. Made you hungry, huh?"

"You followed me," I said. "To the restaurant. You were on my car when I came out. You were . . ." I twisted from side to side, but Mary was watching me. "You were waiting for me?"

"Of course," Mary said. "I thought I'd mess with you a little. I didn't expect you to buy it." She laughed. "Boy, did you ever buy it!"

"But the—the woman in the bed," I said. "They called me about a credit card. Under her name. Why would they call me if she wasn't . . ."

Mary waved her hand. "Rachel had rich parents. She could handle me opening a couple more credit cards for her. They wouldn't let me open any more under my other name, or even under Daddy's. So that's how you found me—the credit cards? No wonder Iker led you to the wrong room."

"The wrong room?" I echoed faintly.

"He led you to Rachel's room." She smiled. "Mine was down the hall."

50

Robin

Leslie pressed herself against the wall, breathing hard through her nose. "I don't understand," she said after a minute.

I rolled my eyes. "Don't you recognize me? I know it's been a while, but man. I expected you to know right away! I mean, Rachel kind of looked like me, but I was definitely the prettier one. Especially toward the end, when she got all twiggy. But that was my fault, I guess."

"Your fault?" Leslie was as white as the wall.

"It's a long story. My ex traded me in for the new model. So I made friends with her, introduced her to some new drugs, and fucked her life up a little bit." I blinked. "I guess it wasn't that long."

"That girl. Rachel. That was her. But . . ." Leslie seemed unfocused. "She had my mother's earrings. They were right there, in her room . . ."

"Mom's earrings? I thought I'd lost them until I saw them on you that day. You'd come out of Rachel's room, and then later you were wearing them in the parking lot, and I realized you'd lifted them right off her, just like she must've stolen them from me. She was always trying to find stuff to sell."

"Stole them. To sell them? For . . ."

I shrugged. "I really didn't think a little heroin was going to end up killing her. I just wanted to fuck her up some, you know? I *liked* that guy." I stopped and looked at her. "You know, Paul. I told you about him. His brother knew James Cameron. He was going to help me with my career. But then he met Rachel. She looked just like me, but she was twenty-two."

"So you punished her," Leslie said.

"No," I said patiently. "I punished *Paul*. I followed her around a little at first—just wanted to know what she was like. Why she was better than me. He'd thrown me away for nothing, so I thought I'd show him so. I told her I was new in town, asked her to be my friend, introduced her to her new favorite pastime. I wanted to know how come he fell in love with her, you know? *I* wanted to fall in love with her. But the more I got to know her the more I knew it wasn't the same between them. I listened to her talk about Paul, how he was getting more distant, and I knew he was almost done with her. She stopped looking good. She stopped eating anything. It happened so fast. When she kicked it, I wanted to be the first one to tell him the news. I thought now that she was out of the way . . . But there he was with some new girl already. He called the cops on me, can you believe it? That cop Sam, he's been following me around for months." I did my best impression of Sam's nerdy cop growl. " 'Give me all your cash, baby. Otherwise I'll take you in for stalking.' I wasn't even stalking Paul, no matter what he told the police. Talking to your ex isn't stalking." I sighed. "At least I got to key Sam's car on my way out. He deserved way worse."

"You killed her," Leslie said.

"I did not!" I said, slapping the carpet. "She did that to herself. I told her exactly what was safe to take. Well, I told her a little more than that, but she *way* overdid it. That is not my fault." I shook my head. "To be honest, I was just as surprised as you when I came home and heard Iker calling your name. I was barely in my room before I saw you peeling out of there like you thought the police were on your tail, and then Iker comes up the stairs, like *Becca,*

Becca—that's the name I gave the housing people—*Becca, Becca, did you know your roommate is dead,* and I thought, Oh, Leslie saw Rachel, that's why she's freaking out—"

"So you followed me."

I threw up my hands. "What else was I gonna do? I hadn't seen you in a decade, and finally you decide to visit me, and you take off before I even get home! I waited for you outside George's to say hi and you didn't even recognize me. You were all, 'Get off my car,' like, immediately."

Leslie drew in a deep breath. "You said your name was Mary."

"It was the least *me* name I could think of. I thought you'd call me out right away." I wrinkled my nose. "Now I wish I'd picked a better name. I mean, do I look like a Mary?" I glanced down at my body. "I really don't think so. It kind of bothers me that you bought it."

"Why didn't you tell me?"

It was the loudest she'd been since I'd walked in and scared her. I winced. "Because you were acting like a crazy person," I said honestly. "I mean, first you don't even recognize me. Then you tell me I'm *dead*. I'm obviously offended that you thought bag-of-bones Rachel was me. Then you say I owe you money. Um, I don't owe you shit! By that point I had no idea what you were talking about, and to be real with you for a second, I was mad about you leaving fake-me for dead and bouncing to find crab cakes at four in the afternoon. So I was just going to wait for you to figure it out, then lay down the guilt trip you completely deserved. But . . ." I took a deep breath. "Then you ask me if I want to impersonate Robin Voigt to the tune of fifty thousand dollars. Do I! I did think about that one for half a second because it seemed to me that you had lost some mental stability in the last ten years and I wasn't sure it was a great idea to poke the bear. But Sam was all over my ass, and after all, *it's my money*—I mean, I'd have gotten it regardless, but how much more fun was it to pretend I was stealing it, huh?"

"But your hair," Leslie said hoarsely. "Your nose . . ."

I felt my face. "Oh. Does it look that different? I got my nose fixed years and years ago. Fixed my teeth too, better skincare . . . it's necessary in the business." I dropped my hand. "You should get yours done too. I can give you the name of the lady who did it."

"No, thank you." Leslie was stiff.

"Whatever." I thought back. "Oh, and the hair. The hair was dye. I knew I'd look cute as a redhead, but blond is ultimately my calling. I always go back."

"I'm going to fucking kill you," Leslie said. Her voice was gravelly.

I let my gaze go flat. "No. You're not."

She shrank back against the wall. "You're a sociopath."

"I'm *fun*," I corrected her. "I had a good time road-tripping with you to Burque. I kept feeling like any minute you'd figure it out, but you never did. You're not that observant, I guess. Or maybe some part of you really wanted me to be dead, enough that you'd ignore what was right in front of you."

Her nostrils flared.

"Ha!" I pointed at her. "That's it! You did want me to be dead! Even though it complicated everything for you! That's fucked up, you know. That's not being a very good sister."

"I *wish* you were dead," she said. "I wish I'd never met you."

"That hurts," I told her. "That's a mean thing to say to someone who helped you pretend to steal fifty thousand dollars. These were incredibly high imaginary stakes for me, you know. I could have pretend gone to prison."

She licked her lips. "What happened to her," she said at last. "Rachel. Did they bury her?"

I frowned. "How should I know? I'm sure someone called her fancy family in Kansas. Don't change the subject. We were talking about you, and the most inept attempt at faking a carjacking there ever was."

Leslie headed for the door, and I cut her off, slamming it closed. "No."

She stared at me, then lunged for the other door. I grabbed her wrist and wrestled her arms behind her back. She brought her foot down on my arch, hard. "Ow, sheesh," I exclaimed.

"Let me go!"

I wrenched her arms closer together and she hurled us both to the carpet. I hit my elbow against the leg of the desk and yelped. "Just hold still!"

Leslie bit me.

"Fuck!" I grabbed her by the hair, sat on her chest, and pinned her arms with my knees. "I just want to know why," I said, panting. "Sheesh, Leslie!"

She spat at me, but it fell down into her hair.

"This is embarrassing for you," I told her.

Leslie writhed for a few seconds longer. At last she went limp. I didn't let go; I wasn't stupid.

"Okay," I said. "So now tell me why you decided to erase yourself."

She stared past me, up at the ceiling. I waited.

"Fine," I said at last. "I'll guess. But you won't like my guess. Here it is: I think you and Mommy had something else in common besides your attractive tendency toward morbidity. It was something you said last night, actually, that helped me put the final piece in place. Do you remember what it was?"

Leslie barely blinked. She looked washed out, frozen.

I leaned in. "You said, *She didn't want us.*" I sniffed. "Well, actually what you said was she didn't want you. But I assumed you were just forgetting about my existence again. It's so easy for you to do that."

Leslie's eyelids fluttered. She'd started to cry, silently, without moving.

"And that revelation came to you not when we were children and she avoided our presence, hated our voices, shut herself in the bathroom over and over—it was after you had your own baby. What's his name again?"

Leslie's throat moved as she swallowed. After a minute, she said, "Eli."

"Eli. That's right. You and Christine, you got yourselves tangled up so quickly. You met Dave and thought your life was fixed. Except he wanted something from you. He wanted a kid. And *you* wanted to give him anything he wanted. So you had the baby. And things with Mom were so long ago. You barely remember her. You didn't

think you were much like her at all. But then you had Eli, and . . ." I
waited for her to finish the sentence, but she only cried some more.
"You didn't love him. Am I right?"

Leslie couldn't answer me. Snot blocked her nose.

"I bet you felt really guilty. I bet you felt just like Mommy. You
tried for a whole year. But you hated being a mother. And so you
wanted to quit."

Leslie squeezed her eyes shut.

"But you can't just quit motherhood, can you?" I sat back on my
heels and ticked off the options on my fingers. "There's divorce and
refusing custody. But then Dave would have hated you, and you
couldn't handle watching your perfect husband see that you were
not the perfect wife. Plus, there's that annoying child support! So,
suicide. But then you'd be just like Christine. That's so embarrassing!" I clutched my cheeks. "And Dave would totally tell on you.
Not like Daddy, sweeping it under the rug. He'd ask for support
from his family members, like a loony. Then there's option three—
you could smother Eli and blame SIDS."

Leslie gasped.

"Aw, see, too scared for that. You don't like to get involved with
the police. Unlike me." I winked. "So you fell on option four. You
decided to run away."

Leslie twisted out from under me. I let her go. She fell against the
bookcase, wiping her nose on her cardigan, leaving long runny
tracks on the cotton.

"What I don't get," I said at last, "is what your plan was this time
around. Without Frank, you couldn't make it look like a real carjacking. What, you were just going to ditch the car and buy a cash
plane ticket?"

Leslie shrugged.

I laughed. "Wait, was that really your plan?"

"I don't know," she said through cracked lips. "I just thought
I'd . . . get out somehow. Leave." She coughed. "I put extra money
in Eli's college fund. Before Clery. For when I was gone."

"You didn't think Dave would look for you?"

She shook her head. "He's in love with Elaine. She's a good

mother. He'd have . . . what he really wanted. And then he wouldn't know that I . . . He wouldn't have to hate me. He wouldn't have to know that I wanted to go. Because if he knew, he'd want to fix it, and I can't fix it." She spread her hands. "I *am* like her. Like Christine. I shouldn't have had a baby at all. I should have known there was something wrong with me. If Dave knew, he would have to think about it every—every time he looked at Eli, every time he thought about me. It would make him sick."

"He loves you," I said. "I watched him. I saw. You found the real thing."

Leslie looked away. There was a long pause. "Did she really kill herself?" she asked finally, staring at the carpet.

"Who? Mom? Of course not," I said, climbing off her and running my hands over my jeans. "She found option five, thanks to you."

"What's option five?"

"I am." I smiled. "I helped."

51

Leslie

"Helped . . . what?" I heard my own voice in my skull.

"You know," Robin said. "Helped her get out. Helped her shuffle off this mortal whatever."

"You're lying," I said. I was shaking. "You're messing with me again. Stop—stop it—"

Robin gave a little shriek of frustration and rolled around on the floor. "Oh my *God*," she moaned into the carpet, slightly muffled. "I thought you were over this by now." She sat up and glared at me. It was nearing noon and the study had been slowly brightening as we spoke. Little flyaway hairs glowed around her head. "You did this all through our teens and it really fucked with my head, you know, Leslie."

She said my name exactly the way she'd said it when we were kids, with that condescending lilt. Like she'd said it on the phone message the night of my wedding. *I love you. I love you, Leslie—*

"You blocked it!" she yelled at me now. "You just . . . *blocked* it out of your head, like it never happened! Well, it did happen, and it was your idea."

My stomach lurched. I got up, clutching my belly.

"Sit down!" Robin snapped.

"I have to—" I gasped. "I'm going to—" I ran into the back hall and flung open the door to the bathroom.

I was dry-heaving over the toilet when Robin came in. She sat on the edge of the tub, next to me. "You haven't eaten anything today," she said after a minute of listening to me choke. "You should probably give up on that."

"I can't stop." But as soon as I said it, the nausea subsided. I sat back on the bath mat.

"See?" Robin said smugly. "Now are you going to listen to me?"

"I don't understand anything you're saying," I whispered.

"I know you remember," Robin said. "You just didn't want to believe it. But it was your fault all along. I was only a kid. I followed you around. I practically worshipped you. And you said to me—"

" 'I wish Mom would die.' " I stared at her.

She nodded. "Exactly. That's what you said to me. I just wanted you to be happy."

"I was so tired," I said. It was coming back in bits and pieces. "I was angry that she wanted to leave us so bad. She kept trying to . . . to leave us. And then Daddy would send her away, and she'd come back and hate us some more—so I wanted . . . I just wanted it to be over . . ." I focused my eyes again. "But you couldn't have done it. You were only a kid."

Robin snorted. "Mom weighed like eighty-five pounds, she was depressed, and they'd put her on downers. She was barely there. I found her half passed out in the bathtub, and I just . . . held her under."

"No," I whispered.

"Yes," Robin whispered back. She laughed. "It wasn't hard. She wanted to go. She didn't fight me or anything."

"I can't," I said. "I can't believe you."

"Well, I can't believe you!" Robin snapped. "When I told you about it, you said I was lying! *I wasn't lying!*"

I stared at her. She was bright against the white of the tub, roundly healthy, pink-cheeked. Beautiful.

She couldn't have killed anyone. She didn't have it in her.

No . . .

The nausea returned.

I'd known for a long time what it was that lived in her.

"I did it because I loved you, Leslie," Robin said, wringing her hands. "I didn't think it would make you hate me. I was just a kid. I didn't know how your brain worked."

Like it was me that was crazy.

"But you did." Her brow wrinkled prettily. She really looked hurt. "You never looked at me the same after that. You acted like I was some kind of monster."

Had I?

I'd spent so much time flattening the memory that now it was fractured. I didn't know whether I'd pushed Robin away. But it was true that before my mother died, we'd done everything together. Spent all our time together.

After my mother died, we slept in separate bedrooms.

I'd always thought it was Robin who'd never liked me, who'd kept her distance. *When I was in middle school she got her own room*, I'd told Mary. *Suddenly she hated me.*

She'd hated me, so I'd hated her back.

No.

She'd loved me, in her own disgusting, sharp-toothed way. And I'd abandoned her. Shut her in the guest bedroom to sleep by herself.

I didn't hate her because she was a monster. She was a monster because I hated her. I'd made her this way, made sure she grew up alone and angry.

I lifted my gaze. There she was. Beautiful, horrible. Alive.

My mouth watered and I spat into the toilet over and over until the bile lurched its way up my throat.

"Now you remember," Robin said, over the sound of my vomiting. "I knew you'd get there eventually."

52

Leslie

When she went to Lakeview the first time, my grandmother came to stay with Robin and me in the house on Riviera. Not my mother's mother—as far as I knew, we didn't speak to her. It was my dad's mother, Grandma Betty. She stayed for months, washing dishes and smoking at the kitchen table. I remember she still wore gloves to go to church, like it was the 1950s. My father joked to her once that you can tell how many generations a family is removed from poverty by how decked out its women get when they go visit God. The more accessories, the newer the money. Betty had frozen him out for the rest of the day. When I was eleven, after Betty's funeral, Daddy told me Betty's parents had been sharecroppers.

That first visit, she treated us like small dogs, letting us in and out of the house whenever we asked and feeding us promptly but otherwise ignoring us unless we made a lot of noise. The kitchen was hers for cooking and reading magazines and having her friends over, and we held almost zero interest. This wasn't especially dissimilar to how our mother treated us when she was home, but for some reason, maybe other kids at school, I had got it in my head that grandmothers should dote on their grandchildren and spoil them and kiss their cheeks, and I was offended that Grandma Betty didn't do any of that. Well, she insisted we kiss *her* cheek every night before bed, and if we made faces while we did it she told Daddy on us.

So it stuck in my head that the one time she treated us like people was the day that our mother was due to return from her sojourn away. She taught us to make snowflakes from sheets of construction paper. We made boxes full, pink and yellow, and when my parents came through the front door at last, we flung the snowflakes in the air like confetti, so that they clung to my mother's perm and the yellow bouquet in her arms, souvenirs of our devotion.

My mother went to Lakeview two more times, and by the third time Grandma Betty was dead and we didn't throw snowflakes anymore.

Robin was a long-legged eight years old, almost nine, when Christine returned. My dad was working all the time back then, sometimes sleeping at his office, and Grandma Betty had died the year before, so there was no one to take care of us. But the decade was different as well. A twelve-year-old was babysitting age; I was plenty old enough to care for Robin, who could ride a bike and make frozen dinners.

After that winter, Robin was not well liked by the nearby fourth-graders, so she spent all her time with me, something that was only now starting to grate on me. She was odd—watched old movies on TV and had recently started speaking in a fake mid-Atlantic accent and wearing clip-on paste earrings from the dollar store. When she wasn't imitating Barbara Stanwyck, she was imitating me. It was something little sisters were supposed to do, so it might have soothed me, but she was uncomfortably possessive in her love, crawling across the room and into my bed at night, sleeping clutched to my arm with her hand in my hair. I couldn't have my newest school friend, Diane Gomez, over without her listening in. We could see the white lumps of her sock-clad feet in the crack of space between the door and the carpet. Later, she'd make me list all the reasons I liked her better than Diane.

I did like her better than Diane, but I wanted space.

So that day I'd locked the door to our bedroom from the outside and gone into the backyard to lie on the tile with my shirt pulled up to my fleshy infant belly, trying to get an April tan before any of the other girls in class had one. Christine had been in the bathroom for three hours, taking one of her interminable baths, which I only later realized were influenced by the pills the hospital had given her. I'd been out there for an hour when I heard a cracking noise and saw Robin braced in the window, pushing up the painted-shut sill. "Leslie!" she called.

I twisted around to look at her. "You broke the window!"

"I did not." She was half out of the house, one thin insect leg hanging down.

"It was sealed!"

"It came up when I yanked." She tumbled out and brushed the dust off her denim skort. "I was tired of being in our room. Can I tan with you?"

"No," I said, but she ran over to my side and spread-eagled out next to me anyway, pulling her shirt up too. I sighed. "Is she still in the bathtub?"

There were three women in the house, but only one *she*.

Robin nodded. "I think she's gonna do it again," she added. "I mean, not today."

"I know what you mean." Christine had always looked through us, like Grandma Betty, but now it was like there was nobody looking at all. She had given up speaking. The second time she'd gone to Lakeview, Daddy had told us she was going to learn to toughen up, but she had come back just the same, if not worse: sleeping all the time, not answering the door. Going to the grocery store required hours of getting ready, and sometimes she'd decide it was too late to go by then, and we'd order a pizza and hide the box in our neighbors' trash can so Daddy wouldn't see it.

Was I angry at her? Yes and no. I had never really been able to put into words what it was like to grow up as we did. Robin was the only one who understood, and that day in the backyard was the last time we would ever really speak to each other for the rest of our childhood. What it came down to, I thought, was that other children had been taught to have an interiority. Their parents tried to befriend them, encouraged them in having preferences, even down to what foods they would and would not try, appealed to their reason when rules were flouted. In our house, no adults ever bothered to justify themselves to children; the idea had a hippie tinge to it. To Daddy, having been raised by Grandma Betty, children were not really people, only people-in-training. There was little to do with them but wait for them to become reasonable.

When no one discusses your feelings, it never really occurs to you that you might *have* feelings. I did have feelings, of course, but sitcom ones, learned from TV and *Are You There God?* and church once a year. For the most part these shallow affectations were sufficient for any situation a twelve-year-old from the suburbs could find herself in, but every once in a while something unidentifiable would pass just beneath my consciousness, like the shadow of some enormous sea creature under the tiny bobbing craft above.

I said, "I don't understand why she can't do it."

Robin was not really listening by this time, having gotten bored of tanning in the few minutes I'd spent lost in thought. She was crouched on the patio, upending her box of chalk. "Do you remember when it snowed?" she asked me.

"I wish she were already dead," I said contemplatively. "Right now, it's kind of like we're all just waiting and nobody's doing anything about it. And I never know what to say to people who ask, because Daddy doesn't want . . . you know, it'd be easier to say, 'She died.' At least people understand that."

Robin pursed her lips. She had no outward reaction to this speech. It was one of her greatest qualities as a kid sister: total unflappability. I appreciated that even as I recognized that she had lifted the pursed-lips expression directly from Agent Scully on *The X-Files*.

I tipped my head back, letting the sun turn my cheeks pink.

Robin scratched away on the tiles next to me. "You're getting sunburned," she told me after twenty minutes or so had passed.

I patted my face. "Really?"

But she was gone, back into the low darkness of the house. Toward my mother.

Did I know what she would do?

Yes and no. It was there, under the surface.

I rolled onto my belly to see the scene she'd drawn: pink-and-green snow falling onto a red adobe house. You could tell it was snow and not rain because there was a pink-and-green snowman beside the house. His arms originated from his ears, and he stood at least one snow-head higher than the two-dimensional roof. Robin had added a little speech bubble. The snowman was saying, I'M TANNING!

I laughed.

53

Robin

I brought Leslie a blanket. She sat at the kitchen table, all emptied out, orange at the corners of her mouth. "You loved me," she said at last.

"I *love* you," I corrected, hugging her around the blanket. She didn't react. "You're my sister," I added anyway.

Nausea passed over her features again, and she almost got up from the table. "I should have stopped you. I should have—"

"Should have." I made my fingers relax. "Her being here was killing us, Leslie. She wanted to die and Daddy couldn't let her, and it was making us *sick*. He never admitted it. You could barely say it. But you were relieved."

Leslie took this in. The kitchen was silent for several moments. "If I had stopped you, would you have stayed?"

"Stayed in Albuquerque?"

She nodded.

"If you had stopped me, you would have been lying to yourself. I like you better when you know what you want. I like you like this." I cocked my head. "Truthful."

"I hated her," Leslie mumbled. "It felt too big for my body. I pushed it out. I hated her for not wanting us. I hated her when she was there and did nothing, and I hated her when she was gone and I missed her. I was alone with you; I didn't know how to make you better. And then it was too late." Her hand rose, and I felt her fingers skimming my hair. "I'm sorry."

"I don't want you to be sorry." My throat felt raw, and I swallowed. "There's nothing to be sorry about."

She receded into her seat. Exhaustion lengthened her features. "Now you know. Everything. Eli. How I'm like her." She turned her face up at me. "Are you going to kill me?"

I coughed out a laugh, astounded. "Kill you? What are you talking about?"

"Like Christine." She was dull-eyed, exhausted. "I let him cry. When Dave isn't around, I—I can't stand it. I used to just go into another part of the house and let him scream. For hours." She blinked several times. "He's behind on his language skills, did you know that? Dave is worried about it . . . It's because I don't talk to him when Dave isn't around. I never told anyone that before. I don't . . . I don't say anything to him. I don't know what to say."

"Leslie, I don't want to kill you." I scooted my chair toward hers with a screech. "I want to help you."

"Help me?" She searched my face. "How?"

"You want to leave," I said. "So let's go."

"I can't." The clock ticked on the wall behind her. She shivered. "There's nothing I can do except stay. That man Frank is in jail. He can't help me. The whole thing was so stupid. I don't know why I can't—" She drew in a breath through her nose. "I mean, everyone does it. Everyone figures out how to be a mother. The whatever-it-is, it kicks in after a while. Maybe when he's three. I kept thinking that. I kept saying that to myself, but it didn't work, and I thought if I didn't do something about it one way or the other I would end up damaging the baby. Eli. That's how I met Frank . . . I went to the pawnshop to buy a gun. And he asked me what I wanted it for. And I couldn't say it was to kill myself, and I didn't even know if I could kill myself, I just wanted the gun in case . . . And he saw it on my face. He knew what kind of person I was. He knew I was desperate. I thought . . . if he can tell, how long until Dave leaves me? And I wished he didn't have to leave me. I wanted to just disappear for him. But now—now he'll have to." Her face creased.

"He's not going to leave you."

"He will," Leslie said. "He'll figure it out. He'll know that I don't—don't feel the right thing." She looked up. "How could you tell—about Eli?"

"Only because I know you," I said. "Leslie, I know you better than anybody."

She stared at me, tears drying on her cheeks. "How can you still love me?"

"Because you know me better than anybody too," I told her.

"They'll put me in a room," she said. "Like her. They'll put me under observation."

"I mean, those places are better than they used to be. But what's important is"—I grabbed her hand and squeezed—"I know the truth now. That's all I wanted. I just wanted to understand what was wrong. You were acting so strange that day in the parking lot when you thought I was dead. I wanted to know why. And now that I do, I can help you." I caught her eyes. "Say it."

"Say what," she whispered.

I licked my lips. "'Robin, will you please help me?'"

She looked at our hands. "How?" she said again.

I smiled and released her. "Not like you were planning, that half-assed attempt. I know a guy. We'll stage a break-in. That's so much more believable. No one wants to jack your three-year-old Honda mom-mobile."

"At the house?" she said. "No, no—Dave—"

"Not *there*," I said. "*Here*, silly. Someone'll break in, take the television and the more valuable records, and knock you out against a wall. Not for real, obviously. But it'll be a good whack. The neighbors will see you being dragged into a car and driven away. He'll ditch you on the side of the road, I'll pick you up, and off we'll go. Easy as pie. And it won't cost you forty grand. This is a fifteen-grand job, max. Clery must have known he could rip you off."

Leslie scrambled off her seat. "You're not serious."

"Of course I am." I sat back. "How do you think I keep from getting booked for shit? I *know* people. Good people."

"Where would we go?" She was pacing. The blanket slipped off her shoulders and fell to the floor.

"To LA," I said patiently. "After that you can skip for Canada or whatever if you want."

"You can get me a fake ID?"

"Leslie, please listen to yourself. I've had fake IDs since I was twelve. It's not hard."

She reached for my arm, just as she had that first night in the hotel room. The same wild look was in her eyes. "How soon?"

I matched her expression. "Tomorrow. Be here at ten A.M. Tell Dave I went back home to Vegas and say you're going to finish packing up my room."

She sucked in a breath. Tears sprang to her eyes. "I don't want Eli to grow up like we did."

"It'll be different," I told her. "Dave is a great dad, and he has about eleven million relatives. He'll be sad, but he'll be fine. And we'll be together."

Her voice was high and thready. "I didn't think I'd ever see you again. Robin, I . . ."

I stood up, almost knocking over my chair, and reached for her. This time she put her head on my shoulder. I felt her face dampen my T-shirt. "You and me," I said. "All you had to do was ask for my help. And everything is going to be okay."

"I don't know how to thank you," she murmured.

I held her close.

54

Leslie

I asked Robin if she needed a ride, but she said she had one—the rental, maybe, although when I went outside my car was still alone in the driveway. A dozen or so cars lined the street on either side. It was impossible to tell which might be hers.

It was a Friday, and I should have gone to work, but instead I called in sick again. I drove home on autopilot, the fifty thousand in the envelope beside me in my purse, next to the burner.

I tried to remember the face of the girl on the bed in Henderson. She'd been thin—so thin. Her open mouth, chin sharp as a knife. People who grew that thin no longer resembled themselves; their skulls peered through their faces. That was what I expected of Robin. The last time I'd seen her in person, she'd been a child. After that, she had deteriorated into missed calls, creditors, drunken messages, like a long, ugly, boring haunting. I'd wished she was dead. I'd wished it.

When I walked into the house in Henderson, I had expected someone like the girl on the bed, someone who was mostly gone already, bones and memory.

I hadn't imagined her the way Mary was—friendly, earthy. The kind of person who would hold your hand in the dark.

I'd been sitting in my own driveway for several minutes. Belatedly, I shut the car off and went inside, upstairs, my feet carrying me to the guest bedroom where Mary had been staying.

It was still a mess, just as it had been last night—just as Robin's room was, I remembered, in the house on Riviera. The yellow dress she'd worn was in a puddle on the floor, the elastic top puckered. Her sheets were wadded at the end of the mattress, streaks of mascara on her pillow. The stub of a thin cigarette lay on the bedside table.

I'd never touched Robin's room, but suddenly I was furious with her for leaving it that way—for always expecting somebody else to clean up after her, just as Daddy had expected me to—

I yanked the sheets from the bed and piled them into the hamper outside Eli's bedroom. Then the stained pillowcase, the cigarette butt for the trash. I went around gathering up each discarded item of clothing, folding them carefully, even the ruined yellow dress. Every time I picked something up, more cigarette butts were revealed, even in odd places like the floor of the coat closet and under the bed. I swept all of them out with my hands and dropped them into the wastebasket. I hung each damp towel in the bathroom neatly from the rack. Her makeup was strewn across the countertop. I organized her brushes and pencils into one of the travel cases underneath the sink, and wrapped the cord neatly around the curling iron, tucking it back into its drawer. All my bath bombs were gone, and when I looked, I found them piled into her duffel. I left those where they were and picked through the rest of the bag, looking for—something. Evidence.

How had I missed it? Why hadn't I wanted to believe it?

Her battered high heels were in there, the ones she'd worn last night, and a long string of fake pearls, tangled in one of the mesh pockets. At the bottom of the bag lolled one of her pink crystals and a prayer candle, which had rolls of five- and ten-dollar bills inside it instead of wax. I pulled them out and counted them. She had two hundred forty dollars. I rolled the bills back up just as she'd had them before and put the candle back into the corner of the bag.

The side of the duffel crinkled under my hand. It took me a moment to work my fingers into the lining and pull out the piece of paper without tearing it, my heart pounding. Something she'd hidden. A secret.

I smoothed out the piece of paper on my lap. It was a receipt—a gas-station receipt, I saw, looking closer, for two packs of Spirits cigarettes. She'd paid with cash at the one just outside my neighborhood.

I stared at it for a minute. Then I curled into myself, my head on my knees, the receipt crumpling again in my lap. It was so ordinary—such a person thing to do—to stuff a receipt in her bag and forget about it. To take all my bath bombs, like she was stealing the complimentary shampoo at a hotel. To leave her wet towel on the floor, like she'd always done.

I went over that afternoon in my memory again. We'd been outside on the patio.

I don't understand why she can't do it.

Do you remember when it snowed?

When had I gone inside? When had I discovered what she'd done?

Whatever had been there was rubbed out. For years now, when I reached for my mother's face, I could only call up images from the photographs I'd seen. I had forgotten it, maybe on purpose, the way I'd forgotten what Robin was like, how it felt to be her double.

I inhaled and sat up. Then I went over to the bed and retrieved Robin's folded clothes and the travel bag of makeup, tucking them carefully into the bag, beside her shoes and her necklace. I zipped the duffel and looked over my shoulder.

It was as if she had never been here.

I had one last night with my new family, before I left with the old. I cleaned the house methodically, with my yellow gloves on, and went to the grocery store, where I bought an entire chicken, several carrots, a bag of pearl onions, a package of cremini mushrooms, and a bottle of wine to replace the one that was currently sitting at the bottom of Mrs. Alderete's swimming pool. When Dave came home, lugging Eli's car seat, I was at the stove. "That smells so good," he said. "I'm starving. Can I have some?"

"No," I said, pushing the onions and garlic around the pan. "I've barely started."

He set Eli's car seat down with a slightly unceremonious *thunk* and came over to kiss me. I smiled against his mouth.

"You look good," he said, pushing my hair behind my ear. "Happy."

"I am happy," I said. "You brought my baby back." It was something a better version of me might say. I knelt down next to the car seat. "It's Eli!" I whispered.

Eli kicked his legs and screeched at approximately fourteen times the volume I'd used.

"Yeah, that's you." I held his feet and bicycled them in the air. "So strong."

Dave wrapped his arms around me from behind. "Pilates so early," he said, biting my shoulder delicately. "I love you."

I leaned back into him, breathing him in.

"Your garlic is starting to smell weird," he said after a while. Eli yelled a string of unintelligible syllables. "That's right," Dave agreed. "He smells it too."

I straightened up. "If you're hungry, there's a baguette on the counter. You could slice that early. I left the butter out."

"You've saved my life," Dave said. "Can I help make salad?"

"You're required to make salad."

"Oh, well, then," he said. "See if I ever do you a favor again." He went to the drawer and pulled out the bread knife.

"Tell me what's on your mind," I said as he took the bread out of its paper sleeve.

"Well, I talked to Elaine today," he said, breaking off the end of the baguette and stuffing it plain into his mouth. Eli babbled to himself in the corner and Dave hustled over to unstrap him from the car seat. "You hungry too, my small auctioneer?"

Eli squeaked.

"Well, I don't think you can have what Mom's making, because

I'm pretty sure that at least half that bottle of wine goes into the stew."

"I cooked some of the carrots and chicken before and chopped it up with a little bit of stock. It's in the fridge," I put in.

Dave raised his eyebrows. "Thinking ahead." He settled Eli in his chair at the table and went to the fridge.

"You were talking about Elaine," I prompted him.

"Oh, right." Dave nudged me aside so he could put the baby portion in the microwave. "She's thinking about dating again." He watched the microwave count down, then opened the door to test the temperature and grabbed the orange plastic baby spoon from the drawer. Eli's eyes followed it like a beacon as Dave stirred the makeshift stew. "She's been," Dave continued, sitting down at the table, "blow on it, Eli, that's it—no yelling at the table—she's been in touch with her ex again recently."

"Is she going to date him?" I pulled the cork out of the wine bottle, careful not to break it.

"I think she was considering it. He's Brody and Tanner's dad, so she didn't want to give up the dream."

"I thought he left her when she was pregnant."

"He did, for some other chick who's not half as cute. Anyway, he said if they were talking again they should share passwords, and then he went through all her accounts immediately and decided that I'm what the Scientologists would call a suppressive person and I need to be excommunicated—"

"He's not a Scientologist, is he?"

Eli puffed his cheeks out and let a little bit of superhydrated carrot dribble onto his chin. Dave laughed and wiped it away. "Do you see me or your mom dribbling food on our chins for fun? No? That's because it's not polite."

"Bah gah," Eli said.

"You question the system," Dave replied, pursing his lips. "I can see you were raised by a suppressive person. No, he's not a Scientologist, just shitty. Whoops. Don't listen to that, Eli. What I mean is that he is an insecure weasel who thinks having control is the same as having character. So he told her not to talk to me anymore, because I told her to ignore him. Well, that's not what he said to Elaine. To Elaine, he said I'm obviously secretly in love with her and trying to steal her away."

"Could you ever be with Elaine?" I asked from the stove.

Dave frowned in the middle of sticking the spoon into Eli's mouth. "Well, we'll never know, will we?" he said, quirking an eyebrow at me. "Anyway, she told him about, uh, a fun activity he could try, and I think that was the last round of him. She's moving on, finally."

"I love you," I said.

He glanced up and smiled. "Thanks, baby. Eli loves you too. Look."

Eli grinned at him, his face mostly orange.

"We should take a picture," I said. "For when he's older."

Dave's face lit up. "Yes!" He dug out his phone. "Wait, come over here and sit next to him."

I left the spoon in the pot and went to the table to crouch next to Eli's chair. Eli glanced at me and slapped one orange hand onto my face. I yelped.

"Yeeees," Dave said, looking at the screen. "I'm so glad we caught that moment. Come here." He leaned in as if to kiss me, and then licked the carrot off my cheek.

"Ew," I said.

He kissed me on the mouth and I gave in, tasting carrot.

"What else happened today?" I asked, going back to the stove. The sauce was reducing. Time to put the lid on. I checked the oven temperature.

Dave thought. "We finished our risk analysis project . . . I gave a little speech . . . Oh, Sarah got in trouble."

"What for?"

"What do you mean what for? For dress code. Joanna's had it out for basically all the women in the department for months. Today Sarah wore jeans with holes in them because it was Friday, but the holes were too far up on her thighs, so now she's been formally reprimanded for the third time and her case is going to HR. Do you think I'd get formally reprimanded if I wore jeans with holes that high?"

"I mean, all they'd be seeing is your boxers. Maybe if you wore tighty-whities."

Dave laughed. "Would you still love me if I wore tighty-whities?"

"I'd still love you if anything," I said.

"Okay, kiddo, you're through," Dave said, wiping Eli's mouth and hands. "Come say good night to your mommy and we'll go get a bath. Is there enough time for a bath before dinner?"

"I'll do his bath."

"You will?"

"Yeah." I stepped back from the counter and collected Eli from Dave's arms. "All you have to do is watch to make sure dinner doesn't explode. It's done in forty minutes, I set a timer."

"Wow. Helpful Fridays. Is it likely to explode?" Dave called after me as I carried Eli upstairs.

The guest room was at the top of the stairs, its door still open. I looked inside and saw that the duffel was gone. She'd come to the house again, maybe while I was at the store, or maybe she'd let herself in while I made dinner, slipping upstairs in bare feet so she'd be quieter.

Eli wriggled in my arms. He'd wet his diaper. I hurried to the bathroom, turned on the water, and set him naked in the tub. He flapped his hands and sent two wings of water arcing up to sprinkle me.

It wasn't hard to wash him, although I hated it, his helplessness; his body was so small. How long until he would be able to wash himself? I didn't remember ever having been washed by my mother, although I was sure she had done it at some point, maybe hating me just the same.

I still remembered what it felt like when Dave and I had started trying to have a baby. The decision was nonexistent; he'd always wanted to have a big family, and I wanted to give him everything. And it was another way to tether him to me and me alone; his family was nearby and we spent a lot of time at their houses before we bought our own, so that he devoted almost as much time to being a Flores man as he did to being my husband, mine.

When I told him I was ready to get pregnant, it was like everything else fell away. Sex became beautifully serious. He made me ride him while he watched with his mouth open, like I was all new to him again.

It took me almost four months to get pregnant. I took a test every month, and on the last month I was too excited to wait until morning. I got up at midnight and went to the bathroom, and then I crawled back into bed and whispered to Dave that it had worked. He started to cry, and I reached for the light so I could see his face.

I blinked. Eli was making spit bubbles, sinking down so that they would float on the surface of the water. He poked one with a stubby finger.

"That's a bubble," I tried.

He didn't respond.

I held his head so he wouldn't hit the metal faucet as he wriggled around. His skull was soft and warm in my palm.

Eli looked up at me. His eyes were dark and glossy like Dave's. I didn't know what his expression meant.

Would he remember me at all?

I had hated being pregnant. The baby sent a ripple across my body, disrupting even the extremities. Pimples broke out across my nose and cheeks, and I carried new weight on my hips and thighs. I'd always been long-legged, easily slender; now I was sluggish and heavy. Everything I ate sat on me like a snow. I had to take an antiemetic, which made dry skin peel off my lips and kept me from sleeping. I lay awake picking at the corners of my mouth and trying not to move too much, knowing it would upset Dave if he woke up and saw me half-dead and angry.

Three months in, I looked in the mirror and saw that a blood vessel had burst overnight, turning the white of my eye an alarming, febrile pink. At the same time my thighs grew hot. My underwear soaked through, purple-black with blood. It was over.

Dave had been desperate to try again. After the experience of pregnancy, I understood my body in a way I never had before, as a kind of receptacle. I read pregnancy books, which called me a vessel, meaning it positively; but it implied a passivity I found demeaning. I could have been anyone under him. I knew he would have denied it if I said it. Later, he would not even remember the way he had looked at me during those nights—as if fatherhood was just behind me on the mattress and I was in his way.

I lifted Eli out of the bath and wrapped him in a towel. He protested wordlessly as I scrubbed his hair dry, twisting his body this way and that, and screeched when I tried to help him use his new teething toothbrush, a yellow banana-shaped thing that Dave had brought home yesterday. "Spit," I instructed. He swallowed.

I sighed, and Eli began to cry.

I opened my mouth to soothe him, and my jaw sent a spear of pain through the right side of my face. I'd been grinding my teeth and hadn't noticed.

Eli wailed.

I picked him up and held him to my chest as I didn't often do when we were alone, and carried him to his room. In the corner was the rocking chair I'd used when he was younger and still on formula. I sat in it now and leaned back.

It had taken me half a year to get pregnant again. When I was congratulated by the doctor I made myself smile at him. I thought, It's only nine months. You can do anything for nine months.

I didn't think of Eli as a person until he began to move inside me. Then I waited to love him. When that didn't happen, I waited for birth; I had read that the body released chemicals in the first five minutes of mother and infant meeting.

I asked Maria if she'd enjoyed being pregnant. She'd said it made her feel strong, and that she used to cry when Joachim sang to the baby through her skin.

People say you don't remember the worst parts of birth, but I remember everything. To make room for Eli's shoulders, they cut me open. Dave held me down while I screamed. The doctor said, *It's only a small incision to avoid any more tearing,* and then Eli was born and they took him away to be cleaned. I lay panting on the bed, Dave's hands still pinning me to the mattress as a nurse kneaded my belly until the placenta came free. It felt like something had been ripped out of me by the roots.

They brought Eli back to me. I was half-conscious, black spots on my vision. I tried to stay awake long enough for the chemicals to release. Instead I felt nothing. I could have been holding my appendix. Dave was crying and I thought, Now we are really separate; he has been changed and I am the same. We can't go back.

Because that was what I was hoping for, secret even to myself: that when I looked at Eli and felt the right thing, Dave and I would knit ourselves back together, and I too would forget the way he had driven himself into me when I was a vessel, and my mind could be open to him again, free of snakes.

I think that was the end of us, that moment. And yet if I could go back, I wouldn't change it. I'd said I would give him everything he wanted. For him, I would let myself be held down and the weeds pulled from me.

Isn't that what love is?

"Your timer went off!" Dave shouted up the stairs.

After a while he came upstairs. "Your timer went off," he repeated.

"I know," I said. "Take it out. We're cuddling."

"Looks like one of you is cuddling and one of you is screaming," Dave said. "Do you want me to put him down for you?"

"Not tonight." I held on to Eli even as he sobbed, red in the face.

Dave cocked his head and went back downstairs.

Eli cried for another twenty minutes until he exhausted himself into sleep. I opened and closed my mouth a few times, stretching my jaw. "I love you," I said aloud. I wasn't sure who the lie was for; Eli wouldn't remember it and Dave wasn't there. "I love you," I repeated.

I set him in his crib and stood over him. The nothingness I felt when I did this terrified me. It was like being a child again. I couldn't help probing for movement in the sea of myself.

Tonight, for the first time since he was born, the numbness abated; I felt something when I looked at him. Not for Eli, exactly; more for my mother. I'd told Robin that I wasn't like Christine, and I did believe that. But she had been dead long before Robin held her under the water, and now I knew what that was like.

It was a relief.

Later, after dinner, I stretched out in the bed. "Tell me about Cadence," I said. "How is she?"

Dave rolled over. "You're going to see her again on Sunday, you could just ask her then."

I shrugged.

"She's good. Nothing new since last week as far as I know. Still waiting on UAD acceptance."

"How about Maria and Joachim?"

He made a face. "What's up with this?"

"I don't know. We just haven't talked about your family all week."

"My family is fine." Dave kissed my eyebrow. "Want to watch a movie?"

What I wanted to do was spend all night asking him every last question that occurred to me before we never saw each other again. I said, "You pick," and walked into the bathroom to wash my face.

When I came back, *My Cousin Vinny* was playing and Dave was sprawled out with his eyes closed, his feet on top of the decorative blanket at the bottom of the bed. I tugged it out from under his feet and wrapped it around me. It had the texture of a placemat. I climbed on top of him and pulled the blanket over our heads, making a little cocoon.

He blinked awake and focused on me. "Why are we in here?"

"It's warm."

"It's warm outside too."

I smiled. "I was cold."

"Well, let's watch the movie." He was annoyed with me.

"In a minute. You're almost asleep anyway."

"I was resting after my long day of not cooking and not putting the baby to bed," Dave said. "Shit's hard. Your food was good, by the way."

"My mother taught me how to make it." I laid my head on his shoulder.

His voice was careful. "I've never heard you talk about your mom without me bringing it up."

"Robin made me think of her."

"She's not here tonight. Did you work out whatever it was with the lawyer? Is she out?"

"She went back to Vegas," I said softly. "I don't think I'll ever hear from her again."

Dave wrapped his arms around me, dislodging the blanket and letting a shaft of light in. "I don't know. Maybe that's not so bad. She really shook you up."

"It wasn't her fault," I said. "I always thought it was the way she acted that kept us apart, but maybe it was me too. I wasn't—I wasn't good family to her. I was harsh."

"You're good family," Dave insisted, pressing our chests tight together. "I have firsthand experience."

I breathed out against his face.

"Okay, let's watch the movie," Dave said. "Stay under this uncomfortable blanket with me. Why did you buy this thing?"

"It goes with our room," I told him.

Was that the last thing I'd say to him?

He was asleep in less than thirty minutes. I thought about waking him up to say something else, but what could I say that wouldn't give me away?

I reached for my phone. *Is everything ready for tomorrow?* I texted Robin.

She replied right away. *Ready if you are. 10 a.m., bring whatever you need. We'll pack some boxes :)*

I'm ready, I replied. Then I shut off the light and curled up against Dave's body, his heartbeat in my ear almost as loud as my own.

55

Robin

I went to the bank after I left Leslie that morning, staying on the east side of the city, as she'd suggested, which was where the only other branch large enough to keep fifty thousand dollars on hand was located. I gave them my real ID, as well as the nearly expired passport. They kept me there even longer than Leslie, since I wasn't a customer. Three different bankers and a manager came by to try to convince me to open a checking account, or put the money in savings, or invest it with one of their financial advisers. I kept smiling until they finally came back with a thick white envelope.

In the car, I ripped off the tape and upended the envelope into my lap. Five bound stacks of bills fell out. I gathered them together; the money was barely thick enough to fill both hands. It wasn't as much as I'd imagined. How long would it last me in LA?

My phone buzzed with messages from Nancy.

The first time I'd left her, I'd done it without thinking. I resented the way she had begun trying to fit me into her future, wondering to me if she should tell her family, if we would stay in Albuquerque if things went badly. I had just met a guy with a truck who had family in Texas; I thought to myself, You don't see me at all. I'm halfway out of here already, and you don't even see it. And when I slung my foot out the window that night in late spring—a decade ago now—it felt like I was fulfilling my own prediction. I'd put everything that mattered to me into my turquoise backpack—high-tops, iPod, star-shaped sunglasses. The guy who was waiting for me in the truck down the street wiped cheese from his fingers, truck still smelling like Wienerschnitzel drive-thru. I'd climbed out of my bedroom window thinking: I'm free, I'm free, I could eat the moon! I'd hung my head out of the car window like a dog, my fingers squeezed tightly by his oily ones, as if he could feel my future straining away from him, too big for my flesh to hold, much less his. And Nancy had faded next to the marquee-bright image of my future self.

Now I saw that I had only been telling myself I was free, just as Leslie had. She had molded me into her perfect companion, fitting my personality around her own. A zero-sum girlhood—you be smart, I'll be charming, you'll cut your hair and I'll grow mine out. You be the general and I your lieutenant. When she'd loosed me from her, I'd been only half a person, Leslie inverted. It was just as Daddy had done: dreamed us up, his children, put his name on us, fleshed us out in his imagination, and then, when we arrived, found us lacking—not pretty enough, maybe, not boy enough; not enough like him, or too much so, idiot mirrors.

It sounds like horror, but it's lovely to be invented, to know what you're for. And awful to know your purpose and be kept from it. If Daddy had invented us because he wanted silent children, we would have been thrilled to silence ourselves. But he'd wanted to love us, and we knew it, and he couldn't really—so we went on straining, contorting ourselves into lovable poses. If he'd loved us more, I would have been less beautiful, I thought, and Leslie less depend-able. In the years that Leslie had refused to speak to me I'd only grown better at being what she needed.

On some level I'd known that when I'd picked out her car in the Vegas parking lot and climbed onto the hood. I had spent ten years coring strangers and spitting them out, covering myself in lesser love, ruining them in the process. I wanted what everybody wants: to see and be seen. But I frightened ordinary people when I grew tired of niceties, and the other ones, the ones like Clery, were incapable of appreciating my infinite tenderness. The only one who had ever got close was Nancy, who let my love suffocate her, who let me dig her fears out of her with my nails. I was desperate to be known again. I think that's why I decided to let Leslie meet me all-new. To see if she would still love me. And she did still love me. She did.

I hadn't been sure of that before. When I ran away, I thought she would be indifferent to my disappearance, as she had been to my presence. Like my mother, I'd made the mistake of thinking I could remove myself from my life in a neat, single motion. But it cost something to disappear—I was older now, and understood a little more. The escape Leslie had imagined for herself would cost her all her old happiness. And mine would cost me Nancy.

I wondered where she was now. I decided I would keep her in my head just as she had been that day at the lookout, small, lean, gold, with her chin tilted up and the bloody smudges of my lips across her face, marking her before she knew I'd done it.

Leslie was gone when I got back to the house, and my things were packed on the bed, the room stinking of lemon cleaner. I went through the duffel bag curiously, but she hadn't touched the vela-dora, only folded my clothes and stacked them inside. It felt like the kind of thing she might have done for me when I left ten years ago, if we'd been friends then.

I carried the duffel bag downstairs and took out my phone, let-ting the back door slam shut behind me. This morning I'd told Les-lie I knew people, good people.

It was true.

56

Leslie

I sat with my father in the sunken living room. The television was on, flickering in the darkness. He couldn't speak anymore, so he wrote to me on a little whiteboard in his cramped lawyer handwriting.

The squeak of the dry-erase marker. He held up the board so I could see.

Where is Robin

"I don't know," I said.

He bent and coughed into his paper towel. I kept the roll right next to his armchair so he could always reach for a new sheet. There was a pile of crumpled dirty ones in and around the wastebasket.

I went back to watching the television. It was an old cartoon, leaping wraithlike figures whose limbs lengthened as they walked. Cab Calloway.

He held up the whiteboard again.

Find her

I opened my eyes. Dave was still next to me under the Chimayo blanket, his chest rising and falling peaceably.

My alarm was bleating into the sheets. I swiped my phone off and got up, moving slowly so as not to rock the mattress. *Going to Daddy's house to pack up the last of the stuff,* I texted him. On the bedside table, Dave's phone made a noise like a triangle.

I didn't take anything with me except my phone and my purse with the fifty thousand dollars in it. That was all I would take if I were going to clean out the house.

It was hot outside even at nine-thirty. Memorial Day weekend. The pool would be open till midnight now. I wouldn't be here to visit.

The sky was a huge flat expanse before me, and the Sandia Mountains recalled their name, the morning light turning them pink as fruit flesh.

Would I miss it here?

I'd never lived anywhere else.

Maybe I'd forget after a while. Rewrite my life as I had rewritten it before. Cut out the bad and ignore the vestigial guilt.

But I knew as I thought it that I would never forget. I could never love anyone as much, or disappoint them as completely.

It seemed to take a long time to reach the house on Riviera, the beginning and end of my life.

There was a white Nissan two-door idling in the driveway, but as I rolled closer I could see that no one was inside it. Were Robin's friends already here? I had thought it would be a surprise, maybe—a few bruises, carried roughly into a waiting car. This one seemed too small, and to walk into an occupied house seemed more daunting than a surprise attack. I pulled up beside the curb and shut off the engine. The lights were on in the house and a muffled noise was coming from behind the door, audible now that the car wasn't running.

I got out and shut the door. My hands were shaking. It took me a long time to find the right key. I hadn't thought about whether it would hurt until this moment. I hadn't thought about how there would be a stranger in my house—someone who would hit me, really hit me.

I had stood in front of the mirror a dozen times while I was pregnant, imagining myself taking my stomach off, leaving it on the floor. After Eli was born, it became clear the problem had not exited with him, but remained inside me, a dead part drifting into my bloodstream. I fantasized that I could locate the poisoned organ and cut it out. I pulled at my skin in the mirror, stretching it to its limit. If it had been as easy as cutting off an arm, I would have done it.

It was different, though, to walk toward my escape knowing that pain was waiting for me. A real man waiting to hit me. I thought about calling Robin. I moved my feet two steps.

The teal gate was open, as if somebody else had come through already.

The noise congealed into something I recognized. It was music. Somebody was playing music in there. It was drifting through the door, left an inch or two ajar.

I glanced behind me, but no one was there. Just the strange car in the drive and the empty street.

I made myself go through the gate and push open the front door. Would I see him right away, the stranger Robin had hired? Would he be like Clery, or would he be the kind of man to introduce himself, apologize before he knocked my head against the wall?

The music grew in volume.

"I was the one came running when you were lonely . . ."

That song Robin had loved. Was she here? She'd said she wouldn't be, that she'd pick me up later, on the highway.

"Robin?" I called. I left my purse on the hook next to the door and went farther into the living room. "Robin?"

No one answered.

The house was nearly empty, covered in boxes. I should have felt alone, but I didn't.

There was another person in the house.

Where was Daddy's record player? It wasn't in the living room. I followed the sound through the house, feeling sick.

The dream I'd had surfaced, jogged by the empty armchair. A stain on it stuck out to me as it hadn't in the months since Daddy had no longer occupied it. I'll have to throw the chair out, I thought, and then I remembered I wouldn't be here to do it. Someone else would have to throw the chair out.

"Robin?"

My room was empty except for the boxes. Dull yellow walls. I closed the door again and went farther down the hallway.

There was a noise like a step behind me. I turned.

Nothing.

At last I reached Robin's room. The door was closed, but the music poured out from around its edges. She was playing the song as loud as it could possibly go.

I turned the knob. It felt hot in my hand.

All the lights were on in Robin's room, bright against the pale blue wallpaper. The faces crowded my vision so that at first all I saw was the record player propped up on the white pouf chair that belonged to Robin's vanity. She'd dragged the chair into the middle of the room for some reason. The record on it spun slowly, blaring its noise.

Then I saw why the chair was in the middle of the room.

Above it, from the fan, hung a length of rope, knotted into a noose.

My mind worked slowly. Was Robin here? Was she going to kill herself?

Then, even more ludicrous: Was it my mother?

I felt something at my back, could feel its breath. The man Robin had hired. But even as I wrenched myself around I knew that wasn't it. The door was yanked shut behind me, forcing me to snatch my hand out of the way to keep from getting caught in the frame. I reached for the knob just as the lock clicked, rattling the wood.

I pulled at the knob. Then again. The door held.

The record player was blaring; I couldn't think. "Robin!" I yelled over its noise. "What's going on?"

She couldn't hear me. I turned and hurried to lift the needle from the record. "Robin?" I called again, going back to the door and pressing myself against it. The painted wood felt sticky against my face.

In the sudden quiet, I heard a car in the driveway. Coming or going? Was she leaving me here? What for?

I looked around. The window—the window—

I pulled up the blinds and looked out into the empty backyard.

The red yucca needed watering. I couldn't see what was going on in front of the house from here, but if I could lift the window . . .

My fingers couldn't gain purchase on the sash. I pushed at the top of the window instead, locking and unlocking it futilely. At last I saw what it was. The sash was nailed to the frame.

I'd put those nails in, years ago. To keep Robin in. She'd pried them out twice to get out from under me. After she'd run away, I hadn't bothered to put them back in again. She must have come yesterday and—and hammered them—so I couldn't . . .

But why? *Ten a.m. We'll pack some boxes.* I remembered holding on to her in the kitchen, the way her fingers had skated over the veins on the back of my hand.

I banged on the window, hard. "Robin!" The glass fogged at my shout. "Robin!" I said again, knocking until the windowpane shuddered. The yard remained quiet, the black pine's needles moving in a breeze I couldn't feel. No neighbors appeared beyond the fence.

I slumped against the window and glanced around the room. A hundred faces stared back at me from Robin's walls.

Phone. I'd call her. I'd ask—But I'd left my purse on the hook as I always did. My phone was in there. I could hear it ringing faintly.

The ringing seemed to go on forever in the empty house, echoing itself a dozen times. I sat down on the floor against the window and pressed my fingers into my forehead.

The noose was like a person in the room. I could barely look at it.

She could have left me yesterday. She had the money; she knew what I'd wanted mine for. But she'd stayed. She'd watched me vomit. She'd helped me plan to run, just as she had run before. Why had she stayed? Just to lock me in the house?

The phone had stopped ringing at some point and a new sound filtered into the room, a whine growing louder as it approached. Sirens. Someone had heard me shouting.

If the police showed up, Robin couldn't come back.

What had she done?

The sirens grew deafening, then shut off. A heavy knock came at the door, and someone said something too muffled for me to make out. I sat shivering at the foot of the window.

"Leslie Flores?" the voice said again, louder. More knocking, and then movement around the side of the house. I turned and watched from the edge of the window as several people in dark uniforms tramped through the backyard gravel. They disappeared toward the back door, and I heard them knock again, and call my name. I was too afraid to reply. After several minutes, there was a cracking noise, and heavy footsteps moved through the house, voices reporting on each room.

"Leslie Flores?" one of them called from just outside Robin's bedroom.

I wiped my mouth. "I'm in here," I said.

"Open the door."

"I can't," I said, too quietly. "The lock is on the outside."

"Okay, I'm coming in." A man, a calm voice. I heard the door rattle and scrambled to stand, knocking the chair and the record player over. A second later, the door burst open, revealing one of the police officers I'd seen in the backyard. He was tall, square-jawed. "Are you Leslie Flores?" he asked.

"Yes," I said. My throat was dry. Another officer stepped into the room behind him. She looked familiar. She'd been in school with Robin. I'd run into her at Sprouts once or twice.

Her eyes were kind. "Leslie, your sister told me you might be here. I'm Nancy Courtenay, if you remember? I'm with the sheriff's department. This is Officer Wright." She turned to her partner. "Can you wait over there for a second? I'm going to talk to Mrs. Flores."

"What?" I could barely think. The other officer—Wright—took one last glance around the room, shook his head, and disappeared into the hallway. "Why would she tell you?"

"She cares about you, Leslie," Nancy said. "Your note really scared her."

"What note?"

"The note you left her," Nancy said, holding a folded piece of paper out to me. "She thought you might go to your dad's house. I'm glad she called us."

I heard voices in the living room, boots shuffling over the carpet.

There were more people here. People Robin had called. I took the piece of paper from Nancy and unfolded it slowly.

> I'm heading out now. I didn't want
> to wake you up to say goodbye.
> I hope you find your way on your own.
> I'm glad our time together is over.
> I can't feel any other way.
> But I'll think about you.
>
>   —Leslie

The bottom of the note, with Robin's Social Security number, had been ripped away, leaving a ragged edge. I could hear my pulse in my ears. "It's not a—a suicide note," I said. "It's—she was leaving town—she was here to work out some legal—"

Nancy came closer, and I stumbled back. "I'm sorry she couldn't be here. She said it was too hard for her, and I hope you understand that. But she hasn't left town. She'll visit you in the hospital."

The voices in the living room muttered to one another. I heard someone chuckle.

"I don't need to go to the hospital," I said to Nancy, my heart rabbit-fast in my chest. "I'm not suicidal. Robin lied to you."

Nancy looked up at the noose. "I wish that were true. But I can't leave you here on your own. I'm required to make sure you're no longer in danger."

Another car pulled up outside. A walkie-talkie burped in the other room, and a garbled voice said, "Everything's okay. We located her."

"Is there someone else we can call for you to meet you at the hospital?" My attention was dragged back to Nancy, who tilted her head. "Someone who can support you?"

"Don't call Dave," I said. "He can't . . ."

"You don't have to worry, Leslie," Nancy said. "We haven't notified anybody yet. I came straight over after Robin's call. If you'd like, we can ask the hospital not to admit him in to see you. You don't have to see anybody you don't want to see. But support can be very important. Is there anybody else I can call for you?"

That car outside. Robin's car. She hadn't packed boxes with me. She'd waited for me, nailed the window shut, locked me in, called this woman.

She wasn't coming back.

I went over the events in my head again. It began to take shape.

The dead girl on the bed in Henderson. The girl who'd been punished for taking something that belonged to Robin.

You and me, Robin had said yesterday in the kitchen.

And I'd said, *I don't know how to thank you.*

"I need my purse," I said to Nancy. "Is my purse in the front room?"

Nancy looked perplexed, but raised her voice to call, "Hey, Alan?" Officer Wright appeared in the hallway. "Can you check if there's a purse in the front room?"

"She can't have anything in it," Wright mumbled.

"We can bring it to the hospital for her, though," Nancy said mildly.

"I need my purse!" I hissed. "There's an envelope in it. I need to know if it's there. Now. Now. Now!" I shrieked the last word at him as he turned to leave.

"There's no need to shout," Nancy said, pulling the door nearly closed. "I promise you, we are here to help."

I sat down on the bed. My face felt like a mask. "You've been fucking her, haven't you?"

Nancy's kind expression evaporated. "That's none of your business. Please don't lash out at me because you're angry at your sister."

"I bet you love her," I said, talking over her. "She told you she's coming back? She lied. She never loved you. She told me so."

"I understand that's your perspective," Nancy told me.

Wright shouldered past the door, holding my purse. "This it?"

I stood up. Nancy put a hand on my shoulder. "Please sit down, Mrs. Flores," she said.

"Give it to me," I said. I had at least five inches of height on her, but she kept me in place on the bed without effort. One of my shoes slipped off as I scraped for purchase on the carpet.

"Leslie, please," Nancy said, lightening her hold on my shoulder. "It's just an envelope. You can get it later." She turned calmly to Wright, behind her. "Should we get going?"

I stopped moving, and Nancy took her hand away. "I don't want to go anywhere," I said, through suddenly difficult breaths.

Wright rummaged around in my purse. "I don't see an envelope," he reported.

Nancy bent and offered me my shoe. "What's in the envelope? Maybe it fell out of your purse."

I curled in on myself, shaking. It was gone. Part of me must have known as soon as I heard the phone ringing, out there where I couldn't reach it, locked in. I felt Nancy crouch and put my shoe back on my foot for me. "Nancy," I whispered, trying to pull myself together. She was still kneeling, her face at chest height. I bent my head to hers, my hair brushing her forehead. "Nancy, you have to help me," I said under my breath. "Robin set it up to look like I was going to do something, but I swear to you, I wasn't."

My words slid off her gentle expression. She wasn't really listening to me. "It's okay, Leslie."

"I can't go to the hospital," I went on, trying to make her understand. "I just need to talk to Robin." If I went to the hospital, somebody would call Dave. He would think that I'd tried to—I could hardly imagine his face. I knew what would happen. I'd gone through it with my mother. She had barely even hidden it from us. I had promised myself I would never do that. No one would ever know. I would eat my shame alone.

If I went to the hospital, no one would help me die. That was their job, to keep people alive. They'd keep me alive to watch Dave divorce me. To watch him turn to Elaine, find somebody better to be Eli's mother. I couldn't be alive for that. I had worked so hard to make it easy for us both. I had left Eli money, packed up most of Daddy's house . . .

I was supposed to be dead right now.

I stared at the noose.

"For what it's worth, what you're going through is very common, Leslie." Nancy's voice broke into my thoughts. "Many women experience it, especially in the year after giving birth. People can be very good at hiding it. I know it may not seem like it right now, but it's lucky that you wrote that note to Robin. You asked for help, and she heard you." She offered me a hand, but I didn't take it.

"If I go, I can't come back," I whispered to her.

Nancy's face softened. "Of course you can come back," she said. "Leslie, don't worry. All that's going to happen is you'll be asked to talk to a doctor about what you've been experiencing this year. Everyone understands what you're going through. You'll get your life back."

I felt something inside me crack. My body sagged, going limp on the bed. Nancy and the other cop propped me up, one hand on each elbow.

"On our way," Nancy said into her walkie. The faces on Robin's walls watched me as I was pulled out of the room. I felt her presence in the house, closer than ever; I understood her, finally, as I hadn't when we were twelve and eight, as I hadn't even yesterday in the kitchen. *All you have to do is ask for my help,* she'd said.

I'd never see her again. She'd trapped me in my life, like an insect under a glass. I'd be in New Mexico until I died.

I love you, Leslie. I love you. It entered my head again. I couldn't get it out all the way to the hospital.

Robin

The phone Leslie had bought me rattled in the cupholder beside me. Music poured over my face from the rental car's speakers, thick as sunlight, obscuring the ringtone. I glanced down, expecting to see her number, but it was Nancy calling me, over and over. When I stopped at a red light, I saw my name on the screen.

Robin, I've got, her message began, then was cut off as the notification ended.

I didn't open it. There was a voicemail too. That one I held to my ear.

"Robin," she said. "I just wanted to call and check in with you. I don't . . ."

She went on, but I started the message over again.

"Robin. I just wanted to . . ."

There were no calls from Leslie. I had cut us free of each other. That was how I had paid for her happiness. A piece of myself thrown into the hole of my death. Hadn't I always done what she was afraid to ask for?

Robin, I've got

I put the phone in my shirt pocket, where it buzzed against my chest, as if Nancy were speaking into the chamber of my rib cage, lips pressed up against my skin.

Robin, I've got

I'd never hear that name again. Nancy was the last one who would say it. I wanted to feel her saying it as long as possible.

At a Shell station in Arizona, I pulled over and went into the minimart with a hundred-dollar bill. "Can you break it?" I asked the guy at the counter.

He was tall and brown, wearing a ball cap and sucking on a piece of licorice. "Just barely," he said around the licorice. "You don't have anything else?"

I shook my head. "Can I put forty toward the gas?"

"Buy something else," he said. "I can't be giving you everything in the register. Grab some snacks. You on a road trip?"

"Sort of," I said, lifting a case of Poland Spring from the stack beside the counter and heaving it into his arms. "I'm moving to LA."

"LA, huh?" he called as I disappeared into the aisles. There was nobody else in the minimart, and I felt his eyes on my back as I snatched up pretzels, sunglasses, a bouquet of fake roses. "You going to be in a movie?"

I nodded, coming back toward him and dropping my loot on the counter. "I hope so. My dad left me some money in his will to get started. A hundred thousand dollars. Can you believe it?"

He whistled, ringing up the pretzels. "Lucky. What's your name, so I know you when I see it?"

"Alice," I told him. The man behind the counter smiled and handed me my change and filled my arms with water and flowers. Against my chest, my phone went on singing, tapping out my eulogy.

AUTHOR'S NOTE

I am not a mother. But, like a lot of women, I've spent a significant portion of my life thinking about whether I would like to be one—or whether I should be one. I'm anxious, a worrier. I don't like to gamble. I'm afraid of pain. I researched all the ways it could go wrong. I imagined the children I might have or not have, the ways my body could change. *The Better Liar* is a nightmare, full of wild shadows and exaggerations, but at the center of it is a real fear: that if I had a baby, I might not feel what I am supposed to feel, and I might be too afraid to tell anyone.

One in seven women experience significant depression, anxiety, intrusive repetitive thoughts, panic, or posttraumatic stress during pregnancy or postpartum.[1] Because intrusive thoughts and anxiety often center around fears of hurting the baby, it can be difficult for people to tell their partners, family members, or doctors about these thoughts. Some even worry their baby will be taken away. You can imagine how many people go on suffering from postpartum depression—an incredibly common experience—because it can be so difficult to get help.

People of color, especially, are blocked from navigating the healthcare system because they are so frequently ignored or disbelieved about their pain.[2] In the United States, Black women are two to three times more likely to die in childbirth than white women,[3] and in New York City, where I live, they are twelve times more likely.[4]

1 postpartum.net/learn-more/frequently-asked-questions/
2 papers.ssrn.com/sol3/papers.cfm?abstract_id=2617895
3 ncbi.nlm.nih.gov/pubmed/17194867/
4 npr.org/2017/12/07/568948782/black-mothers-keep-dying-after-giving-birth-shalon-irvings-story-explains-why

Not even eminence or wealth protects against this racist failure of care. Shalon Irving, an epidemiologist at the CDC, died from complications of high blood pressure after multiple postpartum appointments where she explained, "There *is* something wrong, I know my body. I don't feel well," and was told, "If there's no clots, there's nothing wrong."[5]

I don't say this to scare people. I say it to provoke reflection on how we regard parents who struggle, parents who suffer—and on which parents get more competent care, and why. We owe these parents greater empathy and support.

I want to stress that while it is crucial for people experiencing postpartum depression to receive care, I don't believe it's something that can or should be forced on anyone. What Robin does to Leslie in this book is extremely dangerous in the United States because we have conscripted police officers into mental-health-care work, and that is not their primary training. When you involve the police in an intervention for someone with mental health struggles without their consent, especially a person of color, you risk their life[6]—and, less seriously, you risk incurring thousands of dollars in hospital bills they may be unable to pay.

Instead, encourage them to seek help independently, in a way that prioritizes their comfort and control. It's a blessing that postpartum depression has lost some of its stigma over the past few years and is better understood than in previous decades. This means that it is unlikely for someone like Leslie to experience what her mother went through. Leslie, in today's world, probably went on to meet with a doctor who recommended a therapist who could prescribe an antidepressant that Leslie could take of her own volition.

I know a little of the fear she feels, and I know the shame that follows it. I wanted to write a book that followed my fear to its fullest extent, to see what lived there at the end. I want to make a world where that shame is no longer justified. I hope *The Better Liar* causes us to discuss how we fail parents during and after childbirth. And I

---

5 Ibid.

6 treatmentadvocacycenter.org/key-issues/public-service-costs/2976-people-with-untreated-mental-illness-16-times-more-likely-to-be-killed-by-law-enforcement-

hope, if you are a parent who sees yourself in Leslie's fear and in my fear, that you are heard, and believed, and helped.

The National Suicide Prevention Lifeline:
1-800-273-8255
suicidepreventionlifeline.org for text and chat as well as online support groups

The American Psychological Association's information page on postpartum depression symptoms and treatment:
apa.org/pi/women/resources/reports/postpartum-depression

Postpartum Support International offers a helpline that is answered from 5:00 A.M. to 11:00 P.M. Pacific time. Call 1-800-944-4773 or text 503-894-9453.
postpartum.net

ACKNOWLEDGMENTS

This book exists thanks to the help of dozens of people, but first and foremost, I want to thank my agent, Erin Harris, who found me in the slush and elevated, clarified, and broadened what I had imagined. Erin, you always help me see the skeleton under the text, and I'm so grateful for your brilliant insight and empathy.

Thank you to my editor, Elana Seplow-Jolley. I knew right away that you truly understood the book I wanted to make. You're so generous with your time and your ideas—I'm grateful for the many hours you've devoted to the Voigts, and to me. This book is a binding, but it has unbound me in some ways, and that's your doing. Your work means more to me than I can express.

Thank you to my UK editors, Jade Chandler and Sara Nisha Adams. I never even dared to dream that this book would exist so far away from the place I wrote it, and you made me feel that it could speak to people everywhere. Thank you for your thoughtful notes and your belief in me.

I am grateful to all the people at Penguin Random House who put so many hours into my book, among them Evan Camfield and Pamela Feinstein, who paid close attention to the details; Pamela Alders, who kept us all on track; Diane Hobbing, who made the interior look so beautiful, down to individually created emojis and the running heads I always wanted; Belina Huey, designer of a cover that surprised me and yet made perfect sense, just like the best twists; Taylor Noel, marketing manager and ideal early reader; Melissa Sanford, who let the world know about *The Better Liar;* and Kara Cesare, Jennifer Hershey, Kim Hovey, and Kara Welsh at the helm of Ballantine, who took a chance on my first novel and made my dreams come true.

Thanks to the friends who read my book before it was real: Melissa Mejias Parker, Hannah Allaman, Peter Schultz, Arthur Iannacone, and especially Celina Reynes, for your invaluable encouragement and insight.

Thank you to my family for the books you've written and read to me over the years, the endless word games and puzzles, pennies for memorized poetry, unlimited library rentals on my twelfth birthday, and your belief in me. Thank you for taking me to Albuquerque every year, and to so many other places.

Most of all I want to thank my partner, Matt Sharp. I loved you first when you wrote to me, and you read me as no one else has. You did the work of making room for me to write, sometimes literally, sometimes emotionally. I am so grateful to know you. I won't forget, bird—this will be our year.

TANEN JONES grew up in Texas and North Carolina. She has a degree in American history and spent several years editing law and criminal justice textbooks. A queer author, she writes about queer women in dark spaces. Jones now lives with her partner in New York, where she writes to the sound of her neighbor's piano. *The Better Liar* is her debut novel.

tanenjones.com

Twitter: @TanenJones

Instagram: @tanenjones